BENEATH SHIFTING STARS

THE PATOVIA CHRONICLES
BOOK ONE

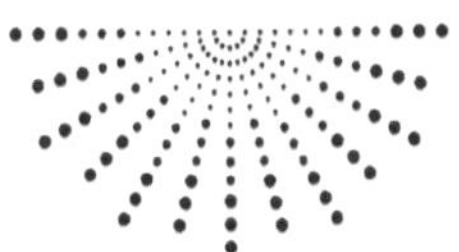

PENNY G. CAVANAUGH

Edited by: Rosa Alonso
Cover Illustration: Kateryna Vitkovska
Map Illustration: Maria Gandolfo
Interior design / Typesetting: AusPix Media / Mary Draganis

ISBN (Print): 978-1-7640859-0-8
ISBN (eBook): 978-1-7640859-1-5

AUSXIP Publishing
www.ausxippublishing.com

ACKNOWLEDGMENTS

Rosa, I've typed and re-typed what you mean to me, over and over again, and I keep hitting that backspace button faster than a Patovian windstorm... There are just no words to describe how deeply I appreciate you, and what an absolute delight it has been to create this adventure with you by my side. I never would have even considered writing another story if I didn't know it would light you up like a goddamn aurora. You're fucking fantastic, and I can finally use that word! FUCK YEAH!¡LO HICIMOS!

AUSXIP Publishing... Mary... Thank you. Your encouragement and belief in me kept my gloves on, and my heart strong. I'm so proud to be sharing my stories under your banner.

My diligent Beta readers, Arielle Strauss Brueland and PT Martin, thank you so much for being among the first to meet my girls, and contributing such fantastic feedback.

To Kateryna Vitkovska, whose exceptional cover art brought Mari to life and captured the Glowing Gardens with such breathtaking accuracy that it brought me to tears. It was exactly as I had imagined and I am profoundly grateful for your talent, vision and patience.

And to Maria Gandolfo, the most extraordinary cartographer I could have hoped to work with—skilled, intentional, and deeply knowledgeable. Thank you for bringing Patovia to life with such clarity and care. You helped me achieve my dream of a book with a map at the front... and oh, what a map she is!

Kat, I'm so grateful for your patience and love while I tapped my keyboard at all hours and talked plot lines out with you until you fell asleep. Goodness, I love our little life and I'm so glad you're by my side. Willow, I did it! Mummy wrote a book! Thanks for being the best cheerleader ever. Remember, we never, ever give up. Even when it gets tough!

To all my teachers whose names are woven into this book... You had a lasting impact and, even during my most cringeworthy teenage years, you gave me a foundation of confidence I still carry.

Dad, thanks for being such a nerd. I know I love the stars so much because of you. I hope I've made you proud.

Finally, to the women in my family who came before me. My ancestors, whose names inspired the places and characters of this story. And, of course, Mum and Jemima, my besties, my mountain and my river. I love you both so much.

DEDICATION

For my Nana Pat and my Grandma Joyce.
Two strong, remarkable women.

For Gladys, Myra, Isabel, and Ada. I didn't know you long, but
I carry you and all those who came before us - in my soul. And
now, I pass that legacy on to my little Willow.

For Willow, may you always have strong threads and bright
flames, my darling.

PATOVIA
the
Elyrian Sea
ELYRIAN FALLS
GLOWING GARDENS
NESBY CAVES
ELYRIAN RUINS
Harcanth
LAKE NESBY
Elyria's Edge
West Myramin
Myramin's Bend
THE CINDER DUNES
Myramin's Shambles
MOUNTAINS
LAKE GLASS
LAKE WARM
THE ISA GLADES
JOYCITA
The Outpost
aine River
Adavale
THE MIDWILDS
enhaven
Brindlemyre
BRINDLEMYRE MOUNTAINS
Lillyford
REN FLOWER GRAPX

CHAPTER ONE

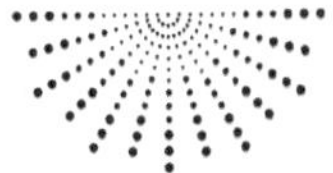

The stars were wrong.

Mari squinted at the star chart on her lap, then back at the sky above her. The constellations, her constant companions for as long as she could remember, no longer sat where they should. The starfield would probably seem like a regular night sky to the casual observer, but Mari had noticed the change instantly, from the moment the first star had appeared at twilight. She had rushed through her evening chores and scrambled into her observatory to investigate further. If the situation hadn't felt so immediately concerning, she would have been excited. This discovery meant that she was becoming, dare she say it, an expert in her field. There was no cause for celebration, though, because a cluster of stars to the north had shifted just enough to unsettle her, and she couldn't explain it.

She frowned as she pulled back from her telescope, her most treasured possession, gifted to her by her mentor a decade before. Huffing a hot breath on the lens and giving it a hasty rub, she leaned over and peered back up. She looked from the chart to the sky and back to the chart again, completely and utterly bewildered. Mari knew these stars like the lines on her own palm. For them to move... It was impossible. It went against everything she had ever learned. Unless she needed an urgent visit to the village healer, this entire situation was troubling in a way Mari had never felt before. She swallowed as she steadied herself, willing her limbs to stop shaking. The involuntary movements were causing the entire structure of her home-made observatory to sway, and she braced her muscular arms against the brittle, aged wood that splintered in every direction to maintain her balance.

Get it together, Mari. Figure it out.

Being careful not to move too quickly, she brought the telescope back up to her eye and looked again, ignoring the way her dark brown hair was whipping into her face, tangling with every twist of the wind.

Her squinty eyes, a habit born from years of peering into telescopes and bright moonlight, narrowed further as she attempted to quell the concern growing in her gut at the fact that the skies above her no longer matched with the charts in front of her—the charts she herself had hand-mapped just days earlier.

Mari took a deep and intentional breath, filling her lungs to calm herself. Could she have made a mistake? No. She never did. Not with this. Her dark golden eyes stared, unblinking, at the blanket of night above her. Something was missing. Something was... wrong.

She needed to get home and pull every chart she had drawn over the past twelve moons. She would cross reference, and cross reference again, and she wouldn't stop until she had found her mistake and corrected it. She had at least nine candle marks until tomorrow's morning light, which was plenty of time to figure this out. She folded the chart and tucked it into her satchel, dropping the telescope in on top. She climbed down from her observatory, skipping the bottom rung on the ladder, and landed with a quiet thud. A gust of wind swept across the field as she stalked through her family's gardens, which were just a sad, crunchy shadow of the lush oasis they once had been. She pulled the gate behind her and gave it a rattle to make sure it had shut properly. Below her, the light of the quiet village commons was barely visible between the dry, browning hedge that marked the edge of her family's land. The drought had stolen much of Greenhaven's foliage, and with it, the colorful character that once perfectly matched its name.

Mari fiddled with the clasp of her cloak, shivering as she pulled it around her shoulders and secured it with a tight knot, the crisp air causing goosebumps to appear across her skin. She glanced again at the night sky as the slightest hint of something caught her eye, gone as soon as she noticed it. Whatever it was, it was enough to make her breath pause. Could it have been...? Surely not. Auroras didn't appear this far south, not in Greenhaven. Certainly not at this time of year. Mari had been saving her coins to travel to Elyria's Edge for the next Festival of Still Waters, the only time of year auroras should be visible in Patovia. She had dreamed of witnessing the spectacle of the dancing lights both above and below her, and the stories of the lights reflecting off the still rivers and through the frozen falls had driven the adventure to the very top of Mari's list as the first place she would visit when she came of age. She was finally old enough, but the festival wouldn't occur for another three seasons, and patience was not one of Mari's virtues.

A voice called up from the base of the hill. "Mari!"

Zeph emerged from the darkness, his broad silhouette ambling toward her, more hurried than his usual pace.

"Hey, Cousin," Mari greeted him with a sigh. She knew he wouldn't be coming to find her unless he had been sent to. She must be late.

"What are you doing out here?" He sounded tired, and Mari decided not to mess with him. "The village meeting is about to start. Elder Amara's been asking for you."

Knew it.

"Just... observing," Mari replied. "The sky's changing, Zeph. Something isn't right."

Zeph glanced upward, frowning. Try as he might, the stars had never been as appealing to him as they were to Mari. "Everything's changing," he said, shrugging. "If we don't figure something out soon, we'll be out of water before the season's end." He turned back toward the village, motioning for her to follow. "Come on. Amara's got some kind of plan. Or at least, she says she does."

THE VILLAGE COMMONS was already crowded by the time they arrived. The villagers' usual energy was wavering, their lively chatter replaced with concerned whispers.

She passed a farmer who was consoling his sobbing wife, his arm hooked tightly around her in a comforting embrace. They both looked terrified. Mari recognized the man as one of her family's regular clients that used their messenger services. Every year, he would send a skyweaver down to arrange transport for his new herd to be shipped from Brindlemyre to Myramin's Bend and then walk the rest of the way back with his animals. He had always had such a strong, stocky figure, but tonight he looked shrunken.

As Mari squeezed through the crowd to the spot where she

usually stood, she offered a reassuring smile to little Ren, the young toddler who would eventually inherit the largest single mountainside of salt ponds in Patovia. Ren was clinging to the skirt of her mother, Lea, who looked just as worried as the rest of the crowd. She was leaning into Jayel, her husband, a protective hand cradling the back of Ren's head. Despite coming from one of the richest families in Greenhaven, Ren's parents were just as affected by the devastation of the drought as everyone else was. Ren's wide eyes darted between her mother and father, absorbing their fear, as they waited along with the rest of the crowd for the village elders to speak. This was the third emergency meeting in as many months. The elders had done their best to offer calm and reassurance, but the panic was starting to get out of hand. The wells had finally dried up, and with them, the last drops of hope that Greenhaveners had been clinging to.

Crossing the Midwilds to secure enough water to support the village was not an option, not only because the frequency of raiders' attacks had made venturing beyond the city walls increasingly dangerous, but because carrying enough water across the hilly forests was plain impractical. And so, once again, the people of Greenhaven had come together to hear the elders' latest plan. Little hope remained, though, if the expressions on their faces were anything to go by.

Elder Amara stood at the center of the gathering, her presence commanding despite her small frame. Her hair, as silver as ever, caught the lantern light as she raised a hand, calling for quiet. "The drought continues to worsen," she said. The group settled as soon as she started speaking.

"It's not just the water, Elder Amara," cried a voice to Mari's left. She was surprised to see that it was her father who spoke. "Our birds are behaving strangely. Messages are delayed, arriving weeks after they should, sometimes days away from their intended location. Many of the skyweavers have been lost altogether! It's unheard of!" His voice cracked as he finished speaking.

"I saw lights in the sky tonight!" a voice from the crowd called.

"I did too! A teal wave... It was incredible!"

The villagers' accounts solidified her suspicions. Mari was sure—she had seen an aurora.

"Mari?" Zeph whispered, giving her a side glance. She beamed inwardly at the way those around her were also looking at her, seeking her confirmation, as if she were an authority on the night skies. It was not quite the moment to be bursting with pride, so she nodded quickly, confirming their stories, and looked back to Amara.

"Our crops wither, our animals falter, and now even the skies are giving us warning signs. We cannot wait any longer to act." Amara's voice cut through the murmur of the gathered villagers. Her hand lifted, commanding silence as tension grew through the uneasy crowd.

Amara's assessing eyes swept the assembly, landing on Mari. The moment their eyes met, Mari's heart began pounding like a trapped bird. "The council is working on a solution, we assure you," she said, though the crowd remained unconvinced. Her eyes remained on Mari, and for a breathless moment, she thought the elder was about call her forward. She shifted slightly, breaking eye contact and trying to melt into the crowd, hiding behind Zeph. But she could still feel the elder's gaze on her, stirring the familiar pressure of expectation, like a thread pulling taut. Amara's eyes moved on, and Mari felt a rush of relief flood her chest, followed quickly by the sting of guilt. She knew she had just sidestepped her moment.

Amara continued. "Now, more than ever, it is crucial that we ALL work together. Solutions may not emerge, but we must unite. Innovate. Find ways to endure the day-to-day struggles, and believe that we will see this through."

"We don't have time," a disgruntled voice shot through from the back of the crowd, hiding his face. It didn't matter. Amara would know who it was.

Fear was taking hold of the village. Mari swallowed and pretended not to notice that Amara was still looking at her. She picked at her nail beds, looking anywhere but at Amara.

The complaints of the crowd got louder as Elder Harrop stepped forward, his deep voice commanding attention. "We will endure this together," he declared. "Rations will be adjusted to ensure everyone has enough to get through the coming weeks. The rules have been posted along the village walls."

"What good is rationing when there's no food left to ration?" came another voice, loaded with panic.

Amara raised her hands again, gently waving everyone out of the commons. "Tonight, return to your homes and rest. In the morning, meet with your neighbors. Speak of solutions. We are strongest when we work as one, Greenhaven."

"More like Brownhaven," Zeph huffed.

The commons slowly emptied, and Mari found herself alone under the darkening sky, the faintest of a wisp present. The skies held the answers—she knew it. As she turned to leave, Amara caught her gaze and gave her a small nod. Apparently, the elders knew it too.

～

NOT MOMENTS after Mari and her family had arrived home was there a knock at the door. Mari showed zero surprise to see her father, Rowan, escorting Elders Amara and Harrop into their home. Jannah, Mari's mother, on the other hand, was so shocked that she all but broke the ration rules, offering them tea and bread. They politely declined, Amara's handwave practically perfected.

"We must send someone to Joycita," Amara said, getting straight to the point. "The capital has resources we need and knowledge we lack. If nothing else, they must be made aware of what's happening here. I saw the warning lights too."

Understanding came crashing down on Mari. The Elders Council wanted her to go.

"Mari knows the skies better than anyone," Rowan said. Jannah nodded in agreement.

"Me?" Mari stammered.

"You've seen the changes?" Amara asked.

Mari nodded.

"You understand them. If anyone can convince the capital of our plight, it's you." Amara said.

Mari's heart pounded. She looked to her father, hoping for some support, but he looked as uncertain as she felt, and that rocked her more deeply than the shifting skies above. He couldn't shield her from this, and while she knew his sense of duty ran deep, she also knew he was fiercely protective of her and would back her in whatever decision she made. It would need to be her decision, though. He wouldn't force her. She knew no one would.

"I...I don't understand them," she confessed, completely unconvinced that she was the right woman for the job, and at the same time, absolutely certain she was the only person who could get it done. "What about the skyweavers? We could send a letter instead. It'd be faster."

Amara's lips pressed into a thin line. "Didn't your father say they had been flying far off their courses and failing to deliver messages?"

Mari nodded. "Yes, but let's send Cel. He's our best. He's never failed us. He'll get the letter into the right hands." She looked to her father for confirmation. He nodded, reluctantly. It was clear he thought Mari's idea was unsatisfying to the elders. Amara's response confirmed it.

"If that's your choice, we'll try it," Amara said with a deep sigh, not hiding the disappointment from her voice.

"Do you think all of this is connected? The sudden drought, the skies?" Mari asked. If they expected her to know what the changes in the skies meant, they were unfortunately mistaken. She should know, though. She had been studying the stars her whole life. What could the connection be? Amara answered as though she could read her thoughts.

"For centuries, Patovia has not been shy to boast about our lush forests, rivers, lakes, and gardens. We've been lucky to enjoy boundless natural resources, harnessing them as we pleased. We all thought this drought was temporary, but..." Amara trailed off.

"It should be over by now. This is sudden. Lasting. Sinister. The air is thinning, Mari; surely, you can feel that?" Harrop finished.

Mari nodded.

"You can't mean for her to go alone?" Jannah asked.

"Raiders' attacks have been more frequent, as you know," Elder Harrop said. "The infantry is exhausted and needed here."

"I know this is a heavy burden," Amara said gently, "but

you've always seen what others can't. The stars speak to you. I believe they chose you for this task."

Mari shifted in her chair. "They might be speaking, but it's in another language, Elder Amara. I don't understand it. Our atmosphere shouldn't be conducive to these auroras." Mari struggled to look at Amara as she spoke.

Amara's voice lowered. "Your charts helped us navigate that early frost two winters ago. Without you, we'd have lost half the harvest. You've already saved this village once, Mari."

"Maybe that was the start of whatever is happening now..." Mari mused, her mind racing as she filed through the recent strange and unexpected weather events.

Amara smiled. "The fact that you made that connection is just further proof that we came to the right person."

Jannah nodded. "When you were little, you used to climb the tree behind the house before we built your observatory. I'd see you up there, scribbling notes about the sky. Even then, you were watching over us."

Despite the situation, Mari felt herself smiling. She hadn't realized how much people had noticed her passion for astronomy. And to think that at one point in time, she had been afraid to tell her parents that she wanted to be an astronomer.

The group sat in silence, the only sounds coming from the twittering birds in aviary that drifted through the kitchen window. It was a familiar melody that settled Mari's nerves.

Rowan looked up at the skies and shook his head. "The lights are faint, but there's no denying they're there."

Astute astronomical observation, Father; well done, Mari thought.

"They're so beautiful," Jannah said.

Amara spoke again. "The lights may be beautiful, but they're not meant to be here. Something has shifted in the balance." Her eyes stayed on Mari for a moment, her resolve faltering. 'I'm sorry to put this on you, but the village needs you.'"

Mari nodded.

"The immediate need is a request for aid. That will keep us going until we can figure out what is causing all of..." Amara waved her hands in disgust, "...this. If we can't figure it out, we will need to leave Greenhaven for good."

Mari poked at her nail beds and swallowed. Abandoning Greenhaven was out of the question. The message could not fail. "Cel will get it done," she said with nowhere near the amount of confidence required from someone who had just been told the fate of her entire village hinged on her.

Harrop grunted, unconvinced.

MARI CLOSED the door behind the elders, standing still for a moment to steady her breath. The pressure of the situation settled over her like an invisible yoke, but she refused to let the elders' expectations incapacitate her. She had faced the intensity of a successful harvest, tasked with sorting and salting mountains of dates... This, she could handle. She caught sight of herself in the small, oval mirror that hung in the front entrance. She gave herself a little wink, a look of confidence the elders hadn't been able to deliver, and headed in the direction of the aviary.

The familiar cooing and fluttering of wings greeted her the moment she stepped inside. As she pushed open the door, a blur of white streaked past her face. She barely dodged the flash of silver-tipped feathers, a squawk of protest cutting through the dimly lit space.

"No, Rih." Mari didn't bother looking as she sidestepped the little menace, whose small but sharp talons had already hooked onto the edge of her shirt.

Rih dug in, flapping wildly as if to physically anchor herself to Mari's side. Tiny, unrelenting claws latched onto the fabric as she let out a loud, "Chirp! Chirp! Chirp!"—or what Mari could only assume was a very clear, "Pick me! Pick me! Pick me!"

Mari tilted her head back toward the rafters, and gave one long, pointed look at the heavens, questioning her life choices.

From the back of the aviary, Rowan's voice drifted over the nesting boxes. "That one was a mistake."

"She was a gift," Mari corrected, prying Rih off and setting her on a perch.

Rih let out an indignant chirp, as if offended at the very idea that she could be anything less than perfect.

"She's definitely not a skyweaver, no matter what her bloodline is. Why you insisted on attempting to train her as one is still beyond me," Rowan said.

Mari rolled her eyes. "Yes, and yet, here we are, over ten years later, and you're still talking about it. Maybe if you hadn't named her after a storm wind, she wouldn't have taken it as a personal challenge."

Her father chuckled. "We should've known from the moment she bit through her first training glove."

Mari smirked and glanced at Rih, who was pointedly ignoring them both, grooming her feathers with an air of exaggerated self-importance. "She has personality."

"She has an attitude," her father corrected. "Not ideal in a bird that's supposed to follow instructions."

Skyweavers were bred for obedience and precision, trained from hatching to follow scent markers and landmarks with unwavering discipline. But Rih had never followed a flight path she didn't feel like taking.

Mari's parents had built their entire livelihood around these birds, ever since her grandfather returned from a long expedition beyond Patovia's borders. He brought back the rare plant cuttings he needed to cultivate an entirely new species of date hybrids, but also three strange birds no one in Patovia had ever seen before.

What began as a simple gift for his daughter, Mari's mother, soon became something far greater. Mari's parents had seen potential, and before long, what was meant to be a gesture of affection had grown into a second family business—one that helped solidify their legacy as one of the most respected families in Greenhaven.

Her father had watched those three birds fly not just away, but back again. Over and over. No matter how far they were taken, they always found home.

That was the beginning of everything.

They bred the first skyweavers from that tiny flock, adding to their numbers with careful selection, training them and selling them across Patovia until their family name became synonymous with speed, reliability, and messages that never got lost.

A skyweaver never wavered. They flew swift and certain, carrying secrets and promises across the kingdom.

And then there was Rih. Mari sighed as she looked at the tiny skyweaver preening herself on her perch. She had been born from the same breeding stock, raised in the same aviary, trained with the same methods as the others, but Rih was a skyweaver in name only—too smart, too stubborn, too much trouble. She had been supposed to follow orders. Instead, she stole food, bullied the other birds, and delivered messages wherever she damn well pleased.

Mari had loved her instantly.

Her father had once joked that Rih had been given a homing instinct, just like the others, but she had simply decided her home was wherever she felt like landing.

"Remember when she stole an entire pouch of salted dates off Elder Amara?" Mari grinned.

Her father snorted. "Or when she delivered a love letter to the wrong suitor," he added, his voice full of mock horror.

They both broke into laughter, and Rih let out a long sigh, flaring her wings just enough to make a show of how utterly unbothered she was.

"Sorry, Rih," her father said. "You're just not cut out for the family business."

Mari reached up and let Rih step onto her forearm. "No," she agreed. "But she's ours."

Rih, apparently pleased with this assessment, nestled against Mari's chest, preening dramatically like she'd just won an argument she hadn't even participated in.

Mari sighed, rubbing her temple. "Alright, you ridiculous thing, get back up there. I need to send someone who actually listens." She lifted her arm and Rih reluctantly hopped back onto her perch, fluffing up like she was deeply wounded.

Mari turned toward the row of trained skyweavers, scanning for Greenhaven's best flyer. Her eyes landed on Cel, a sleek, steel-gray bird with intelligent eyes. Cel was everything Rih was not—reliable, disciplined, and completely uninterested in Mari's antics.

"Hey, handsome." She smiled, slipping her hands under Cel's chest to scoop him up. He blinked at her as she tied the message to his leg, making extra sure the knot was firm but light. "You'll get there," she whispered, stroking the smooth feathers of his chest before stepping outside. Rih let out a begrudging caw from inside, clearly still sulking.

Mari lifted Cel high, and with a strong flick of her wrist, she released him into the night. He took off instantly, his wings cutting cleanly through the air, rising higher and into the sprawling sea of stars.

Mari felt a dash of hope as she watched him disappear in the right direction, but she knew hope alone wouldn't be enough. As Cel slowly vanished into the night, Mari's attention was pulled toward the beginnings of colors that were stretching across the sky. She could now say with absolute certainty that the glow was, in fact, an aurora, crawling across the heavens, beautiful and unsettling. Mari felt the sky spinning above her as she tried to comprehend what she was looking at. The colors were far darker now, and she breathed them in, realizing she was witnessing the beginnings of the most spectacular light show in Greenhaven that shouldn't exist. She found herself agreeing with Harrop's assessment of what they were... sinister. And beautiful, of course... She could sit for hours, unmoving, just staring at them until they disappeared with the night, but she knew they shouldn't be there. And that's when it hit her.

Something was coming.

Greenhaven wasn't ready.

And neither, Mari realized with a chilling certainty, was she.

CHAPTER TWO

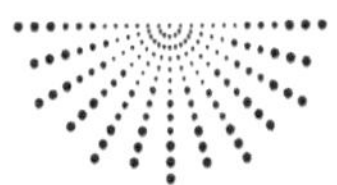

EVERY MORNING LIKE CLOCKWORK, MARI AWOKE AND anxiously scanned the horizon, desperately hoping for Cel's return.

On the fifth day, she stood on the hill at dusk, her heart heavy with every candlemark that passed. By the ninth, she could no longer deny it—Cel wasn't coming back. She stared at the empty horizon, her hands trembling and her spirit deflating. Cel had never failed before. If even the skyweavers couldn't navigate the skies, what chance did she have?

Adding to this failure, village concerns grew over the deepening shades of green that danced across the sky, growing more and more vivid until there was absolutely no question that everyone had to agree with Mari's insistence that they were auroras. Brilliant green ones, at that. If the situation wasn't so dire, it would have been one of the most exciting events to happen to the small village. Greenhaven was starting to earn its name again, although for all the wrong reasons. Wherever she went, Mari heard the panicked whispers, and her guilt grew as strong as the hues overhead.

MARI WALKED out the blacksmith's workshop after having dropped off a broken carrier that had been begging to be mended for over three moons. She knew something was going on the moment she decided to finally deal with it. Her sudden urge to be productive was telling, and she recognized it for what it was: a distraction, a desperate attempt to keep from thinking about Cel. The blacksmith had promised to have it fixed by the next day.

"Want to see if there's anything tasty we can bring home?" Mari asked her cousin, eyeing the fruit stand at the end of the street.

"Always," Zeph said with a grin.

They headed toward the shop, and Mari heard Zeph's stomach grumble. She winced. She knew he'd been forgoing his rations and giving them to their grandmother.

"Do you think the birds will even need cages soon?" he asked.

"Don't say that," Mari said, although her voice lacked conviction. The drought was turning everything brittle. Even hope.

They ducked under the shade of the market awning, a stretch of canvas that had once shielded ripe fruit and jars of honey and was now drooping over half-empty crates. She scanned the offerings... There wasn't much to choose from, but now that they were here, and Gail, the owner, was watching them hopefully, Mari knew she had to buy at least something.

She continued along the stand, scanning for anything she could bring home that wouldn't trigger a disappointed look from her mother. She bumped into someone abruptly and looked up, already apologizing.

Lea and Jayel stood there, looking just as apologetic to have been in her way.

Lea was wrapped in a shawl despite the heat, her eyes sunken and dark. She looked exhausted and afraid, like many other Greenhaveners these days. Her husband stood stiff beside her, his hands shoved into his pockets and his shoulders hunched. Normally, they were the most polished pair in Greenhaven, known for their warmth as much as their wealth, but today, they looked like ghosts of themselves.

Not two moons earlier, Jayel had buried his parents after a tragic accident. Or so the story went. It was widely whispered that his father, having realized what was happening to the salt pools, had decided to exit this plane of existence on his own terms before he had to endure watching his empire evaporate into nothingness. Sadly for Jayel, he inherited the family business as well as the problems, which were increasing by the day. At twenty-two, he had buried his father and now faced the very real possibility of having to bury his family legacy as well.

"Mari," Lea said when she spotted her. "Zeph."

Mari stepped forward instinctively. "Lea. Jayel. I'm..." She faltered. She didn't know what she was. Sorry? Ashamed? Powerless?

Jayel gave a weak smile. "It's good to see you," he said. "We've just come from the pools."

Mari's heart sank. "Is it worse?"

Jayel's nod was slow. "We've lost three more beds."

The salt pools were the pride of Greenhaven—an irreplaceable source of employment, trade, and tradition. Mari's family used their salt for their signature dates and to bake the bread her aunt Kia swore by, among other things. Without the pools...

"If they dry out completely," Lea added, her voice shaking, "there's no coming back. They'll calcify. Permanently."

"We've sent word to Brindlemyre to halt our usual exports," Jayel said. "They'll look elsewhere. They'll move on."

Mari cringed as she recognized the fear in their eyes. Her mind flashed with memories—Ren's chubby hands learning to pack salt into tiny burlap sacks just last season, Zeph's face after negotiating his first contract for the orchard, the village children, their tongues stained yellow from licking salted lemon candies during the harvest festivals.

The salt pools were a family legacy, yes, but they were also a Greenhaven institution at this point. Not to mention a natural wonder of Patovia. Mari was honestly impressed the couple could get out of bed, given what they had been through and what they were facing. If the situation didn't improve... Well, they would have more problems than just tasteless bread.

"I'm sorry," Mari said. She knew it wasn't enough.

"We're trying to figure out next steps," Jayel said. "But it's hard to step into something your whole life was shaped around without the man who was supposed to show you how to carry it."

The group stood in awkward silence, and Mari felt herself spiraling deeper into guilt with every sentence she thought of to say and then discarded as not good enough. Then Zeph cleared his throat. "We'll figure something out."

Lea gave a weak smile, but it didn't reach her eyes. "We're running out of time."

Mari and Zeph didn't speak as they walked to the dry fountain in the middle of the commons. The cracked stone basin was still beautiful, but the greenery that once trailed from its edges was gone, replaced by crumbling husks and looping brown vines.

They sat in silence for a long time.

Then Zeph finally said, "I want to come with you."

Mari blinked. "What?"

"To Joycita. You shouldn't go alone."

Her throat tightened. "I never said I was going to Joycita."

"Come on, Mari, we both know you've already decided that you will."

Mari huffed a chuckle. Her cousin knew her too well.

"I mean it," he said. "The timing's not great, but—"

"But you can't," she interrupted. "You said the first round of interviews for the seasonal workers is about to start."

"I'll talk to Gran. Maybe I can—"

"Zeph," Mari said more firmly. "No. You're needed here."

"So are you," he snapped. Then, reaching out to give her hand an apologetic squeeze, he added, "I just... I don't like the thought of you being out there, facing gods know what by yourself."

Mari offered a humorless smile. "Neither do I."

"Can't you wait a few more days? Just until after the interviews and orientation? I can get them up to speed, and then I can come with you."

She shook her head. "If I wait, I'll miss the convergence. If I miss the convergence, I'll lose the proof." She looked up at the cloud-streaked sky. "I have to go now, Zeph. While there's still time."

Zeph exhaled. "When did you become such a little storm?"

Mari snorted. "I was born this way, sir."

Zeph dropped an arm around her shoulder and gave her a

tight squeeze. "I'll pretend this doesn't suck, but just so you know... This sucks."

Mari leaned her head against his shoulder. "Strong threads, cousin."

He grunted. "I'm too cool for that."

Mari looked down at the shriveled, sad excuse for a mango she'd settled on, turning it in her hand. Everything felt like it was one squeeze away from falling apart.

ON THE TENTH DAY, Mari had fully accepted her destiny.

At breakfast, she looked up at her parents from across the table, over her one steaming hot cup of tea for the day. "Did you know we've been making salted dates for almost a century?" Mari's mother cocked her head. Mari knew the thought probably seemed to have come out of nowhere. "I wonder if, when your great-grandparents planted the first orchard, they realized that they were literally establishing roots for all of Greenhaven."

Jannah chuckled. "Awfully deep for this early in the morning, dear. Were you up late charting again?"

Her parents knew by now that she always got a little philosophical after a particularly successful night with the stars.

"It's just incredible," Mari continued, "how those first few rows of date palms sparked an entire export industry that ended up supporting other families' businesses, and then, before we knew it, boom, Greenhaven became the largest produce exporter in the region."

Jannah nodded while she gathered the empty plates, a proud smile playing at her lips. "Not quite that quickly, but yes, that's just about how it happened."

"We are coming up on the century mark, aren't we, Jannah?" Rowan set his fork down. "Perhaps we should talk to your mother about planning a celebration. She'll insist it's no big deal, but still... One hundred years of salted dates is nothing to scoff at."

"You know," Mari said quietly, "if the salt pools evaporate, they're gone forever."

"The salt pools?" her father asked.

"And the salted dates." Mari put her glass down and looked at her parents solemnly. "I'm going to Joycita."

THE VILLAGE COMMONS bustled as villagers rushed to complete errands before total darkness. Mari made her way toward the forge, already able to see the blacksmith's embers glowing brightly from where she was at the top of the street. She slowed her pace as she approached, hoping she wouldn't see... Lana. The blacksmith's apprentice was leaning over a workbench working away with an intense focus. *Curse it!* The sight of the woman stirred something in Mari—a tangle of messy feeling she could have sworn she had left behind. She took a steadying breath and raked her fingers through her hair, catching on curls as she tugged them free in an attempt to untussle as much of it as possible. If she had known Lana would be here, she might have brushed her hair first. Or asked her mother to come instead. Resigning herself to the interaction, Mari stepped into the street just as Lana looked up, their eyes locking instantly.

Lana wiped her hands on her apron. "Mari," she called out, not sounding anywhere near as bitter as she had the last time they spoke.

"Lana." Mari walked into the workshop, cursing silently and attempting to sound as un-bothered as possible.

"All fixed," Lana said, nodding toward the release crate sitting at the edge of the counter, its latches now secure and gleaming. "You're really leaving, then?" she asked, fidgeting with a cloth as she eyed the sack of supplies Mari carried.

"I am," Mari said simply.

Lana offered a timid smile and then reached behind the workbench to pull out a small, intricately crafted pendant. The metal was smooth and dark, shaped like a crescent moon, with a tiny glass vial embedded in its center.

"An early Lumithra gift?" Mari questioned.

"For the road," Lana said, holding it out. "You'll be missing the festival by, what, a week?"

"Just over a week," Mari corrected her.

"Here." Lana extended her arm further. The pendant swung back and forth in a perfect arc.

Mari's brow furrowed, intrigued. "What is it?"

"A charm," Lana explained with a proud smile. "The vial's sealed with oil from Harcanth. It won't break, no matter what."

"Volcanic oil? Sexy..." Mari admired Lana's detailed work.

"They say it wards off bad spirits." Lana shrugged. "Or maybe it's just superstition. You always said you didn't believe in this stuff, but... just in case."

Mari accepted the pendant, her fingers brushing against Lana's. "Thank you."

Lana offered another smile, shifting her gaze from the ground to the fire... anywhere but Mari's eyes. "My grandmother always used to remind me that Lumithra's not just about giving—it's about putting a piece of yourself into the gift. This... it's just a pendant, but it's something I hope reminds you of home."

Mari fastened the pendant around her neck. "I'll keep it close," she promised.

Silence hung between them for a moment, and a thousand things remained unsaid, waiting at the tip of Mari's tongue to ruin this perfectly sweet moment. Lana finally broke the silence, her voice low. "You could come by later, if you wanted. Just to talk. No strings."

Mari met her eyes, seeking confirmation of the unspoken invitation she suspected Lana was extending. She opened her mouth to reply, but no words came out. Instead, she gave a small, barely noticeable nod before turning to leave.

She stumbled awkwardly as she glanced back, catching Lana watching her, the faintest hint of a smile at the corners of her mouth.

Mari quickened her pace, her thoughts racing. She told herself she wouldn't go back, but the idea was tempting, inviting her mind to open doors to dark treasure chests of memories she swore she would never allow herself to explore again. Perhaps she could go back... it would be rude not to, wouldn't it? Later that night, beneath the cover of darkness, she thought. Maybe then.

DESPITE HER IMPENDING DEPARTURE, Mari was in a spectacular mood on her final day in Greenhaven. She was humming one of her favorite Patovian work anthems when her aunt Kia arrived that afternoon. Mari was surprised to see her aunt at the door, carrying a basket wrapped in a worn but colorful cloth. Mari could smell the freshly baked bread as soon as Kia stepped inside.

"I thought I'd stop by and bring something for the journey," Kia said, her warm smile lighting up the room.

Mari's mother rushed to take the basket, giving her sister's shoulders a squeeze with gratitude. "Kia, you didn't have to. You're already doing so much for the infantry."

"It's no trouble," Kia said, beaming at Mari. "Besides, I couldn't let my niece leave on an empty stomach."

Mari smiled, grateful that the universe had blessed her with two such wonderfully different women. Her mother had never forced her to lean into the "feminine" tasks, and despite her best efforts to gently encourage cooking and baking, it couldn't have been clearer that Mari was utterly disinterested. It helped that her mother wasn't particularly skilled in the kitchen herself. Kia, however, had inherited all the talent and passion for it, serving as the head cook for the village's infantry unit.

Kia handed Mari a small parcel wrapped tightly in waxed paper. "This is for the road. It'll keep for a few days."

"Thank you, Aunty," Mari said.

Kia ruffled her hair affectionately. "Don't thank me yet. You'll have to write to me about all the strange and wonderful foods you find in Joycita. Maybe you'll even learn a recipe or two."

Mari laughed. "Don't hold your breath."

Her mother joined in the laughter, adding, "If Mari's going to learn anything, it won't be cooking. It'll be something far more impractical."

"Impractical?" Kia raised an eyebrow. "Says the woman who can't boil water without burning it."

The three burst into laughter. "No, she's right," Mari confessed. "Although given the journey I've been asked to embark on by the elders of our village," she raised her eyebrows to emphasize the importance of both her task and those entrusting it, "I'd argue that my 'impractical' skills are quite the hot commodity these days." It felt so good to laugh, and she savored the feelings of joy. She expected the next moments like these could be a long way off.

"Hello?" Zeph's voice drifted in from the front entrance.

"In here," called Mari.

Zeph walked in holding a light tan leather waterskin. He held it up to Mari before placing it on the table in front of her. She could tell from the brightness of the red stitching around the edges that it was new.

"Oh, Zeph, how lovely!" Mari's mother reached for the waterskin and rubbed the leather.

"So, does this mean you're on speaking terms with Rissa again?" Mari asked as she picked up the waterskin and held it up to her nose, breathing deeply. The smoky, rich scent doubled her feelings of gratitude for her family.

Zeph blushed. "Maybe. She was more than happy to talk about you, and I was smart enough to stay on topic. She sends her well wishes. She was really touched to be able to make this for you," he said.

Mari stood from her seat and wrapped her arms around her cousin, or as far as they could reach around his sturdy frame. "Thank you," she whispered. Turning to face the three of them, Mari threw up her hands, gesturing to the gift from her aunt and the waterskin, hooked her finger through the necklace around her neck, and showed it off to her family. "And here I thought I would be missing out on Lumithra this year!"

Mari's mother chuckled and pulled her in for a hug, kissing the side of her head and getting a face of Mari's soft, dark hair. "Without you to tell us when the Weavers Arc is directly overhead, I'm afraid that it will be us who miss out on the festival this year."

Mari rolled her eyes. She loved how her parents had always indulged her fantasy of becoming a most important astronomer for her village, a fantasy that was fast approaching reality. A thread of a reminder tugged at her—she wanted to review her charts one final time before she left. Yes, they were ever so slightly off right now, but the study would be helpful to ensure she had her timing right. She wanted to be in Adavale before the new moon, which would allow her one day's rest in a warm bed before she set off on the final leg of her journey to the capital.

"I know that look," Kia said with a grin. "She's about to leave us for her stars."

Mari smiled apologetically. "I still have so much to do."

"Well, I'm glad we were able to give you a little bit of Lumithra before you leave." Kia rested a hand on Mari's shoulder. "Strong threads," she said softly. The traditional blessing usually made Mari cringe because it felt so awkward and corny, but in this moment, she appreciated the sentiment.

Kia leaned in and kissed Mari's cheek. Mari closed her eyes and leaned into the embrace for a moment before pulling away. "Bright flames," she replied, her throat tight.

Her aunt and her mother exchanged a glance. Mari usually only returned blessings to the elders.

With a final squeeze of her aunt's hand, she slipped down the hallway toward her bedroom.

"Before you disappear..."

Mari spun around. Zeph had followed her, his expression unusually serious. "We need to go over some combat basics," he said, crossing his arms.

Mari groaned. "Come on, Zeph, I know this stuff."

The truth was that Greenhaven's combat instructor had long since given up on Mari, as her passion for star mapping left little energy for anything else. Still, she wasn't about to let Zeph think she was completely inept.

"You need to know more," Zeph replied, grabbing her wrist and squeezing it tight.

"Ow!" Mari winced, glaring at him.

"Get out of my grasp," he challenged her.

Mari tried to recall the counter maneuver she'd been taught, twisting her wrist and pulling back. She applied what she thought was the right motion, but Zeph didn't budge.

"Well, if you get attacked out there, maybe you can tell them there's a new moon next week," he teased smugly.

"I'm impressed you remembered that," Mari shot back, panting.

"I didn't," he admitted, grinning. "It's all you talked about at lunch yesterday."

Mari rolled her eyes. "Well, I'm impressed you remembered that far back."

Before she could react, Zeph pulled his arm forward, yanking Mari off balance. She landed on her knees, her elbow bent awkwardly, an intense pressure building, warning her not to move.

"I'm glad I could impress you." He chuckled, releasing her before she could retaliate.

Mari rubbed her elbow, frowning. She hated to admit it, but he was right. Surely, some extra combat skills could come in handy along her journey.

CHAPTER THREE

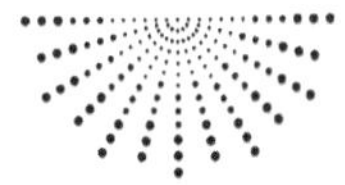

MARI PULLED THE DRAWSTRING ON HER MODEST travel sack closed. She had packed only the essentials. The lighter she traveled, the easier the journey.

She picked up her new journal, a Lumithra gift from Elder Amara, pushed it inside the already tightly packed satchel, and buckled it, but not before checking for the third time that her star charts were rolled neatly and tucked in safely. She looked up to see her mother, standing in the doorway, a proud smile on her face. Damn her parents for being so supportive. Protective, too, but not so protective that they felt the need to accompany her on her journey. While she was sure they would prefer to, the farm and animals needed tending to, and as much as she hated to admit it, her mother wasn't up for the journey. She had been forgoing her rations, saving them in order to send enough sandwiches to get Mari to Adavale without needing to stop anywhere, and as a result, was significantly weakened, though she had been hiding it well. The sacrifice of a mother. Her father had gifted Mari his best knife, the one with the swirls carved into the white handle and filled in with a simple golden resin that looked far more expensive than it actually was.

Before she left, Mari made one final visit to the aviary. She took her time to walk slowly around the entire enclosure, petting every single bird they kept, kissing them gently atop their soft heads and soaking in their vibrating coos. She paused under the sturdy rafters and looked up at the mice that scurried along, having long ago given up any attempt to conceal their existence.

"Bye, little ones," she said to the room. The birds' anxious chirping echoed through the aviary. The feeling permeated through the whole village, animals and humans alike. It all came down to Mari.

MARI TOSSED and turned all night. Eventually, she gave in and just got up. Padding quietly into the kitchen so as to not wake her parents, she filled the kettle with just enough water for a single cup of tea, poked the embers of the fading fire, and dropped in a small log. She heard movement behind her and jumped up quickly, spinning around to face whatever was behind her, only to remember that Zeph had insisted on staying the night so he could be there to see her off. Of course, right before they turned in for the evening, he had made a final offer to accompany her on the journey. He was thoughtful and ridiculously selfless like that, but they both knew that their family needed him here. Zeph tossed under his blanket on the lumpy couch that was far too small for him to fit comfortably. Mari smiled as she watched Zeph's chest rise and fall with each steady breath. There was something so innocent about him when he was sleeping. She sent silent thanks to the stars that Zeph would be here for her parents while she was away.

While she waited for the fire to get hot enough to boil her water, she wandered outside and looked up. The aurora was still alarming, despite its beauty. How wild that this phenomenon that she had spent her whole life dreaming of seeing would end up on her doorstep, an omen of unsettling proportions. Based on where the moon was in the sky, there were probably a good three candlemarks before anyone else in the house was awake. The sky was still dark enough to see the stars. The Weavers Arc, the constellation that signaled the start of Lumithra, was slightly off where it should be this close to the festival. If things were normal, it would be aligning in about ten days from now, but based on her updated calculations, the alignment would be occurring two days earlier. Mari wondered if they should be celebrating based on where the constellation was or where it should be. She felt the dry grass between her bare toes as the heaviness of guilt stabbed at her chest. This was the first Lumithra she would miss. She scowled at the stars in their unfamiliar positions. The whole point of Lumithra was unity, and she was going to be further away from her family and Greenhaven than she had ever been before.

She settled down on a chair under the back canopy and rolled her foot back and forth against the loose pebbles on the ground, enjoying the sensation against her bare skin. She shuddered, anticipation and the crisp morning air settling in around her. Soon, everyone would wake, and the formalities of the goodbye would begin. First, she would have to fight off her mother's attempts to visit the old temple and pay tribute to the ancient gods. Mari was convinced the only thing more insulting than someone not honoring the gods was a nonbeliever rocking up and reluctantly paying them an insincere tribute. Especially when resources were so limited. What was even available to offer? She decided she would offer to accompany her mother, a believer, and bow her head politely. Yes, that would be quite acceptable. To both her mother and to the ancient gods who either did or did not exist. Not that it mattered to Mari. The city of Joycita very much did exist, and as long as her journey went as planned (*come on, ancient gods, do your thing*), she would be there in roughly nine days.

"STARRY MARI'S GOING ON AN ADVENTURE," Mari whispered to herself, claiming the nickname that had haunted her childhood as a badge of honor. "Look at me now, fops," she chided as she jumped over a small ditch. Fragments of the dead grass and crumbling earth flew into the air as she landed and flew into her face. Spluttering, she rubbed her eyes frantically, trying to dislodge the dust particles that filled them. "Stop looking, stop looking!" She coughed, grateful she was mumbling to ghosts of her past and there was no one around to witness her misstep.

When she could blink without feeling like the entire beachside of Elyria's Edge was inside her eyeballs, she continued on. "Starry Mari's gotta slow down a little." She chuckled, adjusting her cloak. The path curved slightly to the left, leading to a gentle incline that gave her a broader view of the landscape. Mari paused at the top, resting her hands on her hips and scanning the horizon. The fields were a lifeless patchwork of dry despair, the goldenreeds' dry husks swaying in the wind.

Mari crouched and picked a fistful of particularly pretty

wildflowers that had somehow survived the heat. Their petals crumbled at her touch, and she frowned, brushing the dust from her fingertips onto her leather pants. Even the weeds couldn't thrive here anymore.

This drought was squeezing Greenhaven dry, strangling everything it touched. Mari shook herself out, a spark of determination igniting within her. It wouldn't be difficult to convince the capital to send aid. It looked like it wasn't just Greenhaven that needed it, either. She wondered how far the devastation stretched. Perhaps Joycita was fighting the same struggles.

She pulled her telescope from her satchel and looked back in the direction of Greenhaven, but she could no longer see the village. She smiled as she recalled the day the telescope became hers. Who would have thought a decade later that it would become such a crucial instrument? It had been years since her mentor had gifted it to her—years since that wiry old astronomer had stood in the middle of Greenhaven's commons and turned her world upside down.

She could see him now, clear as day, his bright blue eyes peering out from under his worn, wide-brimmed hat, as he addressed the curious crowd. "The stars," he'd said, gesturing grandly to the heavens, "are not just lights in the sky. They are history, maps, and warnings, if you care to look."

Young Mari had cared very much to look. That night, while the rest of the village had slept, Mari had crept out of her bed and followed the astronomer to a small clearing beyond the fields where he had set up his telescope. He had laughed when he saw her, all gangly limbs and wild curls, clutching a star chart she had scrawled on the back of an old aviary ledger.

"Ambitious," he'd said, adjusting his spectacles as he

examined her work. "But you've got Nimithra's Bow upside down."

Her cheeks had flushed, but he'd grinned and beckoned her closer. By the time the stars began to fade and the first signs of dawn crept over the horizon, she'd learned more than she ever thought possible. He had stayed three days—three of the most important days of her life, crammed full of constellations, planets, and the phases of the moon. Looking back, those three days completely changed the trajectory of life then, and again today.

"Keep looking up," he'd told her when he left, pressing the battered telescope into her hands, her mouth open so wide that her mother would have threatened to drop a cherry in it.

Shaking off the memory, Mari picked up her pace. The path narrowed as it wound up another incline, this one steeper, with craggy rocks jutting out like broken teeth. At the top, she paused again, turning slowly to take in the view.

She sighed, putting her telescope away before starting down the trail. "Just keep moving, Mari," she told herself. "The answers aren't going to come to you standing still."

As the day stretched on, the wide-open fields slowly closed in until Mari was traveling along a long dirt path bordered by dense trees. The forests in the Midwilds were always green, but even here, leaves were falling off trees when they shouldn't be, the distinct crunches as Mari stepped on them a telltale sign that the forest was thirsty.

The buzzing of insects got louder as twilight arrived. She had been keeping a steady pace and had only needed to stop once to relieve herself. She looked through the brittle tree branches in the hopes of finding a small clearing where she could stop for the night. She cringed at how easily tree branches snapped as she stepped off the path and pushed her way through the brush. Unable to find a suitable space to settle, she easily made her own clearing by breaking off a few low-hanging branches. She pulled a piece of flint from her travel sack, and very shortly after, she had a small fire going. The fire was all but silent, barely crackling, but doing a good enough job keeping Mari warm while she scribbled in her journal about various observations she had made throughout the day.

The journey so far had been uneventful. Mari was in the middle of describing how a particular field of goldenreeds had caught her attention. The tall weeds swaying in the breeze were a thing of beauty, and it took all she had not to stop and stare, mesmerized by the magic of the world.

Mari shook out her hand to release a cramp and glanced up at the sky. The gentle green of the aurora was starting to darken, and she wondered if it was the exhaustion setting in or if she was actually starting to see some tinges of pink creeping in. She made note of it in her journal. The sky was still changing. As she fought an internal battle with her creative mind over the perfect color description, a sudden snap broke the silence, and her body tensed. If it wasn't for the unusually silent fire, she would have assumed it was kindling, but out of the corner of her eye, she spotted movement in the nearby underbrush. She froze.

She glanced at her travel sack, where her knife was stored. *Curse it! Not one more thought of things being uneventful, Namari of Greenhaven. Not one more thought.* She trembled as adrenaline coursed through her body, her mind taking speedy inventory of all the grips, throws, and attacks Zeph had taught her the day before.

Her hand instinctively reached for a branch she'd snapped earlier for firewood, the only thing within reach that could even remotely resemble a weapon. She tightened her grip, bracing herself to parry whatever was about to come at her.

A small rabbit darted suddenly out, its beady eyes locked on to Mari. It paused, only for a moment, its nose twitching, before deciding she was clearly not a threat, and casually hopping across the rest of the path, disappearing into the thick forest on the other side.

Mari let out a nervous laugh, her shoulders dropping in relief. Still, her unease remained, so she retrieved her knife anyway and shoved it down securely into her boot, vowing she wouldn't take a single step in any direction without it close at hand. With a wry smile, she poked at the fire with the branch, its lifeless form a pathetic excuse for a weapon in the thankfully nonexistent battle.

MARI WOKE to birdsong shortly after dawn. She was surprised she had slept so soundly, given that she had been sleeping on a makeshift mattress of tree branches that had no flexibility or bend whatsoever. After a simple breakfast consisting of her aunt Kia's rye bread and some lemon dates, she set off for Adavale. If all went according to plan, she should reach the village by early evening.

She entered a clearing and stopped abruptly when her eyes locked on a figure standing ahead, silhouetted by the filtered sunlight breaking through the trees. The man was tall, his clothes ragged and mismatched, and his menacing grin set every instinct in her body on edge.

"Hello there," he cooed, stepping forward and blocking her path. "A traveler without an escort? Dangerous choice." A smug smile curled across his face.

Mari took a step back, trying to keep her voice steady. "I'm not alone," she lied. "My father is behind me. With our dogs."

"Dogs, eh?" The man asked, not appearing to believe her for even a second.

"Oh, yes. Big dogs. Protective, big dogs."

The man laughed. "Well, you and your 'companions,'" he said, his emphasis making it clear he knew she was alone, "just need to pay the toll and you'll be free to pass."

Mari's mind was racing. "I don't have much," she said, sliding her satchel behind her back as subtly as she could. "But I can share some food."

She reached into her travel sack and pulled out a small pouch of dried berries and bread. She tossed it toward him, hoping it would be enough.

The bandit caught it mid-air and inspected its contents. "Food's nice," he said, his grin widening. "But I was thinking something more... valuable." His eyes drifted to Lana's pendant hanging around Mari's neck. She knew it wasn't worth risking her life for, but there was no way she was going to part with it.

Before Mari could respond, there was a rustling from the trees on either side of the path, and two more figures emerged, each armed with crude weapons—a rusty knife and a long, gnarled stick. They started to close in on her, cutting off any escape.

Panic surged, but she gritted her teeth and took inventory of what was inside her travel sack, an idea forming.

"Fine," she said, trying so hard to keep the tremor out of her voice that she found herself shouting angrily at the trio of bandits. "Take it all and curse you forever."

With a sudden thrust, Mari threw her travel sack to the ground a short distance to her left. The bandits' attention snapped to the sack, their greedy eyes calculating its worth. She didn't wait for them to inspect it.

Mari bolted into the trees on the opposite side of the path, holding her satchel tightly to her hip as she ran, so as not to snag on any close branches. The shouts of the bandits rang out behind her, followed by the pounding of feet as they gave chase.

The forest blurred around her as she ducked under low branches and leapt over twisted roots. At times, the branch was too low to duck but too high to leap, so she would just hold her hands up and run through them, bracing for impact and hitting them hard enough that they would snap upon contact with her forearms and body. This strategy only worked for as long as these trees were thirsty, and for the first time, she prayed there were no healthy trees. Her breath came in ragged, painful gasps, and she glanced over her shoulder once, catching a glimpse of one of the bandits stumbling in her wake. Out of nowhere, an outstretched hand pulled down hard on her shoulder, catching her off guard. She shrieked and made a hard right, running straight into a thicket of brambles. She wrenched her cloak free from the tangle of thorns and pushed her arms in front of her to push a long, chunky tree branch out of her path. The wiry branch moved with her and, as she let it go, it whipped back hard. To her relief, she heard a pained grunt behind her and chanced a quick look over her shoulder. The branch had catapulted the bandit with a furious momentum. His face was bloodied and disfigured, but he continued his pursuit.

"You've gotta be kidding me," Mari breathed, jumping over a mossy rock.

A sharp turn led her down a slope, the loose earth threatening to throw her off balance. She slipped, her knees scraping against the ground, tiny rocks poking into her skin, but she scrambled back to her feet and kept running. The sound of pursuit grew fainter with each step, but she didn't dare slow down.

Finally, after what felt like an eternity, Mari broke through the dense underbrush and collapsed behind a large tree. Her hands pressed against its rough bark as she tried to steady her breathing. Her heart pounded so fast she would surely be heard by anyone nearby, but the forest was eerily quiet, the bandits seemingly far behind.

Mari leaned her head back against the wet tree trunk. She looked down at her bloodied hands and dusty cloak and let out a nervous laugh. Scanning her surroundings, she realized she had no idea where she was and would have to wait for nightfall to use the stars as a guide to get her back on track.

Great. Just like that, I've lost time, she thought angrily. That wasn't all she had lost. The travel sack was gone, along with most of her provisions.

She spat on the palm of her hand and tried to clean away a chunk of clay that had settled into the cracks of the scrapes. It stung as she rubbed it, and a teardrop landed in the mix. She stood slowly and surveyed the forest again. With a deep breath, she took a step forward. *This direction is as good as any,* she thought.

The air was damp. *The air was damp.*

Had she not been so shaken by the attack, she might have noticed sooner. The ground beneath her was alive with flourishing grass. Wherever she was, the drought's reach had not found its way here. Hope rumbled within her.

Mari trudged through the dense forest, her muscles stiff and exhaustion setting in, but her resolve strengthening. She stepped gingerly, cautious not to slip on the exposed tree roots underfoot. The trees here were larger, their branches weaving into a canopy that blocked most of the fading daylight. She picked up a nearby stick and swirled it through a sticky curtain of spider webbing that blocked her path. As she brushed the threads away, she saw a dark opening in the middle of a towering gray cave up ahead, its entrance half hidden by mossy tendrils and a large boulder that appeared to be leaning against an even larger one.

It didn't look like a natural formation; the smooth edges of the stone hinted at intentional craftsmanship. A cold breeze hit her face as she stepped closer, and a shallow hum accompanied the chill emanating from the entrance. Without a second thought, she turned her body sideways and squeezed through the opening.

Goosebumps instantly raised on her skin, and she tried to make her footsteps as silent as possible as she made her way deeper into the cave. Every few steps, she would pause and listen, but the passageway was eerily quiet and undisturbed. So far. As her eyes adjusted, she saw that what she thought was a hallway was just a large, half wall that hung suspended from the roof of the cave, with curved holes burrowed randomly along its smooth face. The room was almost circular in shape, with rectangular pillars jutting down from the ceiling with precise placement. Small beams of light shone through carvings that wrapped around the upper part of the entire room, forming patterns along the walls. She couldn't make out the details, but they looked intentionally carved, as opposed to worn naturally by the wind.

A throbbing in her shin pulled Mari away from her observations. There was a small gash just below her left knee, but without her medical supplies, which were in her long-gone travel sack, there wasn't much she could do to tend to the wound other than a little spit and a gentle wipe with her dirty cloak. It was better than nothing.

Grateful at least that there was no one home, Mari settled on the floor, her back against the unusually smooth wall, and pulled out her journal. The shadows danced through the curious openings as the light outside changed, with the shifting pinks and greens of the aurora peeking through. What was this place?

The designs felt familiar, but that was impossible—she'd never seen anything like them before. At least not in Greenhaven. Perhaps in one of her books? A fragment of a memory poked through her exhaustion, and she recalled flipping through the astronomer's notebook, copying as much as she could to her own journal before he left. He had taught her how to find meaning in patterns.

Orbital patterns? She wondered, running her fingers lightly along the carvings she could reach in the lower part of the wall and tracing their flowing curves. No... they weren't repetitive enough for that. *Orbital...* her mind went blank. Sleep was long overdue, but Mari refused to give in to it. She had too much to do still.

She tried to sketch the carvings, but they were harder to capture them than she expected, since the patterns shifted under the changing light and seemed to throw new shadows and details every time she looked up. Mari frowned. The more she traced the grooves, the more purposeful they seemed. Were these designs meant to channel water, or perhaps light? She shook her head. She had no idea what to make of it all, and try as she might, she couldn't recall a specific enough memory to pinpoint anything helpful. Despite her body's overwhelming desire to curl up in a ball and pass out, Mari knew she still needed to go back outside and determine her exact location.

She had already sacrificed a day thanks to the scumbags who had attacked her and stolen her travel sack. She needed to know exactly where she was going as soon as day broke.

She fought against her tired eyes. It would be so easy to drop her pencil and let sleep take her. Her thoughts drifted back to the astronomer. He had once told her that all the questions of the universe could be answered by the night sky. Her eyes shot open as a sobering chill ran through her body. She mustn't let herself fall asleep until she had recalibrated her location. She gave her cheeks a little slap, far too gentle for the wake-up she needed. She channeled Zeph and tried again.

"Ow!" she exclaimed. This one landed square and firm. She was definitely awake now. She forced herself to stand, shivering as a strong breeze swept through the chamber. Perhaps they were designed to channel wind...

She pulled her cloak back on and made her way outside, pausing momentarily at the ingress to make sure there were no unwelcome visitors outside. She was still alone, accompanied only by the low, gentle hum that seemed to be coming from somewhere within or below the chamber. Mari couldn't tell... at times, it felt like the hum was coming from within her own chest.

She reached for the pendant Lana had given her and pulled it away from her chest so she could look at it properly. The crescent shape caught the moonlight, its shape matching the real thing almost perfectly, although it was a little wider than the moon above her, and for a moment, she felt a pang of homesickness. Mari pushed the feelings down and tucked the necklace back into her once cream but now grayish blouse. This wasn't the time to dwell.

A slender sliver of curved light shone down from above, the delicate arc of the moon heralding the final days of the season before Lumithra began. Mari pulled out her telescope and star charts and got to work.

~

MARI SHOT up out of a deep sleep, the idea hot in her mind.

"Orbital resonance!" she declared loudly, fumbling for her journal and pencil. She scribbled furiously as much as she could remember from her dream. It had been on the tip of her tongue while she was awake, but her unconscious mind drew it to the surface like a well-honed tuning fork. The spacing of the carvings reminded her of the distance required for the perfect balance of harmony between planets and moons.

"So, maybe this is some sort of equilibrium chamber?" she wondered, reaching over to her boots and pulling them on. The sky outside was lightening as dawn approached. Mari brushed the dust from her cloak and gathered her things.

She glanced around the chamber, making a mental note of as much as possible before she left. She felt like she was onto something with the equilibrium chamber. This place, she had decided, was ancient and deliberate—she could feel it in her soul. Despite the crumbling walls and moss-covered floors, it carried an air of something far greater than anything she had ever encountered. It felt like a fragment of Patovia's forgotten past, a past the elders of Greenhaven feared so deeply that they had forbidden even the whisper of ancient technologies, which was something Mari had to learn and respect very early on. Any technology that couldn't be reproduced with the simplest of tools was seen as a threat to their way of life. Creators were banished, and their inventions destroyed. The Elders Council claimed this was necessary to protect their traditions, but Mari had always suspected otherwise. It was fear, fear of the unknown, packaged up and portrayed as wisdom. It really wasn't intentional, convincing the next generation that the Elyrians were nothing but myth, not history. Cautionary tales were turned into bedtime stories, and history eventually faded into legend. And no matter how you spun it, or what you believed, it was understood that the Elyrians had flourished before they crumbled under their own ambition.

As someone with a rather whimsical imagination, Mari hoped the legendary Elyrians had actually existed. Mostly because it was a thrilling idea that such a group of people had walked the same hills and mountain paths that she did. Believing in them meant that there once was something far more exciting and mysterious than the current iteration of Patovia, and that opened the door to the possibility that one day something like that could be a reality again. Especially now, standing here, surrounded by whatever this space was, Mari wondered if the tales were more accurate than she had realized. Perhaps this chamber belonged to one of those lost cities that had dared to embrace the Elyrian advancements only to vanish when they failed. The most famous of these cities, of course, were the Elyrian Terraces, a name spoken with equal parts awe and dismissal in Greenhaven, depending on who you were talking to. The elders would scoff if she brought this back to them, highlighting it as proof of their warnings at exactly the same time as dismissing it as nothing but a myth. But Mari wasn't so sure. This chamber felt more alive than stone should. She couldn't shake the feeling that this was something more.

Whatever this place was—myth, history, or something in between—she wouldn't be forgetting it any time soon.

CHAPTER FOUR

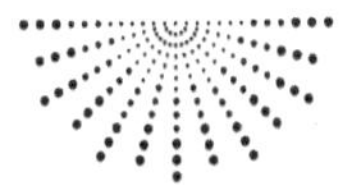

THE STIFFNESS IN MARI'S BODY WAS UNRELENTING AS she set out on the path to Adavale. Her back was tight, her legs aching from her restless sleep in the damp cave, and her shin still smarted from the scrape she had barely tended to. Even so, she pushed on without so much as a wince, her father's, or rather her pocketknife gripped tightly in her hand. This was a precaution she hadn't considered necessary until the bandit attack. Every moving shadow now felt like it held a hidden threat, but Mari was determined not to lose any more time. If she kept a steady pace, she'd reach Adavale just before nightfall.

The path ahead seemed endless, stretching through the forest with no sign of civilization. Mari forced herself to keep moving, using her neighbors' faces and the trust they had placed in her as her motivation. She recalled Elder Amara's voice from one of their last conversations. "Responsibility," Amara had said, "is not a burden, Mari—it's a gift. It means others believe in you." Mari wasn't sure she fully agreed, but the memory of those words fueled her steps, nonetheless.

"Responsibility is not a burden," Mari said to herself

through short, uncomfortable breaths. "It's a pain in my—" She bit her tongue to stop herself from disrespecting Elder Amara.

The birdsong here was higher, almost shrill compared to the calls she knew in Greenhaven. She smiled, grateful for these moments of discovery. Over the course of the morning, a particular bird's rhythmic up-and-down pinging was painfully annoying at first, but by the late afternoon, she found herself quite enjoying the sing-song, walking in time with its rhythm.

Her eyes roamed the forest as she walked, continuing to take in the unfamiliar landscape. The trunks of the trees were impressively thick, their dense leaves weaving together, reminding Mari of the roofing she and Zeph would build for their shelters on their grandparents' farm. Mari's grandparents grew hybrid dates, some of the most sought after in the region.

"The finest in Patovia," her grandfather would always boast, and he wasn't wrong.

Come harvest time, it was all hands on deck to carefully pick hundreds of clusters, push the carts from the sandy beds to the sorting areas where they would discard any damaged fruit, and lay only the very best remaining out in the hot sun to dry. The salted dates then had to be brushed with a special mixture known only to their family. They had to repeat the process as often as necessary to make sure they had enough fruit to fill the orders that would come pouring in. They would also fill baskets until they were overflowing to be featured prominently during Greenhaven's Harvest Festival Feast. It was a lot of work, but no one would ever complain. The unique hybrid fruits were her family's legacy, and they had been growing them since their family settled in the region as one of the founding families of Greenhaven.

Mari was never a big fan of the heat, and unfortunately for

her, both lemon dates and salted dates had to be harvested in the height of summer. Zeph and Mari would collect the biggest palm fronds they could find and set up a crude hut in the sand, central to where they would be working. Then, during their breaks, they would run back to the hut for water and a brief respite in the shade before getting back to work. Mari smiled at the fond memory, her mouth salivating. What she wouldn't do for a lemon date right now.

As rays of sunlight finally started to filter through the thinning trees, Mari's spirits lifted. She always felt uneasy when she couldn't see the sky, so she was grateful for a change in foliage. Small, slender plants with yellow stalks grew more abundant, their diamond-shaped leaves catching the morning sun and glinting like tiny emeralds. So much was different here, and Mari couldn't help but marvel.

The roots and ground-covering ferns that carpeted the forest floor dwindled, and the woodlands on either side of her gave way to neat rows of crops and tended fields. Her eyes lit up when she spotted a herd of drovak grazing lazily in a distant pasture, their sleek black fur glinting in the sunlight. She paused, raising an eyebrow in judgment as she noticed their long, lashing tails, which were much longer than the tails she was used to seeing back home.

In Greenhaven, drovak tails were always trimmed short. It wasn't just a matter of preference but of practicality, as anyone who'd been tasked with grooming the beasts would attest. Drovak were notoriously known for the giant dung piles they would create, and a shorter tail just made sense. Mari's nostrils flared in disgust as she pictured trying to detangle dung that clung to a tail that long. "No, thank you," she said to herself. "You gorgeous beasts look awfully regal, but I bet you stink awfully bad, too."

Their long tails swished with every flick of their ears, and Mari imagined how much "debris" was flying off in every direction with the movement. She shuddered.

The day stretched on, and the landscape continued to change slowly. She was so close to Adavale now.

Mari paused at the top of a gentle slope, swiping a sweaty strand of hair from her forehead. She scanned the sky, a habit she never thought much about, but one that had been ingrained in her since childhood.

There. A dark silhouette glided high above the fields, wings spread wide as it caught a current. Even from this distance, she recognized the distinct broad wingspan and squared-off tail.

Instinctively, she named it: branswift hawk. Female. Young —probably had just started hunting on her own.

Her father had drilled this knowledge into her as soon as she was old enough to sit still.

'You live under the sky, Mari. And we work in the sky. It's important you know who shares it with you.'

For as long as she could remember, Mari had been looking up for one reason or another. Her father's insistence that she had a firm understanding of the family business had been one of the driving factors, but that alone wouldn't have been enough if she didn't have the passion for more. She was never content to simply work—Mari needed to understand.

And so she had learned. She had learned the difference between a kestrel's playful, darting flight and the slow, purposeful circles of a waiting vulture. She could spot a barn swallow by the flash of blue on its wings, and tell the difference between a scout bird warning of a predator and a nesting mother calling to her young.

For most, the sky was just sky. For Mari, it was a language, and she had spent her entire life learning how to understand it.

The same lessons that had once taught her to track the flight of birds had, in time, led her to trace the paths of the stars. Mari wondered what would have happened if she had shown more of an interest in baking bread earlier on. She probably wouldn't be trudging down a dirt path carrying the expectations of her entire village on her shoulders. Unless it was really, really good bread.

As she approached the outskirts of a small farm, she saw a handful of birds pecking lazily at the dirt between rows of barley stalks.

Mari recognized them immediately—the soft gray feathers, the round, sturdy bodies bred for endurance, not speed. These birds weren't wild, and they certainly weren't local... They were skyweavers.

Then, as she got closer, she laughed incredulously. The birds before her were some of the first to have gone missing recently. Jul, Ros, and... Her eyes widened as she saw him... Cel! It was strange seeing them here, in a place that wasn't home. She approached slowly, wondering if their time away from the aviary would make them wary of her. She should have known better. These were Greenhaven skyweavers.

That had always been her family's pride. Greenhaven skyweavers were bred for excellence from generations of the best couriers, each one faster and more reliable than the last.

But here they were—not flying, not on course, and not where they were supposed to be. Her chest tightened. Skyweavers never lost their way. Their sense of direction was stronger than any map, their instincts more accurate than any star chart. This was all just so wrong.

Mari knelt down, pressing her fingers to her lips, and gave a short, commanding whistle. Immediately, all three birds snapped their heads in her direction. It was clear that they recognized her immediately because in a synchronized instant, the trio took flight and landed on her outstretched arm within a heartbeat of her call.

"What are you three doing out here, huh?" Mari asked, looking over their wings and their legs, checking for injuries. "You're lucky you're not hurt."

She looked up at the sun, weighing her options. It wasn't the best time to send them back, but she couldn't take them with her, and it was clear they weren't going to find their own way home.

She stood, facing the direction of Greenhaven, and scooped Cel into her hands. The message she had sent days ago was still tightly attached to his leg. She untied it and dropped it into her pocket. She took a breath. "You go first, my man."

With a push of her hands, Cel launched skyward. She sent Jul and Ros swiftly after him, watching as they got smaller in the sky, their wings beating toward home.

Mari watched the sky long after the last bird had vanished. This was just more proof that something was wrong, but she didn't have time to dwell or worry. The city wasn't far now, so she pushed forward.

TWILIGHT WAS SETTLING into the evening sky when Adavale's village walls finally came into view. She all but broke out into a jog as she approached, trying not to look at the auroras that were visible overhead, bathing the village below in a warm bath of color. She pushed aside her unease and made a beeline to the tavern she had been told about by Elder Harrop.

Inside, the warmth of the hearth enveloped her like a blanket. The barkeep, a stout man with a furrowed brow that didn't match his cheerful demeanor, greeted her with a welcoming grin. "Welcome in! What can I do for you, traveler?"

"I need a room," Mari said, rustling through her satchel for her coin purse. "Please," she added, forgetting her manners momentarily as she melted into the nearest chair. "Elder Harrop of Greenhaven said you might be able to help."

The barkeep's face brightened. "Elder Harrop, eh? Good man. That'll earn you a discount. You're in luck—got one room left." He paused, eyeing her dusty clothes. "And maybe a bowl of soup to go with it?"

Mari nodded gratefully. "That would be wonderful."

"Ellin!" the man called back to the kitchen. "One more soup, love!"

"Be right there, Gil!" a cheerful voice floated through to them.

Not a moment later, a woman emerged from the kitchen, balancing a steaming bowl of soup and a plate of fresh bread in one hand, her other waving at a nearby local as she sauntered through with a smile as warm as the soup she carried. Ellin was short and broad-shouldered, her cheeks flushed from the heat of the kitchen, and her dark brown but graying hair pulled into a loose bun, though a few loose strands framed her round face. Her hazel eyes sparkled with kindness as she approached the table, a faint scent of rosemary clinging to her apron.

She set the bowl of soup down gently in front of Mari and shot the barkeep, Gil, a teasing grin. "Don't think I didn't see you sneaking half my fresh sourdough earlier, dear. Keep that up, and there won't be any left for the paying customers."

She retreated to the kitchen with a wink, Gil chuckling as he held his empty hands up innocently. "She never misses a thing," he said to Mari, his voice loud enough to carry back to the kitchen.

As Mari settled into a corner, hugging her steaming bowl of soup, a conversation at the end of the bar caught her attention. A man who looked like he might be a farmer was carrying what appeared to be a small release crate had approached the barkeep. Mari couldn't hear everything, but her ears pricked up when the man said, "Mari of Greenhaven."

Gil turned to her with a grin. "Well, now. That's you, isn't it?"

Mari stiffened. "It is. Why?"

Gil held up a hand. "No need to worry. Seems you've got a message." He reached under the counter and pulled out a small scroll. "This arrived yesterday. We were all wondering who this mysterious Mari could be."

He walked over to her table and handed her the scroll. Mari's suspicion eased the moment she recognized Zeph's handwriting. She eagerly unrolled the scroll, scanning its contents.

The man at the bar placed the release crate on the counter, the lid still latched tight. A faint scrabbling sound came from inside. When Mari looked up from her scroll, the man unlatched the crate. Then, in a blur of silver and white, chaos erupted.

A screech rang out as a small but furious ball of feathers shot out of the crate—wings flaring, talons skimming the bar as she swooped low, knocking over an empty mug in the process.

"Rih!" Mari gasped, her face lighting up with relief.

Her minuscule menace of a bird landed squarely on her shoulder, and with a sudden tilt of her head, she nipped harder than necessary at Mari's ear, earning a yelp.

"Ow—okay, okay! I missed you too," Mari winced, laughing despite the sting as she reached up to steady the bird.

Rih let out an agitated series of chirps, her feathers puffing up indignantly.

"She's been like that all night," the man explained, rubbing his arm as if he'd been on the receiving end of her sharp little beak.

"Yeah, well, she doesn't like cages." Mari said.

The bird let out a soft, huffing squawk, as if agreeing.

"I could have used you yesterday," Mari told her, scratching Rih's head.

Rih nipped at her ear—not gently—before trilling in satisfaction.

Mari glanced back down at Zeph's letter and read his final line:

"Keep Rih with you. Just in case you need the company."

She rolled her eyes. Zeph knew her too well. "Looks like you're sticking with me," she said, running her fingers through Rih's sleek feathers.

Gil chuckled, returning to the bar and wiping down the counter. "Feisty little thing. Spent the whole day scolding us like she was in charge."

"Oh, she thinks she is," Mari said dryly, scratching under Rih's beak and dodging another affectionate but forceful peck.

Rih hopped off Mari's shoulder and onto the table, puffing up with importance as she surveyed the tavern. Her piercing, silver-ringed eyes locked onto her untouched plate of bread. "No. Absolutely not," Mari warned.

In a single motion, Rih hooked her beak into the crust and yanked off a chunk before Mari could stop her. She flapped once, landing back on Mari's shoulder with her prize, and began to tear at the bread with smug, exaggerated pecks.

Gil barked out a laugh. "She's got good taste, at least!"

Mari hid her face in her hands. "I swear she wasn't raised to be a thief."

Rih ignored her, gleefully tearing apart the bread and throwing it onto the floor, fast having realized the bread was not something she could eat.

"Do you have any raw meat for her?" Mari asked, shaking her head.

Gil scratched his chin, watching Rih destroy and discard the stolen bread. "Got some scraps left over from dinner. But only 'cause she's entertaining." He chuckled and disappeared into the back.

Mari turned to Rih, lowering her voice. "Listen, if you're going to stick with me, you need to be subtle."

Rih paused, twisting her head sideways. Then, with exaggerated slowness, she reached over and stole another piece of bread.

Mari dropped her head onto the counter. "You're impossible."

Rih chirped happily.

Ellin interrupted her reverie, setting another bowl of soup in front of her. "Second one's on the house," she said with a wink. "Long journeys call for hearty meals."

Mari nodded her thanks, already dipping her spoon into the bowl. Rih, however, was not so patient. The failed skyweaver hopped down onto the table and eyed Mari's soup like a predator sizing up prey.

"Don't even think about it," Mari warned.

Rih tilted her head dramatically, the picture of innocence, and edged closer.

With perfect timing, Gil dropped a small dish of scraps onto the table. Rih pounced and immediately began devouring her prize. Mari shook her head, watching as she tore into the meat with all the grace of a wild animal. "You act like you've never been fed before."

The bird ignored her, entirely focused on her meal.

"Smart bird," Gil said. "Doesn't waste time with pleasantries."

Mari huffed a quiet laugh. "No. She really doesn't."

She watched as Rih bobbed her head, ripping the meat scraps apart. With each bite, she snapped her beak closed and threw her head back, swallowing the chunks whole.

Even in the dim tavern light, her feathers gleamed white, tinged with hints of a silvery purple. Her tiny but deadly beak made quick work of her meal.

Mari felt a wave of unexpected relief settle over her. Rih was small but fierce, lovingly aggressive in the way only Rih could be. Zeph had chosen the perfect travel companion for her.

After her third bowl of soup, Mari decided it was time to head to bed. "Thank you again for the soup," she said, smiling at the barkeep. "And the meat," she said, nodding at Rih. "We're both very full."

Gil beamed. "Glad to hear it. Will you be needing anything else?"

Mari shook her head. "Just sleep." She chuckled. "Would you wake me before dawn? I need an early start."

Gil paused, and his cheery demeanor faltered for a hint of a moment before returning. "Before dawn?!"

Ellin's head popped out from behind the kitchen door. "Yes, he can do that for you." She gave Gil a playful glare and whipped him with her dish towel.

"Is that too much trouble?" Mari asked. Maybe she was asking a little too much of their generosity.

"No, no, it's no trouble at all," Gil said. "Anything for

Mysterious Mari." He smiled. "I'll have you up bright and early. Grumbling, maybe, but you'll be up."

"You, grumble? I highly doubt it." Mari smiled. "Thank you," she said again, leaning back as the barkeep collected her bowl and cup. Mari stretched her aching body and glanced out the window. The faint streaks of the aurora were visible even through the glass. She paused before asking, "Have you noticed the aurora?"

Gil frowned, his gaze following hers. "An aurora? This far south? Can't say I have. Don't get much time outside, running this place. Let me take a look." He ambled outside and returned moments later, his face alight with wonder. "Well, I'll be! It's beautiful, isn't it? Like the gods themselves took up painting."

Mari stared at him, surprised by his reaction. "It doesn't... worry you?"

"Worry me?!" He let out a hearty laugh. "Why would it worry me? It's a blessing, that's what it is! Folks travel all the way to Elyria's Edge just to see this kind of thing. Maybe now they'll start coming here instead!"

"You're not even the slightest bit concerned?"

Gil shook his head, grinning. "Life's too short for that. Enjoy it while it lasts, I say. Who knows? Maybe it's a sign of good things to come."

Mari wasn't sure she agreed, but she didn't press the matter. "I suppose we'll see."

"Now, you get yourself some rest. Long journey ahead, eh?"

"Yes," Mari replied, rising from her stool. "Thank you again. For everything."

He nodded, the boyish grin still spread across his face as he looked out the window at the sky. "Sleep well."

Mari made her way to her room. As she climbed the stairs,

she could hear Gil faintly below, calling for Ellin to go outside and look up.

She chuckled. *Unbelievable.*

The room was modest but welcoming, and the mattress was so soft she could cry. She kicked off her boots and collapsed onto the bed, pulling the blankets up under her chin, her legs throbbing with relief.

Rih, however, was not so easily convinced it was time to sleep. The skyweaver fluttered to the headboard, fluffed herself up, and flicked her eyes toward the window.

"Not a fan of the aurora?" Mari asked, already drifting.

Rih let out a low noise, not quite a squawk. She was tired too.

"Me neither."

Rih hesitated for a moment longer, then, apparently deciding she would rather tolerate Mari than the sky, she hopped down and burrowed her warm, feathered body against Mari's side.

Mari let the comfort of the bed and the steady purr of Rih's breathing lull her into an uneasy sleep.

Above them, the aurora danced, silent and looming.

A GENTLE KNOCK stirred Mari from sleep that didn't feel nearly long enough. She groaned and rubbed her face. Rih, however, was already fully alert, perched on the bedpost, blinking down at Mari like she had been waiting for her to get up. And judging her for taking so long.

"Oh, sure, now you're a morning bird," Mari said, throwing off the blanket.

Rih let out a single, pointed, smug chirp.

Mari swung open the door to find Ellin standing there, as rosy and bright as ever, holding out a neatly wrapped, still-warm bundle.

"For the road, love," she said warmly. Mari could practically taste the fresh herbs and butter that wafted from the package. "Gil's still snoring away." Ellin chuckled. "Can't have you traveling on an empty stomach."

Behind Mari, Rih trilled expectantly.

Ellin smiled. "And I suppose you'll be wanting something, too?"

Mari sighed. "Don't encourage her."

CHAPTER FIVE

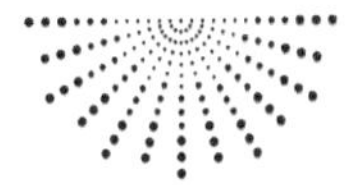

THE FOREST THINNED AS MARI TRAVELED FURTHER, the path widening, sunlight filtering brighter through the trees.

Rih fluttered above her, banking hard before diving down and landing on Mari's shoulder with a dramatic flap of her wings. Mari could barely steady herself before the skyweaver took off again, clearly incapable of staying put for more than a few heartbeats.

The familiar ache in her legs reminded her just how far she had traveled. She was close now. The thought of reaching Joycita spurred her forward.

Rih, however, seemed far less interested in the destination than she was in entertaining herself—swooping low, twisting midair in tight spirals, riding the wind like it was the only thing in the world that mattered.

Mari grinned as Rih let out a piercing cry that echoed through the trees. "Show off," she shouted to the sky.

Rih looped back once more, soaring dangerously close to the top of Mari's head, her hair following in the wake of the bird's speed as she zoomed past her, her feathers gleaming in the sun.

Mari laughed. Of course, she had ended up with the most dramatic skyweaver in existence. She pulled out her water skin and took a long drink. She tapped the stopper back into place after splashing a little on her face with intentional slaps. She picked up her pace, determined to make it to Joycita before the stellar convergence, an event she had predicted would take place in roughly a week. As long as she didn't run into any other unpleasant surprises, she would have no problem arriving on time. She had passed most of the difficult terrain already, and ahead of her now lay only sloping hills and a river crossing. With Rih swooping and looping above her, enjoying herself greatly, Mari pressed on.

THE CITY of Joycita was unlike anything Mari had imagined. She stood at the edge of the main thoroughfare and clutched her satchel as crowds bustled past her. She looked up, marveling at the sheer height of the city. Towering stone buildings rose into the sky, their spires scraping the edges of the clouds that swirled above. Mari had to consciously stop herself from picking at the beds of her fingernails, her eyes anxiously darting from one unfamiliar sight to another. She had imagined grandeur, yes, but not this.

Mari's mouth watered the moment the smell of roasting coffee reached her. It was the first of many smells drifting in from all directions, some familiar, others so strange she couldn't begin to name them. It was nothing like the warm, sweet, dusty breeze of Greenhaven. Every step felt like an intrusion, and she was painfully aware that she did not belong here.

"Just find the library," she whispered to herself, gripping her map like a shield.

The streets of Joycita were a chaotic, endless flow of movement—merchants hawking their wares, messengers weaving between carriages, street performers commanding groups of awed onlookers. The sheer density of people pressed in on her, but she kept her eyes forward, forcing herself to push through the throng until a shrill, sharp whistle cut through the noise, and she jumped a solid foot in the air. She scrambled to pick up her cloak, which had fallen from her shoulders when she jumped. Flushing a furious shade of red, Mari was grateful to realize that no one was paying any attention to her whatsoever. *The perks of bit city living.* She grinned to herself. She turned to locate the source of the sound that had given her such a scare. It had been familiar, not like a childhood lullaby, but like something deeply ingrained in her. She had known instantly what it was... It was a skyweaver's call.

She reached to her shoulder and found Rih perched there quietly, rather unlike herself. Clearly, Rih was as rattled with the city as she was. She frowned and turned instinctively, searching the sea of bodies until her eyes landed on a small market stall tucked between a stand laden with pottery and a textiles vendor. A thin man stood behind it, one hand raised as he whistled again.

A soft gray bird, round-bodied and sturdy, with a gleaming band around its leg, flitted from its perch to his gloved wrist.

The sign hanging above the stall read:

"FINEST TRAINED COURIER BIRDS IN ALL OF PATOVIA"

Mari's heart fluttered.

The man gestured toward the bird and launched into a practiced sales pitch for the cluster of intrigued passersby. "Strong, fast, and trained to return home without fail!" he declared. "For merchants, for nobles, for anyone needing a trusted courier! Nothing is more reliable than a skyweaver!"

Mari looked past him, to the gorgeous birds that were lined along the perches at the back of his stall. There were at least a dozen, all of them skyweavers and undeniably Greenhaven-bred.

She didn't need to see the wing markings or the tiny bands around their legs to know. She recognized their posture, their size, their careful, measured demeanor. These were messenger birds, yes, but they were no ordinary messenger birds. These were hers. Or at least, they had been.

She swallowed. For so long, she had thought of her family's work as small—important, of course, but limited to Greenhaven and the villages that surrounded it. But here, in the heart of Patovia's capital, her family's skyweavers were being sold, traded, and spoken of as indispensable. Her family's work had reached beyond anything she had imagined.

Mari took a step forward, but before she could speak, a wealthy-looking woman in fine, orange traveling robes approached the stall.

"Lady Floris, welcome back! We have Veridi ready and waiting for you!"

The woman placed a pouch of coins on the counter, barely acknowledging the vendor, too deeply engaged in a conversation with one of her companions. The vendor beamed, snapping his fingers toward a younger assistant. "Go on then, lad; fetch the lady her bird!"

The boy hurried to the perches, selected a sleek, gray skyweaver, and secured a tiny parchment tube to its leg. He placed the bird gently into a carrying case and latched the lid shut.

Mari felt something strange and unfamiliar inside her—pride.

The vendor's voice pulled her attention back. "Only the best for Brindlemyre's elite!" he declared, handing the case over to the woman, who gestured for one of her traveling companions to take it before departing. "Thank you again, Lady Floris! A pleasure!"

Lady Floris waved an unenthusiastic hand of thanks as she swished away, chattering loudly away to the gaggle of female attendants who surrounded her.

"Greenhaven-bred skyweavers—none smarter, none faster!" the vendor announced, turning his attention back to the passersby with a flourish.

A flutter of movement at her shoulder broke Mari's trance. Rih had gone completely rigid, her eyes locked onto the vendor's perches.

Oh, no.

She felt Rih's wings flexing as if ready to launch.

"Don't." Mari caught her beak gently but firmly between two fingers.

Rih let out a small, offended squawk.

"Don't even think about it."

The skyweavers at the stall remained completely still, trained not to react to disturbances, and Rih listened... reluctantly. She huffed, but she didn't take off. Instead, she clicked her beak once and then settled back onto Mari's shoulder.

Mari shook out the strange mix of emotions bubbling inside her. She had a library to find.

~

BY THE TIME she finally located the Great Library, the lower skies had transitioned to a brilliant pink, with patches of gold peeking through the soft lilac clouds below the darkening navy sky, not an aurora in sight. The first stars were beginning to appear. Dusk in Joycita certainly was a thing to behold.

The Great Library stood at the end of a long, covered walkway that stretched across the river that ran through the entire city. Lights lit up the library's grand facade, which glittered with tall, arched windows inset between dark bricks, rounded from centuries of rain and wind. A massive set of double doors carved from blackwood and encased in a sturdy but intricate iron design served as the library's main entrance. Above the doors was a circular glass window with ornate ironwork curling across its surface, a hallmark of Joycita's architecture and design. Tall spires, capped with dainty iron points, seemed to pierce the darkening skies above, their angular silhouettes stretching across the water like spindly, outstretched fingers.

Lanterns hung at intervals along the bridge illuminating the passageway with a soft amber light. Mari crossed hurriedly, and below her, the river mirrored the softly rustling reeds that grew at the edge of its shores. Wildflowers and creeping ivy spilled over the bridge's brick walls, their colors muted under the dim glow of the thin, crescent moon.

Mari felt Rih's claws dig into her shoulder, readying herself to take flight. "Stay close," she told her, looking at the water below. The occasional splashes she could hear hinted at a river that was teeming with fish and reassured Mari that Rih would have all the dinner she could get her claws on without needing to try too hard. Rih nipped at her ear in acknowledgment and impatience. "I'll be back soon," Mari promised as Rih launched into the sky and immediately started scanning the river.

Relief swept through Mari as she pushed through the heavy wooden doors and into the cool, quiet interior. She had made it. Rows and rows of shelves stretched high and wide, and she stared in awe as a smile spread slowly across her face. There were thousands of books before her in every direction she looked—ancient pages bound in leather and filled with inspiring ink. The smell was intoxicating. Mari wished she could stand there forever, just breathing it all in.

"Looking for someone?" The voice startled her. Turning quickly, Mari saw an older man with a long gray beard standing behind a polished desk. His bespectacled eyes were fixed on the rolled charts sticking out of her satchel. "If it's astronomy you're after, you'll find no better place in Patovia."

"Teacher," she smiled. "It's good to see you."

MARI APPROACHED her mentor with anticipation. If she didn't feel like she would be disrespecting the grand building, she would have run at him with full force. She forced her bubbling excitement down, the long journey immediately worth every step.

Searsan had not changed much, though his beard seemed a touch longer and his robes bore a few more ink stains. He studied her with the same thoughtful gaze she remembered from years before. "So, Namari," he said fondly, using her full name. "You've come far. What brings you here, aside from those charts you guard as fiercely as a dragon guards her egg?"

Mari chose her words carefully. "Something tells me you already know why I've come."

Searsan nodded, stroking his beard. Mari continued. "I came to ask for help—for Greenhaven. Something's wrong. We've always had a dry season, but this is different. Wells are drying, crops are withering, the salt pools are starting to evaporate... Even the skyweavers aren't flying true anymore." She willed her voice not to waver. "We need help." She swallowed, worried she wasn't emphasizing the stakes. "Fast," she added.

Searsan nodded gravely "I have heard of things such as this happening throughout the region. The skies have been restless. The auroras present where they should not be. And the stars... I expect you've been mapping them diligently."

"I have," she said, unrolling one of her charts and placing it on Searsan's desk. "These are from Greenhaven, and these," she gestured to a smaller, newer set tucked into her satchel, "are from along my journey here. I think something is forcing the stars to realign."

Searsan leaned over her charts. He squinted, frowning in deep concentration as he traced the constellations. "Realignment of the stars is... not possible," he said.

Mari's face dropped. "It is. I'm telling you. I can't make sense of it, but the stars are... shifting."

"Hmph." Searsan's response gave no indication of whether he agreed with her or not. He hummed appreciatively, moving his hands slowly over her inkwork. "Your work has grown precise, Namari. I am impressed."

Mari took a moment to steady her breathing. "You see it,

don't you?" she pressed. She felt the urgency rising up her throat. "The changes? The misalignments?"

Searsan didn't answer. Instead, he reached for a magnifying lens, holding it awkwardly as he peered at the chart. The movement was clumsy, and realization sunk in slowly as Mari noticed his trembling hands. "You don't see it," she said softly.

"That doesn't mean I don't believe you," Searsan insisted. "I've felt it. The imbalance. The way the skies hum with something... unspoken. I've been trying to convince Queen Lyra and her council that the reports of auroras so far south are unnatural, and the changes are foreshadowing a great danger that faces Patovia. But no one wants to listen to a blind astronomer. Namari, my dear, the timing of your arrival is impeccable." His clouded eyes glinted with hope.

Mari's mind spun as she processed his words, and she felt the beginnings of a headache creep across the top of her head. To hear Searsan speak like this... it must be worse than she had even realized. She reached in her satchel and drained the rest of her water skin, pinching the bridge of her nose as she willed the growing ache to stop. "How can I help you?"

Searsan regarded her for a long moment. He reached beneath the desk and pulled out a small brass instrument. It looked like a cross between a protractor and a telescope. A circle about the size of an iris was attached by a slender moving arm that extended across the surface of the semi-circle, the edges of which were adorned with tiny engraved constellations.

"This," he said, placing it in her hands, "is an astrolabe. It's designed to help you track and chart movements more accurately, even under unusual conditions. I'd like you to have it."

Mari's headache seemed to evaporate in an instant, and she turned the instrument over in her hands, marveling at its craftsmanship. "Thank you," she whispered, her throat tight. "But... isn't this yours?"

Searsan smiled faintly, a trace of his old self shining through, just as Mari remembered him. "Instruments like this require more than knowledge. They need precision, patience... and sight." His gaze drifted to the charts again. "You're becoming the great astronomer I always knew you would be. It's yours now."

It was a truly incredible piece of equipment. Mari was already guessing how it would work. "So, we'll be able to figure out what's going on with this?" she asked, brushing her fingers over the detailed carvings.

"With this, we'll have solid proof that the council cannot deny." Searsan grunted and jabbed a finger at the astrolabe. "This will make them understand there's more to be concerned with than just abundance and notoriety. The king's reputation requires a lot of undoing in order for the people to accept Queen Lyra as the true queen. Her councilors think that building Joycita's wealth will prove her position. She needs guidance, and right now, I fear it's coming from the wrong people."

"So if we can get these people to listen, we can find a way to stop whatever is happening?"

"We'll see," Searsan said. "At the very least, we can show the queen that something is amiss."

Mari searched his clouded eyes. He sounded hopeful, at least. "Surely, there are others, more skilled and experienced than I, who could help her?"

"Experience, yes. Skill, perhaps. But precision? Passion? An unjaded eye? Humility?" His emphasis on the last word was pointed. "Those are rarer traits than you realize. And as for myself..." His voice softened. "My time as an observer has come to its end. I can no longer trust what my eyes show me."

Mari wanted to offer reassurance, to say something that would erase the sadness in his tone, but no words she could think of felt appropriate, and she didn't want to seem like she was dismissing his situation. She shot him a half-smile, feeling entirely underqualified to take on what he was suggesting.

Searsan gestured toward the astrolabe in her hands. "You can do this, Namari."

Mari eyed the instrument and held it up in front of her. It felt heavy for its size. "So... the queen will agree to meet with me?" she asked.

"She will," Searsan confirmed. "We may not have long with her, but I will get you as much time as I can."

Mari's mind raced, and both apprehension and determination stirred within her at the thought of speaking in front of the queen. "Okay. I'll do my best." She mustered up her most confident smile, hoping Searsan could at least see that. Images of Greenhaven flashed in her mind, the clearest of all being little Ren, running across their front path, a toy cart in tow, not a concern in the world and completely oblivious to the fact that her entire future and the legacy of her family was at risk. "I need to get this right."

"I know you will," Searsan said firmly. "But be prepared. You'll need more than charts to convince the queen's council."

Mari reached into her satchel, searching blindly until her fingers closed around a familiar pouch. She pulled out the small bundle of soil she had collected in Adavale. She loosened the drawstring and passed it to Searsan. "I have more than charts," she said. "I've been tracking soil conditions throughout my journey. My theory is that the stronger the auroras, the drier the land becomes. The patterns match."

"Impressive."

Mari couldn't help but smile. "Do you think the queen will believe me?" she asked.

Searsan's clouded eyes were fixed somewhere beyond her. "I've tried to find proof beyond what the eye can see, but with my sight as it is, my reach is limited." He turned his face toward her. "She cannot act without evidence, Mari. But now, with you here, we have another chance."

Mari nodded nervously. This was all a lot to process. "When do I meet her?"

"As soon as you're ready," Searsan replied, "And Namari..." He paused. "Her councilors... They have their own agenda. A few may support you, but many will be skeptical. They won't be as willing to listen as Queen Lyra will be. You'll have to fight to be heard. Don't doubt the importance of your own voice."

Mari took a deep breath. "I'll make them listen," she said with a nod. "I can't believe you know me so well, after only three days, and after so much time has passed since then."

Searsan smiled knowingly. "When you discover magic, it isn't easily forgotten."

Mari thought about the humming stone chamber back in the Midwilds. Searsan rolled up her star charts and passed them back to her. "Let's go."

"Now?!" she exclaimed. "I'm not ready!"

Searsan chuckled. "No, first you must rest. Eat something and... bathe," he said, eyeing her dusty cloak.

"That would be wonderful." Mari blushed.

RIH HAD BEEN DUTIFULLY WAITING, perched on the bridge's roof, watching the streets below like a self-appointed sentinel. The moment Mari and Searsan appeared outside, she let out an indignant chirp, as if scolding Mari for taking too long. With a swift beat of her wings, she swooped down and landed on Mari's shoulder, nipping lightly at a stray strand of her hair before settling in.

They headed toward a small side street, Searsan leading the way. Along their walk, they stopped at a small shop where Searsan insisted on purchasing new clothing for Mari. He was adamant that she needed to be dressed appropriately for an audience with Queen Lyra, assuring her it was the council and not the queen herself who would care about how she was dressed.

When they stepped back out into the streets, Mari had a new travel pack, and she was wearing a light orange cotton shirt and a long-sleeved leather overcoat. Searsan had also insisted on a new cloak, which was heavier and lined with hidden pockets. Mari adjusted it around her shoulders, letting it settle on them. It felt safe and secure.

Rih, now perched on her forearm, inspected the cloak as well, plucking at the fabric with a curious tilt of her head. Mari huffed. "It's not for you."

Rih clicked her beak, unimpressed, and flapped back onto Mari's shoulder, where she promptly began preening.

The castle towered above them in the center of Joycita, the gates illuminated by lanterns and manned by guards holding torches. The castle's spires were similar to those of the Great Library but grander, with iron wrapped around each turret in a design that made it look like the whole structure was held together by strong iron threads.

"Strong threads," she murmured in an effort to ground herself, actively ignoring the storm of emotions brewing inside her.

Searsan chuckled. "They do look like threads, don't they?"

"It's actually a Greenhaven blessing," Mari said. "You've never heard of it?"

Searsan tilted his head and gave Mari a puzzled look. "A blessing?"

Mari nodded. "It means... we're connected. Resilient. Now you say, 'Bright flames.'" She smiled.

Searsan returned the smile. "Then bright flames, Namari. Let's see what you can do."

CHAPTER SIX

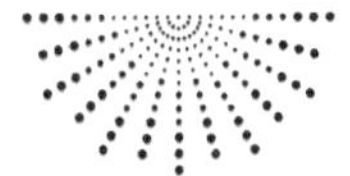

Mari followed Searsan through the winding streets of Joycita. The city's vibrant energy was a stark contrast to the quiet stillness of Greenhaven. Even as night approached, the districts remained lively. Rih's eyes darted in all directions to every deliciously smelling grill they passed, barely able to resist.

Searsan led her to a modest inn tucked between two larger buildings and secured her a room. They found seats at a table by a window, and Searsan ordered them both a hearty stew. Mari all but toppled into her bowl when it arrived, practically inhaling her dinner without a second thought to slow down and actually taste what she was eating. Soon, the conversation was flowing as if no time at all had passed between their last meeting.

"The roads were more dangerous than I was expecting," Mari said between bites of the most scrumptious dessert, which oozed something sweet and creamy, topped with crystals of brown sugar that gave the most satisfying crunch with every mouthful she devoured. "The raiders' attacks are becoming more and more frequent. Greenhaven has had to expand its militia faster than we could have imagined." She took a gulp of the best wine she had ever tasted in her life. "It's all hands on deck now."

Despite what Mari thought to be a satisfactory explanation, Searsan appeared to be confused. "So, even with an expanded militia, no one could be spared to accompany you?"

"Didn't want to risk it." Mari shrugged. "When the general died, there was a scramble to replace him and a bit of a divide amongst the troops. His son was expected to be promoted to the position, but for some reason, it never happened, and that caused a whole commotion."

Mari remembered the awkward conversation between the new general and Elder Amara. He had all but said he had absolutely no faith that Mari would make it, and he would rather lose one young girl than a unit of men. Mari had scoffed, suggesting the only way one of his units would even be able to make it was with her, since the skyweavers were not flying true, and with no tools to lead them, any traveler would be stuck. Mari didn't need skyweavers to find her way. She'd meant it as a brag, but the general had taken her at face value and told her that it sounded like she'd be fine on her own, then. Fop.

"I'm the only one who could make the journey," she told Searsan. "The only others with star navigation skills are far too old to have even attempted the journey. Especially since there wasn't really a guarantee that I would actually make it here at all, and so, I suppose they figured one loss was better than a few."

"Well, you proved yourself capable," he said, tipping his glass in her direction.

Mari nodded solemnly. "Barely." She recounted the story of

her first run-in with the three bandits who had stolen her travel pack. Searsan listened intently, audibly gasping at the part where one of them had grabbed her shoulder. The gasp sent him into a coughing fit, and after draining a glass of water and calming down, Mari continued. "On the final day of my journey, I met a group of strange people hanging around outside the city walls. They seemed nice enough, but they really didn't think much of the queen at all. They said she was selfish and greedy? They even hinted..." She hesitated, lowering her voice. "That whoever killed the king should've taken her out as well." Searsan stiffened, his spoon hovering mid-air. "They said that?"

"Yes," Mari replied. "They seemed... off."

Searsan shook his head. "Well, there certainly are all sorts of people with all kinds of differing opinions... The queen isn't perfect, Namari, but she is not selfish or cruel. A people pleaser, perhaps. She's not young, but she's younger than most queens would be when they find themselves without a king, and she's still finding her footing, especially with certain councilors... whose motives are questionable." He sighed. "But she listens. And she cares. That's more than can be said for many in power."

Their conversation turned lighter as Mari recounted more tales from her journey—the long tailed drovak in Adavale, how she had collected a small sample of soil every time she felt the landscape had changed significantly enough to warrant a new scoop, and her delight at finally finding earthworms in the scoop of dirt she had collected by the outskirts of Joycita. Searsan marveled at her instincts to gather tangible evidence of a connection, and Mari beamed. She neglected to mention the stone chamber, though, and as she drained her cup of wine, she wondered if this was intentional or if she was just too tired to get into all the fascinating details. They would have been up all night discussing it, surely.

Best to leave it till tomorrow, she thought.

As they finished their meal, they made plans for Searsan to meet her at the inn after lunch the next day. "Take the morning to prepare," he advised. "Sort your charts and soil samples. And treat yourself." He handed her a pouch of coins despite her protests. "You'll need more than what you have if you're planning to enjoy the sweetbaths and maybe another dessert or two. Steps, the bathhouse by the river, is well worth a visit."

The mention of dessert sparked a reminder. She pulled a small, brown paper parcel from her satchel. "Oh, I almost forgot," she said, pushing it into his hands. "Salted dates. They almost didn't make it. I nearly threw them to the bandits, but these were tucked at the bottom of my satchel. They're a bit smooshed, but they'll still taste good," she assured him. "The lemon dates didn't make it, I'm afraid," she said with a guilty look that betrayed the sad truth that it had not been the bandits who had eaten them. Searsan's face lit up as he opened the parcel and peered at the three sad-looking, brown dates. "And...If I'm being totally honest, there were more than that originally," she confessed.

Searsan chuckled. "Salted dates?" He popped one into his mouth, savoring the taste. "Namari, you're a treasure."

Mari thanked him again for the coin purse, and the pair stepped back out onto the streets. They walked together until they came to a fork in the road where Searsan was due to turn. Mari bid him goodnight and headed in the direction of the bathhouse. She had a date with some essential oils, and she was not going to miss it.

～

Steps, the bathhouse, was easy to find. Its painted sign hung under the bridge just as Searsan had described, swaying gently in the evening breeze. As Mari approached, Rih gave a loud chirp from her shoulder, tilting her head toward the entrance as if questioning the decision.

Mari chuckled, brushing a finger along the curve of Rih's wing. "You'd hate it in there. Too much steam. Too many people."

Rih clicked her beak in what Mari swore was a huff and then launched from her shoulder, soaring toward the beams of the bridge. She perched high above the entrance, tucking herself into a shadowy nook.

Inside, the bathhouse was warm and inviting, and the girl behind the counter greeted her with a kind but concerned smile, clearly unsettled by Mari's disheveled appearance.

"Long journey?" the girl asked. She was absolutely judging her.

Mari nodded. "Very."

"You'll want the full treatment, then. A hot scrub, a sweetbath, and a rubdown. Trust me."

Mari agreed and handed over a few coins from Searsan's pouch. The girl led her to a room for her first treatment—the hot scrub. Two female attendants rubbed salt and honey into her skin with firm strokes, leaving her feeling raw but refreshed. Her feet received special attention. Mari cringed and even considered apologizing to the attendants who wrapped them in thin, cold, fragrant cloths, interspersing sprigs of lavender and sage between each layer.

The sweetbath was deeper in the bathhouse. The pool was wide and tranquil, its surface scattered with petals of deep pink that floated serenely, their fragrance mingling with the warm steam that curled across the air. Mesmerizing patterns of shimmering light threw a reflection of the gentle ripple of the pool's surface across the back wall. Mari sank into the water and let the warmth seep into her weary muscles. A rhythmic drip from a leaking pipe lulled Mari into a trance, the trickling of the water into the pool a calming, happy accident, and her thoughts drifted with the sounds that ricocheted across the room.

Drip. Drip. Drip.

The quiet was shattered by a sudden bang, and Mari startled as the door to the pool room was pushed open without a thought to the serenity she had been enjoying. A loud clang followed as the door slammed shut, and a woman appeared in the doorway, a metal tool clattering from her hand onto the tiled floor as her gaze landed on Mari. She froze, clearly not expecting to find anyone here.

"Oh! I'm sorry," the woman stammered. "Didn't think this room was in use. I'm here to..." She gestured to the dripping pipe in the corner, "To fix the leak. I'll come back later." Without waiting for a reply, she quickly retreated, her footsteps echoing down the hall as the door slammed loudly shut behind her.

Mari let herself sink under the water, pretending that did not just happen.

Later, as she waited for her rubdown in a small sitting area near the baths, an angry voice drew her attention. Two workers stood near a doorway that led down a hallway a little further down into the bathhouse. One was the woman who had interrupted her earlier in the sweetbath, her posture rigid as she stood opposite a man with an unkind face in a clean but worn uniform.

"You've been here for how long, Kalindi?" the man snapped, his voice carrying. "And you're already causing problems? I told you; no disruptions in the establishments, especially not this one." He was beyond irritated. "Do you think the city's reputation can afford your kind of commotion?"

Kalindi shrank back against the wall. She mumbled a reply, her voice too quiet for Mari to catch.

"Speak up," the man barked. "You think you're still some important engineer, doing as you please without consequences? You're a lowly city plumber now, Kalindi. You're here to do one job. Plumbing. Fix pipes, stop leaks, and keep out of the patrons' way. You're not here to make waves."

Mari raised an eyebrow at the hypocrisy of the exchange. Had she not been so tired, she would have marched up to the angry man and let him know that he was disturbing her far more than Kalindi had. She was tired, though, and didn't want to cause Kalindi any more trouble. She watched the exchange continue with a mix of curiosity and discomfort, noting how Kalindi flinched whenever the man would move toward her.

"I'll take care of it," Kalindi said finally.

"See that you do," the man said with a nod before shooting her a dirty look and stalking away with a saunter that indicated he thought himself far more important than he probably was.

Mari turned quickly and tried to pretend she hadn't just watched the entire conversation as Kalindi began walking toward her. She stopped a foot in front of her, and Mari pulled her towel up a little higher, covering more of her chest than before.

"Miss, I apologize for earlier. If my interruption caused any displeasure in your experience, please allow me to purchase you another." Kalindi's eyes remained fixed on the tiles.

"It was not an interruption at all," Mari said kindly. "You

probably saved me. I was so close to falling asleep, I might have drowned if you hadn't come in."

Kalindi looked up, grateful and relieved at the response, and Mari gave her a quick wink and a smile. Kalindi returned a half-smile, dipped her head in a short bow, and turned back toward the direction the angry man had walked.

"Hey," Mari whispered after her.

Kalindi turned back.

"Toss that man in the river," Mari said with another wink. Kalindi put a hand over her mouth to stifle a giggle. She nodded in thanks again and took off.

When Mari left the bathhouse, she was beyond ready for bed. She only hoped her bed was as inviting as Steps had been. A familiar flutter of wings stirred the air overhead. Rih swooped down from her perch and gave a small, expectant chirp, as if commenting on Mari's refreshed state.

"Yes, I'm clean now. No more smelling like sweat and battle."

Rih clicked, unimpressed, as if to say she hadn't minded the scent to begin with.

Shaking her head fondly, Mari knelt by the edge of the path, carefully scooping up a soil sample into a small leather pouch. She tied it off with five knots at the end of the cord, marking it as the Joycita sample. She let herself get lost in the feeling of stillness that surrounded her.

The bathhouse had been exactly what she needed. She strolled back toward the inn, taking slow, intentional breaths, feeling lighter than she had in weeks.

She reached up, running a finger gently along the ridge of Rih's beak. "Remind me to thank Searsan for the recommendation."

MARI WOKE WITH A LAZY STRETCH. The scent of last night's sweetbath oils smelled so good on her skin that she buried her nose into the crook of her arm and inhaled deeply. Her body, though still weary from her journey, carried a satisfying looseness. Rih perched at the end of the bed frame, her midnight eyes fixed on Mari with what could only be described as silent judgment of the time of day at which she had awoken.

"What?" Mari said defensively, stretching again, feeling her spine pop as she groaned deeply in relief. "It was a late night."

Rih, apparently, did not approve of this.

Her stretch was interrupted by a sudden tug on the blanket, which was yanked clean off her body in one swift, merciless motion. She barely had time to react before the cool morning air hit her bare skin. Her eyes snapped open.

"Rih!" she hissed, scrambling for the stolen fabric as it fluttered to the floor. She caught it just in time, pulling it up to her chest before she flashed the entire street below.

Rih, unbothered, stood at the edge of the bed, feathers fluffed with smug satisfaction.

Mari groaned again, louder. "You're a menace," she shot at her, flopping back onto the mattress.

As if to prove a point, Rih grabbed the edge of the blanket again.

Mari glared at her. "Don't you dare."

Rih released the blanket from her beak and, with an exasperated chirp, flitted off the bed, only to return seconds later, dragging one of Mari's boots awkwardly across the floor.

Mari snorted. The boot was almost as big as Rih, and the

bird was clearly struggling under the weight of it but refused to give up.

"Alright, alright, I'm up!" Mari laughed, swinging her legs over the edge of the bed.

Rih immediately released the boot with a triumphant little shake.

Mari arched an eyebrow at her. "Happy now?"

Rih chirped a familiar chirp that Mari recognized instantly.

Mari sighed. "Oh, you're starving?"

"CHIRP!"

"Why didn't you just say so?" Mari laughed. She made her way to her pile of clothes to dress for the day.

ONCE PROPERLY DRESSED AND BOOTED, thanks to Rih's insistence, Mari set out on a morning stroll through the streets of the capital. The last thing she wanted was more walking, but she knew that keeping her body moving was essential to avoid stiffness setting in. The thought of hobbling into the throne room, aching and rigid, while attempting a curtsy in front of Queen Lyra made her chuckle. She extended her stride, stretching her muscles just enough to feel that satisfying, restorative ache.

At a quiet corner by the city's outskirts, along the banks of the Myramin River, Rih finally had enough of waiting. With a cry, she launched off Mari's shoulder, cutting through the air in a blur. Mari tracked her movement, watching as Rih flitted low along the base of a stone wall and then, with a downward dive, snatched up a fat mouse scurrying for cover. She returned seconds later, the unfortunate creature dangling triumphantly from her beak.

Mari moved her head as far away from the mouse as possible. "Good catch!"

Rih flipped the mouse in her grip and gulped it down in two quick bites.

Mari grimaced.

Rih ruffled her feathers, fully content now that she had something in her belly. She would repeat this routine several more times throughout the morning—three mice in total, a breakfast gathered on her own terms.

Mari turned her attention toward the lively sounds of Joycita's morning markets, back in the direction of the inn where she was staying. Stalls were now bustling with shoppers, vendors shouting over the clatter of coin and barter, haggling over fresh cuts of meat, crates of fruit, and handfuls of grain. She had a hefty coin purse at her disposal, and if she was going to be here for a while, it was time to start navigating the rhythms of city life.

She stopped at the closest market stall, her senses pinging in every direction. Smoky, grilled tomatoes drew her in, their blistered skins topped with a blend of herbs she had never smelled before. She made a mental note to buy a jar of them to bring back to her aunt Kia. She eyed a delicious-looking round ball, roughly the size of her fist, and she asked the vendor to add one to her plate. She pointed at a jar that contained pinkish strands amongst round slices of lemon, which turned out to be the most incredible pickled onions she had ever tasted in her entire life. The vendor added a wedge of charred cheese that melted against the heat of the tomatoes and handed it over to her with a chunk of grilled flatbread topped with the same herbs that flavored her tomatoes. The combination of smells was intoxicating. She couldn't resist adding a small squat pie filled with some type of cold meat and topped with a glossy jelly she was desperate to taste.

Rih eyed the pie like it was a personal challenge.

Mari angled her plate away from the skyweaver, shooting her a warning look. "No."

Rih let out an innocent chirp, but Mari wasn't fooled. "Why don't you go stretch your wings?" she suggested, not particularly interested in spending her morning defending her breakfast from the very companion meant to be protecting her.

Rih warbled with delight, as if Mari had just granted her the greatest of privileges, and took off instantly, launching herself into the morning air without a second thought.

Mari finished off her plate with a honeyed pastry that the vendor assured her was the best in the capital. Balancing her haul, she perched on a low stone wall to enjoy the impromptu breakfast, savoring each bite as the morning shoppers moved around her. It felt like the perfect companion to the city's indulgences she had experienced the night before. A pang of guilt hit her as she remembered her family back home, rationing flour and water for the most basic of meals.

CHAPTER SEVEN

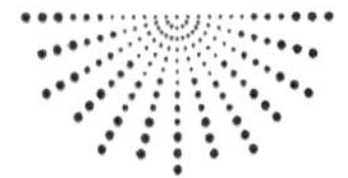

Back at the inn, Mari made her bed in an effort to resist lying back down again under the comfortable, cotton sheets. Her full belly threatened to put her to sleep, but she had work to do. She unpacked her satchel and arranged her pouches of soil samples with care, each tied with leather cords knotted to signify their origin. Greenhaven had one knot, Adavale two, and so on, forming a chronological map of her journey. The soil samples were lined neatly above her star maps, which bore careful notations of Mari's own intensity rating system, scribbled in the small margins. The notes told the story of the auroras' presence across the regions: Greenhaven, a vivid 10, still held the record for the most brilliant display she had seen, as well as the driest soil sample.

She hunched over her maps, her eyes darting back and forth comparing the placement of the stars over the past week with the stars from the past month, and finally, from last season's Lumithra mapping, noting the subtle shifts she had been tracking. She compared her observations with the annotations on Searsan's chart from the night before. The pattern was there; it was undeniable. She wished she had a satisfying explanation to present to the queen along with the unsettling information before her. She hated that the facts she would be presenting only prompted more questions... and hoped Searsan could help her find the answers.

When she tired of poring over her charts, convinced she had committed every detail and trajectory to memory, she perched herself on the edge of the bed, her satchel at her feet, and gazed at the quiet side street below.

The waiting felt interminable. She shifted restlessly, idly retying the knots on her sample pouches.

By the window, Rih sat watching the street with keen-eyed interest, her head flicking to track the occasional passerby. When a young boy suddenly dashed past, a toy bow and arrow clutched in his hands, Rih perked up instantly.

A Greenhaven boy his age wouldn't be running around with a toy—his bow and arrow would be real, well-crafted, and lethal enough to bring down small game. The differences between Greenhaven and Joycita were unsurprisingly vast, but Mari still enjoyed being shocked whenever she discovered yet another way the two were dissimilar.

She had learned that Joycita did not celebrate Lumithra, and while it partly comforted her to know she wouldn't have to witness celebrations and feel apart from her family, she also felt sad to not have the opportunity to observe the festival that meant so much to her. She was silently calculating the optimal time and location to make her observations that night when she suddenly remembered her astrolabe tucked into one of her many cloak pockets. She made a mental note to bring it with her, wondering if it would give her a more accurate location of where to set up. She tingled with anticipation at the thought of stargazing. If her calculations were correct, there would also be a short shower of stars that would rain across the skies in gentle cascades over the course of about two candlemarks. She was excited to see if she had adjusted the timing correctly, but given the shifting of the stars, she wasn't confident she would actually see anything.

Her focus broke only when her stomach growled again, and she reluctantly packed away her soil samples and headed downstairs for a quick meal. Bread and boiled eggs were delivered promptly to her table. It was far less exciting than her exquisite breakfast had been, but it did the job.

As she tore a piece of bread, she glanced at Rih, who was perched nearby and watching her with interest.

"Comfortable enough to hunt for your own lunch?" Mari asked, raising an eyebrow.

Rih tittered, considering. Then, with a squeak, she launched herself toward the open window, disappearing over the inn's roof.

Mari ate absentmindedly, her mind focused on the next lunar observations she hoped to make that night—the ones that would mark the start of Lumithra.

A sudden tap at the inn's window broke her trance. She looked up to see Searsan's flustered, rosy face peering in at her. A moment later, he strode inside, his robes disheveled and his beard looking as though he had run his fingers through it one too many times.

With a tired sigh, he dropped into the chair across from her. "What a day."

"Everything okay?" Mari asked, concerned, casting her gaze over his harried appearance.

"Yes, yes. By the skin of my teeth, I've managed to secure you a very brief meeting with the queen." He held up a hand, preemptively silencing her protest. "Between two of her councilors' appointments."

"So, barely enough time to bow and introduce myself..." Mari grumbled, not bothering to hide her disappointment.

"There'll be no time for pleasantries, Namari," Searsan said, cutting her off and giving the back of her chair a little shake—a not-so-subtle nudge that she should vacate the seat. "Come on, come on; we must go now." Mari stood quickly, and Searsan motioned toward the stairs that lead to the lodgings. She hurried upstairs to gather her belongings as Searsan followed and added, "You'll need to present your findings succinctly and convincingly. The queen is willing to listen, but her time is not easily given."

"Are we coming back here after?" Mari asked, straightening the blanket on her bed. Her mother would be so proud.

Searsan's face tightened. "From this point on, it would be unwise to make any assumptions about our next movements."

His cryptic reply unsettled Mari, but she had no time to dwell on it. She wrapped her cloak around her, clipped her satchel around her hip, and descended the stairs.

Once outside, Searsan took the lead, his pace relentless, weaving through the crowded streets with surprising agility for a man of his age. Mari kept up, her anxiety increasing with every step.

MEETING QUEEN LYRA was absolutely nothing like Mari had imagined. There was no grand hall, no gilded throne, no ceremonious procession, nothing official at all. Instead, it happened in the unassuming curve of a staircase, the stone steps winding up into the muted light of the castle's upper levels. Mari and Searsan were ascending when the queen appeared, descending from above, a tall man close by her side, his hand cradling her elbow, as if he were supporting her. The moment the man noticed the pair, his body stiffened. It was clear that he was not expecting the meeting, and Mari began to wonder if a meeting had actually been arranged.

"Queen Lyra," Searsan greeted, bowing with a subtle flourish. "Good afternoon, Your Majesty."

"Hello, Searsan," the queen replied warmly. She was enchanting.

Mari suddenly forgot how to breathe.

Queen Lyra was the most beautiful creature she had ever seen. Her soft skin seemed to glow, as though she carried the magic of the universe that Mari had been searching for her entire life. The low light of the stairwell should have dulled her presence, but instead, it only made her more intense, more mesmerizing, more entirely and unfairly radiant.

Mari felt her legs falter beneath her, her entire soul tipping dangerously toward the abyss, her heart hammering, her hands shaking. She mentally conjured up one of Zeph's slaps to the face, determined to keep herself present in the moment. The queen's gaze settled on her like a slow, intoxicating unraveling, and a knowing gleam in her bright blue eyes told Mari she had been expecting this encounter. She waited for Mari to speak.

Mari's mind screamed for focus, for stability, for mercy. Her body had already surrendered.

"Your Majesty," Mari somehow forced out, her voice wavering like a crumbling site of ancient Elyrian ruins. She stumbled into a too-quick, too-low curtsy—an awkward mess of limbs and instinct, neither correct nor warranted.

The queen's lips curved in the softest, most damning smirk Mari had ever witnessed.

Amusement. She was enjoying this.

Mari felt heat flood her face, her skin betraying her.

And then Lyra winked.

Mari stopped breathing entirely. She was getting nowhere fast. She was going to die in this very spot, in the unbearable, all-consuming presence of Queen Lyra.

Curse this impossibly gorgeous woman.

Searsan cleared his throat and caught the eye of the man at Queen Lyra's side—tall, with a calculating gaze, and dressed in the deep green of the royal councilors. Searsan took a deliberate step toward the clearly contemptuous councilor and placed himself directly in view, despite the man's attempts to ignore him. "Councilor Bomi." Searsan made himself heard. The man turned reluctantly, a sneer tugging at the corner of his mouth that he didn't bother to hide.

"Searsan," Bomi replied, his voice cool, "What is it now? I assume this interruption is of some pressing importance?"

"It is," Searsan said, unbothered by the man's obvious disdain. "The coordinates I provided you for the Opal Tower were mapped before the stars started shifting..."

Bomi frowned. "And? Can't you just remap them?"

Searsan folded his arms. He gestured for Bomi to step aside. Bomi's reluctance was clear in the severity of his glare. With an audible sigh, he followed Searsan a few paces away to the edge of the landing, leaving Mari alone with the queen.

Mari watched, impressed, as Searsan pushed forward the unwanted exchange. Then, before she realized what was happening, Queen Lyra's hand was on top of her own, her milky complexion a beautiful contrast against Mari's olive skin, her touch impossibly soft. The contact sent a jolt of awareness coursing through her veins. Mari stiffened as the queen turned to her fully, stepping in just enough to erase the safe space between them.

Too close.

Mari's breath disappeared somewhere in her chest as the queen's warm, keen eyes set upon hers. She had thought Lyra was beautiful, but as she got even closer, she realized that had been the understatement of the century. Up close, she was devastating.

She attempted to catch herself before she fell into the depths of Lyra's celestial blue eyes, and she swore she could see entire galaxies swirling there, drawing her in, undoing her completely.

The queen spoke with urgency. "How can I help you?" She leaned in, her eyes wide, and Mari was thrown back into the reality of why she was there.

This was it. The moment she had journeyed so far for. Her mind swam, spiraling into half-formed sentences, her thoughts scattering like startled birds.

Elder Amara's terrified eyes.

Dry salt pools evaporated into nothingness.

Goldenreeds swaying ominously in the wind.

The sky shifting into something it shouldn't be.

What should she mention first? And why, in the name of every constellation, could she only think about how close Queen Lyra was standing to her?

Searsan had prepared her to convince the queen that the skies were the looming problem, but in that moment, Greenhaven thundered in Mari's heart. *The skies, or the drought? The drought, or the skies?*

She glanced at Bomi, whose eyes flicked impatiently toward them. The moment was slipping away.

"Your Majesty," Mari began, her voice trembling. "I've come

from Greenhaven, far to the southwest. The drought has worsened beyond anything we've ever faced. The Sharaine River has been reduced to nothing but a muddy trickle. Our salt pools are evaporating. My village..." Her voice broke, just for a moment, but she pressed on. "My village won't survive much longer without aid. Please, can you help us?"

The queen paused. This time, it was her who seemed caught off guard.

Mari exhaled shakily, waiting for a response. She looked down nervously, and only then did she realize that Queen Lyra was still touching her hands. It would have been so easy to let go. Instead, she turned her palms upward, her fingers closing gently around the queen's hands, holding them in place.

"And, I think it might be connected to the appearance of the southern auroras," she added hesitantly, silently cursing herself for forgetting to mention that part sooner.

She could explain it all—the shifting constellations, the dried-out soil, the air that felt so humid despite not carrying a drop of moisture behind it... But Mari knew that this was not the moment to fumble through parchments and data. She swallowed. "I have proof."

The queen's expression softened, concern flooding her face. "You believe the drought is tied to the auroras?"

Mari hesitated.

This was it—her chance to bridge the logic and the concern, to convince her of the connection between the shifting stars and the drought. To show Queen Lyra she wasn't just another villager begging for grain rations. But time was slipping. So instead, she held Lyra's gaze, steady and sure.

"I believe they're connected," she said finally. "The skies are shifting, and the land is suffering. There's something unnatural about it."

Queen Lyra nodded slowly, her eyes searching Mari's, but before she could respond, a voice cut between them.

"Your Majesty."

Queen Lyra released Mari's hands at once. The loss of warmth was immediate.

"Aid is not something we can spare at the moment," Bomi interjected coldly. "Our resources are tied up in projects vital to the city's future. Rural aid is... a low priority."

The queen's jaw tightened, and she looked at Mari with something that resembled regret. "This young woman has traveled a great distance," she said firmly. "At the very least, we can spare a small team to assist her village."

Bomi bristled. "A team? We've just approved the construction of the Opal Tower. Every engineer and scientist is needed. This request is not possible."

"Please," Mari begged. She met Bomi's angry gaze, her eyes determined as she stepped toward him defiantly. There was a long, tense pause. Bomi sneered at Mari, but she didn't let it stop her from trying again.

"Your Majesty," Mari began, turning back to the queen. "I believe I can show you the connection. Tonight, if you meet me in the Great Library's lower gardens, I can demonstrate what I mean."

The queen appeared to waver, and for a moment, Mari thought she might agree, but Bomi's presence loomed over her, and her eyes transitioned from warm to glassy and distant. "Thank you, but that won't be necessary," she said almost coldly. "You'll have aid for your village, but I'm afraid that's all we can spare."

The drastic change in the queen's demeanor jolted Mari, but she wasn't deterred. "Wait!" she called, desperation creeping into her voice. She raised her hand, her words tumbling out before she could stop them. "Please, Your Majesty, I can show you how these are connected."

Bomi's eyes snapped to Mari, scanning her face with sudden interest.

The queen turned her head slightly, casting a pointed glance back at Mari. Was it an apology? A warning? Mari couldn't tell. "Let me show you," she pressed, the urgency in her voice clear.

The queen shook her head lightly. "I'm not available; I'm sorry," she said curtly. Turning again, she started descending the stairs. Her councilor was quick to follow, his hand once again on her elbow, guiding her as though she were a ship in need of steering.

Bomi paused just long enough to shoot Mari a withering look. "I've told Searsan before that the queen cannot be bothered with silly stargazing. She's busy holding together a fractured kingdom, in case you hadn't noticed."

Mari's shoulders sagged, and she hung her head. "Of course," she murmured. "I'm sorry."

The door at the base of the staircase closed with a resounding thud, leaving Mari in silence. The feeling of failure settled in her chest like an iron stone. She felt like she'd had the wind knocked out of her. She turned to Searsan, her voice breaking as she spoke. "I didn't say enough. I—"

Searsan rested a hand on her shoulder. "It's all right," he said, though his voice was laced with disappointment. "We can try again."

Mari nodded, although her spirit was already crushed. The queen's sudden unease, Bomi's barely concealed hostility—she highly doubted they would get another opportunity. The queen seemed to be guarded at every moment, shielded by layers of protocol, politics, and people who clearly didn't want this conversation to happen.

Perhaps she could scale a turret, sneak into one of the royal washrooms, and catch the queen in a moment of privacy. Surely, no one would follow her there... She stifled a laugh at her own absurdity. And then, just as quickly, the humor curdled. She felt a pang stab her side as she realized she had failed everyone. Her throat tightened, her nose burned, and tears threatened the corner of her eyes.

"I'm so sorry," she confessed.

Searsan stopped, focusing his eyes on hers. "This isn't over, Namari," he said firmly.

She found it hard to believe him.

CHAPTER EIGHT

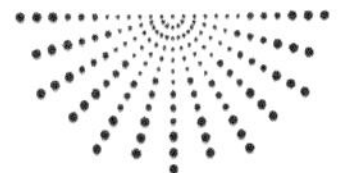

MARI SAT AT A CORNER TABLE FOR HER EVENING meal, a plate of roasted chicken and boiled potatoes in front of her. The meal did little to stir her appetite, and she absently pushed the food around with her fork, her thoughts spiraling back to the staircase encounter. She could put the food in her mouth and even chew, but she couldn't bring herself to swallow. She felt sick in the wake of her absolute and utter failure. With a sigh, she finally gave up on the meal. She left a few coins with the barkeep and carried her plate up to her room.

Rih was perched on the windowsill, her eyes scanning the street below. When Mari set the plate on the bedside table, Rih's head snapped toward it. In an instant, she hopped down eagerly, landing with a light thud, her feathers flaring just slightly as if to assert her claim, and began tearing into the offering as though the food might vanish if she paused.

Mari huffed a quiet laugh. "Better you than me." She watched Rih pick apart the chicken with precision, her hooked beak working methodically through the best bits first.

Mari pulled out the most recent chart she had been working on, plotting the stars above Joycita.

Despite her performance today—or perhaps because of it —she still felt the pull of the stars. She couldn't let her disappointment keep her from observing the stellar convergence that marked the beginning of Lumithra.

"Strong threads, starry Mari," she whispered to herself.

THE STREETS WERE QUIETER NOW as Mari stepped outside, her eyes stinging with tears from a moment of weakness she allowed herself in the privacy of her room. She bit her lip and balled her fists as she made her way to the Great Library's lower gardens. She found a secluded spot beneath the arching branches of an old willow tree, its silvery leaves swaying gently in the breeze.

The sky above was unusually clear, and the Weaver's Arc glittered faintly against the black night sky. Mari's hands trembled as she calibrated the astrolabe, her first time doing it alone. Aligning it with the stars overhead, she adjusted for their unexpected shift. The convergence should have been due south, but the instrument's calculations placed it three degrees west.

She leaned into the buzzing of insects, a sharp contrast against the trickling of the nearby river, the gentle current lapping at the moss-covered banks.

She got to work setting up her telescope, trusting the astrolabe's guidance over her instincts. Searsan had loaned her a heftier telescope, one with a stand and a bigger barrel, so she could see everything more closely than she would have been able to with her own telescope. Closing one eye, she peered into it, nodding with satisfaction. This was her space, where the tension of the day faded into the background, and she felt lighter, alone with her stars.

A rustling behind her broke the stillness. Startled, she whipped around, her hand instinctively reaching for the small dagger at her side.

Rih reacted faster.

The skyweaver launched from a low branch, her wings flaring wide as she swooped toward the movement... Then, she stalled. At the last moment, Rih veered upward, landing high in the tree instead, watching from above with her piercing eyes.

Mari's heart pounded. She turned, her knife still half-raised, and found herself staring at a figure cloaked in deep purple with emerald-trimmed edges stepping out from behind the willow's thick trunk.

Her hood was pulled low, but her striking features were unmistakable.

"Good evening, Mari," Queen Lyra said softly.

Even in the darkness, Mari could see the glint of her bright eyes, assessing her reaction.

Mari tried to stand, but she stumbled, and her dagger hit the ground with a dull thud. Her elbow knocked against the telescope, and she nearly toppled the entire instrument over in her rush to compose herself.

"Your Majesty!" she blurted. "I... What are you doing here?"

Lyra smiled the knowing smile of a beautiful woman who was familiar with the effect her beauty had on others.

Mari wondered if her body was still there or if she was just a floating head, for all that she could feel. That smile. That devastatingly, ruinously, unfairly beautiful smile.

Stars save me.

"Forgive me," Lyra said, taking a step closer. "I didn't mean to frighten you."

Mari highly doubted that.

"I couldn't stop thinking about what you said earlier. About the skies. About the connection." She took a step closer, her voice dropping to a whisper. "I'm sorry for how that meeting unfolded," she continued. "I have to be careful... I can't speak freely in the presence of my councilors."

Mari's breath caught. She had suspected as much, but hearing it aloud from the queen herself made the air around her feel heavier and her heart feel lighter.

She swallowed, her tongue suddenly useless in her mouth. "I... I understand, Your Majesty," she said, though her words felt small, and she really didn't understand at all. "Shouldn't you trust those folks?" she asked, chancing the bold question.

Queen Lyra sighed. "The council has been invaluable since I took the throne. Since the king was... since he died. The transition period has been incredibly difficult for all of us."

Mari nodded. She couldn't imagine what it must feel like to have lost her husband and then be expected to rule.

"There are a few I trust, yes—Councilors Sannah and Thammond, without question. And Councilor Varella... She's been supportive in a way that doesn't make me feel like a fool. Maybe the others are fine too, but I'm second guessing every step I take. I'm no politician, Mari. I'm not cut out for any of this."

Mari was surprised. That wasn't what she had expected to hear.

"Their guidance has been crucial," Lyra continued "But there are times I don't agree with their decisions, although I'm not sure I could tell them no, even when I want to."

Mari studied the queen's face closely, sensing an unease

that ran deeper than she was letting on. This wasn't just hesitation... It was fear.

"Are they... holding something over you?" she ventured cautiously.

Lyra's expression darkened. "Let's just say," she said slowly, "if I told you too much, it could put both of our lives at stake."

Her words sent a chill down Mari's spine. "Your Majesty, I —" she started, but stopped herself. This was bigger than her village. Bigger than the drought. She wanted to push, but she didn't want to be just another person forcing the queen into conversations or situations she was clearly uncomfortable with. She knew when someone wasn't ready to give an answer.

"I'm glad you're here. I can show you what I meant," she said, gently shifting the conversation.

Lyra nodded, stepping closer. "Please, call me Lyra."

Mari blinked, momentarily caught off guard. She finally managed to speak. "Alright... Lyra." It felt strange on her tongue. Strange, but right.

Encouraged by the queen's warmth, Mari motioned toward the telescope.

"Look here. See the Weaver's Arc?" Lyra leaned over, her hands brushing the tops of Mari's fingers as she braced the telescope and peered through.

Mari steadied herself. Her heart was not going to race over this. She was a scientist. A scholar. A woman on a mission. She was a melting mess. Shoving the distraction aside, she pressed on. "That arc," Mari continued, "should extend perfectly toward the moon, like a hand reaching out. But tonight..." She adjusted the lens to strengthen the focus. "The moon is cradled within it, like it's nesting. Beautiful, yes, but it's not how it's supposed to be. Not for Lumithra."

Lyra's lips parted in awe as she gazed at the alignment. It was spectacular to behold, despite how wrong it was.

After a long moment, Lyra looked at Mari. "Lumithra is...?"

"It comes from an old Patovian word that means 'woven light.'" Mari's voice had settled into a natural rhythm now, her knowledge carrying her forward, picking up where her nervous system had dropped the ball. "It's tied to the legend of the Elyrian Weaver. Have you heard of her?"

Lyra shook her head.

"She was said to have woven a magical tapestry that brought rain and prosperity to the Elyrian Terraces during one of the harshest droughts in Patovia's history." Mari let out a soft chuckle, shaking her head at the irony. "We sure could use some of that rain now."

She found herself absentmindedly tracing the green and golden filigree that edged Lyra's cloak. "The festival is our way of honoring creativity, resilience, and the strength of community—everything the first Elyrian Weaver embodied."

Lyra smiled. "That's a beautiful story." She shifted slightly, leaning just a fraction closer toward Mari's frame.

Mari shuddered. She hadn't even realized what she had been doing. Her fingertips still rested against the fabric, Lyra's presence far more distracting than it had any right to be.

Quickly, she pulled her hand away and self-consciously brushed a curl of hair behind her ear.

Lyra didn't seem to notice, or if she did, she didn't call attention to it. "So many of the old Patovian legends have been forgotten here in Joycita."

Mari cleared her throat, willing herself back to steady ground. She glanced toward the towering silhouette of the Great Library. "I bet you could find them all in there."

Lyra laughed softly. "I bet I could."

Mari turned her attention back toward the sky, willing her unease to settle. With Lyra around, that was not likely. "It's not just the placement. It's the timing," she added. "It's early. It shouldn't be this close to the moon for at least another two days."

Lyra looked a little lost. "What does it mean?"

Mari chewed her lip, struggling to articulate the unsettling feelings that accompanied the shifting stars. "It's... a disruption. The skies have a rhythm, a balance, and when they fall out of step, the world below often follows. Like ripples in a pond. The auroras, the droughts—they're all a result of something larger. And tonight..." She gestured upward. "It's happening faster than it should. What we're looking at right now... It's not supposed to happen for another six days."

Lyra followed Mari's gaze. The moon sat neatly inside a semi-circular arc of stars that cupped the lower half of the moon like a perfectly round ball of golden rice in a silver dotted bowl. She was silent for a long moment, her eyes fixed on the heavens. "You're certain they're connected?"

Mari exhaled, her breath misting in the cool air. "I am. The auroras are strongest in Greenhaven, where the drought is worst. The soil grows richer the closer you get to the capital, where the auroras fade. I can show you, if you want. I can't explain it better than that, but the skies... they're trying to tell us something. I just wish I knew what." Her voice lowered with her confidence, and she shook herself out of it. "But I'm going to figure it out!" she said, as convincingly as she could muster.

Lyra turned to her fully, her blue eyes gleaming in the soft starlight. She studied Mari with an intensity that sent a slow, curling heat down Mari's body.

"You're remarkable, Mari," Lyra murmured.

Mari swallowed, her breath catching.

"The conviction with which you speak... I saw it earlier, on the steps. Even when you faced resistance, you didn't balk."

The words settled deep in Mari's chest, and she fought to ignore the screaming voice inside her head that insisted she wasn't good enough. Wasn't doing enough. Wasn't enough at all.

"I thought I'd failed," she admitted, her voice barely above a whisper. "I thought I'd ruined my one chance."

Lyra shook her head, stepping closer. Too close. And also not nearly close enough.

"You didn't fail." Her voice dropped lower, the distance between them charged with the kind of energy that made Mari feel like she could scale the nearest tree and backflip back down to earth without so much as a scratch. "You made me listen. That's why I'm here."

The admission sent a rapid heat wave through Mari's body.

"I wish I had your courage."

Mari's eyes widened. "Me? Courageous?" She let out a breathless laugh, but Lyra didn't smile. She just watched her, her eyes burning with sincerity.

"I wasn't always like this," Mari confessed. "Even a week ago, I couldn't make a decision without looking to someone else for reassurance."

"The roads hardened you," Lyra suggested.

"No." The intensity in Mari's own voice surprised her. "Not hardened. Strengthened."

A slow, knowing smile spread across Lyra's fac. She reached out, her fingers grazing Mari's, tentative at first but only for as long as it took her to realize that Mari was ready to throw herself at the queen's feet, should she command it.

"There's nothing hard about you, my dear," Lyra murmured as she laced her fingers fully with Mari's.

Mari was still processing the words when Lyra turned her hand over, brushing her thumb across her palm. It was a featherlight touch, but it sent a deep, aching pull through Mari's chest.

Heat flooded through her, utterly consuming, pooling deep, her skin rippling with sensation. She felt too warm, too aware, every nerve drawn tight with anticipation.

She wasn't sure which of them had stepped closer, but suddenly, there was only a whisper of space between them, a roaring of heat where their bodies nearly touched.

The moment stretched, the stars above a silent witness.

Lyra's gaze dropped to Mari's lips.

Mari stopped thinking entirely.

The queen leaned in, her movements both deliberate and hesitant as if she were asking a question Mari already knew the answer to.

And Mari answered. She closed the gap and their lips met —slow, tentative, unbearably soft at first, before a desperate need took over.

Lyra kissed her like she had been waiting for this, waiting for Mari, and Mari melted into its longing, her body pressing instinctively closer, like it was the most natural thing in the world, the kiss both tender and electric all at the same time.

The tension of the day, the failures, the doubts... They all unraveled, fading into nothingness beneath the swaying branches of the willow tree.

When they finally broke apart, Lyra didn't pull away. She rested her forehead against Mari's, their breaths mingling, their bodies still radiating heat.

"You're incredible," Lyra whispered. Then she kissed her

again, gentler this time, as if her lips were moving in slow motion, as if she wanted to savor the moment.

"Thank you," Lyra murmured between them. "For showing me. For trusting me."

Mari gave a shaky, blissful laugh. "And you?" she asked softly. "Do you trust me?"

Lyra pulled back a bit, searching her face. Finally, she nodded. "More than I've trusted anyone in a very long time."

Mari's head spun, her thoughts tripping over themselves, a racing mess of 'what the fop just happened here?!' Had she really just kissed the queen of Joycita? Twice?!

Lyra saved her from the spiral before it could take hold. "I believe you," she said earnestly. "That they're linked. And that you'll find out what's causing it. I promise to do everything I can to help."

Mari didn't hesitate this time. She reached for Lyra, pulled her back in, needing to taste the warmth of her lips again.

This time, there was no uncertainty.

Her telescope sat forgotten as Lyra led her to the base of the willow tree and laid out her cloak. Mari moved to the ground and pulled Lyra in close. She settled against the trunk, her back pressing into the rough bark, one hand tangling into Lyra's perfectly soft hair, the other intertwining with Lyra's fingers, tracing idle patterns against her skin.

"Tell me more about Lumithra?" Lyra asked, looking up at her.

"We believe it signifies unity, light, and hope being woven into the fabric of life, even when everything feels bleak." Mari said, dotting a faint kiss on top of Lyra's head. She ran her fingertips along Lyra's open palm. "Villagers exchange handmade gifts—things like woven pouches, carved trinkets, tapestries, or tools. It's not about extravagance. It's about effort and care, even when times are hard. Every gift symbolizes that, even in scarcity, we can create something meaningful. It's a way to remind ourselves that we're stronger together."

Lyra listened intently as Mari spoke, asking questions about Mari's family, the gifts she gave growing up, and the spiritual observances connected to the phases of the moon.

They stayed in the garden until the first light of dawn began to creep over the horizon, sharing stories and quiet moments beneath the fading stars. Lyra spoke of her struggles with the councilors, of feeling trapped by their expectations, forever navigating their demands and scrutiny. Mari spoke of her journey, of the aching worry she carried for Greenhaven, of the hope that had pushed her forward even when she doubted herself.

The sky slowly lightened, the remains of the night fraying into pale gold.

Lyra sighed, brushing Mari's cheek, her eyes searching Mari's. "I have to go. I wasn't lying earlier when I said I have a busy day ahead."

Mari's heart sank, but she nodded. "Thank you for coming."

Lyra smiled, a glimmer of mischief shining behind her desperately beautiful blue eyes. "Thank you for being impossible to ignore."

Before Mari could think, before she could find something clever to say, before she could do anything at all, Lyra had pulled her hood up and disappeared.

Mari stood frozen beneath the willow. How on earth was she still standing? What in the sweet salted date had just happened to her?!

A giddy laugh escaped before she could stop it. She hurriedly packed up her equipment, her mind a storm of tangled thoughts—the queen's words, the press of her hands, the taste of her lips.

Still buzzing, she whistled for Rih.

The skyweaver swooped down from her perch in the high willow, landing gracefully on Mari's shoulder with a knowing glint in her eyes.

Mari flashed her a breathless, wide-eyed grin. "That did just happen, didn't it?"

Rih twittered, tilting her head. Mari huffed a laugh, deciding that was a firm congratulations.

Somehow, she made it back to the inn and stumbled into her room with the reckless urgency of someone who needed to lie down before their brain shattered into a thousand pieces.

She barely managed to kick off her boots before crawling into bed and pulling the blanket over her head. And for once, the stars weren't the only thing she was dreaming of.

CHAPTER NINE

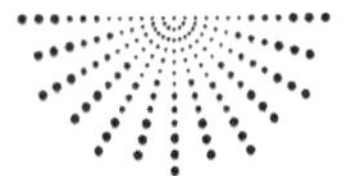

THE NEXT MORNING, MARI AWOKE TO A BANGING ON her bedroom door. Rih was flapping aggressively above it, her wings flared like she was prepared to attack whoever dared disturb them.

Mari stumbled forward, still half-asleep, and reached for the handle. "Alright, alright," she grumbled, pushing Rih aside with one hand as she pulled the door open. There before her was Searsan, completely out of breath, wide-eyed, and with a mad grin on his face. "I don't know what happened, but Namari, you've been requested to appear in front of the queen's council today!" he exclaimed.

Mari smiled. She knew what had happened. Twice.

Perhaps it was the queen's turn for a demonstration of strength. She pushed Searsan back out the door and clumsily dressed herself, her insides churning with excitement and anticipation. She had another chance! Although, she thought as she ran a brush hurriedly through her hair, if she was being honest with herself, she was more nervous about the prospect of being in the same room as Lyra again than she was about how she would convince the council that aid to Greenhaven was imperative. She'd deal with both when she got to the castle. First, she needed breakfast, and then she needed to fill Rih's belly enough that she wouldn't complain when she was left behind at the inn.

THE COUNCIL CHAMBER was not the cold, dark room filled with calculating minds bent on dismissing her that Mari had imagined. Instead, it was warm, almost welcoming, and the golden light of midmorning streamed through arched windows draped in silken curtains. The room's circular shape gave it a softer energy, and a set of arched double doors opened up to an outdoor balcony where tiny pink and white flowers were blossoming.

At the center of the room stood a round, dark, gleaming redwood table. The chairs surrounding it were high-backed and sturdy, upholstered with deep green velvet. Queen Lyra sat in seat on a stone platform, raised a little higher than the others, indicating that it was the head of the table. The councilors took up the remaining seats, their faces ranging from disinterest to veiled hostility.

Mari stopped in the open doorway, taking in the details of the room. Tapestries hung between the windows, depicting great moments from Patovian history. Above, a massive chandelier crafted from iron and emeralds hung low. It was beautiful, but it did little to calm her nerves.

"Namari of Greenhaven," an official-sounding voice announced. Mari jumped. Not a small, cute jump like she had been startled, but a huge, both-feet-left-the-floor-and-her-arms-flew-out-at-weird-angles kind of jump. One step down from a being-chased-by-a-bear jump. She cringed.

Off to a great start, she thought. She cleared her throat and shook out her nerves, delivering another one of Zeph's imaginary slaps to her face. She would have to thank him for all the support when she got back to Greenhaven. She channeled the brightest, boldest version of herself. She had no idea what was about to come out of her mouth, but she knew she wasn't going to back down.

Mari stepped forward.

Queen Lyra's eyes met hers, and Mari all but melted. She flexed her hands to shake off the tell-tale tremor that threatened to betray her. Her heart thudded with frantic palpitations, each beat a reminder that Queen Lyra's presence did things to her that no amount of composure could suppress. She forced herself to focus on the councilors, who were already murmuring amongst themselves.

"Namari," Lyra said, her voice steady. "We would like to officially welcome you to present your request to the council."

Mari nodded and looked around the room. The queen appeared to be the only individual at the table who was at all welcoming the presentation of her request. "Yes, Your Majesty. Thank you for granting me this audience."

From her right, Councilor Bomi threw his hands up. "We've already discussed this matter," he snapped. "The kingdom's resources are stretched thin as it is. Aid to the rural south is simply not feasible."

Mari's chest tightened. "With respect, Councilor, Greenhaven isn't asking for the impossible. We need support—tools, expertise, someone who can help us navigate this crisis."

"And what," Bomi interjected, "do you propose we do about the weather, Miss Namari?"

Mari's cheeks flushed, but she refused to let him make her look like a fool. "It's not just the drought," she said, her voice rising with conviction. "It's tied to the skies. The auroras are strongest in Greenhaven, where the drought is worst. The closer you get to the capital, the weaker they appear, and the richer the soil grows."

She reached into her satchel to pull out her star charts and soil samples, which she placed carefully on the table. "I've documented the changes across my entire journey. This isn't a coincidence."

The councilors exchanged skeptical glances. One, a woman with silver hair pinned in an elaborate braid, picked up a soil sample and examined it with mild curiosity. "What do you expect us to do with these findings?" she asked. "You're an astronomer, not a hydrologist."

Mari swallowed her frustration. "I don't have all the answers, but I know this: if we don't act now, Greenhaven and other villages like it will collapse. If you send someone to help us, to buy us some time at least, I can continue my research and find the connection."

"And if there is no connection?" Bomi pressed. "What then?"

"There is," Mari insisted. "I just need time to prove it."

The room fell into a tense silence. "This council exists to serve all of Patovia. If you want to spend time researching your little theories, might I suggest you attend our university, Miss Namari?" Bomi said, his face spread with a condescending sneer.

Queen Lyra considered Mari, her mouth tightly closed, her chest rising slowly with each controlled breath. For a moment, Mari thought she had lost. Then the queen spoke. "We cannot turn our backs on those who depend on us."

Bomi stiffened. "Your Majesty, the resources required—"

"One person," Lyra interrupted. "Surely you can spare one person to assist Namari in her efforts."

The councilors exchanged uneasy glances, but no one dared to argue further. Bomi bowed his head. "As you wish, Your Majesty."

Mari wanted to squeal with delight, but she forced herself to remain composed. "Thank you, Your Majesty," she said, bowing deeply.

Lyra smiled. "You'll have your assistance, Namari. Make the most of it."

As Mari gathered her charts and samples, her gaze flicked to Lyra's, and she flashed her a bright grin. Of course, she was grateful that she would be returning to Greenhaven with help, but she was also extremely proud of the queen for speaking up. She bowed her head again quickly, and as she turned to leave the room, she could have sworn she saw Lyra throw her a quick wink.

Mari blushed a ferocious red as she left the council chamber and trampled down the castle steps two at a time. She stepped out into the lower quadrangle and raced toward Searsan, who was waiting for her by a spectacular water fountain that towered above the lush gardens and stone wall surrounding the area. Searsan seemed out of place next to such grandeur, his scholarly robes too practical for such extravagance.

As Mari approached, she saw Searsan's smile of relief morph into something dark. His eyes shifted past her, and she turned just in time to see Councilor Bomi following her closely.

"Well, Searsan," Bomi began, his voice laced with venom.

"It seems your protégée has been quite the busy little messenger this morning." He glared at Mari.

"Councilor Bomi," Searsan replied curtly. "I trust the queen's court deliberations went smoothly?"

"I hope you're not planning any further unscheduled interruptions today, Searsan."

"Councilor Bomi, I was under the impression it was the queen who requested the meeting with Namari today."

Bomi smiled unkindly, his eyes cold. "Mmm. And as a result, the queen's schedule has been... delayed."

Mari bristled, but Searsan placed a calming hand on her shoulder.

"Which means, in turn, my schedule has also changed." Bomi sighed dramatically, clasping his hands before him. "Unfortunately, I'll have to push back our meeting to finalize the Opal Tower's next phase. I've had to rearrange my priorities. Again."

"The queen's priorities seem clear to me—helping her people," Mari countered.

"Help, yes," Bomi said smoothly, his eyes switching to Searsan. "Which is precisely why ensuring the Opal Tower's construction stays on schedule is so critical. Don't you agree, Librarian?"

"I agree that ensuring the tower stands the test of time is critical. But hastening the project for appearances' sake will only create problems later."

Bomi's smirk faltered, just for a second.

"An architect as renowned as Haldic should have answers when I come to him with questions about the foundation. So, perhaps you could tell me why it is that he insists I speak with you instead?" Searsan was pushing it.

Irritation flashed briefly in Bomi's face, and Mari caught it before he was able to adjust back to his neutral arrogance. "We shall have to address them when we meet this evening, then, won't we?" He kicked at the ground, a cloud of dust rising and scattering dirt over Searsan's boots. "I look forward to your insights. It's always such a pleasure to hear how our Great Library can contribute to the kingdom's progress. After all, we're not just building a tower here, Librarian. We're building this queen's legacy."

"Looks to me like she can build her own legacy." Mari shot him a glare.

"You're becoming tedious," Bomi said, waving a hand as if to dismiss Mari entirely. "Enjoy your brief moment of relevance, girl. It won't last." He turned back to Searsan again. "The council has no time for more of your hypotheticals. You may be the head librarian, but do not overestimate your influence here. The queen's patience is not infinite, and neither is mine. See you tonight. Don't be late."

Without waiting for a response, he turned and strode off towards the castle, his robes swishing behind him.

"What an absolute drovak's ass." Mari scowled, kicking a cloud of dirt in Bomi's direction.

"Bomi doesn't like interference, Mari. Not from me, and certainly not from you."

Mari crossed her arms, still fuming. "He's just upset he's losing control over his precious queen." *MY precious queen*, she thought. *Stop it, Mari.* A grin started to form despite herself.

Searsan seemed to have caught the expression on her face because his tone changed. "You have a journey ahead of you!" he exclaimed. "I can see the gleam in your eyes... Greenhaven awaits! Come, let's get you ready."

Mari declined to correct him. She wasn't exactly sure how

"Actually, I'm replaying the kiss I shared with Queen Lyra for the thousandth time" would go over.

MARI RETURNED to the Great Library gardens that evening, hopeful that perhaps Lyra might appear again. She waited beneath the willow tree, trying not to let her expectations get the better of her.

Nearby, Rih was perched on a low branch, preening her feathers, occasionally ruffling them as if she could sense Mari's restlessness. Mari busied herself setting up her telescope, pretending the ache in her chest wasn't there as she kept glancing toward the path. Every sound made her heart jump, only for it to settle back with a thud when no one appeared. The moon moved higher in the sky, and higher still, but the queen never came. With a resigned sigh, Mari packed up her equipment, her steps slower than usual as she left the garden.

Rih fluttered down to her shoulder and nuzzled her gently. Mari tried not to be too disappointed. It's not like they had made plans. Tomorrow, she thought, there would be one more chance.

By the time she got back to the inn, Mari was exhausted. She trudged toward the stairs, miserable and exhausted. All she could think about was collapsing into bed.

"Oi!" the barkeep called.

Mari blinked, startled. "Me?"

"This came for you," he said, holding out a folded piece of parchment.

Mari frowned. The ink was smudged, and she didn't recognize the handwriting. It was untidy and looked self-taught. The sight of her name scrawled in black sent her body cold. She opened the parchment to find only three short words scribbled across the page: "The Lantern District."

She stared at the note, confused. The Lantern District was one of Joycita's older quarters, known for its winding alleyways and markets that stayed open late into the night. She had never even visited, let alone known anyone from around there.

"Do you know who left this?" Mari asked the barkeep.

He shrugged. "Just said it was important. Left it with a coin to ensure I delivered it tonight. You had me worried for a while there... I was wondering where you were."

It could be a trap, she thought. Or... something else. She stuffed the note into her cloak.

"Thanks," she said, leaving a coin on the bar and stepping back into the chilly night. "Shall we go and see what all this is about?" she asked Rih. The bird responded with a sharp flick of her tail feathers.

THE LANTERN DISTRICT was alive with color despite the late drift of darkness overhead. Strings of glowing paper lanterns crisscrossed the crooked streets, bright and beautiful, but Mari felt a stab of unease as she wound her way through the maze of alleyways. Rih sat on her shoulder, alert as ever, her eyes tracking every movement she made.

Mari looked around, her senses on edge, her breath shallow as she tried to gauge her next move.

Where was she supposed to go?

She slowed, finally stopping by a deteriorating wooden bench, its edges splintered with age. Settling onto it gingerly, she scanned the area nervously. A dark figure slipped from a nearby side street, and Mari started to pay more attention to them when she realized they were approaching her.

"Mari," said the figure.

The voice was female, and Mari felt the tension in her body loosen a little.

The slender woman stepped closer. "Follow me."

Something in her tone put Mari at ease right away. She obeyed, trailing silently behind the woman. They wove through cramped alleyways, and it wasn't too long before they came to a modest, yellow door tucked between two unassuming storefronts. The woman knocked rapidly six times, then again three times with slightly less speed. The door swung open, revealing a staircase leading downward.

"This way," the woman said.

Mari glanced around. "What is this place?"

The woman didn't reply, disappearing instead down the winding staircase.

Mari reached up to brush over Rih's feathers, feeling safer knowing Rih had her back. She was just about to take the first step down when the woman's head appeared again from around the wall.

"Hurry up!" she whispered curtly.

Mari pulled the door closed behind her and followed the woman into the dark.

She fumbled her way down the pitch-black staircase, touching the rough stone walls to keep her balance. As she got to the bottom, she waited for her eyes to slowly adjust to the candle lights that lined a long hallway.

"Where are we? And who are you?" Mari asked more firmly this time, expecting a response.

"I'm Elisa," she finally replied.

"Oookay... And where exactly are we going, Elisa?"

No answer.

Elisa kept moving. Rih let out a small, inquisitive chirp as Mari hurried to follow.

"We've come this far... may as well," Mari whispered.

Despite knowing the woman's name, Mari's unease deepened as they wove through a maze of tight, barely lit hallways. A sweet, woody smell filled the air, and Mari strained to listen to muffled conversations from behind the curtained doorways that they passed every ten or so steps. Elisa led her to the very back of the corridor, pausing before a closed door.

Mari's heart began to pound again. Was this a trap?

Elisa opened the door, and Mari tensed, her hand once again inching toward her blade. But when she stepped inside, her breath caught.

CHAPTER TEN

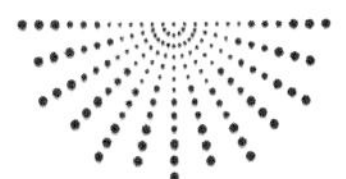

QUEEN LYRA SAT AT A LOW TABLE, HER HOOD already pushed back, her golden hair tied back neatly and secured with a simple band. A freshly lit candle in the middle of the table told Mari she hadn't been waiting long. Her eyes smiled as they landed on Mari. "I'm glad you came," she said warmly.

"Welcome to Zećira's Tea House," Elisa said with a small curtsy.

Mari stared at her, too shocked to say anything. She blinked, glancing around the room, then back at Elisa. "So, definitely not a trap, then."

Rih let out a short trill before promptly taking flight, flapping up to a high rafter where, if Mari had to guess, she'd already spotted a small rodent.

Mari sighed. "Glad one of us feels at home."

The queen smiled. "Thank you, Elisa." She turned to her fully and spoke with warmth in her voice. "Please, tell your mother how much I appreciate her accommodating us."

Us. Mari's heart wobbled.

Elisa curtsied again. "Of course, Your Majesty. It's her pleasure. Our pleasure. She was so proud when I got a job in the castle kitchens; you can only imagine how delighted she is to host you tonight. Not that she can boast to anyone, 'course."

The queen smiled again. "I appreciate the discretion."

Mari swallowed hard. "Lyra," she murmured, finding her tongue.

Elisa raised an eyebrow at Mari's familiar greeting.

"Please. Sit."

Mari slid into the seat across from Lyra as Elisa left the room and closed the door behind her. The queen motioned to a steaming teapot and two porcelain cups on the table. She poured the tea slowly and slid a cup over to Mari, all without breaking eye contact for even a moment. She lifted her cup, inhaling the fragrant steam. "Tangerine and lemon balm," she said, taking a sip. "It's my favorite."

Mari followed suit, the warmth of the cup calming her nervous energy. "It's lovely," she admitted, though her focus was entirely on the queen.

They sipped in silence for a while, their eyes meeting often; each glance lingered just a moment longer than necessary, and their smiles spoke volumes.

"I couldn't let you leave without seeing you again," Lyra finally broke the silence. She set her cup down, her index finger lightly tracing the delicate, golden rim. "I owe you an apology for earlier today, too. The way my council regarded you... it wasn't right."

"Why do you let them act like that? You're the queen."

Lyra sighed. "Yes...I wear the crown, but it's not as simple as that." Her gaze dropped to the table. "When my husband, the late king, was murdered, the kingdom barely paused to mourn before they thrust the throne at me. Overnight, I went from being dismissed as a pretty face to being expected to hold an entire region together."

Lyra took a long sip of her tea before continuing. "I swore I'd be different from him—he was so arrogant. I wanted to listen, to trust my advisors. But..." She let out a bitter laugh. "Now I wonder if I've gone too far the other way."

Mari leaned forward. "It doesn't have to be all or nothing, Lyra. Listening is great and all, but you're the one with the title. You should be making the final call."

Lyra's eyes smiled, and she reached for Mari's hand. Her thumb started to stroke it absently. "You make it sound so simple. Bomi already undermines me at every turn. If I push too hard, I risk alienating the entire council..."

"No, it's not simple," Mari admitted with a small laugh. "But you're the queen. You can do it."

Lyra smiled and squeezed Mari's hand. "I'm glad one of us has faith in me."

"You hold the power, Queen Lyra," Mari said with a cheeky wink. "Own it."

Lyra poured the two of them some more tea. "You remind me of myself," she said. "Though I was much older than you before I dared speak so boldly."

"So, what changed?

"Power," Lyra admitted. "When I became queen, I thought I would have the power to make whatever changes I wanted... but I quickly learned that power isn't always yours to wield. It can be taken, twisted... held against you."

Mari frowned, unsure of how much to push. "You don't have to be like him to lead. And you don't have to let them push you around to listen. If you let them overshadow you, Patovia will lose its queen." She looked down and noticed Lyra's fingers gliding over her hand. Her arms were instantly covered in goosebumps. "If I'd noticed this sooner," she said with a sheepish chuckle, "I don't think I'd have been able to hold up my half of this conversation at all."

Lyra followed Mari's gaze to their joined hands. She laughed, and Mari could have sworn she saw her blush ever so briefly as she pulled her hand back. "Forgive me. I didn't mean to make you uncomfortable."

"You didn't," Mari said quickly. "I just... I wasn't expecting it."

Lyra reached for Mari's teacup, smiling. "May I?"

Mari frowned. "May you what?"

"Read your leaves," Lyra said, tilting the cup slightly. "I used to do this with my grandmother when I was a girl."

Mari handed over the cup, watching as Lyra studied the dregs. "Hmm," Lyra murmured. "I see conflict ahead. A fork in the road, both literally and figuratively. You'll have to choose carefully."

Mari grimaced. "That's not exactly comforting."

Lyra's expression grew somber. "About your trip tomorrow. I've been assured the person accompanying you is capable, but if there's danger..." She trailed off, her brow furrowing.

Mari snorted. "Capable? From your council? I'll believe it when I see it."

Lyra's lips twitched. "They'll surprise you. Perhaps."

In an effort to lighten the mood, Mari reached for Lyra's cup. "Your turn."

Lyra raised an eyebrow. "Are you an expert in tea leaves?"

"Absolutely not," Mari said with a grin. "But I am very good at making things up." She squinted at the dregs. "I see... an epic battle. You, speaking in tongues, vanquishing your enemies one by one."

Lyra laughed, a sound so warm it made Mari's chest ache. "In tongues, you say?"

"Very impressive," Mari confirmed, then hesitated. "I... I hope you don't think I'm making light of this." She gestured to the tea leaves in the bottom of the cup. "I just... wanted to be cute."

"You are... very cute."

Mari's cheeks burned. "Oh?"

"Mmhmm." Lyra nodded, a strand of golden hair slipping loose from behind her ear. Without thinking, Mari reached up and tucked it back into place, her fingers grazing Lyra's skin ever so slightly as she pulled back. Lyra shivered. Their eyes locked, and for a breath, just a breath, Mari swore she felt Lyra's heartbeat in her own chest.

She quickly hid her giddy grin behind her teacup, squeezing her eyes shut. *Get it together, you absolute fop.*

As if sensing Mari needed a lifeline, Lyra graciously shifted the conversation. "What's your favorite constellation?" she asked. Her voice was genuinely inquisitive.

"The Weaver's Arc," Mari said without a doubt. "There's something so graceful about its curve, like it's reaching for something just out of sight. And the stories—how it represents weaving light and unity into the world... I think we could all use a bit of that."

"That's beautiful."

"What about you?" Mari asked. "Do you have a favorite?"

Lyra's face turned wistful. "The Healer's Crown," she said. "My grandmother would point it out to me when I was little. It was the first constellation I ever learned to find on my own."

"Tell me the story behind it?"

"I would have thought you knew it."

"I do," Mari confessed, "but I want to hear you tell it."

"The Healer's Crown is said to belong to an ancient figure who could mend anything—broken hearts, broken possessions, broken stars. My grandmother used to say it reminded her that even in the darkest times, there's always a way to heal, to rebuild." Lyra paused, a wistful smile on her face. "She had a charm with the constellation on it. She would wrap me up in these big hugs, and I would just snuggle into her and play with the charm on her necklace. It was so comforting to me. When she passed..." Lyra paused to take a steadying breath. "When she passed, she left the charm to me."

"She must've been a remarkable woman."

"She was," Lyra said. "She would have liked you."

Mari blinked, surprised. "Me?"

Lyra chuckled. "Yes. You remind me of the stories she used to tell me about people who dared to reach for more, no matter how far away it seemed."

Mari felt her cheeks burn yet again under Lyra's gaze. She gestured toward the queen's teacup, deflecting the conversation. "Careful, or you're going to inflate my ego."

Lyra laughed, and the two fell into a comfortable rhythm once more, trading stories and questions until the teapot ran dry.

Some time later, a soft knock interrupted them. Elisa peeked her head in. "Your Majesty, I'm sorry, but we need to get you back to the castle."

Lyra sighed. "Duty calls," she murmured, but she didn't take her eyes off Mari. "I'll see you tomorrow."

Mari stood, her heart pounding. "You will?" she asked, the words feeling more vulnerable than she intended.

Lyra stepped closer, the space between them charging instantly. Her fingers brushed along Mari's cheek affectionately. "Yes," she whispered. "I promise."

Mari's lips parted instinctively as Lyra leaned in. Her mouth captured Mari's in a soft, drawn-out kiss. Mari melted into it, her breath stolen, her thoughts scattered like stars across the sky as the impossibly tender embrace deepened.

When they finally pulled apart, Lyra's eyes shone bright with what Mari would confidently call a renewed strength. "Goodnight, Mari."

All Mari could do was nod as Lyra stepped out of the room, leaving her standing there, breathless and utterly undone.

MARI WOKE with a spring in her step. She was a bundle of nerves and excitement, and she fumbled as she dressed quickly, fastening the cloak Searsan bought for her around her neck and tucking the astrolabe securely into her satchel. She paused at the mirror and took a few deep, calming breaths while she contemplated her own reflection. Pressing her eyebrows down, she tossed her hair and gave herself a little wink. She tightened her boots, clicked for Rih to follow, and made her way downstairs for the last time. She said goodbye to the innkeeper on the way out, and he wished her luck for the journey ahead of her. Today, she would begin the journey back to Greenhaven.

The queen's council had decided who would accompany her, but Mari remained in the dark about their choice. The uncertainty gnawed at her, although it was dulled by the knowledge that she'd get one last moment with Lyra before leaving. She could still feel the warmth of her touch on her hand, a sensation she wouldn't likely forget any time soon.

The castle gates stood open, the courtyard alive with

activity. Horses snorted and pawed at the road as stable hands saddled them. Mari weaved through the commotion, heading toward the stables as instructed.

When she arrived, she looked around, but no one else had arrived yet. A gorgeous gray horse with a pink-splotched nose caught her eye, and she reached out, stroking its velvety muzzle. The horse huffed softly, nudging her hand, and Mari couldn't help but smile. She leaned in for a snuggle.

A clinking noise drew her attention to the next stable. She peered over the wooden partition, her brow furrowing in recognition. There, crouched by a trough with tools spread around her, was Kalindi, the plumber from the sweetbaths. She was focused on tightening a bolt, her curls falling into her face as she muttered under her breath.

Mari cleared her throat. "Kalindi?"

The woman didn't look up immediately. "Hmm?" she replied absentmindedly, turning the wrench one last time before setting it aside. She glanced over her shoulder, looking mildly confused. "Do I know you?"

Mari grinned. "The sweetbaths. You came to fix the pipe. Your boss was a jerk."

Kalindi's eyes flashed with recognition. "Oh, hello..."

"I'm Mari."

"Mari. What are you doing here?"

Mari stepped closer, brushing a piece of floating straw out of her face. "I'm getting ready to leave. Back to Greenhaven."

Kalindi raised an eyebrow. "Greenhaven?"

Mari nodded. "My village is struggling, and I came here to ask the queen for help."

"And?"

Mari sighed. "I was hoping for a real solution. Maybe a team of people to help us rebuild and fight the drought, but instead, they're giving me one person. Just one. How is that supposed to make a difference?" She bit her lip. "Probably not even anyone useful," she added with a disappointed huff.

Kalindi leaned back on her heels. "One person, huh?"

"Better than nothing, I guess." Mari shrugged.

A harsh voice interrupted from behind them. "I see you're both here. At least you're prompt."

Rih screeched a warning as Mari snapped her head around just in time to see Bomi standing at the stable entrance, his hands clasped behind his back. She frowned, glancing around in confusion. *Both?* Her eyes darted back to Kalindi, who was already standing and brushing dirt off her hands. That's when she noticed the large travel pack propped against the wall near Kalindi's feet.

It clicked.

"You've got to be kidding me," Mari said, the words slipping out before she could stop them.

Kalindi gave a flat, tight-lipped smile and widened her eyes so Mari could see the white all the way round. She hefted the pack onto her shoulder. "Better than nothing, right?" she quipped, her voice dripping with sarcasm.

Mari cringed. "That's not what I—"

"Don't worry, Stargazer," Kalindi interrupted, adjusting the strap on her shoulder. "I'll try not to slow you down."

Bomi, oblivious to the tension crackling between the two, stepped forward and cleared his throat. "Namari of Greenhaven, you are hereby granted the services of the engineers of Joycita. Should you no longer require these services, you may release the engineer, who is expected to return to the city immediately. Do you understand the terms of the assistance?"

"Um... yes?" Mari finally managed after what felt like an excruciatingly uncomfortable amount of silence.

Bomi gave her a flat look. "Convincing," he said with a sigh. "Goodbye."

"Wait. What about the queen? Isn't she—"

Bomi laughed, bitter and dismissive. "The queen doesn't make a habit of bidding farewell to every lowly engineer or villager she helps. You've had your audience." He spun around and marched away, leaving Mari standing there with her mouth open.

Her heart sank as his words settled over her. She turned to Kalindi, who appeared quite amused.

"I thought you were fixing the trough..." Mari's voice trailed off as she tried to process what was happening.

"I was. While I waited for you to arrive. I can't help it. I see something broken and I have to fix it," she said with a shrug.

"Well," Mari said with an awkward smile. "I guess we should get going?"

Kalindi snorted and started briskly toward the stable gates without saying a word. Mari scrambled to grab her travel pack, slinging it over her shoulder as she hurried after her. Rih took flight from the rafters, following from above.

As they rounded the corner into the castle's quadrangle, Mari saw Searsan leaning against a small garden wall. His skin seemed paler than usual, his posture slouched, and his robes pooled loosely around him.

"You look awful," she meant to tease him, but she couldn't help feeling some concern as she got closer and realized she wasn't wrong.

Searsan gave her a weak smile. "I'm fine. Just didn't sleep well."

"You sure it's not something else? You look like you've been dragged through a swamp."

"I'm fine, Namari," he assured her, rubbing his temples.

Mari scanned his eyes. "If you say so," she said, unconvinced.

"All set?" he asked.

She nodded. "Thank you, Teacher. For everything." She threw her arms around his neck and pulled him in for a hug.

Searsan nodded. "Travel safe, Namari. Keep looking up." He sounded proud, and Mari beamed.

"Let's move," Kalindi's gruff voice interrupted the moment.

Mari rolled her eyes and jabbed her head toward Kalindi. "This is Kalindi. She's a plumber."

"I'm an engineer. And a scientist," Kalindi emphasized.

Searsan eyed them, a bemused look on his face as they bickered.

"She was expecting someone taller," Kalindi said sarcastically, pushing through the pair and walking toward the gates that would take them to the main road out of Joycita.

With one last hug, Mari parted from Searsan and raced to catch up with Kalindi.

"Wait!" A booming voice called out from an overhead tower.

"Are you kidding me?" Kalindi threw her arms up in frustration. "We're never going to reach the outskirts by sunset if this is our pace," she said impatiently.

The quadrangle suddenly stilled. Mari frowned and looked for the cause of the abrupt silence that had swept over the area. A low, imposing rumble started up around them. Mari turned toward the source of the commotion to see two rows of guards appear, dressed in brown leather vests and bronze helmets that shone brilliantly as if they had just been polished that morning.

The unit stopped by the castle's front entrance, and multiple pairs of guards distributed themselves evenly along the tall, stone walls. The doors of the keep opened, and a dozen more guards filed out in two straight lines. They headed straight for Mari.

The double row of guards parted and Queen Lyra emerged, her presence as commanding as ever, though she was flanked by her ever-present councilors. Mari's heart soared, and then immediately plummeted back to earth as she recognized Bomi beside the queen, gripping her elbow like a leash. Any hope for a private moment evaporated faster than a Greenhaven salt pool as the group approached. Lyra smiled at Mari, but her smile was gone as soon as it had arrived when Bomi stepped closer to them.

"Her Majesty, Queen Lyra," Bomi announced flatly.

Mari shot him a smug look.

"Your Majesty," she said with a deep bow. Kalindi and Searsan followed suit.

The queen approached Mari and extended her hands in farewell. She took both of Mari's hands in her own briefly and gave them a squeeze. The touch was fleeting, and as Lyra pulled away, she left something small and cool in Mari's palm. Without daring to look down, Mari slipped it into her pocket, her pulse quickening. Lyra delivered a regal kiss that barely touched Mari's cheek. That whisper of a kiss sent a shiver down her spine, and she nodded, unable to muster more than a quiet "Thank you."

Queen Lyra's eyes focused on Kalindi. "You must be Kalindi," she said with a smile. "Thank you for accompanying Mari to Greenhaven. Please take care of her. The success of your mission is of great importance to Patovia."

Kalindi nodded. "I'll do my best, Your Majesty," she said stiffly.

"Thank you. I asked the kitchen to prepare some provisions to keep you going. We've arranged lodging for you at General Clar's outpost. There is also a letter you can give the general requesting they give you anything you need for your journey ahead," Lyra said.

Elisa appeared from behind her, holding a small brown parcel bundled with a golden twine. She handed the parcel to Mari with a wink.

"Thank you," Mari whispered, not expecting this kind gesture. Kalindi simply nodded again.

"Safe travels," Lyra said softly.

Bomi reached for Lyra's elbow, once again taking hold of the queen. Mari's eyes narrowed as she watched the interaction, noting Lyra's rigid frame as she allowed herself to be led away, glancing back one final time before she was swallowed up by the guards who marched in formation behind her.

Searsan placed a hand on Mari's shoulder. "This isn't the end."

"I'll make you proud," Mari promised. She felt a lump the size of five lemon dates lodge in her throat, but she shoved it back down from where it came. She would not cry in front of Searsan. Gods, even more mortifying, she would certainly not cry in front of Kalindi.

Kalindi crossed her arms. "Can we leave now?" she asked impatiently, her irritation radiating.

CHAPTER ELEVEN

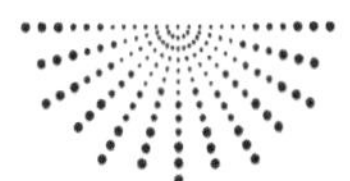

THE JOURNEY OUT OF JOYCITA BEGAN IN AWKWARD silence. Kalindi walked a few paces ahead, kicking at the rocks and dirt that littered the road with each step. Rih flitted between the two women, chirping occasionally, as if trying to bridge the gap.

"So," Mari ventured after a while, "you don't seem thrilled about this arrangement."

Kalindi snorted. "What gave it away?"

Mari sighed, trying to keep her tone light. "Look, I'm not exactly happy either, but we're stuck with each other. Might as well try to make the best of it."

Kalindi stopped abruptly and turned to face Mari. "I've spent the last four years building a life in Joycita," she snapped. "I was finally starting to feel settled, like I belonged. And now I'm being sent off to who-knows-where to babysit some stargazer."

Mari bristled. "Babysit? Do you even understand what's at stake here?"

"I do, actually." Kalindi glared at Mari. "When I was told I would be joining you, I was scared and angry. And then I realized that this was my opportunity to do some actual good!

"I stayed up all night designing schematics for Greenhaven. I even went to the library and found old maps so I could make sure what I designed would work with the climate. I was so excited that I was sure to arrive early, so as not to keep YOU waiting. So I'm sure you can imagine MY raging disappointment to discover that you're a whiny, ungrateful baby with puppy dog eyes for the queen just like everyone else in this city!"

Mari's mind went blank as she processed everything Kalindi had just yelled at her. But Kalindi wasn't done. "You might not have any faith in me, but I'm telling you now—I can help. With everything."

"What did you mean this is your opportunity to do some actual good?" asked Mari.

Kalindi scoffed. "I don't want to talk to you!"

Mari frowned. Now who was acting like a whiny baby? She had half a mind to say just that, but decided, wisely, to bite her tongue. Kalindi stomped forward and didn't say a word for the next two candlemarks.

During a short water break, after Kalindi had accepted some pastries from the parcel Elisa had given them, Mari tried again. "Where did you live before you came to Joycita?"

Kalindi rolled her eyes and said nothing. Mari vowed to try again once they reached the outpost. Their getting off on the wrong foot was entirely her mistake, and she had to fix it.

Her thoughts drifted to the queen.

"Just like everyone else," Kalindi had said. She wasn't surprised. The queen was beautiful. Who wouldn't fawn over her? But the comment had planted a seed of doubt in her mind. Lyra had confessed she was a people pleaser. Could she have been leading Mari on? What would be to gain on her end? Mari had nothing to offer—not armies, not money, and certainly not power. Still, though, she found it difficult to shake the feeling that perhaps the queen had overemphasized her affection for Mari, and it settled in her ribcage like a heavy pit, dulling the delight that had been bubbling away before, whenever she had thought of Lyra.

The tension between them simmered as they continued. As the sun started to set, Kalindi slowed her pace and turned to face Mari with obvious reluctance.

"Is this the right way?" She squinted in the direction they had been traveling.

Mari nodded. "Yes, we should be getting close."

"But I can't see anything ahead. Who gave you directions? Perhaps we should just verify..."

"Searsan suggested this route because it's just slightly off the main road, so we're less likely to bump into anyone else. It should take us more or less the same time as the main road."

Kalindi looked uncertain. She jumped when Rih suddenly puffed up, the sharp-eyed skyweaver fixating on something in the brush—dinner, most likely.

"You're welcome to look at the map, if you'd like." Mari did her best not to sound condescending.

"Thanks," Kalindi said, taking the map from Mari. She bent over, resting the map on her legs, struggling with the edges that rolled in on themselves. She huffed and grunted. "Where are we? Here?"

Mari peered over her shoulder and hummed in confirmation.

"Where's the outpost? I don't see it on this map..." Kalindi looked at Mari with wide eyes.

Goodness, this girl is anxious.

"It's here." Mari pointed. "It's not outrightly mapped, probably for security purposes? Searsan told me it was right here in this river bend." She tapped at the thin line of river that ran a little further west of the spot where Kalindi had pointed out as their current location.

Kalindi pressed her lips together and scrunched them to one side. "Here?" She jabbed at the map, roughly in the same spot Mari had.

"That's right," Mari said, putting as much kindness and patience in her voice as she could muster, despite her growing irritation. *Could this girl just trust me already?*

"Alright. Let's keep moving then," Kalindi said, taking off at lightning speed. She looked entirely unconvinced, her knuckles white as she gripped her travel pack tightly.

Mari pulled out her astrolabe and pointed it above. The sky was ever so slowly beginning to darken, but there were no stars visible yet. She spun on the spot and pointed the device back in the direction they had just come from. After some quick math, she quickened her pace to catch up to the engineer, who was a solid thirty paces in front of her already.

"Um, Kalindi? We should be there well before it gets dark," she said. She did her best to sound as reassuring as possible.

"Not if you don't put that thing away and start moving," Kalindi snapped, pulling away from her once again.

Mari gritted her teeth and took a deep breath. "What a butt," she mumbled.

"What?"

"I said I'm moving my butt!" Mari said, skipping a step and lengthening her stride.

～

MUCH TO MARI'S ANNOYANCE, it was evening when they arrived at the military outpost on the far outskirts of Joycita. Kalindi shot a smug look in her direction as they reached the outer walls, which were built from black stone and reinforced with iron bands. The barracks inside were modest but sturdy, its walls covered in black banners bearing the royal crest of Joycita—a soaring falcon over crossed swords. Inside, soldiers moved about leisurely, their uniforms dirty, but not a pin out of place.

They were greeted by a young soldier by the name of Calen, his enthusiasm for protocol tedious after their long journey.

"What business do you have here?" he asked.

Mari handed him the letter bearing the same royal crest that adorned the barracks' walls behind them. "We're traveling to Greenhaven," she explained. "The queen has requested lodgings and supplies."

Calen's eyes widened as he read the letter. "Of course," he said quickly. "Anything you need."

"Anything?" Kalindi asked, a mischievous glint in her eye.

Mari sighed, pinching the bridge of her nose as Calen led them inside, his gaze flicking uneasily to Rih's sharp beak.

"She's harmless," Mari reassured him, "unless you're a mouse. I promise."

Calen chuckled, although he sounded more nervous than amused.

"But if you're a rat..." Kalindi threatened, letting her words trail off.

Calen swallowed. Mari shot Kalindi a scowl.

Calen walked them through the outpost, pointing out details with the passion of someone who clearly loved his post. "This is one of the oldest outposts in the kingdom. It's said the stone for the walls was quarried from the same mountains that birthed the Elyrian Terraces."

Mari studied the grayish blue walls, their surface etched with what could have been faint carvings but were probably just wind-weathered grooves. She made a mental note to ask Calen about them later.

"And this is our armory," Calen said as they rounded a corner and stopped in front of locked double doors. "It's where we keep all the good toys," he added with a wink.

Kalindi's face lit up. "The queen's letter said we could take what we need, right?"

Mari groaned. "We're not looting the armory."

"It's not looting if we have permission," Kalindi replied with a grin, already heading toward the armory door.

OVER DINNER, they sat with Calen and his unit in the mess hall while Rih skimmed the skies on the outskirts of the barracks in search of her own food. They listened to the soldiers as they recounted their stories of what brought them to the outpost. It was clear that this small barracks had a tight-knit community of dedicated servicemen and women.

Calen shared stories of his childhood in Brindlemyre, a village Mari had only heard of in passing. "Each month, my grandfather would journey with me to Joycita's Great Library and let me pick out as many books as we could carry back home," he said with a wistful smile. "I remember looking up at the very tops of the castle spires and deciding that when I was old enough, I would join Joycita's guard so I could see them every day." He looked around the dark mess hall, the crowded space buzzing with camaraderie. "I almost made it," he said with a bittersweet chuckle.

After dinner, Calen took them to meet with General Clar. His office was small and impeccably neat, and he gave them a warm, welcoming smile when they entered, offering them his outpost's full support and assuring them of any help they might need. It was a short meeting, but enough for the pair to feel at ease with their stay.

As they left General Clar to his work and moved on to the final leg of their tour, the lodgings corridor, Kalindi marveled at the kindness displayed by the general.

"He can't command too much respect being that lovely," she mused.

"Oh, on the contrary," Calen said, slowing as they reached two doors that faced each other. "I'd die for that man."

"And the others?" Kalindi asked, raising an eyebrow. Calen was perhaps an eager exception.

"Long before he was General Clar, he was Commander Clar," Calen began, his voice overflowing with excitement at the opportunity to recount the tale. "He led a small unit out to investigate a disturbance a little further south from here, near a small town called Lillyford. At first, it seemed like it was nothing but reports of raiders harassing trade routes and some land disputes—the usual. But when Clar and his men arrived, they discovered something far worse."

Mari and Kalindi exchanged a glance, drawn in already.

"What was it?" Mari asked.

"The story goes that a group had taken over Lillyford—a faction of self-proclaimed 'visionaries' who called themselves the Stewards."

Kalindi raised an eyebrow. "The Stewards? Never heard of them."

"Most haven't," Calen said with a shrug. "Their name's been wiped from every record I've ever seen. Officially, it's like they never existed, but around here, the story is legendary."

Mari frowned. "Why? What did they do?"

"They weren't just raiders," Calen explained. "They came with plans—ambitions, even. They promised Lillyford's people that they'd make life easier, richer, and safer. But it wasn't long before the villagers realized those promises were lies."

Kalindi crossed her arms. "What happened?"

"They enslaved the town. Forced labor, stole land... anyone who resisted disappeared. Some say they were executed, but others... Well, some think the Stewards used them in their experiments."

"Experiments?" Kalindi asked curtly.

"That's the story," Calen replied. "The Stewards claimed they were trying to harness the power of the ancient Elyrians."

"The ancient Elyrians," Kalindi snorted. "Like the Elyrian Terraces? Those are just bedtime stories for little children."

Mari shook her head. "No, I believe them," she said.

"That's because you're a child," Kalindi chided.

Mari ignored her. "What did Clar do?"

"He arrived with just twenty soldiers—barely enough to defend a village, let alone take on a group as organized as the Stewards. They had more men and better weapons, and they'd fortified their position in the woods around Lillyford. Clar could've turned back or sent for reinforcements, but he didn't."

Kalindi tilted her head. "Why not?"

"Because he believed in the people," Calen said simply. "He spent his first night in Lillyford listening to their stories and earning their trust. Then he made a plan—not to fight the Stewards directly, but to outsmart them."

"How?" Mari asked, completely captivated by the tale.

"Clar staged an offering," Calen said. "He sent word to the Stewards' leader, asking if he could join them, offering wagons of 'tribute'—grain, coin, some basic weapons. He even tied up his own men and made them look like prisoners. The Stewards, arrogant as they were, marched right into the village square to claim their prize."

"And then?" Kalindi asked. For someone who had started off this conversation with such skepticism, she was clearly quite intrigued by the story.

"The wagons were a trap," Calen said. "Clar had loaded them with oil, and he'd hidden villagers and soldiers in the shadows, armed with whatever was on hand. When the Stewards gathered to collect their loot, he gave the signal. The wagons went up in flames, cutting off their escape, and Clar's forces struck. Clar himself took down their leader in single combat—barehanded, if the stories are true. Without their leadership, the rest of the Stewards scattered."

Mari's heart raced. Calen was a fantastic storyteller. "He really pulled that off?"

Calen nodded. "By the time reinforcements arrived, the threat was gone. Clar had saved Lillyford and all but destroyed the Stewards in one fell swoop, with barely a drop of blood spilled on his side."

"Why isn't this common knowledge?" Kalindi asked.

"Apparently, the king decided the Stewards were too dangerous to let the story spread. They buried the whole thing. Lillyford was told to rebuild and forget." Calen shook his head. "The Stewards have friends in high places, and spreading fear could destabilize the kingdom. Our job is to avoid that at all costs."

"'Have' friends?" Mari caught his use of present tense. "You think the Stewards are still out there?" Images of the strange symbols in the equilibrium chamber she had stumbled upon flashed through her mind.

"If they are, we haven't heard anything about it. But we don't forget. The legend lives on," Calen said with a wink in Mari's direction.

"How do you know it's true, then? If it's just a legend?" Kalindi asked, back to her usual, skeptic self.

Calen wasn't deterred by her questions, and simply shrugged. "Maybe it isn't true. Maybe it's just a great story. But I believe it."

THAT NIGHT, Mari lay awake, staring at the ceiling of the modest room they'd been given. Rih slept silently, tucked on the back of a chair in the corner, her head nestled beneath one wing. The day had started out long and frustrating but ended pleasantly enough. She and Kalindi seemed to have started to mend the tension between them, although she was fairly certain Kalindi still didn't trust her at all. Mari didn't exactly trust Kalindi either, but tomorrow was a new chance for both of them.

Mari punched the pillow under her head. She just could not manage to fall asleep. The story of Commander Clar and the Stewards spun in her mind like a gnat hovering around a plate of near-expired lemon dates. She was trying desperately to weave together the seemingly unconnected details.

The Stewards. Their name, erased from history, made Mari's skin crawl. What else had been hidden about them? Calen's mention of the Elyrian Terraces had hooked her. Could the Stewards really have been trying to recreate something from the Elyrians? She had always believed there was truth to the tales that the Elyrians' mastery of the elements was more than just folklore, and with everything unfolding around her as it was, those stories were starting to feel closer to fact than to fiction. The strange equilibrium chamber, with its mysterious symbols and faint hum in the air, drifted to the forefront of her mind. Could it have been connected to the Elyrians? Or to the Stewards? The possibility sent a shiver through her. If the Stewards had truly sought to harness the Elyrians' power, what had they uncovered? And if they were still out there, as Calen seemed to believe, what were they doing now?

Her blood ran cold as the possible connection clicked. Could the shifting skies play a part in all of this?

She shook her head. She was really reaching now.

Mari turned onto her side, punching her pillow again in an effort to give it some volume. She wondered if the queen had heard the story of the Stewards.

Then, she suddenly remembered the gift that Lyra had pressed into her hand at her farewell. Quickly but quietly, so as not to wake Kalindi, who slept restlessly in the bed on the other side of the small room, Mari threw her blanket aside and padded over to where her cloak was draped on a chair. She dipped her hand into every pocket, each dive becoming more frantic as she attempted to locate the item, relaxing the moment her fingers closed around the small object in one of the interior pockets.

She couldn't believe she had forgotten about this! In the darkness she wasn't quite able to make out what it was. A coin, perhaps? It was small and round, but she would need to find a light source if she was to see it clearly. She scanned the room, the only light creeping under the door that opened to the main barracks corridor. She slowly eased the door open a crack, the creaking hinges reverberating loudly through the silent room. Mari cringed.

From the back of the chair, Rih rustled awake, ruffling her feathers with an irritated flick before settling again.

Kalindi stirred, her body tensing as she murmured something unintelligible, her voice tight and panicked.

Mari stopped moving immediately, the low light from the corridor spilling into their quarters in a thin line that ran down the center of the room. She didn't dare breathe until Kalindi settled, the small round object from Lyra cutting into her hand, her tight grip wrapped around it.

After a moment of stillness, Mari turned back to the light source. She opened her fist, revealing a delicate, silver charm that bore a tiny, intricate engraving of a constellation. Her breath caught—it was the Healer's Crown. The charm glinted faintly in the light of the hallway, and she traced its delicate lines. Mari felt an overwhelming amount of affection for the queen as she realized the significance of the gift, and she closed her eyes, balling her fist around the charm, holding it to her chest as she willed her heart to beat a little less fast. For a moment, she felt treasured. She felt unstoppable.

Mari climbed back into bed and wriggled about, creating friction to warm herself up. The thought of Lyra brought warmth and unease equally. Her presence had always seemed so steady, so calm, but she wondered if there was more to the situation. She recalled the way Bomi's hand had gripped Lyra's elbow, both the day she had first met the queen and the day of her farewell. The tension in Lyra's body as she was steered from place to place... The queen was keeping secrets; of that much, Mari was sure.

What could Lyra want from her? Why would she shower her with so much affection, so ardently certain and reassuring?

If it was to gain allegiance, it had worked. Mari would crawl on broken glass the entire way back to Joycita if it meant she could return to Lyra's embrace. She had known her for barely two days, and already she was willing to all but lay down her life for the woman.

Giving up on sleep, Mari left her bed again and crossed the room, grabbing her cloak on the way out.

In the quiet of the corridor, Mari laced the charm from Queen Lyra onto a thin leather cord that she had stored in one of her cloak pockets. She silently thanked Searsan for insisting he buy her a cloak with ample pockets. She lifted the charm over her head and pulled her thick, gentle curls through. The charm felt comforting against her skin, like a quiet promise. She closed her eyes, picturing the constellation it represented, and then imagining the sweet, soft kisses of its gifter. She shivered in the coolness of the corridor, or maybe it was the thought of Queen Lyra's lips against hers. Licking her lips, she decided to venture down the hall and see if the kitchen was still open at this time of night.

CHAPTER TWELVE

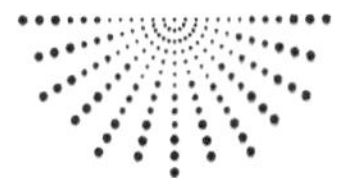

THE DAWN BROKE CRISP AND CLEAR OVER GENERAL Clar's outpost. Mari and Kalindi stood near the gate, Kalindi sporting a brand-new dagger tucked into her boot and a shortsword at her hip. The silver earrings that encased her ears glinted in the sun, peeking out through her black cascading hair that had been pulled up into a bronze clasp high atop her head. Wrapped around her wrist was a flat leather strapping that held a stunning black stone that glinted flecks of blue when it caught the sunlight in a particular way. She was leaning on a quarterstaff, a thin wire cord wrapped around one end, the crest of Joycita carved at the other. Rih was flying circles above them, stretching her wings and searching for breakfast. The soldiers moved about, their morning routine in full swing. Kalindi impatiently tapped her boot on the floor. Calen had insisted that he must sign them out before they could leave.

"For someone who is such a stickler for the rules, you'd think he'd be on time," Kalindi huffed.

A full figure hurried around the corner toward them. The long, bright face of the kitchen attendant who had caught Mari rustling through the dry goods baskets the previous night beamed as she approached them carrying a wrapped package.

"Mari!" the woman called, her voice warm.

Mari's face lit up. "Brenna! You didn't have to do that."

"Nonsense," Brenna said, shoving the package into Mari's hands. "You've got a long road ahead, and you'll need proper food, not just dried rations." She lowered her voice conspiratorially. "There's honey cakes in there too, and something tasty for Rih. Don't tell the quartermaster."

Mari grinned. "You're a lifesaver." Brenna squeezed her tightly and hurried back to the kitchen before she was spotted by anyone who might mind.

Kalindi leaned against a nearby post, watching the exchange with a raised eyebrow. "Making friends last night, were you?"

Mari nodded with a smile while she made room for the bundle of goodies in her pack.

"Why does everyone find you so charming?" Kalindi asked, her voice half-teasing, half-skeptical.

Mari turned to her, fluttering her eyelashes dramatically. "Because I am charming," she said with a grin.

Kalindi snorted, rolling her eyes. "If you say so," and then "Ah, Calen! Good morning."

Calen approached them awkwardly, his chirpy demeanor unusually strained. He shifted, not making eye contact, clearly wanting to say something.

"Thank you for your hospitality," Mari said, breaking the silence.

Calen nodded. "It was an honor to host you. If you're ever back this way..." He extended two small brooches. "The royal crest," he explained. "It's a bit of a good luck charm 'round these parts. It'll mark you as a friend of the outpost."

Mari accepted it, touched by the gesture. "Thank you, Calen. I'll treasure it."

Kalindi nodded her thanks as she took hers and pinned it to her cloak.

Calen hesitated again in front of Mari. "I, um, I really enjoyed meeting you..." His voice trailed off.

Was that a question or a statement? Mari wondered. The man was a shadow of the charismatic soldier that had shown them around the previous night.

"It was a pleasure. Thank you for sharing your hospitality and your gift of storytelling with us."

Calen blushed.

"Charming strikes again," Kalindi teased under her breath.

Mari shot her a look. "Jealous?"

"Hardly," Kalindi replied, but her expression softened into something resembling a smile.

As they stepped through the gates, Calen raised a hand in farewell. "Safe travels!" he called after them.

THE FIRST CANDLEMARK passed in relative quiet, the camaraderie of the morning lingering in the air. Kalindi was five strides in front of Mari, as if she owned the path. Ahead, the road split into two directions. Kalindi slowed as they approached the fork, her sights fixed on a signpost pointing to Myramin's Bend.

"We're going right," she announced.

Mari frowned. "No, we're not. The straight path is faster."

Kalindi crossed her arms. "We need to go to Myramin's Bend."

"For what?" Mari asked, irritated. "We're already carrying more than enough."

Kalindi sighed. "I told you; I need materials."

"Materials?" Mari raised an eyebrow. This hadn't been discussed.

"Quartz, preferably in rods if I can find any. Zinc, copper, and iron. Assuming you have ceramics and clay back in Greenhaven?"

Mari was shocked, unable to answer.

"I can't build the device unless we have this stuff, so it really is non-negotiable."

Mari stared at her, frustrated. "Why didn't you just say that?"

"I didn't think I'd have to justify myself," Kalindi snapped. "The queen trusted me to ensure this mission does not fail, and that's what I'm doing."

Mari was torn. Kalindi's determination was clear, but so was her arrogance. She really hated having to dig for every piece of information. Their lack of trust was starting to become a problem. If they were going to succeed together, one of them needed to start trusting the other first, and Mari had a feeling it wasn't going to be Kalindi.

"Fine," she said finally. "We'll go to Myramin's Bend, but if this turns out to be a waste of time, I'm throwing all your new weapons in the river."

Kalindi gave a smug grin. "Deal."

Kalindi strode ahead toward Myramin's Bend, her strides unwavering. With each step, her quarterstaff struck the ground with purpose, a rhythm that matched the renewed energy in her gait. The dark stone secured by a leather strap around her wrist caught the high afternoon sun, flashing sparks of brilliant blue. Mari's attention was drawn to the subtle details about

Kalindi that she hadn't noticed before, and she couldn't help but feel a growing sense of confidence. She was determined, unyielding, and unapologetically herself. Perhaps Kalindi, annoying and stubborn Kalindi, with all her quirks and grit, might just be exactly what Greenhaven needed after all.

Her thoughts drifted to Queen Lyra as the charm around her neck stuck to her sweaty chest. The way Lyra's electric blue eyes, threaded with dancing waves of olive green, would look deep into her own, freezing the world around her, aware only of the queen's cool, calming touch... The way the queen moved in slowly, stopping just particles above her lips, waiting for Mari's unspoken permission before she pressed a light, leg-destroying kiss against her partly open mouth... The way Mari had let her tongue hover below her top lip, ready to welcome Lyra's, should it venture in... She was trying to curtail the shivers rippling throughout her entire body when a high-pitched click snapped her rudely out of her daydream.

She blinked, only now registering the familiar sensation of Rih on her shoulder. At some point, the skyweaver had landed unnoticed, and now, with a nip at her ear, she made sure Mari was paying attention. Mari had slowed her pace without realizing it, and Kalindi was already far ahead, disappearing fast. If she didn't move now, she'd lose her around the next turn.

Mari pursed her lips and gave her shoulders a little shake, quickening her steps to catch up with the engineer.

Dusk approached, and Kalindi strayed from the path to find a place to stop for the night. Mari let her take the lead. They found a small clearing that had obviously been used as a campsite by previous travelers. A solid tree trunk sat parallel to a ring of rocks, the blackened ground in the center of the circle indicating the fire that had burned there the night before. The rush of the Myramin River, the powerful waterway that had given rise to Myramin's Bend, could be heard in the distance. It wouldn't take them long to get to the town once they woke.

"Let's camp here tonight," Kalindi said, sitting down and taking a long drink from her waterskin.

Mari dropped her pack next to Kalindi's and sat beside her, but not too close. She knew how to treat a horse who spooked easily, and something told her Kalindi might be the same. They'd been doing so well so far, and she didn't want to mess it up now.

They worked together in silence, gathering firewood. A rumbling overhead threatened a thunderstorm, and Mari was equal parts excited and concerned. It had been a long time since she had witnessed a storm. Noticing the wide, twiggy branches that lay on the ground around them, she gathered up enough of them to build a crude but effective hut that would shield them from the rain. Kalindi watched, obviously impressed, as Mari wove the shelter together, securing the branches in place so no water would seep through.

As the evening settled, the tranquil symphony of the forest unfolded around them. The dark night sky that Mari had grown accustomed to in Joycita had been replaced by the faint flow of an aurora. Gentle whisps of an almost white light green stretched from the tops of the trees upwards toward the center of the sky. *Makes sense,* Mari thought as she watched the aurora's slow, easy dance above. She felt a warmth within her as she realized that the brighter the auroras got, the closer to home she was.

Mari and Kalindi sat side by side under the shelter, the steady patter of the light rain drizzle creating a soothing backdrop to the occasional hiss of water droplets meeting the fire.

Kalindi poked idly at the fire with a long stick, watching the tiny hypnotic embers dancing upwards. "Water is incredible, isn't it?" she said.

Mari nodded, her hands outstretched to the warmth. "It's life and destruction all at once. Too much of it can be devastating. Not enough, also devastating. It has control over our livelihoods, but we have no control over it."

Kalindi's lips curved upwards ever so slightly. "My grandfather used to say something like that. He believed water was the only true force we could understand but never truly control."

Mari tilted her head, intrigued. "He did?"

Kalindi nodded. "It didn't stop him from trying, though. He was a master of water systems. He built aqueducts, irrigation channels, and even showed me how to build a water-catcher. That's what inspired the design I came up with for Greenhaven, actually."

Mari smiled. "He sounds wonderful."

Kalindi huffed an uncomfortable breath, her eyes wistful, and sad, almost. "He was brilliant. He wanted me to carry on the legacy, to be better and brighter than him, always pushing me to learn, to innovate, but I..." She trailed off, staring into the fire. "I couldn't do it."

Mari studied her, sensing more behind her words than she was letting on. "Why not?"

Kalindi leaned back against the tree trunk with a quiet sigh. "I didn't want to be part of something I didn't believe in. He thought the world could be fixed with enough ingenuity and effort, but the truth is, people, or systems, don't work that way. They're messy. And sometimes, the things we build only make it worse."

There was something in Kalindi's voice that Mari couldn't

quite place. "What do you mean? Did something happen?" She pressed gently, careful not to push too hard.

"It doesn't matter. I let him down. That's the only part that stuck." Kalindi turned her face toward the skies, and Mari caught the tear that escaped the corner of her eye before she surreptitiously wiped it away.

"He wanted so much for me, and I just... walked away," Kalindi said, her voice flat.

Mari felt her heart pang at Kalindi's moment of vulnerability, her tough exterior nowhere to be seen, allowing Mari a glimpse of some actual human emotions from the stoic engineer. "Walking away doesn't mean you failed him. Sometimes, the bravest thing you can do is carve out your own path."

Kalindi shot her a weak but grateful smile. "Maybe," she whispered.

Mari gave the fire a poke, allowing Kalindi the space she seemed to need. She couldn't help but feel there was more to Kalindi's feelings than she was letting on. Her story definitely seemed to hold an awful lot of guilt that ran far beyond disappointing a grandfather.

The rain started to come down a little heavier, and the fire crackled louder, filling the silence. Eventually, Mari spoke again, doing her best to keep her voice light and unassuming. "For what it's worth, I think you're pretty remarkable. You've got this fire in you, Kalindi... I like it."

Kalindi snorted. "You like it, huh?"

Mari shoved her playfully with her shoulder and chuckled. "Don't get too excited; I don't like it that much."

"Mmhmm. That's what they all say at first," Kalindi teased, but she flashed her a grateful smile. "Thank you, Mari, but don't go making a habit of getting sentimental on me."

Mari grinned and leaned back against the shelter. "No promises."

The conversation drifted to lighter topics as the night wore on, with Mari remarking how interesting it was that, despite the aurora being present, it had rained.

"So maybe they aren't connected?" Kalindi asked.

"No," Mari said with certainty. "They're connected."

They unpacked what they needed to settle in for the night and agreed to take turns sleeping in order to keep watch over the fire and the nearby road. Mari had agreed to keep watch first, with Rih perched high above, nestled among the leaves, ever watchful. Kalindi tossed uncomfortably, murmuring her distress as she had at the outpost. Mari wondered if she'd ever free herself of the burdens she carried. Perhaps that's what this journey was truly about for her—proving herself worthy of the legacy her grandfather had left.

Mari stared into the dancing firelight, turning the charm from Lyra over in her hands to keep herself awake.

THE PAIR ARRIVED in Myramin's Bend a little after midmorning the next day, the sun reflecting across the water that rushed through the lively riverside town. Ferries covered the river, their comings and goings the heartbeat of the trade route that connected the town with the rest of Patovia. Mari's first impression was awe. It was nothing like Greenhaven's quiet fields and modest cottages. Here, the village pulsed with energy, its lifeblood the deep waters of the Myramin River.

"This place is... huge," Mari said, her eyes flitting between the ferries and the long redwood docks.

Kalindi shrugged, her quarterstaff propped against her

shoulder. "Yep. It's just as I remember it, too," she said nonchalantly.

Mari's brow furrowed. "You've been here before? What for?" she asked.

"To shop, obviously," Kalindi said, pointing to the lines of stalls.

Mari considered her with a head tilt. Kalindi didn't seem like someone who would shop for fun. It made her wonder if there was another reason she had insisted on Myramin's Bend. Another detail withheld. She felt her trust in the engineer waver.

They headed to the nearest inn, not having the energy to spend comparing options. They got lucky that the first place they came across was a clean establishment tucked along a paved street just off the riverfront. After securing a room for the night, they ventured to the town's famed markets. Stalls lined the riverbank beneath long, curving concrete arches that reminded Mari of the giant ribcage of some great beast. The off-white arches, a tribute to the marine life that thrived in the Myramin, framed the bustling market before them. The atmosphere reminded her of her first steps through Joycita, and she felt comforted by the energy that enveloped her as they entered the rows of market stalls. The smell of fish, salts, and burning oils mingled with citrus fruits was rich in the air, and Mari felt her mouth fill with saliva as she looked at Kalindi, who was already eyeing a small riverside eatery nearby.

Above them, Rih let out a loud shriek and made a left turn, gliding low over the river's surface. Drawn in by the flash of silver scales beneath the water, she swooped toward the shallows, circling with keen interest, assessing whether dinner could be caught fresh. Mari watched her for a moment before deciding to leave Rih to fend for herself. She and Kalindi headed inside, led by the smoky warmth of grilling fish.

They shared a meal of grilled river fish and crispy flatbread, the fish accompanied by a tangy green sauce, and Mari licked her fingers without any thought of the table manners her mother had painstakingly drilled into her a long time ago.

"What exactly are you going to build?" Mari asked, breaking their comfortable silence.

Kalindi wiped her mouth, guarded. "An atmospheric water generator."

Mari's eyes widened. "That sounds... complicated. And you need all these supplies for it?" She had looked at the list Kalindi had written out while they waited for their food.

Kalindi bristled. "It's more complicated than it sounds. I still need to survey Greenhaven to see if it'll work. No promises."

Mari did her best to withhold an eye roll. *Guard's back up again. Great.*

There was an edge to Kalindi's voice that hinted at something... self-doubt, perhaps, but she didn't press. "Fair enough."

Wanting an early night, they agreed to split up and work their way through opposite ends of the market to locate the required items as swiftly as possible. The faster they got to bed, the more sleep they would bank before rising early to continue the long journey to Greenhaven.

As she wandered the market stalls looking for quartz rods, Mari's attention was caught by a small silver ring displayed on a cloth-lined table. The band featured an intricately etched lion, his mane transitioning seamlessly into a bold flame. She thought of Lyra instantly—the ring would be the perfect gift to remind her of her strength. She shook her head. *You are not going to buy a ring for a woman you kissed briefly,* she thought, admonishing her ridiculous notion.

"Kissed twice, briefly," she clarified under her breath, her cheeks heating.

"What's that, dear?" asked the shopkeeper.

Mari held up the ring. "How much is this?"

BACK AT THE INN, a commotion in the connected tavern drew their attention. A woman, her face tired and worried, was pleading with the barkeep. "Please, just a bowl of broth," she begged, her voice trembling. "She hasn't eaten in days. She's so weak."

The barkeep looked uncomfortable. "I'm sorry, Gura. The boss made it pretty clear; I can't just give away food or I'll lose my job."

"Not even the scraps? Jai, please! She's going to die!" Gura's already desperate voice got louder, and her face twisted into a panic.

Mari stepped forward. "What's going on?"

Gura turned, her eyes raw. "My daughter... She's sick. She won't keep anything down, and I don't have the supplies or money to make her a broth. She's all I have," she said, her voice breaking. "I just need a little. Something. Anything."

Kalindi placed a steady hand on Mari's shoulder. "Let's see the child."

Gura led them across a simple rope bridge suspended over the river to a small, rundown home in a much less attractive part of town known as Myramin's Shambles. The dilapidated houses in the area, which Mari would better describe as shacks, reeked of a darker side to Myramin's Bend. Clearly, not all the villagers benefited from the town's prosperous trade route.

Rih circled high above. Mari whistled once, loud and clear, calling her down. She landed on the crooked windowsill and looked to Mari for instruction.

Mari nodded in the direction of the street. "Keep watch," she instructed.

Rih let out a soft click in acknowledgment and fixed her gaze on the lane ahead.

They squeezed through the entryway, ducking to avoid the top of the door frame, which was hanging on by one, struggling nail. Inside, a young girl lay on a thin cot, her face pale and her breathing shallow. A threadbare blanket was pulled tightly around her frail body, and what looked like puddles of vomit pooled on the floor beside the cot.

Gura looked ashamed and dropped a nearby pillow over the mess, covering it as best she could. "This is my Jannah," she said quietly, brushing a trembling hand over her daughter's damp forehead. "She's been like this for days. I don't know what else to do."

Kalindi knelt beside the cot, her face clouded with concern. She reached out to check Jannah's pulse and pressed a hand lightly against her cheek. She turned to Mari. "This isn't just hunger. She needs mooncap."

Mari's suspicion flared again. "How do you know that?"

Kalindi shrugged. "I know the area. I've dealt with this before. Trust me."

Mari frowned but said nothing, respecting that, at the very least, Kalindi seemed confident in her diagnosis, which was more than she was able to come up with.

Kalindi turned to Gura. "Mooncap is the only thing that'll help her."

Gura's face crumpled as she sank into a chair. "We can't get that here."

"That's okay," Mari said, standing. "We'll go get some."

"It's not that simple," Kalindi replied sheepishly.

Mari crossed her arms. "What now?"

"Mooncap is rare," Kalindi explained. "It only grows in the Glowing Gardens, and..." she trailed off.

"What?" asked Mari, her frustration growing by the instant. *When is this girl going to lead with all the information up front?* she thought. "So, do we need permission to access the gardens or what? What's the problem?"

Kalindi sighed heavily. "The gardens line the edge of a cliff."

Mari blinked. "A cliff?!"

"In Elyria's Edge," Kalindi said, her voice barely above a whisper, her gaze dropping to the floor.

Mari threw up her hands. "Of course. Why not? Anything else? Is it guarded by wolves? A raging river? Surrounded by fire? What?"

"That's it," Kalindi said with an apologetic half-smile. "Just the cliff."

Mari wanted to scream. Elyria's Edge was far. She looked at the little girl, lying limply in her cot. She took a deep, steadying breath and nodded. "Fine. We'll go first thing in the morning."

Gura clutched Mari's arm. "You'd do this? For us? I can't offer much, but I have a locket—" She reached inside her loose blouse and fished for the chain hidden beneath it.

"Keep it," Mari said firmly, resting her hand on the distraught mother's arm. "You don't owe us anything. Just take care of Jannah."

Kalindi looked surprised by her quick agreement. "Are you sure? It's dangerous."

Mari's expression hardened. "We need to get back to

Greenhaven, but this family needs our help. My entire journey has been about helping our community, and we're all Patovian. We're going."

Kalindi stood, brushing off her knees. "We'll leave at first light," she said. "The journey's not easy. We'll need rest."

Mari nodded, shooting Gura a reassuring look. "We'll get the mooncap. She's going to be fine."

Gura's eyes filled with tears. "Thank you. Thank you so much."

CHAPTER THIRTEEN

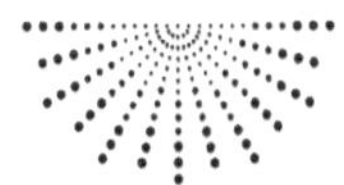

On their way back to the inn, Mari fought against the rising tide of overwhelm. Their journey was growing more complicated with each passing candlemark while Greenhaven remained at the mercy of the drought.

She thought of the ring at the market, wishing she'd purchased it—not for Lyra, but as a token of strength for herself.

Rih glided soundlessly above, a shadow against the night sky. Mari lifted her gaze, watching her for a moment before letting it drift to the stars beyond. A pang of longing tightened in her chest. It had been days since she had peered through her telescope, and her spirit ached for the comfort of the stars.

By the time they reached their room, exhaustion had settled deep, pressing down like a cartful of lemon dates. Rih fluttered in after them, landing lightly on the foot of Mari's bed and tucking her head under one wing.

Mari sighed, sinking into the mattress as sleep pulled at her from every direction. "Jannah is my mother's name," she whispered, breaking the silence.

"Oh," Kalindi murmured. "That explains your swift agreement."

The faint sounds of the Myramin River drifted through the open window, mingling with the gentle rustle of leaves. Sleep claimed Mari quickly, shielding her from the muffled stirrings of Kalindi's restless dreams.

IT TOOK two and a half days of travel to get to Elyria's Edge, one "tiny" detail Kalindi had failed to mention, and by the time they arrived, Mari had more or less resigned herself to the detour. Kalindi's answers about the device she planned to build in Greenhaven remained vague, and the lack of clarity frustrated Mari. Perhaps Kalindi didn't want to promise too much or risk raising false hope, but Mari felt dismissed, and it bothered her to know their trust was yet again at a standstill.

Elyria's Edge itself was incredible. The remote town was nestled in a lush valley of towering green hills that took Mari's breath away the moment she saw it. The famed Elyrian Falls cascaded over the sheer limestone cliffs into the Patovian Sea below, creating a mist that drifted back to the town and left a permanent dew throughout. Even in the warmer months, the falls were a magnet for travelers from across the region. Mari had dreamed half her life of visiting Elyria's Edge, but she had never imagined she'd be planning to scale them.

The town's beauty wasn't its only draw. Nearby, the Nesby Caves boasted staggering formations that seemed to hang suspended from their ceilings, a labyrinth of glistening rock that lured explorers and artists alike. During the darkest months, the valley transformed into a snow-blanketed wonder, and the Festival of Still Waters drew crowds to watch the once-rare auroras dance across the frozen falls and rivers, a spiritual and breathtaking spectacle.

This wasn't festival season, though. Elyria's Edge was quiet and unhurried, the perfect pace to match the off-season lull. As Mari and Kalindi strolled through the breezy streets, the town's beauty was on full display. Colorful umbrella awnings fluttered in the wind, paved limestone paths wound gracefully through carefully cultivated greenery, and the ever-present sound of the falls could be heard in the distance. It didn't take long to find a place to rest. A tall, rectangular inn stood on the corner of one of the main streets, its open design inviting the drifting breeze in, giving motion to the flowering vines that draped from the cheerful, bold red sign. The corrugated iron roof wrapped around the midsection of the two-story building like a skirt. The quieter season worked in their favor; the innkeeper offered them their pick of rooms.

Mari sat on the end of her bed with her foot tucked under her knee, grateful that the establishment only offered one bed per room, and even more grateful for a night's sleep that didn't involve panicked cries and accidental face-punches (Kalindi had been mortified when Mari told her the next morning). She did her best not to look directly at the metal roof below her window, which jutted out, reflecting the blinding afternoon sun.

The inn they'd chosen wouldn't allow Rih to stay in the room, and the feisty skyweaver was not handling it well. Banished to the rafters of the nearby stables, she had made her displeasure known before finally taking off to hunt, vanishing into the rolling hills on the horizon.

Mari had seized the opportunity to get some work done—undisturbed, for once.

Her eyes darted back and forth between the two maps

spread across her bed in front of her. She hadn't charted the skies this far north before, and she was itching to reach for her telescope as soon as night fell. Her stomach growled, breaking her concentration. With a sigh, she rolled up the charts and tucked them carefully into her bag. Her load was becoming cumbersome, but she didn't dare risk sending anything back to Greenhaven—not when the innkeeper confirmed they were having issues with some skyweavers that were sent to certain destinations.

Mari found Kalindi sitting on the floor, tinkering with a copper coil. "Hungry?" she asked.

"Famished!" Kalindi dropped the coil and scrambled to her feet, following Mari downstairs.

The inn's tavern was rather dark, with bulky curtains pulled tight over its small windows. A squat red candle adorned each table, the flames coming close to extinguishing every time the draft that seeped through the cracks blew through. The only other patron, a cloaked figure seated in the farthest corner, barely stirred.

They chose two stools at the bar, opting for the barkeep's recommendation: sea crabs tossed in a thin pasta with lemon butter sauce and Elyrian capers. It was a dish unlike anything Mari had ever tried before, and she could barely sit still as she waited impatiently for the kitchen to deliver it.

Mari drained her glass of water almost immediately. "Why is this water so good?" she asked, glancing at the barkeep.

"It's from the gardens, not the wells," he replied with a wink. "Tastes different, doesn't it?"

Kalindi nodded enthusiastically. "I could drink a whole jug of it. I've never tasted water like this."

The barkeep chuckled. "Sounds about right. Most folks can't get enough once they've had a taste."

Before their meals arrived, Kalindi excused herself, shifting restlessly in her seat. "Nature calls."

Mari stretched back to study the carvings along the tavern's blackwood beams above her. The designs captured the swirls and curves of the Elyrian Falls, each detail so lifelike that the water almost seemed to move and flow. She was so engrossed she didn't notice the cloaked figure approach her until they spoke.

"Looks like it will be a beautiful night to stargaze," the voice whispered softly.

Mari jumped. She turned to see the figure, their hood still pulled low.

"Sorry?" Mari asked.

The figure tilted their head, revealing electric blue eyes, cut with the familiar green Mari had seen emblazoned in her dreams for days.

"Lyra?!" Mari gasped, having the sense to keep her voice a hushed whisper. "What in all of Patovia are you doing here?"

"Tonight," Lyra said, glancing toward the door. "Meet me at the top of the smallest hill on this side of the gorge."

Before Mari could respond, Lyra turned and left, disappearing as suddenly as she had appeared.

When Kalindi returned, the food was already waiting. "Why didn't you start without me?" she asked, cracking her knuckles.

Mari forced a smile, suddenly not at all hungry, twirling the pasta on her fork, but never picking it up. "What? Oh, just...," she mumbled, trailing off mid-sentence.

～

MARI PACKED HER TELESCOPE QUICKLY, her movements hurried and her mouth dry. She paused just long enough to stick her head through Kalindi's door on her way down the stairs.

"I'm going to do some charting," she said briskly, surreptitiously shuffling down the hall as fast she could, hoping to the gods that Kalindi wouldn't suddenly be interested in joining her.

"Hey—Mari, wait!" Kalindi's voice trailed after her, and Mari heard her jump up and follow her in a rush. By the time Kalindi made it to the top of the stairs, Mari was already halfway down.

"Everything okay?" Kalindi called.

Mari nodded without looking back. "Fine."

"You sure?" Kalindi pressed, descending a few steps to follow her. "You seemed... off at dinner."

Mari gripped the railing. "I'm just tired," she lied, not turning around.

"Right. You're tired, so naturally you're off to stargaze all night. Makes perfect sense."

Caught, Mari's cheeks flushed. She glanced over her shoulder. "I won't be late," she promised.

Kalindi raised an eyebrow. "I've made some sketches of what the mooncap looks like, so you know what we're looking for. I was hoping we could be off at first light. You know, to get this over with."

Mari shifted her weight impatiently and let her head drop backward with a silent protest. *Now she wants to hash out every detail of her plan?*

"First light. Got it." Mari turned and hurried down the stairs before Kalindi could question her further, leaving the engineer frowning in her wake.

~

THE NIGHT WAS UNUSUALLY QUIET, save for the distant roar of the fall. Mari slipped on the damp, grassy slope as she ascended the hill Lyra had described, fighting the winds that coursed through the gorge and blew her hair into her face. At the top, the gusts settled down as the land leveled out, offering an unbroken view of the stars above.

The vast sky unfurled above her, a tapestry of blues and blacks that seemed to stretch on forever, dotted with infinite stars, their light twinkling like bright, scattered diamonds. Each constellation stood out sharply, and tiny galaxies swirled faintly behind them. In the far distance, the moonlight spilled across the surface of the sea that shone like a liquid mirror, creating a silver path that seemed to stretch endlessly toward the horizon, as though leading to the very edge of the world.

Mari took it all in, her breath catching at the sheer, unbridled beauty above her. She felt a sense of unease when she realized that here, in the most secluded area of Patovia where she would not be surprised to see auroras, there were none.

She kneeled and ripped a handful of grass out from the ground. Digging through her satchel, she produced an empty pouch, using her fingers to scoop dirt from the hole she had made and filling the pouch with a new sample. She tried to remember how many knots the cord needed... Was she up to seven or eight? Rather than guess, she tucked the pouch away, opting not to tie any knots at all.

She scanned the area, her heart sinking when there was no sign of Lyra. The queen's tense demeanor at the tavern had been hard to ignore. As she looked down at Elyria's Edge from above, she felt sick. She was certain there was absolutely no way the queen would be there unless something catastrophic had happened.

She pulled out her telescope, aiming it upward and doing her best not to catastrophize. Her mind refused to comply. Where was Lyra? Why wasn't she here yet? Was it foolish to have trusted the queen's instructions? A sudden movement caught her eye, and she turned around.

Lyra emerged from the nearby tree line, her face pale and her eyes wide with fear. "Mari," she said, her voice trembling.

Mari stood immediately, rushing toward her. "Lyra, what happened? What's wrong?"

Lyra hesitated, as if struggling to form the words. "Searsan is dead," she said finally.

The words hit Mari like a punch to the chest. "What? How? What happened?"

Lyra took a shaky breath, her cold hands trembling as she clutched Mari's. "It happened not long after you left. Poison, they think, although no one will say for sure."

Mari's mind raced. Poison? Who would do this? And why? She fought the urge to vomit as she gathered her thoughts. "Lyra... whoever killed the king—"

"No," Lyra interrupted, desperation tinging her voice. "It's not the same. It can't be."

Mari frowned. "Why not? It makes sense."

Lyra's grip tightened, her voice dropping to a whisper. "Because... I killed the king."

A deadly silence followed.

"Wh...what?" Mari's heart thundered in her chest. "You?"

Lyra's eyes filled with tears as she continued her confession. "I was... convinced. By Bomi."

"Manipulated," Mari corrected her.

Lyra's face crumpled with discomfort. "He told me it was

the only way to save Patovia. That the King was driving us to ruin, and if I didn't act... the kingdom would fall apart."

Mari stared at her. "He used you."

Lyra nodded in agreement. "And now he's using that to control me."

Mari's mind raced, piecing together the implications. "And now Searsan..."

"He was the only one who could see through them. I think they killed him to isolate me," Lyra said, her shoulders shuddering as she fought to keep her sobs silent.

Mari felt a surge of anger. "Lyra... you have to fight this. Find a way to get out of his clutches."

"I am," Lyra said, her voice breaking. She took a moment to regain her composure and cleared her throat. "That's why I'm here. I think I heard something useful. I couldn't send a messenger—it's too dangerous. I had to come myself."

"What did you hear?"

Lyra pulled a small piece of parchment from her cloak. She was shaking, and Mari wanted nothing more than to wrap her up in her arms, press a kiss to the corners of her eyes, and promise her that everything would be alright. But the truth was she had no idea what she had stumbled into, and no right to offer reassurance when she wasn't sure there was any to give.

"After we discovered Searsan was..." she trailed off and her eyes found Mari's, a look of compassion in them. "After I heard about Searsan... Bomi told me he was going to handle the arrangements. He left me alone. I haven't been alone outside of my bedchambers for forever... I knew this was my one chance. I sent Elisa's brother, Eldane, to follow your trail immediately. To keep eyes on you. Then, I broke into Bomi's chambers and I looked for anything I could hold over him. It took all of about three seconds before I found this book... a ledger of sorts; I'm not sure what it was, but it was filled with names, maps, sketches... I couldn't copy all of it, and I definitely couldn't take the book, so I just copied this." She handed the parchment to Mari.

The hastily sketched lines looked familiar to Mari. She recognized the patterns from the cave she had passed through on her way to Adavale. Her thoughts raced. "This... this might be important. Thank you."

Lyra nodded, her eyes darting nervously toward the horizon. "There's more. I heard him coming back before I could get out, so I climbed out the window and hid on the ledge."

"You what?!" Mari couldn't help but gasp a laugh at the thought of Queen Lyra standing on the stone ledge of the window, floors above the ground, spying on Bomi.

"I don't know who he was talking to, but I overheard him say, 'The echoes are expanding; the Stewards will follow.' I don't know what it means, but it felt... significant."

Mari felt her blood run cold. "The Stewards."

"Does that make any sense to you?"

Mari swallowed, nodding. "But the echoes..." she murmured, her mind racing.

"Mari, be careful with Kalindi. I did some digging to try and find out more about her... anything about her. I had to know you were safe." A gust of wind whipped across the hilltop, and Lyra pulled her cloak tighter. "I couldn't learn much at all, except that she hasn't lived in Joycita for long... Something about her isn't sitting right with me. What if she's a plant?"

Mari recalled Kalindi's evasive answers and the unsettling feeling that she definitely knew more than she was letting on. "I've noticed something off about her too. It's been hard to find a genuine connection. It's possible she could be working with Bomi..."

"I instructed Eldane to inform me immediately if your journey veered off in any direction other than to Greenhaven. When you headed north, he sent word and I set out to beat you here. I watched you come in so I knew where you were staying... I wasn't sure I would make it in time." Lyra paused to take a breath, her hand on her chest. "What are you doing here?"

"We're helping a woman," was all Mari could think to say. Her mind was still processing Searsan.

Lyra smiled. "Of course you are." She reached into a small, purple satin pouch that hung from a bronze cord over her shoulder. "I told the council I was visiting my mother," she said. "They'll send someone to check my story, so I have to go." She pressed a bulging pouch of coins into Mari's hands. "Take this. You'll need it."

Mari accepted the pouch. "Be safe." Her voice caught in her throat.

The queen turned to leave but paused and turned back to Mari, her eyes catching both the moonlight and Mari's breath. She reached out and took Mari's hands in hers. "Mari, before we part ways tonight, I need to say something."

Mari swallowed against the tight knot of anxiety that lodged itself in her throat at the unease in Lyra's eyes, which conveyed a level of vulnerability Mari hadn't yet seen. "What is it?"

"I owe you an apology."

Mari blinked, surprised. "For what?"

Lyra's mouth fell into a disappointed smile. "For... for being so forward when we met. For kissing you."

Mari wanted to respond, but Lyra held up a hand, shaking her head. "Let me finish."

Mari nodded, her heart pounding in her chest.

"The truth is, I've been... overwhelmed. By you," Lyra admitted. "When I look at you, I see a strength I've long since forgotten in myself. Your conviction, your courage—it's like a fire, and I couldn't help but be drawn to it. You reminded me of what I used to be, before the Crown, before the council and the endless compromises."

She broke eye contact and looked up to the stars above them. "I let those feelings take hold of me, and I got carried away. Not because they weren't real," she added quickly, looking back at Mari with an intensity that stole her breath. "But because I shouldn't have acted on them. You came to me for help, Mari. For your people, your home. And I... I shouldn't have let my emotions complicate things. You deserve better than that."

Mari swallowed again, hard, unsure how to respond now that she suddenly had the chance. "Lyra, I—"

The queen's hands tightened around hers, her eyes brimming with regret. "I don't regret the feelings," she confessed. "But I do regret the timing. I can't let myself get in the way of what you're trying to do, what you're trying to save. And I certainly can't let myself take advantage of you."

"Take advantage?" Mari echoed, her voice almost a whisper. "That's not how it felt."

Lyra looked at her sympathetically. "You're kind to say that, but I've lived long enough to know how power can blur lines, how it can create dynamics that... shouldn't exist. I don't want to be that person. Not with you."

Mari's chest ached at the raw honesty in Lyra's words. She wanted to argue, to tell her she wasn't that kind of queen, that whatever was between them felt too real to be just a mistake, but the words caught in her throat, tangled with the complications of everything else that was piling up on her plate—the drought, the stars, the growing unease that shadowed their every step.

"I understand," she said finally, her spirit utterly crushed.

Lyra's lips pressed into a bittersweet smile. "I hope you do. Because whatever happens, I need you to know that I believe in you, Mari. I trust you. More than I've trusted anyone in a very long time."

Lyra squeezed her hands one last time before letting them go. For a moment, the queen looked as though she might say more, but she only turned toward the hill's edge, her silhouette framed by the endless sky.

"Take care of yourself," Lyra said, her voice carrying a hint of a plea. "After Searsan... just be vigilant. Okay? And if you ever need me... you know how to find me."

Then, Lyra mounted her horse, kicked it into a quiet canter, and rode down the hillside, her cape billowing behind her.

CHAPTER FOURTEEN

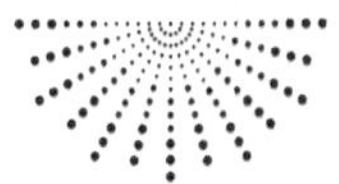

KALINDI WAS WAITING FOR MARI IN THE DOORWAY of her room, arms crossed and eyes intense. "Where have you been?"

Mari forced a casual shrug, even as her heart raced. "Just needed some air."

Kalindi's eyes narrowed and Mari knew she didn't believe a word she said, so she was relieved when she didn't push further. Instead, she pulled a folded sketch from her pocket and handed it to Mari. "This is what we're looking for—mooncap."

Mari examined the detailed drawing. It looked like a mushroom, but Kalindi had drawn thin vein-like lines along the top of it.

"It grows anywhere in the gardens, but it's rare. We'll have to keep a sharp eye tomorrow. Hopefully, we won't need to venture too far in. Or too far down," Kalindi continued, her tone clipped.

"Got it," Mari said quietly, studying Kalindi's face more than the drawing. *What are you hiding? What's your endgame?*

Kalindi didn't seem to notice Mari's scrutiny. "Get some

rest," she said, her stern voice relenting just enough for Mari to feel like she might be off the hook. "It'll be a long day tomorrow." She was already turning away.

MARI CLIMBED INTO BED, but sleep refused to come. Her mind churned with everything Lyra had told her: the echoes, the Stewards, Kalindi's possible role in it all, and the queen's regretful confessions. And Searsan.

Searsan.

The ache in her chest deepened as the realization that she had lost her mentor settled heavy in her heart with tiny, painful stabs. She felt the tears well in her eyes, and she readied herself to let the floodgates open.

She turned toward the window, hoping the stars would offer some semblance of comfort, but they were wrong, and it just made her angry. A movement from across the street below caught her eye. She stiffened.

A dark figure crept toward the inn, moonlight flashing across his face as he darted from one shadow to the next, revealing a bushy beard and cold, dark eyes. He slipped between the buildings and paused at the foot of a nearby tree to pull his hood up so that it obscured his face. Mari's blood ran cold as she watched him deftly scale the tree and then leap across to the stables that were attached to the inn. He wobbled briefly as he made his way along the iron rooftop, pausing to catch his balance, his steps silent.

As the figure came closer, Mari was doused with dread as she realized that she and Kalindi were the only two guests staying at the inn. This man was coming for her.

Mari jumped to her feet and frantically collected her

belongings, which were piled together where she had dropped them upon arrival. She threw her satchel over her head in one swift motion, pushing it down around her hips tightly, and quickly clipped the leather strap around her thigh. She raced across the room and pressed herself flat against the wall beside the window, holding her breath. The curtains fluttered in the breeze as the intruder silently crept into her room. He moved with slow, controlled steps across the old floorboards, each one a gamble, trusting that none would betray him with a creak that would shatter the silence and give him away.

Mari could see his outline now, a shadow among the shadows. He crept toward her bed, the knife he held glinting faintly in the moonlight. She had moments to decide what to do.

Moving as silently as he had, she went through the open window and onto the roof, almost slipping on the slick iron. She edged toward the neighboring window, determined not to panic but desperate for an escape. She paused and glanced back. The man, quiet as a phantom, was closing in on her empty bed.

She climbed into the next window, landing softly in Kalindi's room. "Kalindi," she hissed, shaking her awake.

Kalindi bolted upright, a bundle of confusion. "What—?"

Mari clamped a hand over her mouth. "Shh," she whispered. "We need to move. Now."

Kalindi had barely grabbed her boots and bag before Mari dragged her toward the door. The sound of a creaking floorboard in the next room spurred them forward. They ran down the stairs, heading straight for the stables.

"What's going on?" Kalindi asked, but she didn't stop or slow even the slightest.

"We need to get Rih, and we need to run!" Mari replied.

The assassin was on them before they reached the stables. He moved with terrifying speed, his knife flashing as he threw it at Mari. She ducked, and the blade embedded itself in the wooden beam that framed the stables behind her.

Kalindi stalled for a moment, as if she were processing everything that was happening in front of her. Her eyes darted back and forth between Mari and the assassin, who was now moving toward Mari, his hands rigid and outstretched. Kalindi launched herself at the man, locking an arm around his neck and pulling him back. He staggered but managed to throw her over his shoulder with brutal force. She hit the ground with a grunt, scrambling to her feet as Mari snatched the knife from the beam.

"Who sent you?" Mari demanded, holding the blade to the man's throat.

He sneered at her, and with a sudden twist, he wrenched the knife from her grasp and slashed at her. Mari jumped back, narrowly avoiding the blade. The assassin advanced forward as Mari backtracked, hitting a wall behind her. To her left, a horse blocked her path, and the assassin's heaving figure took up the only opening available for her escape. She was trapped.

A shriek split the air as Rih dove from her perch on the rafter above, her beak driving into the back of the assassin's neck. He screamed, thrashing as blood spurted from the wound. Rih tore into him, severing the connection between his head and body. His screams faded into gurgles before he collapsed, lifeless.

Kalindi, her face pale, shoved a handful of straw into the man's mouth to muffle the dying sounds. Blood splattered the horses, the walls, and their clothing. Rih's crisp white breast was streaked with red. Mari stared at the scene, her chest heaving.

"We need to get out of here," Kalindi urged. "This doesn't look good."

Mari nodded, forcing her legs to move. They grabbed water from the trough behind them, washing their hands and faces as best they could. Kalindi snatched the man's bag before they sprinted across the street, leaving the bloodied stables behind.

They raced to put distance between themselves and the stables, their breaths visible in the chilly night air, their bodies numb with shock.

With Rih soaring above them, they crossed a long, weathered rock formation worn into the perfect shape of a bridge that spanned the steep gorge below. The Myramin River roared beneath them, but Mari barely blinked as she crossed it without a second thought—a feat she wouldn't ordinarily be able to manage under any other circumstances. Adrenaline and fear will do incredible things to one's determination. When they finally stopped running, she staggered against a tree, clutching her side.

Kalindi dropped to her knees, hands braced against the ground. Their ragged breathing was the only sound that bounced off the short, bushy trees until Mari's stomach eventually gave in to the situation, twisting violently as she doubled over and emptied its contents all over the forest floor.

Kalindi cast Mari a look of sympathy, although she couldn't entirely hide her disgust when the remnants of Mari's ill-fated sea crab made a sour return, the lemon-acid stench crawling up her nostrils. She pulled a waterskin from her pack and handed it to Mari.

"Here. Take some long, slow breaths. You'll slow your heart faster that way."

Mari took the waterskin gratefully and took little sips of the water slowly, trying to process everything.

Rih landed heavily on Mari's shoulder and nudged her cheek with her beak—once, twice—before letting out an impatient chirp.

Mari blinked. "I'm okay," she managed, shaking as she reached up to stroke Rih's feathers.

Rih didn't budge. Instead, she pressed closer, another quick nudge against Mari's temple, and a slightly louder, more insistent chirp.

Mari let out a breathy laugh, scratching her fingernails gently against Rih's wing. "Really. I'm fine. Just needed a second." She pulled back just enough to glance at Rih's bloodstained breast, her brows furrowing. "Are you?"

Rih clicked softly, readjusting her weight, but she stayed firmly perched, unwilling to leave just yet. Mari leaned her head into Rih and nuzzled her softly, grateful for the moment. She let the quiet between them settle, her breathing slowing, her pounding heart finding a more regular rhythm.

She finally lifted her head and surveyed the immediate area. The trees were too dense for her to see the sky, leaving her unsure of how far they had traveled, but she was fairly certain they had put quite a distance between them and Elyria's Edge.

"So..." Mari started, not really sure what she was going to say. What in the old Gods were they to do now?

Kalindi rubbed her face, a look of terror suddenly spreading across it as she started to frantically pat her wrists. "No. No, no, no!" Her voice cracked, and her face drained of color.

Mari sat up, alarmed by the sheer panic in Kalindi's voice. "What's wrong?"

Kalindi's fingers clawed at her wrist, her eyes wide with disbelief. "It's gone. My wristband—it's gone!"

Mari frowned. "The one with the stone? Are you sure?"

Kalindi nodded furiously, appearing to be teetering on the edge of devastation. "It was my mother's... It's all I have left of her." She stared at her empty wrist as if willing the band to reappear.

Mari crouched down beside her, placing a hand on her shoulder. "I'm sorry," she said. "Do you want to backtrack a little, see if we can find it?" She hoped Kalindi would decline. There was no way she wanted to go anywhere near that scene again. She shuddered as the memory re-ran in her mind.

"No," Kalindi said. "I didn't drop it. Someone must have taken it."

"From your wrist?" Mari asked, confused.

"When you were gone, I went down to the baths and washed up a little. I always take it off when I bathe since the leather gets weak when it gets wet, you know? I... I left it with my clothes... someone must have taken it. I remember rushing to get dressed. I thought you would be back sooner than you were." She paused to give Mari a glare. "I didn't want you to wonder where I was... I must not have realized it was missing."

Mari measured her reaction curiously. She seemed to be panicking about more than a lost heirloom.

"Kalindi..." Mari watched as Kalindi's fidgeting hands ran through her hair and she buried her face in her hands. "Is there... more to that stone than you're telling me?"

Kalindi looked away before she answered. "It was my mother's," she repeated, but the edge in her voice gave her away.

Mari studied her for a moment longer, suspicion growing. She absolutely did not believe her, but without outright saying that, there wasn't really much more she could add in the moment.

"Come on," Mari said, standing and offering a hand to help Kalindi up. "We need to keep moving."

Kalindi took Mari's hand. She looked beyond terrified, and it gave Mari's stomach another churning rumble. If that stone was more than she was letting on—and at this point Mari was convinced that was the case... Who had taken it? And were they in more trouble now than before?

The pair pushed on through the wet forest and came to a clearing that allowed Mari to chart their location. Kalindi busied herself by digging through the assassin's bag. She pulled out various bits and pieces, but Mari couldn't really tell what she was looking at through the subdued light. She stopped at a particular item that she appeared to be examining intently.

"Let's go this way." Mari dropped her astrolabe down and pointed in the direction of a slight hillslope covered in trees. "I think staying off any roads is the best idea for right now."

Kalindi nodded in agreement and threw everything back in the assassin's bag. Mari took the lead, keeping a brisk pace, with Rih still on her shoulder—uncharacteristically silent and still.

EVENTUALLY, they had to stop. Exhausted, they looked for a secluded shelter. They were far from Elyrian's Edge at this point, but once you witness a man have his spinal cord severed and drown in his own blood, the edginess tends to stick around. A tiny trickle of water ran past a small cave opening, and they took the opportunity to drop their gear and rest for a few candlemarks. Neither moved for a long time.

Kalindi was the one to break the stillness as she started to dig through the assassin's bag. She pulled out a crumpled parchment and began to examine it.

"What is it?" Mari asked, still on edge.

Kalindi looked unsure. "Just a map," she said, folding the parchment and putting it into her bag.

Mari wasn't sure if she should believe her. "A map of what?"

"Patovia," Kalindi said too quickly, flashing the parchment at Mari long enough for Mari to recognize the region but too fast for her to see any specific details.

Mari didn't press, but Kalindi's evasiveness was impossible to ignore, and Lyra's warning echoed in her mind: *Be careful with Kalindi. She could be a plant.*

Kalindi glanced over her shoulder. "If we're staying off the roads, why don't we just go around Lake Nesby and get to Greenhaven from the North? We could cut through the mountains easily enough at this time of year, go through the salt pools, and be back half a week sooner."

"No," Mari said firmly, stopping in her tracks. "We promised to get the mooncap. I'm not leaving without it."

Kalindi sighed, her frustration evident. "Mari, we need to go. The longer we stay, the more danger we're in."

Mari put her hands on her hips to prove to Kalindi that she wouldn't be deterred. "Then you can leave, but I'm going to keep my promise."

Kalindi stared at her for a long moment, then huffed. "Fine. But let's not rest any longer. If we go now, we can be back in Myramin's Bend by the end of tomorrow."

They left the cave and made a hard right, heading straight for the cliffsides where the Glowing Gardens lay.

CHAPTER FIFTEEN

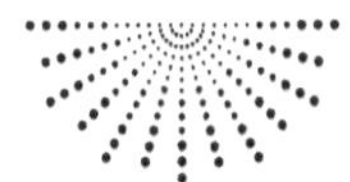

THE SIGN AT THE ENTRANCE TO THE GLOWING
Gardens was weathered but legible, etched into smooth stone
with ornate carvings that mimicked the twisting vines around
it. A smattering of soft moss framed the edges, its faint
luminescence casting a gentle glow that gave the sign an
ethereal aura. In an elegant, flowing script, the inscription read:

"The Glowing Gardens: Protected Natural Wonder of
Patovia. Removal of any Natural Elements is Strictly
Prohibited. Penalties Enforced by the Elyrian Natural Wonders
Council."

Mari let out a low whistle, and ran her hand across the
engraved words. "This is more of a warning than a welcome."
She grimaced.

"With beauty like this, they have to be protective. It's one
of the last places untouched by greed," said Kalindi.

Mari hesitated. "Should we—?"

"It's one cutting," Kalindi said firmly, tugging Mari past the
threshold and into the Glowing Gardens. "It's not like we're

harvesting the whole species. Trust me, the balance here can handle it."

The two ventured into the gardens, their steps slow as they took in the living expanse that unfolded before them. The "gardens" were anything but cultivated—they were a wild masterpiece. Towering bioluminescent trees glowed faintly in hues of turquoise and lime, their leaves twinkling like distant stars. Flowers below shone bright with pinks, yellows, and blues. Ferns taller than Mari brushed their shoulders, the curling purples and deep reds swaying above their heads, and the air around them seemed to vibrate with an energy unlike anything Mari had ever felt before. Tiny warm lights danced in front of them, blinking in and out of sight, adding to the surreal beauty that surrounded them.

"This place is... alive," Mari murmured, tilting her head back and spinning slowly to take in the glowing expanse.

Kalindi crouched beside a cluster of plants, her face full of intense wonder. "It's thriving. Most of these plants only exist here, and even the ones that grow elsewhere are... diminished by comparison. It's all connected—light, motion, energy—perfect harmony."

The air shimmered faintly in front of them, illuminating their path ahead.

"Look at the fireflies!" Mari exclaimed in awe over the tiny, glimmering insects.

"Those aren't fireflies," Kalindi corrected. "They're pappus spores."

Mari watched as hundreds of the spores flustered past them, a faint, high-pitched tone accompanying their flight.

Kalindi stood still, her arms outstretched and her palms upturned, as if she was breathing in the moment, taking in everything around her with her soul just as much as her senses.

When she spoke, her voice wobbled with overpowering emotion. "I always thought the Glowing Gardens were named for the way the auroras reflected off them, or maybe the moon... I never imagined they would actually glow by themselves."

Kalindi was beaming. Her smile was about as genuine as Mari had ever seen, her eyes wide and bright as she reached her open hand out and carefully captured a glowing spore that spun lazily across the pathway in front of them.

"Incredible," she said as the spore dimmed when it touched her skin. "Most of the plants here are lit from within. It's like their biology produces certain light waves, but these... they're porous, and the air flows through them, generating friction with the electric energy that vibrates from its core." She twirled the spore between her thumb and forefinger, and it glowed momentarily. "Incredible," she said again, breathlessly.

Kalindi released the spore, and it spun to the ground in a glow of golden-pink effortlessness. Kalindi wiped a tear from her eye.

"You're glowing too, Kalindi," Mari said, smiling.

Kalindi caressed a low-hanging branch of a brilliant coral and purple fern, its enchanting light glowing brighter with her touch. "A clumping tengar," she whispered. Mari watched her, struck by Kalindi's reverence. "For an engineer, you sure know a lot about plants."

Kalindi smiled. "It's all the same thing, really—life, machines, ecosystems. We're all just moving parts in a greater design."

~

TIME TICKED on as they combed through the gardens. Every now and then, they would stop to inspect a plant that seemed promising, only to find it was something else entirely. At one point, Kalindi crouched by a concentrated patch of fungi with silvery caps that seemed to glimmer under the light. "This might be it," she said cautiously. "Hand me my book?"

Mari knelt beside her and pulled out the book from Kalindi's bag. Underneath the book, the assassin's map unfolded slightly, and Mari's eye was drawn to markings on the edges that looked similar to the sketches Lyra had shown her back in Elyria's Edge. She scanned he rest of the map, picking up on some notations over areas just outside of the Isa Glades and Adavale. Her curiosity had to be ignored for now, and she cinched the bag closed and handed the book to Kalindi, who hadn't noticed Mari looking since she was far too engrossed in the plant she was examining.

Kalindi's face fell as she compared the plant to the book. "No, look here." She ran her finger along the top of the cap and turned her hand up—a silver dust residue painted her fingers. "These are widow's caps. Poisonous." She stood, wiping her fingers against her pants, leaving silver streaks. "We're wasting time."

They pushed further into the gardens, the terrain growing more rugged until the bioluminescent glow gradually dimmed behind them, swallowed by the encroaching darkness. Ahead, the silver streak of moonlight danced across the Patovian Sea far below, its vastness stretching beyond the cliffs into what seemed like eternity.

As they neared the edge, the eerie, high-pitched ringing that had echoed through the gardens began to quiet, overtaken by the distant roar of waterfalls. The ground beneath their feet shifted from damp earth to coarse sand before vanishing entirely into a sheer drop of limestone.

"There," Kalindi said, pointing to a clump of something nestled about the length of a person below the jagged cliff's edge. The mooncaps gleamed beautifully in the moonlight, their iridescent pearl glow matching the description of what they were looking for perfectly.

Mari squinted. "That has to be it."

"On the... face of a cliff. Great." Kalindi nervously chuckled.

"You said mooncap grows on the cliffsides," Mari reminded, peering anxiously over the steep drop.

Kalindi looked down the edge. "I was hoping it meant near the cliffs, not over them," she admitted.

Mari looked around. "So... what now?"

Kalindi was already pulling vines from a nearby tree. "We'll need to anchor these. If it's too far down to reach—"

"Wait," Mari said, growing more concerned with every moment. "Do you really think we should..." She trailed off as Kalindi looped the vines around herself.

"I'll go. You hold the line," Kalindi said, thrusting the other end of the vine into Mari's hands.

Mari caught the vine and gripped it as tightly as she could. "Are you sure about this?"

Kalindi's usual confidence wavered as she glanced at her, and Mari could practically see her shoving her fear deep down, as far as it would go. "No," she admitted. "But someone has to."

Mari swallowed and wiped her brow.

Kalindi's bravado returned with full force as she flashed a bright grin and stuck her tongue out at Mari teasingly. "What's wrong? Afraid you'll let me fall?"

Mari rolled her eyes.

With that, Kalindi descended, disappearing almost immediately into the limestone cliffside. Mari moved as close as she would allow herself to get to the edge of the cliff and braced herself against a nearby rock, securing her footing, all the while maintaining a visual on Kalindi. She held the vine steady as Kalindi moved lower and lower. The glow of the mooncap drew closer, and Mari allowed herself a sliver of hope.

Then she saw it.

A luminous plant with long, brilliant tendrils like a jellyfish that belied its predatory nature quivered near Kalindi's arm. Mari's heart dropped.

"Kalindi!" Mari hissed. "Don't move—there's something near you!"

Kalindi froze, her head tilting. "What? Where?"

"The plant—right by your arm. Don't touch it!" Mari's voice shook but she tried to keep as calm as possible. The last thing she needed was a panicked Kalindi, dangling by nothing but a vine. "You'll be fine, just..." she paused to emphasize her words, "don't touch that plant."

Kalindi glanced to her side, her breath catching as she spotted the hypnotic, glowing tendrils. Of course, she immediately reached out and touched them. As soon as her fingers glanced the tendrils that snaked out from its base, one of them brushed her sleeve, creeping like a curious constrictor. The plant shuddered, its tendrils spreading wider, moving faster.

"Mari—" Kalindi began, but her voice broke as the plant lunged, its tendrils wrapping tightly around her arm. She yelped, trying to shake it off, but the plant tightened its grip further.

"Hold on!" Mari shouted, her heart racing. She anchored the vine around her waist and scrambled dangerously close to the edge, reaching desperately for Kalindi. "Don't move! I've got you!"

Kalindi's breaths came in short, pained gasps as she struggled against the plant. Its tendrils glowed brighter, the light pulsing like a heartbeat. Mari grabbed a nearby stick and threw it at the plant, but it bounced harmlessly off its surface.

"Use the knife!" Mari yelled, her voice cracking. "Cut it off!"

Kalindi fumbled with her belt and pulled out her dagger. She slashed at the tendrils, releasing a burst of glowing spores with every cut. The plant recoiled, its arms snapping back like a wounded animal. Kalindi yanked herself free, but the motion caused her to slip, pulling Mari forward with a jolt.

Mari screamed, gripping the vine with all her strength and digging her feet into the gravel as she was dragged slowly closer to where Kalindi was dangling precariously over the edge. "I've got you!" Mari cried again, her voice hoarse, her feet sliding. "Hold on!"

Mari looked frantically around for something, anything, to grab hold of. The rock was just out of reach, but there was a mound of lavender to one side, and she slowly reached out to grab a tuft of the grass at the base, urging it to hold tight. She gave the grass a tug, but it didn't move. Using every ounce of strength, Mari pulled Kalindi back up, the vine burning her palms as it slid through her grip. When Kalindi finally collapsed onto the ground beside her, Mari fell to her knees, trembling.

"I've got you," Mari whispered, her voice shaky. "I've got you..."

Kalindi coughed, her face pale but her eyes still clear. "You didn't let me fall," she said weakly. She reached out and found Mari's trembling hand, and gave it a grateful squeeze.

Mari let out a shaky laugh, tears stinging her eyes, and let herself crumble onto the floor beside Kalindi.

They sat there in silence, catching their breath. Mari looked at Kalindi with a mixture of relief and newfound respect, letting her body relax into the moment, unconcerned by the bits of gravel she was certain were latching onto her thick curls as she lay in the dirt.

Until a cold realization hit her like a punch to the gut. Mari jolted upright and whipped around, scanning the edge of the cliff.

They hadn't completed their task.

Her face fell. "We need to try again..." she cried.

Kalindi winced, exhaustion long since having set in. But before either of them could move, a piercing screech echoed across the cliffside. Mari's head snapped up just in time to see Rih's purple-silver outline streak past, a rush of wind hitting her face as the skyweaver cut between them, soaring high, then diving over the cliff's edge.

"Rih!" Mari cried, scrambling forward, her heart leaping into her throat.

She reached the edge just as Rih reappeared, rising fast, nearly colliding with Mari as she shot up along the sheer cliff face.

The moonlight caught the gleam of her talons, and clutched within them, something was glowing.

The mooncap.

Mari's mouth dropped open as Rih swooped low, releasing the plant with perfect precision, dropping it directly into Kalindi's outstretched hands.

Kalindi gasped, staring down at the glowing plant, blinking in disbelief.

Rih swept into a wide, high arc before perching triumphantly on a nearby branch, puffing her chest with unmistakable smugness.

Which was, of course, entirely deserved.

For a moment, Mari and Kalindi just stared. Then, Mari burst out laughing, shaking her head.

"You, unbelievable little champion," she chortled, glancing up at Rih, beaming with pride.

Kalindi cradled the mooncap carefully in her hands. She grinned, still breathless. "I mean, if I knew that was an option from the beginning, it might have saved us some time and a whole lot of stress."

"And a near-death experience," Mari added.

"Yes, that too," Kalindi said. "But I have to say, I'm not even mad. That was incredible."

She carefully wrapped the mooncap in a small piece of cloth pulled from her bag before tucking it safely away.

"Alright," Mari said, standing. "Let's get out of here before someone else decides to almost die."

AS THEY LEFT THE GARDENS, the glow of the forest fading behind them, Mari's curiosity got the better of her. "You really know your way around plants," she said. "So then... why engineering?"

Kalindi shrugged. "It's practical. Engineering puts food on the table."

Mari frowned. "And plants?"

"Plants... they're not something you fix. You nurture them. Watch them grow. But the world doesn't pay you to care for beauty. It pays you to build."

Mari fell silent, matching her pace to the steady rhythm of Kalindi's staff tapping against the earth.

CHAPTER SIXTEEN

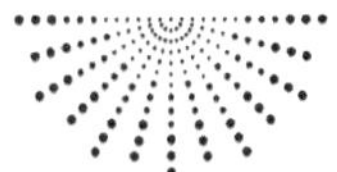

They walked until they had to stop. Mari had suggested they rest at the Elyrian ruins, an ancient site about halfway between Elyria's Edge and Myramin's Bend. The ruins were a somber reminder of the ingenuity of the ancient Elyrians, their crumbling stone walls a shadow of their former glory, and as Mari looked at the remnants, she tried to imagine what they might have looked like in their prime. They ventured into the opening of one of the larger ruins, choosing it for the safety of its small entrance that would be easy to keep watch over.

The ruins were hauntingly beautiful, the bluish gray stone fighting a losing battle against the creeping greenery that wove through the cracks in the walls and arches overhead. Kalindi eyed the vines suspiciously as they walked under them, but they were decidedly unanimated, much to both women's relief. Mari ran her hand over a carved pattern on one of the walls, fascinated. The design reminded her of the symbols she had seen in the cave outside Adavale, a thought that sent a shiver down her spine.

The ancient Elyrians were fabled to be a powerful empire, rich with resources, knowledge, and infrastructure. She had always dismissed the idea of their floating terraces mostly as an exaggerated legend, but after seeing the Glowing Gardens that morning she was more convinced than ever before that the stories were true. The Elyrian Terraces were said to cascade down vast slopes, their elaborate network of waterways flowing through carved stone channels, feeding lush, suspended gardens. The ingenuity behind it all was enough to make Mari want to board the nearest ship and go in search of the fabled land. Some claimed their carvings held the secrets of their technology, which was supposed to have been so powerful that it elevated the Elyrians to a level of sophistication that saw them flourish... until they fell.

Mari sat at the mouth of the ruins, a fresh parchment in front of her, as she got to work drawing lines on the new chart, pausing every few moments to peer back into the astrolabe. Kalindi sat in the direct path of the moonlight, leafing through her book about native plant life that she had picked up during their stop in Myramin's Bend. Eventually, she drifted off to sleep, and the book fell from her hands, hitting the floor with a loud clap.

Mari scrambled quickly to her feet, seizing the opportunity to look through Kalindi's pack for the map she had seen earlier, curious for a closer look at the assassins notes. She pulled it out quickly and scanned the page. What she saw made her skin crawl. Several locations were marked, all with notations near caves, including the area near Adavale. Why hadn't Kalindi mentioned this?

She glanced at Kalindi, who looked peaceful for the first time in quite some time. She considered waking her and demanding to know why she hadn't mentioned the markings on the map earlier. She decided against it.

She paused, trying to decide whether she should continue to look through Kalindi's bag. She had been hiding the details about this map... What else might she be hiding? Didn't Mari owe it to her own safety to look?

She shook her head, pushing the thought away. She had her limits. For now. She folded the map and pushed it down into her satchel.

Instead, she lay back, staring up at the sky that was starting to lighten. Her mind raced with questions, her trust in Kalindi hanging by a thread. Her gaze moved to the engraved swirls that framed the top of a pillar nearby. The Elyrians had achieved such incredible feats, but they had also destroyed themselves. Greenhaven's elders had long taught that it was the Elyrians' hubris and overreliance on technology that had led to their downfall. The ruins around her were a blatant warning.

She wondered if Kalindi's designs for Greenhaven's water generator would fall into the same trap. Would the elders see it as a gift or as a threat? Mari continued to mull similar thoughts over until it was time to wake Kalindi to take over the watch. Mari fell asleep almost instantly.

She slept just long enough to feel like she could put one foot in front of the other without wanting to vomit. She was shivering when she woke, exhausted and on guard. Kalindi had shaken her gently, and when she looked into Kalindi's tired, wide eyes, she wanted to pull a blanket over her head, roll over, go back to sleep, and tell Kalindi to do the same. But there was no time for that. They needed to get back to Jannah to deliver the mooncap before she got any worse.

Mari put her boots on and started to pull the laces tightly.

The last thing she needed right then were blisters. Kalindi looked up at the ruins, observing the carvings that adorned the walls.

"They're beautiful, aren't they?" Mari said.

Kalindi nodded. "Stunning," she whispered, her voice tired. Probably from the lack of sleep.

"The ancient Elyrians were incredible. They harnessed powers beyond anything we understand today. Mechanics, resonance, plant life—things that would be right up your alley."

Kalindi's head snapped abruptly in Mari's direction. "They did?"

Mari gestured to the carvings. "The Elyrian Terraces. Those children's tales' you were so quick to dismiss back at the outpost? Apparently, they were so resourceful that they even used sound to enhance their technology. But... something happened and everything was destroyed. We're not sure if they imploded or they were attacked... There's not much evidence at all. How do you go from being the most advanced civilization to nothing? That's why Greenhaven keeps things simple. The elders believe it's safer that way."

Kalindi's eyes twitched as she turned back to the carvings. She seemed to be considering more than just what Mari was saying. "I see," she said, although her mind seemed elsewhere.

Mari picked up her satchel and wrapped it around her hips, securing the thigh strap with a snap. "Hope whatever you're planning to build for Greenhaven isn't too technical. If the elders can't understand it, they won't agree to it."

Kalindi didn't reply. She was still staring at the carvings as if she were trying to solve a puzzle of sorts.

Mari started toward the path leading out of the ruins. When Kalindi didn't follow, she glanced back. Kalindi hadn't even picked up her pack. Her hands were now pressed against the stone of the ruins.

"Kalindi?" Mari called, her voice harsher than she intended. Rih took off from Mari's shoulder and landed on Kalindi's, giving her hair clip a quick tug.

Kalindi blinked and pulled her hands away as if burned. "Coming," she called, and she hurried to catch up.

As they walked, Mari felt herself getting more worked up with each step. This journey so far had been anything but easy, and the one thing she needed was a friend she could trust. At this point, Kalindi was not that person. Mari wondered how she could justify welcoming Kalindi to Greenhaven or presenting her to the elders or her family if she didn't trust her. The uneasiness seeped into her spirit as they pressed onward.

They stopped for a brief rest at a fork in the river. Mari scanned the area for a bridge, but there was none. "We're going to have to wade through," she said with a sigh. She was tired, and this was just one more delay that added to the long list of things that were bothering her. She kicked her boots off with force, and one went flying further than she had intended. She grunted.

Kalindi shot her a look from where she was bent down, rolling her pant legs above her knees, and Mari felt her anger bubble up like molten lava spewing from a Harcanth volcano. "How can you be so agreeable and easy to travel with and be so secretive at the same time?" she growled, throwing her weapons to the ground as she unbuckled her belt.

"What?" Kalindi asked, clearly confused by the sudden onslaught of emotion aimed squarely at her.

Mari stormed toward Kalindi, the assassin's map clutched in her hand like a weapon. She waved it in Kalindi's face, her voice firm. "When were you planning on telling me about this?"

Kalindi looked up from her boots, which she had been unlacing, with a frown across her face. "What are you talking about?"

"This!" Mari snapped, shoving the map at her. "It's not just a map; it's a map from the Stewards!"

Kalindi blinked, her expression blank. "The Stewards? You mean that tale Calen told us about?"

"It says it right here, Kalindi!" Mari jabbed at the parchment. "Are you seriously telling me you didn't see that?"

Kalindi's eyes darted to the map. "I... I didn't see it," she said simply.

Mari's lips thinned. She was furious now. "You saw these, though, right?" She pointed to the markings scattered across the map. "Look at this!" Her finger hovered over the big black X near Adavale. "This spot—this is the cave near Adavale. I recognize it. You can't tell me you didn't notice that."

Kalindi shrugged. "I saw the marks, yes, but—"

"And look here," Mari added, pointing to other locations marked with similar notations. "There are more of them!" She thrust the map closer to Kalindi, her voice transitioning from frustration to intensity. "This isn't random. These places mean something. We should check them out!"

Kalindi took the map and shoved it into her pack without even looking at it. "Are you crazy, Mari? We barely survived that assassin's attack! The only reason we're even standing here is because Rih came to the rescue!"

Rih gave a smug chirp from Kalindi's shoulder.

Mari planted her hands on her hips, unwavering. "I don't know what we're caught up in, but I owe it to Searsan to find out what's going on. Something tells me that if we crack this, we solve everything."

"Owe it to Searsan... What do you mean?"

Mari kicked herself mentally, realizing her slip. "I just mean... I want to make him proud," she said, thinking quickly and hoping for the best.

Kalindi's dragged her hands down her face and flung her hands in the air. "We can't go there. We would be backtracking. We need to get back to Greenhaven to help—"

"This is bigger than Greenhaven!" Mari interrupted. "Don't you see? This thing is affecting all of Patovia—or it will, even if it hasn't yet. The auroras started out faint, right? But they're growing stronger. They're disrupting the atmosphere, and water sources are draining. Greenhaven hasn't had rain for months, and the Sharaine River has been dry for even longer. It's a pattern! The Stewards have regrouped, and they're running something catastrophic. If we don't figure this out, the entire region will be in ruins. We're going."

Kalindi stared at her, clearly torn between frustration and something else, but what, Mari couldn't quite figure out. Finally, she let out a loud breath. "Let's just get the mooncap to Jannah first. After that, we'll see."

Mari turned her back with a huff and gathered up her boots and belongings. She flung them over her shoulder and stomped into the river. The cold hit her unexpectedly, and she gasped as she misstepped on a rock underfoot. She shouted a wild gurgle for help before losing her footing completely and crashing bottom first into the river. The water was flowing gently, so there was no risk that she could be pulled away by the current, but she still resented Kalindi for laughing at her when she came up for air.

"You fall off the edge of a cliff and I risk my life to save you, but a girl almost gets swept away by a raging river and here you're laughing!" she pouted.

Kalindi rolled her eyes and extended her quarterstaff. Mari grabbed it and yanked hard, pulling Kalindi into the river with her. Not expecting the attack, Kalindi plunged headfirst, and Mari took her opportunity to laugh at her in return.

Kalindi splashed Mari with a wave of water, and Mari dove under the surface to avoid the attack. She swam closer to Kalindi and burst upward, breaking through the surface and showering Kalindi with water droplets. Kalindi braced herself against Mari, pushing her playfully. The pair dripped with water as their laughter died down, and the moment transformed into a slower, more peaceful one. Mari lay backward, letting her body float on the river, the sun above warming her.

The image of the map flashed in her mind, the markings like a giant red flag waving right in front of her. She let her body sink into the water and cast a sideways glance at Kalindi, who looked relaxed, almost at peace, as she squeezed the droplets from her long ponytail.

The assassin had been after both of them—of that, Mari was sure. But why? It didn't make sense. If Kalindi was working with the Stewards, wouldn't they want her alive?

"Kalindi," Mari said cautiously, breaking the silence. "What do you really know about the Stewards?"

Kalindi lazily cupped water into her hands and dropped it on her body, the water cascading over her chest and trickling into the river. Mari made a conscious effort not to look at her very attractive, very wet body. She was only human.

"Not much more than you do. Stories, rumors. Why?"

Mari studied her carefully, searching for cracks in her

composure. "Back at the outpost, you said you'd never heard of them before..."

She waited for Kalindi's response, but Kalindi continued to wash her arms, not giving her much more.

Mari continued. "I'm trying to piece this together. Whoever sent that assassin wanted us both dead. Either that means we're caught up in something bigger than we realized, or..."

"Or what?" Kalindi turned, her eyes daring Mari to say out loud what they both knew she wanted to.

Mari hesitated. "Or you're not working with them."

Kalindi's jaw tightened. "I'm not working with the Stewards."

Mari wondered if her choice of words was deliberate. "Are you working with someone else?"

Kalindi started toward the bank of the river, using her quarterstaff to push herself out of the water. "I'm working with you," she said. She turned to Mari and looked her dead in the eyes.

Mari stared back, not moving. "Okay," she said with a sigh. Kalindi had to know she wasn't satisfied with her response, but what more could she ask? Mari reluctantly climbed out of the river, shivering from the breeze that hit her as she squeezed the water out of her clothes.

Rih preened herself from the cracked stump of a toppled tree, her feathers flaring as the others dried off nearby. Mari watched Kalindi brush her hand over her bare arm where her leather bracelet used to be. "When did you lose your mother?"

"A long time ago," Kalindi said, her eyes sad. "I would have been... twelve? Maybe thirteen... It was the worst year of my life."

Mari shook her head as she wrung out her travel cloak and

laid it out in a spot of sunlight for as much dry time as she could get before they had to move on. "So you lived with your father after that? Or..." she dug.

"My brother and I spent time with a few different family members. My father traveled a lot for work, so we went wherever we were told while he was gone. Eventually, we ended up with our grandfather, my father's father, until..."

Kalindi trailed off, her gaze fixed on the rippling river waters, as though she was reliving a memory too painful to share. Mari stepped closer, her breath caught in her chest, waiting for Kalindi to continue. The pause stretched into what felt like forever before Kalindi finally decided on the right words.

"Until I was old enough to leave for Joycita and live my own life," she said at last.

"Was it a culture shock for you, too? Joycita?" Mari asked, remembering her first steps through the crowded city.

Kalindi chuckled. "Oh, yes. The city itself is overwhelming at first. The noise, the pace, the sheer size of it... It's enough to rattle anyone. But what really struck me was the politics. I don't know why I thought it would be like the villages, where decisions were communal and made with everyone's input. There, everything seemed to be so calculated. Every word, every decision—it's all part of some larger game. I thought it would be different..."

Mari considered her words. She felt like Kalindi had been trying to outrun something far more sinister than small village life where she was shipped from caregiver to caregiver. It explained why she was so willing to head for Greenhaven. She tilted her head. "What made you go there?"

"I had heard a rumor. They were planning to build a grand arboretum on the northern side of the city. They said it would rival the Glowing Gardens. I wanted to be part of that. But after actually seeing the Glowing Gardens..." She snorted with a smile, shaking her head. "There's no way they'll ever create anything that even comes close to them, though. They're not gardens... They're a whole other universe that just happens to be sharing the same plane as us. They're alive in a way that nothing we could build could ever replicate."

Mari watched as Kalindi's smile faded. "That queen of yours... She prioritizes all these grand expansions and these massive projects meant to dazzle and impress. Meanwhile, the outer regions of Patovia are barely getting by. Sometimes, I think they've forgotten about the people outside the city walls."

"You think the queen doesn't care?"

"I've heard people say she does. That she's trying to rebuild, to unite the kingdom, but actions speak louder than words. And the actions coming out of the castle don't exactly scream compassion for the people struggling to make it outside the city walls," Kalindi replied. "My mother always said, 'Show me, don't tell me,'" she added.

Mari nodded slowly, her gaze drifting to Kalindi's bag. Her mind was already working, weaving together fragments of conversations and memories. Something about this didn't add up. She couldn't shake the nagging feeling that Kalindi still wasn't telling her everything. "Actions speak louder than words," she murmured.

Kalindi's eyes narrowed when she caught Mari staring. "You've been eyeing my bag for a while now," she said sharply, though not entirely unfriendly. "What is it you're so curious about?"

Mari grimaced, but she didn't look away. "The map," she said plainly. "I'm sorry, I just don't buy that you didn't see the markings."

Kalindi stiffened, then let out a long, slow exhale, and reached into her bag. She pulled out the parchment and unfolded it with care. "Mari," she said, her voice quiet now.

"Yes?"

"I noticed the markings," she admitted.

Revelation of the century, Mari thought, keeping her eye roll internal.

"I didn't want to say anything because I wanted to focus on Greenhaven. That's the task I was given. I wasn't lying to you when I told you that I was excited to help. I've spent days designing a system that could ease the drought—something that might actually work."

"Okay," Mari said, expecting more. Kalindi's words sounded sincere, but she had already heard all this before. It was starting to sound rehearsed. Maybe it was Kalindi's tone or the way her hands fidgeted, but Mari remained unconvinced. She decided to push a little harder. Reaching her hand out, she gestured for the map. Kalindi handed it over without hesitation. Mari looked at it again, scanning the marked areas, her fingers tracing the roadways and landing on a mark close to Myramin's Bend. "This one," she said. "It's near the Isa Glades. I want to check it out."

Kalindi looked at her with timid eyes. "I promise I'm not trying to dissuade you from going, but Jannah needs the mooncap, Mari."

"We'll get Jannah the mooncap first. The cave is on the way to Adavale," Mari said. "See?" She jabbed a finger at the map again. "We need to go this way to get back to Greenhaven."

Kalindi studied the map for a long moment before agreeing. "Fine," she said, resigned. She handed Mari her cloak and pulled her pack over her shoulder. "Let's go."

Mari shoved the map into her satchel, her eyes flicking to

Kalindi's face, which revealed nothing, leaving Mari to wrestle with her thoughts. Why had Kalindi agreed to this so easily when she was so adamantly against it earlier? The shift felt too abrupt, too convenient. Was she finally piecing things together and willing to help, or was this a calculated move to throw Mari off the trail?

She wished Lyra were here, ready with tea and her steady presence. Mari had too many questions and not nearly enough answers.

CHAPTER SEVENTEEN

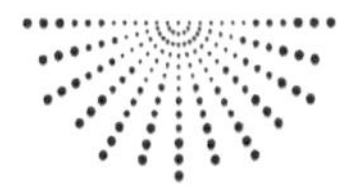

THEY TREKKED THROUGH THE WILDERNESS UNDER the cover of darkness, which was perhaps a reckless decision, but the risk paid off and they arrived undiscovered as the sun started to peek over the horizon. The journey through West Myramin was quiet, the early morning sun throwing warmth upon them as they walked. The small settlement was stirring to life, its residents beginning their daily routines. Mari and Kalindi exchanged few words as they trudged through, both too focused on their thoughts to make conversation. Birds dipped high and low from the treetops above, seeking out their morning meals, and Rih took flight to do the same, gliding easily on the soft breeze. The stains from her breast had faded to the point where they just looked like nothing more than natural markings, much to Mari's relief. She hadn't been eager to explain why her bird was covered in blood stains.

By the time they reached Myramin's Shambles, Mari was ready to drop the mooncap on the doorstep and head to the nearest inn for the hottest bath and the longest sleep she could afford. She hadn't noticed earlier just how dangerously disheveled the relegated village was—crumbling stone walls lined the crooked streets, and weeds were the only visible vegetation. The neglect was overwhelming, and she wouldn't realize until much later how Myramin's Shambles would make her feel grateful for just having grown up somewhere beautiful.

Mari noticed Jannah's house immediately. The roof of the home was sagging, and the siding was blackened from years of water damage. Gura greeted them at the door, her lined face hopeful and also a little shocked.

"You came back!" she said. "I didn't think... Well, I wasn't sure you would."

"We promised," Mari grinned.

"I was worried you'd been caught... They don't take kindly to anyone meddling in the gardens."

Kalindi's gave her a reassuring smile as she stepped inside. "We were careful."

Jannah lay in the same cot where they'd left her, her face still pale, her breathing shallow. The room was poorly lit, the single, dirty window casting a pale rectangle of light onto the floor. Mari's heart ached at the sight of her, so small and fragile under the worn blanket.

Kalindi knelt by the cot and unwrapped the mooncap with care. The mushroom's iridescent glow was almost invisible, but it gave off a subtle warmth that seemed to brighten the room.

"You'll need to dry this by the fire first. Once it's dry, grind it into a fine powder. Add a little powder to some hot water— just enough for a spoonful at a time. Feed it to her slowly. Make sure it's not too hot, but not cold either," Kalindi explained.

Gura nodded, her hands wringing the hem of her apron. "Will it work right away?"

"No," Kalindi said. "It takes time. Give her some of the drink every day. You'll start to see the color come back to her cheeks little by little."

Mari watched as Gura reached out hesitantly. "Is it... glowing?" she asked. She stared at the mooncap's surface with apprehension. Kalindi nodded.

"How?" Gura asked. "You're sure it's safe?"

Kalindi set the mooncap on the table. "Everything in this world has a vibration... a rhythm. Every part of us is connected in ways we don't always see. The mooncap emits a small vibration. It's part of its healing properties."

"A vibration?" Gura was understandably nervous, and she glanced over at Mari, who offered an encouraging nod.

"Like a hum," Kalindi explained. "Think of it like a heartbeat. Everything has a heartbeat, right? You just have to listen for it."

Gura stared at the mushroom, her brow furrowed in thought. "And the powder... What should I do with the rest?"

"Keep it hidden," Kalindi warned.. "Somewhere cool and dry. Don't tell anyone you have it. It will glow brighter at night, and that could attract attention you don't want."

Gura's hands trembled as she wrapped the mooncap in a cloth, and she looked over at her daughter's still form. "Thank you," she whispered. "Thank you both."

Kalindi reached out, brushing a gentle hand over Jannah's forehead. She leaned down and pressed a soft kiss to her temple. "You'll be alright," she murmured, glancing up at Gura as if her words were meant for both of them.

They stepped back into the sunlight, the door closing quietly behind them, and Mari glanced at Kalindi. "You didn't have to do all that, you know."

Kalindi shrugged. "Maybe not, but it felt like the right thing to do."

They walked away from the house, the relief of the task lifting from their shoulders. As they turned onto the main road, Mari glanced back once, catching a glimpse of Gura standing in the doorway, clutching the wrapped mooncap to her chest like a lifeline.

"She's scared," Mari said softly.

"Good," Kalindi replied. "Fear will make her careful."

Rih gave a little squawk, as if in agreement.

THEY HEADED BACK to Myramin's Bend, to the same inn they had stayed at before, stopping by the tavern to visit the barkeep, Jai, the man who had denied Gura food when they were there last. As Kalindi dropped a pouch of coins on the counter, she insisted that it be used to set up a tab for Gura and Jannah the next time they came in.

"Thank you," Jai had said, gratefully accepting the pouch. "I used to give her whatever was left at the end of the night, but the boss got wind of it and told me he'd let me go if I continued. Said he wasn't in the business of giving away food to a potential paying customer." Jai scoffed and weighed the pouch in his hand. "This will make a difference. May the Gods bless your families."

Kalindi looked at him, her eyes steel. "Keep your blessings. Just see that Gura and Jannah are fed whenever they need it," she said, leaving before Jai could say any more.

Mari trudged slowly to her room, her head throbbing. After making it clear to Kalindi that their next movements would be to head towards the Isa Glades, she headed straight for bed and slept until the early evening.

When she woke, the night sky bore a gentle aurora above her. She stretched her body as long as it would go, her muscles aching. She could easily turn over, hoist the soft, heavy blankets over her head, and sleep through the night, but her belly growled, and she knew she would just lie awake until it was full. Rih perched quietly on the windowsill, surveying the road below.

"Keep watch for me, girl," Mari asked, giving her tiny head a kiss. She pulled on pants and threw her jacket over her shoulders before heading downstairs to see if she could find something to ease the hunger pains.

Inside the tavern, spiced wine and tobacco mingled with the low murmur of the patrons' voices. Seated at a table near the bar was a man with intense eyes who seemed out of place. His dark hair was cropped neatly, and his jawline dusted with stubble. Though he appeared relaxed, his steel sapphire gaze was fixed intensely on the person sitting opposite him, and by his posture alone, Mari could tell he felt himself superior. Their conversation appeared heated, and the man made small, abrupt movements as he spoke. Curious, Mari approached the bar, positioning herself close to the man and the person he was talking to. From the corner of her eye, she recognized the defined arms that peeked out of the cloak covering the other person... It was Kalindi. Mari leaned in and turned her head slightly to hear the conversation.

"Don't insult me, Kiron. You know exactly what they're doing. There's nothing good about it."

The man, Kiron, reached his hand out to touch Kalindi's, but she pulled away. "You don't understand. I see it differently now. They're trying to—"

"Save it," Kalindi snapped, cutting him off. "You're either blind to their schemes or a willing accomplice. Either way, I want no part of it."

"Anything to drink, miss?" Mari spun to see a new face behind the bar. The late-night barkeep's voice drowned out the conversation behind her.

"Please, just water," Mari said. "And something to eat. Anything," she added, willing for him to go away.

Mari tuned her ears back to the conversation behind her, but it had gone silent. She cast another sideways glance and saw that Kalindi was looking right at her.

"You're awake," Kalindi said, brushing a dark curl from her face and giving a hard swallow.

"Everything okay?" Mari asked, noticing that Kalindi's hands were shaking terribly.

Kalindi nodded. "This," she gestured to the man opposite her, "is my brother. He's come to try to bring me home."

Mari took the opportunity to scan the man from head to toe plainly now. "Kiron?" Mari asked, making sure Kalindi knew she had overheard her conversation.

Kiron stood. He was tall, imposing, and radiated confidence. "Mari," he said. So, he knew who she was. He extended his hand and Mari took it. He greeted her with a rigorous shake, clasping his other hand over the top of hers. "So this is the woman who has been gallivanting across the countryside with my sister."

"Gallivanting?" Mari asked with a single eyebrow raise.

"Kalindi's family misses her. Our grandfather sent us to bring her home."

Kalindi's laugh was harsh, almost panicked. "Home? You mean the web of lies and manipulation I fought to escape? No, thanks."

Mari was still stuck on gallivanting. "Don't you think Kalindi's old enough to decide to spend her time however she wishes?" She stared Kiron directly in his eyes.

"The family needs her," he said. He turned back to face Kalindi. "Things are changing. We're doing good work—work that matters. And we need you, Kalindi."

"What kind of work?" Mari asked.

"Family business," Kiron said, his attention still firmly fixed on Kalindi.

"I'm not interested," Kalindi spat back. "How did you find me, anyway?"

"You know the reach Grandfather has," Kiron said. "I suspect someone saw you... It only took four years. So you either resurfaced publicly because you want to come home, or you got lazy and made a mistake. Either way, we're leaving together. Tonight. You can understand the strict instructions I was given not to return without you."

With that, Kiron reached out and took Kalindi by the wrist. "Where's your bracelet?" he asked. Mari studied his face in an effort to work out whether that question was genuine or a clever way of letting her know he knew something that she did not.

"You tell me, Kiron," Kalindi said, seething.

Mari stepped between them. "Kiron, as lovely as this little family reunion is, I think it's time you leave. Without Kalindi. I'm sure your grandfather will understand that Kalindi is her own woman, and she can make her own choices."

When Kiron didn't so much as glance at Mari, she placed a hand on top of his, his grip still wrapped around Kalindi's forearm. She pressed her thumb and her finger into the soft, fleshy part of his hand below his thumb and squeezed firmly. Kiron let out a small yelp and immediately released Kalindi's arm and tried to pull his arm back, but Mari maintained her pinch.

"You will leave now, Kiron," she said, increasing the pressure. She saw his eyes water, but his lips remained tight. "You will leave, because none of us wants any trouble, do we?"

Mari stopped breathing as she waited for his response, praying that her hunch was right and that he wasn't looking for any attention. She lightened her pinch, and Kiron took his hand back, rubbing the area she had been locked on.

He glared at Mari before turning back to Kalindi again, his voice thick with warning. "You can't keep running, Kalindi. You know they won't stop."

Kalindi's response was a low growl. "Let them try."

Kiron shook his head, a sneer across his chiseled face. "You think you're safe out here, wandering around with no plan? They'll find you. You need me."

Kalindi's hand drifted to the hilt of her dagger. "Who says I don't have a plan?"

Kiron snorted.

"Stay away, Kiron. I mean it. If you follow us, I'll consider you my enemy."

Kalindi looked Kiron dead in the eye with a glare that demanded nothing but consent. Mari thought she saw a flash of regret cross Kiron's face, but if she did, he managed to control it well because, before she could blink, his lip had curled into a scowl. "Eventually, you'll come home. And they'll be waiting."

As Kiron turned and walked away, Kalindi grabbed Mari's glass with a trembling hand and drained it. She stared at the door Kiron had just left through.

"Are you okay?" Mari asked quietly. She tried to shake off the adrenaline she was feeling. As much as she felt concern for

Kalindi, she also felt equal parts suspicious over her alleged brother's sudden arrival.

Kalindi's glare cut through her. "Don't. Just... don't."

The barkeep put a plate of grilled fish, rice, and pickled river greens in front of Mari, who pushed it in front of Kalindi, ordered her to eat it, and requested a second plate for herself.

"Mari?"

"Yes?"

"Can I stay with you tonight?"

Mari gave Kalindi a sympathetic smile. "Sure."

KALINDI HAD INSISTED she was fine sleeping on the floor, with Mari's cloak as a pillow and her own as a blanket. Instead of claiming her usual perch on the back of a chair, Rih had nestled down beside Kalindi, snuggling in close as if standing watch. Kalindi didn't seem to mind. In fact, she welcomed the tiny sentinel's company, resting a hand lightly on Rih's back.

As they settled in, the door firmly locked and their bellies full, Mari couldn't hold her tongue.

"Kalindi, you need to tell me what's going on. Who was that man? Why is he after you?"

"He really is my brother."

"Why was he acting like such a fop?"

Kalindi sighed, her frustration evident. "Please drop it, Mari. This is my past, my problem. I didn't ask to be followed, and I certainly didn't ask for your curiosity."

Mari huffed and turned onto her shoulder, her back to Kalindi. *Why is this girl so difficult?*

MARI AWOKE in the gray predawn light, her body restless after having slept most of the previous day. The inn was still, the faint sounds of distant birds the only sign that morning was on its way. An early start to the Isa Glades would mean more daylight to explore, so she shook Kalindi awake gently.

Kalindi groaned, pulling the blanket over her head. "The sun isn't even up yet, Mari," she mumbled.

"And we'll have more daylight to find this cave if we start now," Mari countered, tugging at the blanket until Kalindi reluctantly rolled out of bed.

Despite Kalindi's initial grumbling, the pair were back on the road before the first stirrings of Myramin's Bend began. The cool morning air shook off the last traces of sleep, and Mari couldn't help but notice Kalindi's unease. Her eyes darted to every single sound that came from the underbrush.

"Would it make you feel better if we had Rih scan our perimeter?" Mari asked after Kalindi flinched at a particularly loud rustle.

Kalindi cast her a wary glance. "She can do that?"

Mari smiled. "She can do a lot of things. She's a brilliant bird."

Kalindi frowned. "Why isn't she affected like the other skyweavers?"

Mari snorted. "She's definitely not your typical skyweaver... But she's also not flying long distances, so maybe that's why? Honestly, I'm not keen to find out."

Kalindi nodded, her tension appearing to ease slightly. "Yeah, especially after Elyria's Edge. Let's keep Rih and that sharp little beak of hers close by."

Mari reached out, placing a hand lightly on Kalindi's arm. "You don't ever have to go back," she said, her eyes steady.

Kalindi stiffened, then nodded slowly. "I know." She patted

Mari's hand briefly before stepping ahead. She still moved briskly, but her shoulders seemed a little less rigid.

Mari smiled to herself. Not a full rejection. Progress.

THE ISA GLADES WERE BREATHTAKING. The landscape shifted as they neared, the dense forest giving way to sprawling marshland. Tall grasses swayed in the humid breeze, and two large lakes gleamed like twin mirrors across different levels of the glades—Lake Glass, a salt pool nestled into the eastern side of the Maiyma Mountains, and Lake Warm, a shallow basin surrounded by mud and reeds. Their surfaces were still, broken only by the occasional ripple of a fish or a water bird.

Kalindi's mood improved as they entered the glades, her earlier tension disappearing, her energy lighter. She paused to study the landscape, clearly appreciating the abundance of plant life. "This place is gorgeous," she murmured, impressed. Mari smiled as she wondered how many other people would marvel at a glorified swampland, bright green weeds in every direction, as far as the eye could see.

They wandered the area for what felt like half the day, searching for any sign of a cave. "Maybe Rih could help?" Kalindi suggested with a laugh. "Want to find a big cave for us, girl?"

Rih circled above and gave a screech before swooping low over a cluster of dense bushes. "Looks like she's already on it," Mari said, nodding toward the spot.

Nestled among the bushes was a compact opening, barely visible through the foliage. The two exchanged a glance before pushing their way through, their knives drawn. As they stepped inside, they heard the faint trickle of water, the stone beneath them wet. Lake Warm ran through the cave, and true to its name, the temperature of the water created a crawling mist that hovered an inch above the floor, disappearing when they walked through it.

Halfway in, Mari paused. "This isn't a natural cave," she said, running her hands along the walls. "Look at this—it looks convincing, but..."

Kalindi followed Mari's lead and traced the markings she had found.

"It's like the cave near Adavale," Mari noted. The similarities were undeniable. Openings in the roof allowed shafts of light to illuminate the space. The markings around the edges felt familiar, but the space was completely empty.

"Okay, we've checked it out. Doesn't seem like there's anything here. Can we head to Greenhaven now?" Kalindi's voice was suddenly impatient.

"Wait," Mari said, her hand brushing against what she thought was a corner. Instead, it curved, revealing a passage that continued deeper. "There's more."

The path led them to a round chamber where sunlight poured through carefully carved openings in the ceiling that illuminated the room like natural spotlights, revealing a pile of discarded metal rods and brackets.

Mari knelt and picked up one of the pieces. "What do you suppose this is?"

Kalindi frowned as she turned one of the brackets over in her hands. "Not sure," she said, examining the metal.

She moved around the room, inspecting each piece. Meanwhile, Mari felt her disappointment growing. They'd come all this way only to find remnants. No answers.

"We tried," Kalindi said quietly.

Mari shook her head. "Something happened here. We're on the right path. I know it."

She glanced up through the ceiling openings. The skies had darkened, the auroras above blazing with a much more intense brilliance than the night before. Vivid greens and pinks swirled above, almost pulsating with energy.

"The auroras are getting even stronger," Mari whispered, pulling out her map. "Look, we're here. The outpost is there. The auroras around here were faint just a few days ago, but look at them now! Whatever the Stewards are doing, it's accelerating."

Kalindi stared at the glowing sky, her jaw tight. "And you think this..." She gestured to the cave walls. "...is part of it?"

Mari nodded, her mind racing. "This place is connected to Adavale. I'm sure of it. And there must be more. Check the map again."

Kalindi handed it over. Mari's eyes scanned the markings, her finger landing on a spot farther south and to the east. "Brindlemyre," she said. "We need to go."

Kalindi frowned. "That's a huge town. You really think they'd risk exposure there?"

Mari's thoughts raced. "I... I don't know," she confessed. She was starting to feel completely confused.

"Mari, we need to get back to Greenhaven. Your people are waiting for us."

Mari's eyes flashed. "I already told you, This isn't just about Greenhaven. The Stewards are planning something catastrophic. If we don't stop it—"

Kalindi threw her arms up, her frustration boiling over. "Stop! Do you want to help your town or do you want to chase shadows and stories?"

Mari's mouth gaped open, insulted. "Why are you so against looking into this?"

"I just want to get back to Greenhaven and implement my systems. It's important!" Kalindi snapped back.

"What systems? What are you talking about, Kalindi? What's so important that you're willing to just ignore whatever this is?" Mari gestured to the cave and the metals around them.

"It's complicated, but I can build something that will generate water, and I have a design for a system of water canals that will eventually direct the water throughout the different areas of the village as well. That's part one, anyway. Part two is...complicated. I'm still thinking it through."

"Does it have anything to do with this?" Mari reached into her pocket and pulled out the parchment that Lyra had given her back on the hilltop in Elyria's Edge, covered in the elaborate drawings that looked similar to those on the walls of the caves.

"Yes," Kalindi said simply.

"When were you going to fill me in on the fact that you clearly know more about this than you're letting on?"

"It's complicated."

"It's complicated, it's complicated, it's SO complicated!" The sarcasm in Mari's voice was rife. "Why don't you let me decide for myself how complicated it is?" She snatched Kalindi's bag from her hands and pulled out the metal pieces that she had just collected. "This isn't a shadow. It's a pattern. And if we don't figure it out, there won't be a Greenhaven left to save."

"There will," Kalindi said softly.

"What do you mean?" Mari glowered. She was tired of the games.

"The Stewards..."

Mari waited for Kalindi to go on. Kalindi inhaled deeply

and leaned back on the cave wall, sliding her back down until she was slumped on the floor.

"The Stewards will sell water back to Greenhaven. Greenhaven will still exist... They'll just be indebted to the Stewards, just like everyone else will be, eventually."

Mari's mind raced. She tried to process what Kalindi was saying. "How do you... what makes you... how do you know?"

"Because I was a Steward."

CHAPTER EIGHTEEN

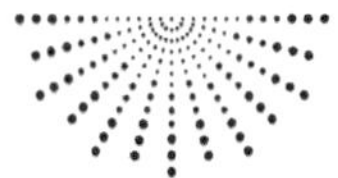

Mari shook her head and rubbed her temples. "Tell me again. Slower this time, please. I'm... I think I'm getting there."

Kalindi sighed. She had already explained it twice, but she went through it again with profound patience. Her grandfather was one of the most powerful high-level executives of the Stewards, and their work on what was known as "The Echo Project" is what caused the atmospheric shifts, which resulted in the auroras and the perceived distortion in the night sky.

Mari's brows furrowed. "So, the stars haven't actually moved?"

Kalindi nodded, her face grim. "Exactly. They're where they've always been. It's the vibrations in the atmosphere that make it look like they've shifted."

"And all this... just so they can control water supplies? Generate it and ration it on their terms?"

Kalindi nodded again. "And sell it back to the villages."

Mari's chest tightened. The enormity of it all—the

manipulation, the suffering caused by something so calculated —was suffocating. Her hand instinctively went to the charm around her neck, gripping it as if it would bring her closer to Lyra. "Does the queen know?" she asked, her voice shaking.

"The Crown is funding it," Kalindi said flatly.

"She's funding it?!"

"No," Kalindi said, still full of patience. "The Crown is funding it. Not the queen herself. The kingdom was infiltrated decades ago. The plans were laid out long before she ascended the throne. The Stewards have been biding their time, experimenting, making sure the technology works. I didn't see it at first. I thought we were developing it ourselves." A bitter laugh escaped her lips. "Now I'm starting to realize..." She looked up at the markings engraved on the ceiling above them.

"It's stolen technology," Mari finished for her, her voice barely above a whisper.

Kalindi nodded, her humiliation clear. "When we were at the ruins, it hit me. All this time, I thought I'd created something revolutionary. What an idiot, thinking I could come up with something as advanced as the Elyrians' systems."

Mari stared at her. "You thought you created it?"

"My grandfather," Kalindi said, her voice tinged with self-loathing, "dripped information to me little by little. He had the framework but couldn't figure out how to make it all work. So he used me. Fed me just enough until I pieced it together."

"You figured it out?" Mari's voice was incredulous.

Kalindi's nod was small, her head hanging low. "And when I realized what I'd done—what it was really for—it was too late. The first device, the one in Adavale, worked perfectly, but a man on the project couldn't keep his mouth shut. He bragged about how we'd control everyone and everything. Got way too excited. Grandfather was livid. Killed him on the spot. Right in front of me." She rubbed her eyes, her voice cracking. "That's when I understood. His talk of growing a flourishing empire? It wasn't about Patovia. It was about the Stewards."

"Why now? Why are they ramping things up?" Mari asked.

"They've been ready for years," Kalindi said, her voice weary. "But the king wouldn't cooperate. He resisted them—he wanted all the power for himself. Anyone with a new idea was a threat."

Mari's eyes bulged wide. "So they had him killed."

Kalindi nodded grimly. "And with him out of the way, they moved forward."

"Bomi." The name left Mari's lips like a curse. Her mind raced, piecing together fragments of conversations and memories of Lyra's warnings. "Bomi IS a Steward." Her blood ran cold. "I need to warn the queen," she said, her voice rising as she whistled for Rih.

"No, you can't!" Kalindi grabbed Mari's arm, her grip firm. "Don't you see? If you tell her now, you're putting her at even greater risk. The less she knows, the safer she is."

Mari shook her head, pulling free. "The Stewards are running Patovia, Kalindi. She needs to know!"

"She's not clueless, Mari. She probably doesn't even want to know... She strikes me as someone who willfully looks the other way and keeps her hands clean by never digging too deep."

Mari fumed. "She's being used. You have no idea who she is."

Kalindi rolled her eyes. "Neither do you! She's weak. What do you think she will do with that knowledge? Nothing. She doesn't have an ounce of courage in her pretty little body."

"She's not weak," Mari said fiercely.

Kalindi's lip curled. "If she were stronger, none of this would have happened."

Mari glared at her but didn't argue. Instead, she turned back to the auroras above, their colors burning brighter, fiercer, the way she felt inside. "Why did you leave them?"

"What?"

"The Stewards," Mari said.

Kalindi sighed. "When I realized what the project was really trying to achieve, I destroyed the device. Smashed it to pieces. I thought that would be the end of it. And then I ran as far as I could."

"And hid out in Joycita?" Mari asked.

Kalindi nodded. "For four years. I thought I'd done it. I thought I'd saved Patovia. Then I heard about the auroras... and I realized I'd been naive."

"They built another device," Mari guessed.

Kalindi gave a slight nod. "Without me. My guess is that they've been moving it from town to town, setting it up, adjusting the vibrations, and drying up the land. They'll save Elyria's Edge for last."

"Why?" Mari wondered.

"I remember my grandfather promising to take me to the Glowing Gardens one day. Whenever I asked when, he would just say, 'During the final phase.'"

Mari's heart pounded. "And then?"

"The Stewards are strong, Mari. They stretch far and wide. Look how quickly they found me when I poked my head up out of Joycita. They'll mobilize, take Elyria's Edge, build a wall, and use it as their stronghold."

"They always build walls when they've run out of better ideas," Mari said bitterly. She shook her head. She was used to having ideas and coming up with solutions to almost any problem she faced, but in this moment, her mind was blank. "This only works if people are willing to pay for water..."

"They'll pay," Kalindi said with disdain. "The device can be set to another frequency that will harness rain. Villages will have to pay the Stewards to let it rain."

"Do you think Brindlemyre is next?"

"Probably," Kalindi said with a sigh.

"Then let's destroy it again!" Mari said, her eyes blazing.

Kalindi shook her head. "It's not that simple. They'll just rebuild, and we'll get killed trying."

"I can't do nothing," Mari said, struggling to keep her voice level.

Kalindi hesitated. "I've been working on a design—a disruptor. Something that could counteract the vibrations and make their device useless."

Mari's eyes widened. "That's why you're pushing so hard to get to Greenhaven."

Kalindi confirmed with a nod. "It's the safest place to build it. The mountains will shield us from prying eyes."

Mari sat silently for a moment, staring at the sky. The auroras danced mockingly above, their beauty taunting her with how little control she had. "Everything's connected," she murmured, echoing Kalindi's earlier words. She blinked back tears, but she was fast becoming overwhelmed by everything she'd learned. "You told me you weren't working with the Stewards," she said, her voice betraying her disappointment.

"And I'm not. Not anymore. I know I should have told you all of this from the start, but once I realized how well-acquainted you were with the queen..." Kalindi trailed off, running a hand through her hair. "I was scared you'd turn around and tell her everything."

Mari flushed, her thoughts darting to how quickly she had been willing to send Rih off with a warning.

"But also," Kalindi continued, her voice tight, "I'm so deeply ashamed of my involvement..." She hung her head, wiping her eyes with her arm. When she looked back up, her faint smile was brittle. "It's stupid, isn't it? Thinking I could outrun my past."

Mari reached out instinctively, her hand resting gently on Kalindi's hair, stroking it once. "I'm sorry if working with me put a spotlight on you," she said.

Kalindi sniffed. "It's not your fault."

"Do you think Bomi knows who you are?"

Kalindi gave a small shrug. "There has to be a reason I was chosen to help you. I think... I think they set us up, not expecting us to succeed."

"Explains the assassin."

Kalindi nodded grimly. "So... shall we head to Greenhaven? Build my device? We have everything we need."

"Kalindi, your new device... I'm afraid the elders will never approve of this kind of technology."

"They won't have a choice unless they want to see Greenhaven crumble."

THEY CUT through the Isa Glades, doing their best to keep a steady pace, but as they trudged deeper into the lowlands, the landscape turned against them. What was once firm, green terrain gave way to a swampy expanse of hot mud, tangled roots, and buzzing insects that seemed hellbent on ensuring neither of them made it out unscathed. Overhead, Rih drifted in slow circles, patiently waiting for them to choose a path and actually commit to it for more than ten steps.

"This is definitely not the way we came in," Mari said, tugging her boot free from the muck with a squelch. "Are you sure you know where we're going?"

Kalindi shot her an incredulous look, her arms full of long, thin reeds she had gathered along the way. "Am I sure? You're the one with the fancy astrolabe, remember? You tell me where we are!"

Mari huffed and pulled the astrolabe from her satchel. She flicked it open, scanning the faint alignment of stars through the hazy evening sky. "I'd love to help, but it's hard to chart a course when half the constellations are hidden behind... whatever that is." She gestured vaguely toward a thick plume of swamp mist rolling toward them like a lazy ghost.

Kalindi, now kneeling by a clump of marsh grass, held up one of the reeds triumphantly. "We're not lost, Mari. I know exactly where we are."

Mari raised an eyebrow. "Oh, really? Enlighten me."

Kalindi grinned, holding up the reed as if it were a trophy. "This is *Typha Patovica*. Common cattail, but the marsh variety. It only grows near running water. That means if we follow this," she gestured vaguely with her reed, as if pointing into the abyss of mist, "we'll find a stream."

Mari squinted at the reed in her hand. "That's your big plan? Follow the weeds?"

"They're reeds, not weeds," Kalindi corrected with mock indignation, brushing mud off her pants. "And yes. These reeds are my backup plan. My primary plan is all on your shoulders, Starry Mari."

Mari scowled at her, regretting sharing that story with her the night before. "I'll follow you and your reeds," she said. "You can take the lead. Just so you know, though, if they lead us to a crocodile instead of a stream, I'm not saving you this time."

Kalindi stood, clutching her collection of plants like they were priceless artifacts. "If I lead us to a crocodile, I'll wrestle it myself. You can watch and cheer me on."

They stared at each other for a moment and then both burst out laughing.

A candlemark later, they were still wading through the deep marsh, both soaked to the knees and covered in a variety of questionable substances, considerably less agreeable. Somewhere above, they could hear Rih's occasional warble, faint and muffled, but any hope of following her had been lost to the dense fog curling just above their heads, blocking out the sky save for a few scattered, shifting gaps.

Mari squatted on a slick rock, staring up through tiny pockets in the mist-obscured sky while Kalindi fiddled with her reeds nearby.

"Any luck with the stars?" Kalindi called, waving a particularly muddy reed in the air like a flag.

"I swear they're mocking me," Mari said, her tone equal parts frustration and amusement. "I'm starting to think the stars shifted just to spite me."

Kalindi snorted. "Yes, the universe conspired against you, specifically."

Mari ignored her, focusing instead on the faint glimmer of a constellation breaking through the mist. "Wait! There's Quirkey's Loom!" she said, pointing skyward. "It's low in the sky. That means...factoring in the shift...we need to head..." She turned an abrupt ninety-degree angle from the direction they had been heading. "This way."

Kalindi grinned. "See? I told you we'd get out of here."

"You told me we'd follow weeds—sorry, reeds—and hope

for the best," Mari shot back. "Looks like this head of mine, fixed so firmly in the stars, has saved the day."

Kalindi chuckled. "All right, fine. Lead the way, Navigator."

As they trudged in their new direction, the ground grew firmer and the mist began to thin. Just as Mari was about to declare victory, Kalindi suddenly stopped, her hand shooting out to grab Mari's arm.

"What now?" Mari asked, alarmed.

Kalindi pointed ahead. A massive, mud-coated shape loomed in the distance. Mari's heart leapt into her throat. "Is that... a crocodile?" she whispered.

Kalindi squinted, then burst into laughter. "No, it's a log."

Mari frowned, her heart still racing. "It's the size of a horse!"

"Congratulations, you've discovered the rare and elusive Horse-Log," Kalindi said, wiping tears of laughter from her eyes. "Quick, chart us a safe course before it attacks."

Mari shoved Kalindi playfully. "You're impossible."

"You're the one who keeps me around," Kalindi teased, giving her a light shove back.

By the time they finally stumbled out of the swamp and onto solid ground, both were grinning through their exhaustion. The ordeal had left them muddy, sore, and mosquito-bitten. Despite all that, their spirits were high.

CHAPTER NINETEEN

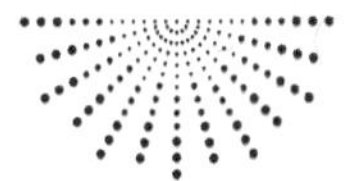

After two days of steady travel, they found themselves in Adavale once more. Mari insisted on returning to the inn she had stayed at originally, assuring Kalindi that she would love Gil, the friendly barkeep, and his just as lovely wife, Ellin.

Gil greeted them warmly, his face lighting up as he welcomed them back. "Well, our Mysterious Mari and Rambunctious Rih are back again, and with a traveling companion." He beamed and cast a glance over a very dirty Kalindi.

Rih puffed up proudly.

"Kalindi," Mari supplied.

Gil gave Kalindi a welcoming nod. "Come in, come in. I'll bet you haven't had a proper meal in days."

Mari grinned. "You're the best, Gil."

"All part of the service," the innkeeper said with a wink, ushering them inside.

Kalindi eyed the flaking paint on the doorway and the carpet that had all but worn away to the dirt floor below as they entered. "I was hoping for something... less likely to fall over," she whispered, shooting a side-eye look at Mari, who hushed her with a quick frown.

THE COZY DINING room smelled like heaven, and the duo picked a table as close to the fire as they could get without actually dining in the embers. Ellin had insisted they get comfortable while she prepared something "special." Around them, locals nursed their drinks and chatted cheerfully, not so loud that they had to struggle to hear each other, but not so quiet that they felt they had to keep their voices hushed to discuss their next steps.

When the plates arrived, they were heaped with tender roast duck, glazed with honey and herbs, served alongside roasted root vegetables and a chunky slice of crusty bread slathered with fresh butter, plus a bowl of fresh fruit for good measure. For Rih, a bowl of deep burgundy organs, more than likely from the same duck.

"This," Kalindi said, staring at the food as if it were a rare fern from the Glowing Gardens, "might be the best thing I've ever seen."

"You haven't even tasted it yet," Mari said, tearing into a piece of bread.

Kalindi took a bite of the duck, her eyes widening. "Okay, correction. This is the best thing I've ever tasted."

Ellin beamed from across the room. "They like the food, Gil!" she shouted to her husband as she made her way back into the kitchen. Gil was serving a pair of customers at the bar but shot the pair a thumbs up as they tucked into their steaming meals.

As they ate, the conversation flowed more easily than usual. The warm atmosphere and full bellies seemed to lower Kalindi's defenses, and Mari took the opportunity to push.

"You never told me how you got into botany," she said, mopping up a pool of honey with a piece of bread.

Kalindi paused, her fork stabbing at a chunk of charred pumpkin. "My mother," she said finally. "She loved plants. Our garden was her pride and joy."

"Did she teach you?"

Kalindi nodded. "She used to say plants had their own language. If you listened closely, they'd tell you what they needed."

"That's beautiful," Mari said sincerely.

"Yeah, it was... for a while." Kalindi drained her glass. "What she didn't tell me was that sometimes, you can learn more from what's silent than what's loud. Plants don't scream when they're dying—they just... fade. Quietly. And if you don't pay attention, you'll miss it. I guess people aren't all that different."

Mari studied her for a moment, smiling. "You're full of surprises, Kalindi."

Kalindi shrugged, focusing on her plate. "What about you? How'd you end up with your head in the stars?"

Mari's smile faltered. "Searsan," she said, her heart giving a little stab. "He always said the stars told stories. I wanted to hear them all."

"And did you?"

"Sometimes," Mari said, with a sigh. "And sometimes, I just made up my own."

Kalindi's chuckle was low and genuine, something Mari wasn't used to hearing from the engineer. "Figures. You don't seem like the type to wait for answers."

"And you seem like the type who already knows them."

Kalindi looked away. "Not always."

The moment was interrupted by Ellin. "Shall we have some pudding, girls?" She hovered a foot back, as if realizing too late that she had interrupted an awkward moment.

"Oooh, what do you think, Mari?" Kalindi asked, shaking off the darkness in her face and giving an over-the-top nod.

Ellin clasped her hands together, rubbing them gleefully, and headed back to the kitchen.

Mari laughed. "Oh, this is going to be good," she said, her mouth watering.

Kalindi grinned, raising her almost-empty mug. "To Ellin."

"Hey," Gil's mock-hurt voice appeared over them as he set down two fresh mugs of cider.

"To Gil!" Mari said with a grin, flashing Gil a wink.

"That's better," the barkeep said, scooping up their empty plates.

"To not getting lost in a swamp again," Mari added.

They both laughed, clinking their mugs together, and for a moment, Mari almost found herself relaxing.

LATER, as they prepared for bed in their small shared room, the energy between them felt lighter.

"I'm glad you suggested this place," Kalindi said, sitting on her bed and pulling off her boots. "It's... cozy."

"Told you," Mari said, grinning. "I'm always right."

Kalindi rolled her eyes. "Don't push it."

"I'm going to chart a little," Mari said. "Would you like to join me?"

Kalindi punched her pillow to fluff it. "Absolutely... not. I enjoyed the stories, but I'm getting as much sleep as I can."

Mari looked at Rih. "You coming?"

Rih fluttered down from the bedpost and landed gently on Mari's shoulder.

MARI INHALED a deep breath of fresh evening air as she sat comfortably cross-legged on the flat rooftop of the inn. She took a moment to let herself just exist, to be a smaller part of a greater whole. Around her, insects chirped, the occasional dog barked, and the distant grunts of the drovak from the paddocks just outside the village walls made her miss home. She was glad to be headed back. She put the parchment down, sliding it under her satchel to keep it from blowing away.

She leaned back on her elbows and gazed upward. The height offered solace, a peacefulness she'd grown to crave. Perhaps it was a trauma response after Elyria's Edge, or perhaps it was her yearning for familiarity—it reminded her of the observatory back in Greenhaven. Up here, she was closer to the stars.

The sky was veiled with thin clouds, not perfect for charting the skies, but just clear enough for Mari to make it work. Light from the aurora scattered through, and the streaks of green danced with a wild fervor, stretching through the backdrop of deep pink, even brighter than it had been just days before. She thought of Searsan as she watched the stars peek occasionally through the light cloud floating overhead. She was on the edge of understanding this entire thing. Kalindi's revelation from the Isa Glades certainly filled in a lot of the blanks.

She lay back fully, the world tilting away as her gaze fixed on the heavens. Her mind churned over Kalindi's words about her mother and their garden. What kind of woman could inspire such passion in someone as guarded as Kalindi? There had to have been a time when she wasn't so closed off. Mari was determined to crack that shell, to become someone Kalindi could trust. It was painfully clear that Kalindi trusted no one but herself. Kalindi's words to Jannah's mother echoed in her mind: *Everything hums. Everything has a heartbeat.* Mari let the night wind caress her face, her fingers stretching skyward. The breeze rushed through them like threads of silk, carrying with it a strange energy.

Realization ripped through her, and her eyes flew open. The air had changed. She bolted upright and grabbed her astrolabe, her hands trembling. She trained it skyward, watching the clouds drift.

They shifted in peculiar ways, their movements erratic, their heights uneven. Mari stilled her breathing to feel the air around her... The pressure had dropped. It was subtle, the kind of change you could only detect if you were paying close attention. Her heart quickened.

"Hep! Hep! Hep!" Mari shouted into the night, her voice ringing out loudly. She paused, tilting her head to listen as the sound bounced back, distorted. It was almost as if it was being pulled off course.

Rih's answering screech startled her, the bird wheeling high in the sky above, her dark wings slicing through the auroras' glow.

Mari cupped her hands around her mouth and called again, her voice louder this time. The vibrations carried farther, catapulting across the treetops, but still drifting to the left. She settled herself, shutting her eyes to the world and letting her senses guide her. It felt like the entire atmosphere was vibrating in a way she had never felt before. She stood still, letting the wind whip her hair and clothes as she shouted once more. "Hep! Hep!" The echoes pulled left again, bending her voice unnaturally, and she was now completely convinced. Rih swooped down, her flight uncharacteristically unsteady as she landed awkwardly on Mari's shoulder, possessing none of her usual grace.

Mari struggled to think fast, weighing up her discoveries. She felt a tingle of satisfaction as she realized she had caught the signs far earlier than she ever had before. A storm was coming. And it was going to be a big one.

She scrambled down the ladder as fast as her numb feet would allow her to move, her entire body shaking. A storm of this magnitude wasn't supposed to happen outside of the Cinder Dunes, but then again, auroras shouldn't be blazing above her right now, so logic was out the window.

Bursting into their shared room, she found Kalindi sprawled across the bed, a hand flung lazily over her eyes.

"Kalindi! Wake up!"

Kalindi groaned, rubbing her eyes as she sat up. "What now?"

"Listen!" Mari paced the room, her hands flying as she explained. "There's a windstorm coming!"

Kalindi gave her a skeptical look and sat on the edge of her bed. "A windstorm? This far west? That doesn't happen."

Mari strode to the window and wrenched it open. The curtains billowed gently in the soft breeze, the earlier gusts having calmed. She winced at the underwhelming stillness... It was the ultimate anticlimax.

"Oh, wow, brace the beams; she's a big one," Kalindi said with a yawn, flopping back down onto her pillow.

"No, it's brewing, I'm telling you. The air pressure has shifted, and the echoes... I listened to the vibrations, like you said... It's coming, and it's big, Kalindi. I'd bet my life on it."

Kalindi sat up and crossed her arms, skeptical but not dismissive. "You're predicting this storm based on vibrations and echoes?"

Mari planted her hands on her hips, meeting Kalindi's gaze head-on. "You told me to trust you with the echo project. How about you try trusting me, too?"

Kalindi sighed and leaned back against the wall. "Fine. How long do we have?"

"My guess is around ten days until it reaches here. Maybe less. But Greenhaven... it'll probably hit in a week."

Kalindi shot to her feet. "Then we leave now. Push as hard as we can. We need to get there, build the device, and get out again before it hits."

Mari nodded, grabbing her gear. "We should take a different route this time. I don't want to run into those thieving fops again."

"I'm sure they'd love a rematch, though." Kalindi laughed.

Mari went to retort, but she paused, drawn to the clouds she could see in the sky outside. "Look at that formation—it's thinning on one side but staying dense on the other. That shouldn't happen unless something's disrupting the flow, right?"

Kalindi smiled as she followed Mari's pointing finger. "You're smarter than I gave you credit for, you know?" she said.

Mari blinked, caught off guard by the compliment. "Thanks, I guess," she said, catching her satchel as Kalindi tossed it to her from across the room.

"Let's go," Kalindi said, breaking eye contact and shaking off the moment.

Mari rolled her eyes. This engineer just would not allow her to get close.

"What happened to you, Kalindi? You've got walls higher than the castle gates in Joycita. Why?"

Kalindi's face darkened, and she stiffened. "The topic is off-limits, okay? I trust you. I wouldn't be here if I didn't. And believe me; that means more than you know. But some things stay buried."

Mari frowned but didn't press.

"Right," Kalindi said, hoisting her pack. "We'd better move it."

Mari scribbled a quick note to Ellin and Gil to explain their sudden departure.

As they stepped out into the night, the wind whispered gently through the streets of Adavale, and Mari suddenly started to question her decision.

"Kalindi, I..."

"Don't doubt yourself now, Stargazer." Kalindi said, giving Mari's shoulder a playful punch. Mari grinned despite herself and quickened her strides to match Kalindi's. Together, they veered sharply to the right, passing through the narrow doorway in the village walls that opened to the open stretch ahead, the stench of ungroomed drovak hitting them in the face instantly.

CHAPTER TWENTY

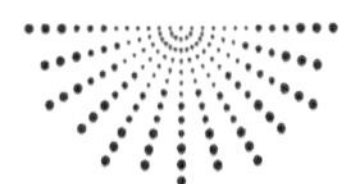

Mari blinked back the sting of happy tears as Greenhaven appeared on the horizon, a tiny dot at first, growing steadily more distinct with each step. The sight of her home stirred a whirlwind of emotions—relief, anticipation, and a longing so fierce it made her chest ache.

Overhead, Rih chirped excitedly, looping in wide, eager arcs as the familiar hills came into view, her joy as palpable as Mari's.

As they neared, the sensory rush of her surroundings hit Mari like a brick wall, and she had to resist the overwhelming urge to break into a run, burst into the commons, and hug every Greenhavener she saw.

Kalindi grabbed Mari's cloak and yanked her back. "We can't let anyone know we're back," she said, her voice low.

Mari frowned, her joy faltering. "Kalindi, this is Greenhaven. I know you find it hard to trust people, but I promise you—we haven't been infiltrated."

Rih let out an impatient trill, ready to make her grand

return, dipping low before reluctantly rising higher into the sky, as if even she understood the need to stay out of sight.

Kalindi's glance cut through Mari's optimism. "Unless you can be one hundred percent certain of that, we need to lay low."

Mari wanted to argue, but the truth was she couldn't be absolutely sure. How long had she been gone? Long enough for strangers to come and go unnoticed. She sighed begrudgingly. "Fine. I'm going to find my cousin, though, and that's not up for discussion. Zeph can help us gather supplies, bring food, and connect us with the elders. You'll need their support if we're going to make this work. Besides, we still have to warn everyone about the windstorm."

Kalindi tilted her head, considering this. Finally, she gave a reluctant nod. "Only Zeph. And we stay out of sight until nightfall."

They crouched under the cover of dense shrubbery, Kalindi idly plucking a sprig from a nearby bush. She brushed it along her palm and the crook of her arm absentmindedly. Mari smiled, the gesture stirring childhood memories. She had done the same thing with her school friends—brushing leaves across each other's arms during story time, delighting in the shivers and goosebumps the simple motion would provoke. As they reviewed their plans, Mari kept a watchful eye on the shifting air pressure and the steady winds, still indicating an impending storm. She felt restless, though, and she knew she couldn't fully settle until her feet were back on the familiar soil of Greenhaven.

As the first hues of twilight painted the sky, Mari took the lead, crouching low as she darted along the back fence of a paddock on the village outskirts. They skirted her family's property, slipping unnoticed into the shadows of the observatory her father had built for her. The old wooden structure was a tight squeeze for two adults, but it would work for now.

Rih had flown up to the treetops the moment they arrived. The small skyweaver perched on a high branch, scanning the field below with an air of satisfaction, clearly recognizing the familiar terrain. She let out a soft screech, her eyes gleaming in the fading light.

Mari glanced up, a smile creeping across her face. "She's happy to be home," she said. "Probably more than I am."

Kalindi gave a wry chuckle as she watched Rih's head flick from left to right, looking everywhere, all at once. "Seems like she's already settled in."

"Stay close, Rih!" Mari called, cupping her hand around her mouth to keep her voice low.

Rih gave a twitch of her head in what Mari could only hope was acknowledgment, clearly more interested in scouting for dinner than listening.

Mari shook her head fondly. "She'll stick to the trees," she said with confidence. "She knows this place. She won't stray far."

Kalindi gave a nod of approval. "Smart bird. She's earned the rest."

Mari smiled as she dropped her pack and lowered herself onto the floor of the observatory, comforted by the rustling leaves overhead and the knowledge that Rih was still up there, keeping watch.

Kalindi followed suit, sitting cross-legged, rustling through her pack, and fishing out her notes. "These are the materials I still need for the anti-echo device," she said, handing the list over to Mari. She zipped her pack back up and leaned against it, her head rolling back to convey her lack of energy.

Mari read the parchment and nodded. "I'll get Zeph right away. Anything else?"

Kalindi grinned. "Some of those famous dates sound pretty great right about now."

"Lemon or salted?"

"Yes," Kalindi replied, her grin widening.

Mari laughed and disappeared down the ladder, leaving Rih perched nearby with Kalindi, who definitely looked relieved to have the skyweaver's company while Mari would be gone.

THE JOURNEY to Zeph's room felt like muscle memory. Mari hopped the red dirt wall, keeping low enough that she wouldn't be seen from the kitchen on the off chance that her aunt was still awake at this time. Her foot slipped as she swung herself up, misjudging the effort required and toppling onto the balcony floor with a graceless thud. She froze, listening for her aunt Kia's footsteps from below. When no one came, she pushed aside the fluttering tapestry that she herself had made and gifted to Zeph for their fifteenth Lumithra and stepped into Zeph's room.

She crept toward his bed to wake him, but before she could, someone grabbed her suddenly from behind. An arm hooked around her neck, squeezing tight. Reacting instinctively, Mari bent her knees and thrust her hip, flipping her assailant over her shoulder. They landed on the bed with a crash, and she winced as her hand struck the edge of the bedframe.

"Mari?!"

She blinked, realizing the figure sprawled before her was none other than her only cousin, Zeph, his head dangling upside down off the bed as he gaped at her in disbelief.

"Zeph!" she hissed, clutching her throbbing hand.

He scrambled upright and pulled her into a bear hug. "What do you think you're doing?! Couldn't just use the front door like a normal person?"

Mari laughed, squeezing him as tightly as she could before stepping back to take him in. He looked gaunt. "Gods, you look terrible!" she said, her tone half teasing, half concerned.

"And you're not exactly the radiant queen of Patovia," he shot back with a grin.

"She is radiant, by the way," Mari said with a wink. "Most gorgeous woman I've ever seen."

Zeph rolled his eyes. "Figures. You go to the capital to save the world and end up swooning over royalty."

"Who said anything about swooning?" Mari retorted, giving him a playful shove.

"Nice moves, by the way," Zeph said, rubbing his shoulder where he'd landed. "You've kept your wits sharp."

"You have no idea," Mari said, but before she could launch into her tale, a voice bellowed from below.

"Zeph!"

"Yes, Mother?"

"If I have to tell you one more time—bring that nice girl through the front door, or don't bring her at all!"

Mari raised an eyebrow. "Nice girl?"

Zeph waved her off, brushing past her to the balcony. "Come on, before she comes up here and makes tea for everyone. Let's go to the farm."

"Who does she think I am?" Mari asked, desperately curious to know the answer..

"Uh... we'll talk about that later," Zeph mumbled, vaulting over the wall.

Mari followed more gracefully this time, landing lightly beside him. As they headed toward their grandparents' farm, a location where they knew they could safely talk without being witnessed, she began to recount the events of her journey, and Zeph listened intently, his expression darkening with every revelation.

ZEPH HAD BEEN DRAGGING his feet for most of their walk, offering grumbles about "this Kalindi person," and Mari's patience was wearing thin. Every time she mentioned Kalindi's name, he made a noise—whether it was a scoff, a snort, or some other creative display of disapproval, he made it clear exactly how he felt about their new engineer.

"Okay, look," Mari finally snapped, stopping mid-row and turning to face him. "You have to give her a chance. She told me everything."

Zeph leaned against one of the date palms, arms crossed and one eyebrow raised in mock curiosity. "Yeah? After how long hiding it from you? Would she even have said anything if you two had come straight to Greenhaven? You backed her into a corner, Mari. She had no choice but to admit it. She's a liar, and I don't trust her. Neither should you."

Mari frowned. She wasn't sure how any of this was going to work without Zeph's support. If she couldn't even convince him to give Kalindi a chance, what hope did she have of persuading the elders? And she had to tell the elders the whole truth, no matter how complicated that made things.

"Okay, well," she said with a forced cheerfulness, trying to redirect the conversation, "can we focus on food first, please? And figuring out where we should lay low? I was planning on using the observatory, but Father built that for 12-year-old Mari, not a fully grown adult Mari... plus one."

A mischievous glint creeped into Zeph's eye. "I know exactly where we can go," he said. "Frankly, I'm disappointed in you that you didn't think of it first."

Mari cocked her head curiously. "The granary rafters?" she guessed. "I did think of that, but I don't know how big this device is that Kalindi is planning to build. I don't fancy our chances of carrying it down those ladders without someone breaking a leg."

Zeph rolled his eyes dramatically, pushed off the tree, and began jogging down the orchard row. "Hey!" Mari called after him, quickening her pace to catch up.

By the time she saw where he was headed, Mari's cheeks flushed with embarrassment. Of course. How had she not thought of it? "The prop cellar," she breathed. "Zeph, you're a genius!"

"I know," he said, throwing her a wink as he raced ahead to the sage-green double trap doors at the far end of the orchard.

Nestled into the side of a gently sloping hill, the propagation cellar was a tribute to the family's dedication and ingenuity. Mari's great-grandfather, great uncle, and grandfather had dug the hillside out and built the cellar together decades prior. Over the years, the cellar had become a sanctuary for the cousins—part workspace, part archive, and part refuge. Even as children, Mari and Zeph had loved sneaking in to marvel at the rows of saplings and jars, much to their grandfather's chagrin. He'd always grumbled about their muddy footprints disrupting the sacred order of his space, but Mari suspected he secretly enjoyed their curiosity.

Now, it was Zeph who carried on the tradition, meticulously maintaining the cellar with a mix of pride and reverence. This space was as important to the family's future as the orchard itself.

Zeph opened the slanted trap doors with ease, the hinges groaning. "After you," he said with a mock bow.

Moonlight streamed in from the slanted window panels above the propagation tables, illuminating the rows of knee-high date palm saplings lined neatly in clay pots.

For a moment, Mari simply stood there, taking it all in—the propagation tables, the seed storage shelves, and the sturdy workbench where her grandfather's hand-built irrigation system lay waiting. It was all so familiar, so much like home. She grabbed a handful of dates from a nearby crate and brought them to her nose, inhaling deeply, the sweet smell enveloping her soul. Then, she dropped a few carrots into her satchel, looking for anything else she might be able to pilfer while her mind buzzed with plans.

"We'll have to push the prop tables to the side," she said finally, glancing at Zeph to make sure this wasn't an entirely sacrilegious suggestion.

His lips pressed into a tight line, and for a moment, Mari thought he might argue, but then he gave a reluctant nod. "Yeah. Fine. But I take the lead down here, Mari. Please."

"Deal." She gestured toward the steps. "Let's grab some food and head back. You can meet Kalindi, and we'll bring her here to get started."

Zeph scrunched up his face. "Do we have to?"

"Yes, we have to," Mari said firmly. She glared at him,

crossing her arms for good measure. "And you will be nice, Zepharon of Greenhaven."

"No promises," he said, but his voice lacked the venom it had carried earlier.

As Mari started up the steps, she paused at the shelves near the entrance of the propagation cellar, her eyes catching on a row of unfamiliar jars filled with golden, mahogany, and amber-colored liquids. She picked one up, turning the long, thin bottle in her hand to examine the label: "Rosemary Date Seed Oil."

"What's all this?" she asked, looking over her shoulder at Zeph.

"Oh, that," Zeph said, brightening. He stepped closer, grabbing a bottle of his own and holding it up like a prized trophy. "I've been experimenting. Oils, syrups, all kinds of blends. Trying to see if we can expand our presence in the food market. You know, take the Greenhaven name beyond dates, salt, and skyweavers."

"Experimenting?"

Zeph grinned. "Yeah, experimenting. Look at this." He reached for another jar and held it up. "Date syrup with garlic. Sounds weird, but trust me—it's incredible. You dip fresh bread in this stuff, and I swear you'll die of happiness."

Mari made a face, skeptical but intrigued. "Date and garlic? As a syrup?!"

"I'm serious, Mari. Grab a bottle. I'll swing by the house and nab a fresh loaf of bread on the way."

Mari slid the jar into her satchel and hummed in interest. "This could be the way to crack Kalindi's shell. The girl does like to eat."

"I'm not looking to get to her heart. I'll be happy if she does what she needs to do and is on her way back to Joycita," Zeph said.

Mari shrugged, her grin unfazed. "Well, you never know. Food works wonders. Speaking of which... Aunt Kia's going to kill you for stealing a loaf," Mari said knowingly.

"I'll tell her it's for Lana," Zeph replied so casually that it took Mari a second to process what he'd said.

Mari's head snapped away from the jar she was inspecting, suddenly no longer interested in rosemary-infused oils. "Lana?" she asked, her voice rising slightly. "Lana, the blacksmith's apprentice?"

Zeph rubbed the back of his neck awkwardly, looking down at the dirt floor. "Uh... yeah."

"You two..." Mari's voice trailed off.

"Yeahhhh." Zeph said, grinning sheepishly, although it quickly morphed into a wince. "I'm sorry... She said you two weren't... Uh..." He was struggling, the unimpressed look on Mari's face not helping one bit. "And honestly, it started because she missed you, and—"

Mari waved her hands frantically, cutting him off. "Eurgh! Stop, stop, stop! No, thank you, I don't think I require the details. That's... great, if that's what both of you want."

Zeph grimaced, shifting awkwardly. "I'm not sure it's more than just... you know, what it is right now." He scrunched up his face, baring his teeth in an expression that made Mari snort despite herself. She did know. Intimately.

"Oof, poor Lana," she said.

"No, I mean, she was the one who—"

"Arghhh, stop! Stop! Remember I said no details!" Mari interrupted, holding up both hands like a shield. "No details! I'm quite aware of how forward that woman can be... with the eyes, and the glances, and the hands—"

"Yes! The hands! She's strong!"

"She's a blacksmith, you fop; what do you expect?"

Zeph's laughter echoed off the cellar walls. "Anyway," he, recovering, "Mother really likes her. She wants it more than we do, I think."

"Well, Aunt Kia and Lana's sister work together in the infantry kitchens," Mari said. "That's probably why."

They both fell silent for a moment, the conversation halting awkwardly. Mari was acutely aware of the sudden discomfort she felt. She had no right to feel this way—not about Lana, not about Zeph. Whatever had existed between her and Lana was long over, and she had no claim on her.

Still, the idea of Lana lingered, sparking an idea in her mind. "Wait!" she said suddenly. "We should ask Lana to help us."

Zeph tilted his head. "What?"

"She's got access to all the materials on this list," Mari said, her excitement building. "We could borrow her tools, and anything we can't do down here, she could do in the forge and bring it back to us."

"You think she'll go for it?"

Mari shrugged. "I think if anyone can talk her into it, it's you."

Zeph rubbed his neck again. "I actually think you might have a better chance."

Mari raised her eyebrow again.

Zeph dropped his voice to a whisper. "She talks about you a LOT, Mari."

Mari groaned. "Ohhh, this is going to be SO delightfully awkward."

"It'll be a nightmare, but it's a smart idea. And I think she'll be down."

Mari gave him a sly smile. "Well, if date and garlic syrup doesn't work, you can always woo her with your charm."

Zeph laughed. "I'm pretty sure it's your charm she's interested in."

"Let's just get this food to Kalindi and go from there," Mari said.

Zeph scoffed at the mention of the engineer's name.

"Good ancient gods, Zeph!" Mari shoved him back up the steps as she made her way out into the night.

THE GROUP SAT on the grass beneath the observatory, their modest meal spread out before them. Mari had taken great care to portion out the food—dried dates, a loaf of stolen bread, the carrots, and Zeph's date and garlic syrup.

"Dip the bread," Zeph encouraged her way too enthusiastically. "I'm telling you; it'll change your life."

Mari obliged, tearing a piece of bread and swirling it in the glistening syrup. The flavors hit her tongue all at once: sweet at first, with a garlicky tang that balanced perfectly. She let out a surprised hum of approval. Even Kalindi, hesitant at first, couldn't suppress her smile after taking a bite.

"Alright, that is good," Kalindi admitted begrudgingly. "You might actually be onto something."

Zeph preened at the compliment but said nothing, keeping his eyes fixed on the leaves above them that swished in the evening breeze.

Rih made quick work of a few plump Greenhaven voles, clearly thrilled to be back hunting on familiar ground and looking quite pleased with herself and her all-you-can-eat countryside buffet.

As they ate, Mari and Kalindi began discussing their next steps. "We need to get down to the prop cellar and set up the space," Kalindi said. "Lay out all the materials; figure out what we have and what we still need."

Zeph, behaving, refrained from scoffing. Instead, he leaned back against the tree trunk, his arms crossed. "Why can't we just go public with this?" he asked. "Expose the Stewards and let everyone see the corruption for what it is? If we trigger a revolt, the militia will back us. We can destroy them."

Kalindi laughed. "That's exactly why we can't do that," she said obnoxiously. "You think the villages of Patovia—spread out and barely scraping by—are going to unite into some kind of organized front? Against the Stewards, who've been consolidating power for decades? Their plan is too far along. They have near-total control over the Crown, which means no support from the royal militia. The queen has her supporters, sure, but her network is small and disorganized. They act without strategy and take hit after hit because of it."

Zeph glanced at Mari with a look that silently questioned why she hadn't mentioned this before. Mari could only offer a clueless shrug in response.

Kalindi pressed on. "She can barely sneak out of the castle for a midnight kiss without arousing suspicion."

Mari's cheeks flushed hot in the low light. "She managed to get out long enough to meet me in Elyria's Edge that night," she said defensively.

Kalindi turned to her, surprised. "She did?"

Zeph gloated. "Guess you're not the only one keeping secrets."

Mari's fist found his arm with a swift punch. "I didn't know if I could trust you," she admitted. "It was right before our... visitor." Her words trailed off, and she shook off the memory of that harrowing night. "She has people in the castle helping her," she added quickly, hoping it would be enough to make Kalindi see this wasn't as hopeless as it seemed.

Kalindi sighed, her frustration clear. "Yes, she has people. Chambermaids, cooks, stablehands—sure, they might help her fake a quick day trip to visit her flame of the month. But they're not strategists, Mari. They don't hold any real power. Don't you see? The Stewards hold all the power. They've built an empire of fear and control, and they've stacked the deck against us."

Mari noticed the suggestion that she was nothing but a 'flame of the month,' but she let the comment slide, noticing how tightly wound Kalindi had become.

"If we've learned anything from General Clar, it's that subterfuge is the only way. We need to outsmart the Stewards, not overpower them," Kalindi pushed.

Zeph screwed his face up. "Outsmart them with your devices? The same device that started this whole mess in the first place?" His eyes narrowing at Kalindi. "You're a manipulator, Kalindi. And a liar."

Kalindi didn't even so much as blink. "You're half right," she said calmly. "I am a liar. But I'm not manipulative. I call it like it is and I suffer the consequences. Sure, I'm a liar; hell, I'm even a traitor... but I'm trying to make it right."

"What do you mean?" Mari asked quietly.

Kalindi opened her mouth, but the words seemed to catch in her throat. She shook her head. "I'm finished. Can we go?" She stood abruptly, brushing crumbs off her hands. "It's going to be getting light soon, and I want to be set up and ready to work as soon as we have everything."

"I need to sleep," Mari confessed, lying back against the grass.

"Then sleep," Kalindi said. "But the air pressure hasn't changed. The windstorm is coming. If we can't get this built and get to Brindlemyre before it hits, we might not be able to stop the expansion. If they take Brindlemyre, they'll control the end of the Myramin River. It'll be like dominoes falling from there."

Zeph nodded with a grim reluctance. "I'll head to Lana's at first light," he said, not looking at Kalindi.

They packed up their things in silence.

CHAPTER TWENTY-ONE

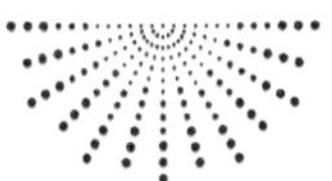

THE FIRST RAYS OF DAWN WERE CREEPING OVER THE hills by the time they arrived at the propagation cellar. Kalindi stepped inside, and her eyes widened as she took in the space. "This is... unbelievable," she breathed, running a hand along the edge of one of the tables. She eyed the potted baby date palms that lined one of the propagation tables against the wall, their tiny green leaves stretching toward the light. "Are these salted dates? Lemon dates?"

"Neither," Zeph said shortly. "It's a new hybrid I'm trying."

"What kind?" Kalindi asked, with genuine curiosity.

"It's none of your business."

Kalindi rolled her eyes. "Relax, I'm not going to steal your ideas. I'm an engineer, not a botanist."

Mari, watching the exchange, couldn't help but interject. "I think you might be both, Kalindi."

Kalindi ignored the comment, her attention drawn to the seed storage shelves. "Look at all these seeds," she wondered, reading the carefully labeled jars. "These are from all over Patovia."

Mari stepped closer and gave a hum of confirmation. "My grandfather collected them. He had all these plans to expand the farm beyond dates, but the hybrids took off so well, he never had the chance."

As Kalindi moved closer to a crate filled with round bulbs, Zeph snapped. "Don't touch my bulbs!"

Kalindi threw her hands up in mock surrender. "Believe me, I'm not looking to touch your bulbs," she said, shooting Mari a look of wide-eyed disbelief.

Zeph pointed to the table. "You can stick to working there."

"Great," Kalindi said briskly, trying to sound unmoved, but Mari knew her well enough by now to see that Zeph's dismissal would have bothered her greatly, and for a fraction of a second, she caught a flash of the hurt in Kalindi's eyes.

By mid-morning, Zeph returned with Lana, who carried a bundle of tools slung over her shoulder. She greeted Mari with a kind smile, pulling her into an embrace, but when she leaned in, aiming for a kiss, Mari stepped back awkwardly. Lana's hurt was immediately obvious, and Mari felt her heart twinge at the look on her face.

"Is this because of Zeph and me?" Lana whispered, pulling Mari into a corner. "Mari, that was just some lighthearted fun... After we spent the night together before you left for Joycita, I thought that you felt there was something between us."

Mari blinked, stunned. "Lana, you said no strings attached!"

"Well, that was before all the—"

"Hey," Mari interrupted, glancing at Kalindi and Zeph, who were openly staring at them. "I don't think we have complete privacy here."

Lana's gaze dropped to the charm around Mari's neck, her

brow furrowing. "What's this?" she asked, reaching out to lift it closer.

"That," Kalindi interrupted smoothly, "is a token of love. A promise, if you will. It says, 'Mari's spoken for.'" She shot Mari a self-satisfied grin.

Mari cringed internally. *Does she think she's being helpful right now?*

"Oh," Lana said, stepping back. She stood at the workbench, her arms crossed, watching Kalindi with a cold, scrutinizing gaze. "I'll start gathering materials," she said finally, "but I need to see the schematics first."

"Why?" Kalindi asked, suspicious.

"Because," Lana replied, her voice firm, "if we're building something that goes against Greenhaven's laws, then I won't have any part of it without the elders' approval."

Mari winced. She'd known this was coming. It was only a matter of time before someone demanded to know exactly what they were working on. She'd just hoped it wouldn't be this soon.

Kalindi made no move to oblige, but after a moment of reluctance, she reached for her pack and unrolled the blueprints. "Fine," she said, spreading them across the workbench. "Here's the design for the first device."

Lana leaned over the table, studying the detailed diagrams and calculations. "Is this just a dew collector?" she asked, frowning.

Kalindi bristled. "It's an atmospheric water generator," she corrected. "Also known as a dew collector, yes."

Zeph snorted from his position near the seed storage shelves. "I have one of those here," he said, striding over to the bench. He picked up a dry irrigation kit and held it out as if to prove his point. "Been using it for years. Works just fine."

Kalindi glanced at the small contraption in his hands. "That's small potatoes," she said bluntly.

Zeph's knuckles tightened around the device. "Small potatoes?"

Kalindi winced. "Sorry," she said quickly. "I mean, it's great —obviously. It works perfectly down here, but we're not talking about a single cellar or a few seedlings. We need to think grand scale. Big enough to support all of Greenhaven."

Zeph looked thoroughly unimpressed.

"And now's not the time for a joke about whether size matters," Mari said, cutting Zeph off before he could open his mouth.

"I'll go get some of the basic tools," Lana offered. "You three can figure out how you want to explain this to the elders."

Kalindi nodded but didn't look at her. Mari murmured a quiet "thank you," but Lana was already heading for the door.

When she returned a few candlemarks later, carrying a bundle of tools, the tension in the propagation cellar had intensified. Lana set the tools down on the workbench with a distinct thud, her movements betraying her mood. She wouldn't even look at Mari.

Kalindi noticed, of course, and raised an eyebrow in Mari's direction. Mari caught the glance and cringed internally.

Lana unpacked the tools abruptly and then turned to face Kalindi. "I need to see the blueprints for this... anti-echo device or whatever you're working on next," she said flatly.

Kalindi's face hardened. "No."

"Then I'm not helping you." Without another word, Lana turned and left again, her footsteps stomping up the cellar steps.

"Wow, she's really perfected the dramatic exit," Kalindi exclaimed.

Mari rounded on Kalindi, her frustration bubbling to the surface. "You know she thinks we're together."

Kalindi shrugged, unfazed. "And?"

"So why didn't you correct her?!"

Kalindi crossed her arms, tilting her head. "You could have corrected her too."

"I kept waiting for you to say something!" Mari shot back.

"I didn't think it was my place," Kalindi said, a hint of mock innocence in her voice.

Zeph, who had been leaning against the seed storage cabinet, decided this was the perfect time to interject. "Wait... so you're not together?" he asked, unable to keep the desperate curiosity out of his voice.

"No!" Mari exclaimed, throwing her arms up and glaring at him.

Zeph looked between them, clearly enjoying himself. "But she is with someone, isn't she?" he pressed.

Kalindi grinned playfully and propped her hands on to her hips, enjoying this far too much. "Oh, she's with someone alright."

"We really don't need to be going into this now," Mari said through gritted teeth. She could tell her cheeks were getting hotter, and she felt like someone really should go after Lana.

"It's an older woman, isn't it?" Zeph said, his grin as wide as the orchard rows above them. "She always was into the older women."

Mari's blush deepened. She wanted the floor to swallow her whole.

Kalindi, sensing an opportunity, delivered her next line with a wicked grin. "The Queen of Patovia, actually."

The silence after Kalindi's revelation was stark. Mari's cheeks burned a furious red as she avoided Zeph's pointed gaze.

His mouth opened wide, clearly not ready for such a juicy piece of news, and he stood like that in silence for far longer than was comfortable for Mari.

"She's joking," he said finally, staring at Mari, a look of shock on his face.

Mari pinched the space between her eyes and gave in to the situation. "She's not." She scowled, glaring at Kalindi. "And I don't know why she felt the need to say anything about something that was shared in confidence."

Kalindi shrugged. "Secrets have a funny way of spilling out eventually. Better now than later, don't you think?"

Zeph scoffed. "Oh, that's rich, coming from you."

Kalindi turned to him, her eyebrows lifting with curiosity. "What's that supposed to mean?"

"You heard me," Zeph said, his tone curt. "What are you even doing here, Kalindi? Tagging along on Mari's mission. What's the angle, huh? You had a taste of power once, working for the Stewards, and now you miss it?"

Kalindi's playful attitude fizzled away as Zeph started up again.

"That's it, isn't it? You're trying to climb back into someone's good graces. Following Mari to get closer to the queen—because that's what you do. You latch onto people with power, people who can get you what you want."

"That's enough," Mari said, utterly fed up with the bickering and accusations at this point..

Zeph wasn't finished. "You should be questioning her, Mari. Why else would she suddenly show up, throwing herself into all of this? She wants something. Admit it."

Kalindi looked at Mari with a face full of surprise at his undisguised rudeness. Then, Mari recognized Kalindi's expression change, from resignation to determination. She turned in Zeph's direction and took slow, intentional steps toward him.

"You don't know anything about me," Kalindi said quietly, her voice cold.

"Oh, I know plenty," Zeph snapped back. "You were working for the Stewards, right? Helping them consolidate their power? And now you're cozying up to Mari, hoping she'll hand you a free pass to the queen's court. You're just as selfish and manipulative as you were back then."

Kalindi's fists clenched at her sides, and Mari breathed a sigh of relief when she finally stopped inching closer to Zeph, not quite within arm's reach of him. "You don't know what you're talking about."

Zeph barked a humorless laugh. "Don't I? You think people can't see right through you? You're still that same traitor. Still chasing power, no matter who gets hurt along the way."

"Stop it!" Mari said, her voice rising. "Zeph, that's enough!"

But Kalindi's composure had already cracked, and her voice rose above Mari's. "You want to know why I'm here?" she snapped, moving even closer to Zeph. "You want to know what I'm chasing?" Her hands trembled as she pointed a finger at him, her voice shaking with barely contained fury. "I'm not here for power. I'm not here for your precious queen." She glared at Mari. "I'm here because I can't outrun what I've done. I'm here because it's my fault my mother is dead."

Her cold words hung in the air.

Zeph blinked, silent. Mari's breath caught in her throat as she stared at Kalindi.

"She died because of me," Kalindi continued. "Because I

thought I was smarter than everyone else. Because I built their damn devices. And when I tried to stop them, I paid the price."

Kalindi turned away, barely managing to hold herself together as she gripped the edge of the workbench for support. "So go ahead," she said, her voice raw. "Judge me. Call me a liar, a traitor, whatever you want. But don't stand there and pretend you understand."

Mari rubbed her eyes, willing the hot sting of tears to fade. She swallowed hard, her voice breaking when she finally spoke. "I thought your mother died when you were twelve?"

Kalindi flinched. She took a long time to answer Mari's question, her head hung low between her shoulders. "They told me she was gone," she said, her voice brittle. "For years, I believed them. I believed she was gone. And I let that belief fester until it consumed me."

Mari stepped forward cautiously, her heart twisting at the look of anger on Kalindi's face... or was it grief?

Kalindi pressed on, her words coming faster now, tumbling over themselves like a stampede of startled drovak. "But she wasn't gone. I found out years later—by accident, not because anyone told me. She was alive. Alive, and living in Joycita."

Zeph's brow furrowed, his usual skeptical comments nowhere to be found. Instead, he seemed so shocked that he actually listened for a change, without trying to respond. Mari didn't know what to say. There was no appropriate response to an admission like this. She simply waited, sensing that Kalindi still wasn't finished.

"I thought she had run away... escaped their control, like I dreamed of doing. That's what gave me the strength to finally leave too, even though I was scared. If she could get out, so could I. I left for Joycita to find her."

Kalindi's voice cracked, and she laughed bitterly, though

there was no humor in it. "She wasn't just alive. She was one of them. Doing their bidding. She was embedded in the queen's court, a Steward plant, feeding them information, pushing their agenda. My mother. The Steward." She spat the last four words like they burned her tongue.

Mari couldn't even begin to imagine what that must have meant for Kalindi. "What... what did you do?" she asked softly.

"I sought out the Mycelium, a resistance group known to oppose the Stewards. It took a while for me to find them, but once I proved who I was, they were more than happy to work with me," she said, her voice low. "I thought... I thought if I gave them information, they could capture her. Save her. Maybe she'd been forced into it, like me. Maybe she was trapped, and I could help her escape."

She paused, her breathing uneven. "I thought I could save her. I thought..." Her voice broke entirely, and she blinked rapidly, tears welling in her eyes despite her effort to hold them back. "Instead, I gave them the information they needed to find her. And they didn't take her hostage. They didn't question her. They didn't even try to reason with her. They..." Her voice faltered again, and she pressed a shaking hand to her mouth.

Mari moved closer, her instinct to reach out warring with the knowledge that any touch she could give Kalindi at this moment would likely make the tension and emotion more intense. She pinched her hands and squeezed her fingertips together. "What happened?" she asked gently.

"They killed her," Kalindi whispered, her voice hollow. "They called it 'neutralizing the threat.' Neutralizing—" Her breath hitched, and she turned away again, her head bowing as tears slid silently down her cheeks. "They killed my mother. Because of me."

Zeph's hostility seemed to drain from him in an instant. He

stared at Kalindi, but he didn't speak. Mari, however, couldn't hold back any longer. She reached out, touching Kalindi's arm lightly. "Kalindi... I'm so sorry."

Kalindi pulled away, her walls slamming back into place as quickly as they had cracked. "Don't," she said harshly, wiping at her face. Her voice hardened. "Don't pity me. Don't tell me it wasn't my fault. I know what I did."

Mari chose her words carefully. "You were trying to do the right thing."

Kalindi laughed. It sounded sharp and painful. "Was I? Look where it got me. Look what it cost me." She gestured around the cellar, at the blueprints and the tools scattered across the workbench. "You think I'm here for you? For Greenhaven? I'm not. I'm doing this for me. To make it right for me." She turned to look Zeph dead in the eyes. "So you're right... I am selfish. But at least after this, I might be able to live with myself."

Mari stepped closer again. She took a steadying breath before she spoke. "You don't have to trust us, Kalindi, but we trust you."

Kalindi's face was a masterpiece of disbelief. "Why?" she asked, her voice barely audible.

"Because," Mari said simply, "you could have run. You could have kept running, but you didn't. You're here. And that means something."

Zeph, his voice quieter than usual, added, "You've paid a heavy price. No one can take that from you."

Kalindi stared at them both. For a moment, she seemed on the verge of saying something, but instead, she turned back to her blueprints, unrolling the designs for her anti-echo device. Her demeanor was still tense, but Mari could already tell that her walls were coming back down. "Let's get to work," she said quietly.

And although she didn't say it, Mari recognized something new and promising in her eyes. Not trust—not yet, but maybe, just maybe, the beginning of it.

CHAPTER TWENTY-TWO

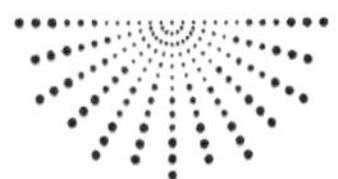

Zeph stood across from Kalindi, looking down at the sets of blueprints on the workbench.

"You're good at this," he said finally, nodding toward the elaborate designs.

Kalindi raised an eyebrow, clearly not expecting the compliment. "At what?"

Zeph gestured toward the schematics. "Engineering. These are... well, impressive." He stepped closer and pointed at one of her diagrams. "The way you've integrated the water generator with the canals... It's smart. Really smart. You've thought of everything."

Kalindi shrugged, but Mari could see relief pooling behind her eyes. "It's just what I do."

"Yeah," Zeph said. "And I think... I think you're doing it for the right reasons. Despite everything."

Kalindi looked at him, searching for any trace of mockery or sarcasm, but found none. "You don't have to say that," she murmured.

"I'm not just saying it," Zeph replied. "You made mistakes.

Big ones. But I can see you're trying to make it right. You're not doing this for power, or glory, or... whatever I thought before. You're doing it because you care. I'm sorry I said what I said."

Kalindi cleared her throat, her usual quick retorts failing her.

"As for your anti-echo device..." Zeph pulled the second blueprint out from the bottom of the pile. "I honestly don't understand a single word of it."

Kalindi laughed. She sketched a quick diagram on a piece of parchment. "Think of the echo chambers as tuning forks," she said, tapping the parchment for emphasis. "They emit vibrations that disrupt natural cycles—water, air pressure, the atmosphere in general. My device counters those vibrations. It works by emitting opposing frequencies, creating a kind of... canceling effect. Once it's close enough to their device, it'll neutralize the echoes entirely, like cutting the strings of an instrument mid-song." She glanced at Zeph, gauging his understanding. "It won't destroy their device outright, but it'll render it useless. And over time, the natural balance will start to restore itself."

"Although it can't hurt to locate their device and smash it into lots of tiny pieces, right?" Mari asked.

Zeph looked at Mari, impressed. "You spend a few weeks with this girl and suddenly you're ready to smash things? Where did my sweet, docile astronomer go?"

"Oh, she's still here," Mari said with a wink. "She can just flip you on your butt if she needs to."

Zeph laughed. "Don't remind me," he said, rubbing his lower back. "How do you generate the vibrations, though?" he asked.

Kalindi grinned at Zeph's question, clearly in her element. "That's the beauty of it," she said, pointing at the sketch she had drawn. "The core of the device will use resonance frequencies. We think that Elyrian technology was centered around the idea that everything in the world vibrates at its own frequency. Stones, water, air... even light. Their device amplified those frequencies to manipulate the environment."

She grabbed a fresh piece of parchment and quickly sketched a plant. "But here's where my part comes in. I've been working on a theory about bioluminescent plants, like the ones we saw in the Glowing Gardens. Those spores don't just glow—they vibrate subtly, at a frequency that can amplify or disrupt other vibrations. If I can harness that resonance and pair it with the Elyrian framework, I can generate a counter-frequency strong enough to neutralize their device."

Mari watched Zeph's face as he processed the information.

"So you're telling me," Zeph finally said, his voice incredulous, "that you're combining ancient Elyrian technology with... plant spores... to build something that can stop a device capable of controlling the weather?"

Kalindi gave him a cheeky smile. "More or less, yeah."

Zeph leaned back in his chair, letting out a low whistle. "You ARE an engineer and a botanist. That's... that's genius."

Kalindi shrugged, though the grin on her face betrayed her pride. "I prefer the term innovator, but I'll take genius."

Mari nudged Kalindi with her elbow. "Told you she was full of surprises."

"Well, it's just a theory right now, and it's not like we have the time to test it, so... Let's hope this device does a good enough job with the hollow core and we don't need the supercharged power of plant spores to come to our rescue, yeah?" Kalindi said quickly, looking suddenly uncomfortable.

Zeph shook his head in disbelief, impressed. "So," he said,

straightening with a determined glint in his eye, "I'll get you an audience with the elders."

Kalindi blinked, clearly caught off guard. "You will?"

He nodded firmly. "Yeah. They need to hear this. The anti-echo device, the atmospheric water generator," he paused, flashing a playful wink as he emphasized the name of Kalindi's dew collector, "the canals—everything. They need to know how you can help us and what's coming if we don't act."

Relief swept over Mari and she felt her face break into a grateful smile. "Thank you, Zeph."

"And... I'm sorry for what I said before. I underestimated you," Zeph said with a genuinely apologetic look.

Kalindi nodded her thanks and even managed to send a smile back Zeph's way. "Maybe you can be the one to talk to Lana, then? Undo the damage I did?" she asked, a spark of hope in her voice.

Zeph chuckled nervously. "I'm not sure she'll believe me, but sure... I'll talk to her. Set the record straight. Maybe even convince her to come back. Who knows? She might help us present all this to the elders."

Mari exchanged a glance with Kalindi. "Let's do it," Kalindi said with a rare, genuine smile.

THE ELDERS' home was modest, located close to the heart of the village, making it tricky for Zeph to get there without drawing attention. Mari and Kalindi were awkwardly squashed under a blanket in the cart he pulled, their elbows jabbing into each other every time the wheels hit a bump. Zeph had piled various supplies from the prop cellar on top of them as camouflage.

"A late Lumithra gift," he called cheerfully to Mel, the baker who passed by with a questioning glance as Zeph heaved the cart across the commons.

They had decided it would be smarter for Rih to stay out of sight, just in case someone recognized her and made the connection to Mari. In protest for being left behind, Rih had nipped Mari a bit harder than could reasonably be described as affectionate, her little beak making her feelings perfectly clear.

Zeph rounded a corner under a canopy of fruit trees and the elders' home came into view, surrounded by a low garden wall draped in creeping vines. Like many homes in Greenhaven, the front bore a tapestry, and this one was by far the most intricate in the village. Its woven patterns told the story of Greenhaven's history, marked by generations of villagers who had added their own threads as gestures of respect and gratitude to the elders.

Zeph wheeled the cart through the gate and into the courtyard. A navy-blue awning stretched taut above a weathered, circular table, the fabric rippling gently in the breeze, and around the edges of the courtyard, simple clay pots overflowed with flourishing herbs. On the table sat bowls of dried fruits, jars of honey, and a kettle of freshly brewed tea— small gifts from the people of Greenhaven, who ensured their elders were cared for despite their modest lifestyle.

Elder Amara and Elder Harrop were seated at the table, waiting expectantly. They seemed calm and blissfully unaware of Mari's presence, let alone the revelation she was about to drop in their laps. Lana was already there and sat beside Elder Harrop, her hands tucked between her knees, staring blankly down at the table as Zeph entered. At the far end of the table, the third and silent elder, Elder Corrin, sat quietly, clasping a small cup of tea. Elder Amara, her hazel eyes framed by her braided silver hair, was the first to look up when Zeph arrived, and she smiled at him as he set to unloading the contents of the cart after greeting them good afternoon. Zeph moved slowly, clearly nervous to reveal what, or rather who, was hiding at the bottom. He set down a bottle of date seed oil with obvious pride before finally pulling back the blanket with a dramatic flair to reveal Mari, who was curled up at the bottom of the cart.

Mari sat up, peering over the edge of the frame with a sheepish grin.

"Mari?" Elder Amara's voice was filled with disbelief as she stood. "By the stars, is it really you?" She embraced Mari tightly. "It's so good to see you, child. We feared we'd never see you again."

Elder Harrop's weathered face broke into a rare smile as he rose, his towering frame still imposing despite his years. "I thought we'd lost you to the capital," he said, stepping forward with open arms.

Mari relaxed immediately, the warmth of their welcome washing over her. Memories of childhood flooded back as she returned Elder Amara's embrace. "It's good to be back," she said, realizing how tired she sounded. She willed herself to perk up. It was possible that the future of Patovia would depend on her ability to deliver their news and proposal effectively. No pressure.

Elder Harrop placed a firm hand on her shoulder. "Come, sit with us. You must tell us—" He stopped abruptly, his eyes drifting past her to Kalindi, who was still lying in the cart. His brow furrowed as he took in her appearance: her simple, worn clothing, the dagger at her hip, the piercings in her ears, and the tightly rolled blueprints she was clutching.

"And who is this?" Elder Harrop asked, immediately suspicious.

Off to a great start..

Mari gestured for Kalindi to climb out of the cart. "This is Kalindi," she said. "She's here to help."

Lana scowled and folded her arms with a huff. Kalindi rolled her eyes in response.

Elder Amara's sharp gaze flicked over Kalindi, noting every detail. Though she said nothing, her skepticism was unmistakable.

Mari looked to Elder Corrin to gauge her reaction to all of this. She had not risen to greet them since age had left her largely confined to her chair, yet her piercing blue eyes missed nothing. She had been a little girl during the first fall of Harcanth, one of the last refugees to escape from the ships that had waged war for the precious minerals abundant there. Though she rarely spoke, the weight of her approval—or disapproval—was felt in every decision made. She gave no indication one way or another what she made of the situation so far. Mari appreciated that at least one of the elders was willing to reserve judgement until she was able to explain.

"Sit," Elder Amara said, gesturing to the open seats at the table. "Tell us why you're here."

Mari didn't sit. Instead, she planted her hands firmly on the table and prayed that the words that were about to come out of her mouth did not waver. "We're all in incredible danger, and if we don't act now, Greenhaven will be nothing but dust before the season's end."

From the far end of the table, Elder Corrin let out a dry chuckle. "How delightfully apocalyptic. Please, continue."

Mari didn't miss a beat. "The stars aren't wrong," she said. "They just look wrong."

Beside her, Kalindi unrolled her blueprints onto the table, pressing down the curling edges, and gave a little nod toward the elders, encouraging them to move forward to look. Zeph stood behind them, his arms leaning against the back of Mari's empty chair, watching the elders' reactions closely.

"There's a group called the Stewards," Kalindi began. "Zealous idealists who believe Patovia should return to an era of so-called 'glory'—one where they hold all the power. They want to reshape the region to be completely under their control, disbanding the Crown and pushing technological advancements that will ensure their dominance. The Echo Project is just the beginning. If they succeed, they won't stop at Patovia—they'll use their control over the elements to seize power over the surrounding regions as well."

"What's the Echo Project?" Harrop asked.

Mari tapped a sketch on Kalindi's blueprints. "It's a device, or a weapon, designed to reshape the entire climate." She paused as she waited for the elders to take in the designs before them. "You've felt it—the drought, the skyweavers flying off course, the auroras that don't make any sense this far south... These aren't coincidences. They're consequences." She met their eyes, her own dark and determined.

Elder Harrop leaned forward, a look of deep concern etched across his old face. "So, let me get this straight. You're saying none of this is natural? It's all because of some device?"

Kalindi nodded. "It's disrupting the atmosphere through vibrational resonance. Think of it like an enormous tuning fork, sending out waves that ripple through the air itself. The auroras? They aren't real. They're light distortions caused by interference. The stars haven't moved—it just appears that way to us."

Mari unfurled her own star charts beside Kalindi's

diagrams, the inked constellations crisscrossed with fresh red markings. "These charts show my observations before the Echo Project was activated. And these," she tapped a second set where the lines had shifted, "are how the stars have appeared since. The distortion follows the exact locations where the Stewards have set up their device."

Elder Amara studied the marked points. "And the drought? How does their device explain that?"

Kalindi flipped open a tattered notebook filled with sketches of pressure systems and wind currents. "Because it's doing more than bending sound and light. The Stewards have been setting up resonance caves—chambers that amplify their device's vibrations. These pulses are altering the appearance of the sky and disrupting weather currents, pushing moisture away from Greenhaven... And that's just the things we know about."

"The drought isn't a side effect. It's an intentional strategy. The Stewards are suffocating Greenhaven on purpose. No rain means no crops. No crops mean desperation. And desperation means power for those who control the water." Mari felt beyond tense as she delivered her warning. "This isn't just about Greenhaven. It's happening all over."

Silence stretched over the courtyard. Elder Corrin finally set down her tea. "I've seen something like this happen before." Her gaze sharpened. "Not as advanced, but equally as concerning. When the Kethlians attacked Harcanth the second time, they vowed if they couldn't take the land with us, they'd take it without us. They poisoned the water supply... gave us no choice but to leave... of course you know the story, but still... it was a clever move."

Mari nodded. "It's only going to get worse. We uncovered their plans." She reached into her satchel and produced the replicated Steward document that Lyra had risked copying from Councilor Bomi. She laid it on the table, the ink slightly smudged but the message clear. "Their next deployment is Brindlemyre. If they activate another resonance chamber there, it will escalate beyond recovery. And that's why we're going to stop them."

Elder Harrop let out a loud breath. "You expect us to believe that a group of men can manipulate the sky and steal our water? You sound like the fools who believe in Elyrian ghosts."

Kalindi's patience frayed. "This isn't magic—it's science. The Elyrians understood it long before we did, and the Stewards have taken their knowledge and turned it into a weapon. If they control the water, they control who lives and who dies. And right now, they've decided Greenhaven—and villages like yours—are expendable."

Mari crossed her arms. "That's why we're building a counter-device—one that will send out inverse frequencies to neutralize theirs." She pulled Kalindi's blueprints from beneath her charts back to the top of the pile, the details of the device schematics drawn with such care and precision.

Elder Amara watched intently, her hands folded neatly in her lap. Elder Harrop moved closer to study the diagrams, and it was clear that he was paying more attention than earlier. Elder Corrin remained still, her eyes fixed on Kalindi's schematics.

Kalindi held the scroll in place as she waited for their response now that they knew what they were looking at.

Finally, Elder Amara broke the quiet. "You're suggesting we use Elyrian technology." Her tone was carefully neutral.

"Yes," Kalindi replied. "But—"

"We don't use Elyrian relics in Greenhaven," Elder Harrop interrupted firmly. "Not ever."

"They're not relics," Kalindi said, not even attempting to hide her frustration. "They're tools. And they could save your entire village."

Elder Amara shook her head. "Greenhaven has survived this long without relying on dangerous technologies. We won't risk it now."

"The matter is closed," Elder Harrop said, his tone brooking no argument.

Zeph shifted behind Mari, about to speak, but she placed a hand on his arm and stood abruptly. "Sorry, Zeph," she said. She let her hands fall to her sides, palms outstretched in an effort to appear as unthreatening as possible, as she readied herself for what she was about to say next. "Elders, I'm not here seeking approval or advice. I'm telling you that we're building it."

A stunned silence followed.

Mari grabbed Kalindi's notebook and snapped it shut, tossing it back to her. She swept up the remaining scrolls and maps with swift movements.

"All my life, I've looked to others for guidance—for reassurance that I was making the right choices. I've relied on people to tell me where to go, what to do, and how to act. But not this time." She planted both hands on the table and met each of the elders' gazes in turn. "This time, I know what must be done—not just in my mind, but in my heart. And I won't waste another second asking for permission."

Elder Amara's frown deepened. "Mari—"

"No," Mari cut in, her voice resolute. "Patovia is at great risk, and step one is stopping the Stewards. We're building this anti-echo device, and when it's done, Kalindi and I are going to

Brindlemyre to shut down the next phase of the Echo Project before it's too late."

She cleared her throat before adding, "This is a water generator." She pulled the smaller blueprints out so they were unobstructed, jabbing at the diagram in an effort to make the elders understand how much work had gone into this plan. "It will stay here and it should buy Greenhaven time, and if we fail in Brindlemyre, it may be our only bargaining chip. Either way, we leave as soon as the devices are built."

Elder Harrop raised a grizzled brow. "Then why come here at all?"

"Because we need Lana," Mari explained plainly.

At the mention of her name, Lana squirmed where she sat and huffed another loud sigh.

Mari turned to her. "You're the best smith in Greenhaven. We can build the device, but we need materials—iron for the frame, copper for the wiring, and reinforced casings to withstand the vibrations. Without you, it'll take weeks. We don't have that kind of time."

The elders exchanged glances.

Lana's fingers drummed against her elbow. "I won't work without the elders' approval."

Mari's eyes turned pleading toward the elders. "Then give it to us. If you back us, we can move faster. But make no mistake —this is happening. Without Lana, we'll lose time we can't afford." She tried to sound stern.

"If this is going to work as widespread as we need it to, we must align the deployment of the anti-echo device with the windstorm," Kalindi explained. "We need to have the devices built and be on the road in no more than three days."

"Which is why we need to start immediately," Mari

emphasized. She stepped back. "I'm leaving now. Keep this quiet, or you risk all our lives."

Mari turned to Lana and pulled a folded list from her satchel, slapping it down on the table in front of her. "Here's what we need. Deliver it to my family's backwoods by first light tomorrow. If you don't, I'll understand that to mean we're on our own."

Lana looked at the list but didn't move to pick it up.

Mari climbed into the cart and pulled the blanket over her lap. She looked back at Lana. "Please," she added.

Kalindi climbed in beside her.

The courtyard was silent. The elders sat motionless, deep in thought, until Elder Corrin spoke, her voice soft in spite of the command it carried. "Wait."

Mari paused, looking over her shoulder.

Elder Corrin's blue eyes locked onto hers. "Sometimes, pet, trust is not given freely—it is earned. But I see your conviction, and I trust that conviction." She turned to Amara and Harrop, a slow smile creeping across her wrinkled face. "If there's one thing I've learned in my many years, it's that you always back the horse with fire in its eyes."

The power of her words silenced any potential objections. Elder Amara looked at Harrop, and after a moment of hesitation, he gave a slow nod. Amara sighed deeply and turned back to Mari, resigned. "You have our support."

Mari nodded gratefully. She lay back in the cart, pulling the blanket over her head. She closed her eyes, exhaustion finally creeping in, but the image of Queen Lyra's face burned in her mind, keeping her strong. Her voice floated through Mari's memories. Lyra had been the first to tell her she admired her conviction. Mari smiled, feeling, for the first time, not only that she was making her queen proud, but that she was finally making herself proud.

CHAPTER TWENTY-THREE

THE SUN HAD BARELY REACHED ITS PEAK WHEN ZEPH emerged from the tree line, brushing dust from his hands, his grin triumphant. "It's all there," he reported. "Every last piece."

Mari felt the relief cut through her nerves. "Alright. Let's move fast."

She pushed through the underbrush and ran in a squat across the back field of her parents' property. Kalindi and Zeph followed, silent and swift. They reached the cart, half-covered with sacks of grain to mask its true cargo, and Kalindi sorted through the materials. "None of the metals I requested," she huffed with irritation.

"I can head into town and buy whatever we need," Zeph offered. "It'll be pricey—"

"Price doesn't matter," Mari said, her voice firm. She grabbed a coil of rope that had fallen to the ground and threw it into the cart with a little more force than necessary. "Damn it, Lana. I thought you'd come through for us."

Zeph shrugged. "She got us most of what we needed."

"Most isn't good enough," Kalindi said. "Without the right materials, we're improvising, and I hate improvising."

Mari was already adjusting the tarp over their haul. "We'll figure it out later. Right now, we need to move."

GETTING the supplies back to the prop cellar was tedious work, and with each trip, Mari grew more and more concerned about how long the whole ordeal was taking. The backwoods behind the observatory provided cover, but the village was still too close for comfort. They kept to the outskirts of Greenhaven, using the orchard rows and the remnants of the once-luscious hedges that bordered her family's property for concealment, now just a tangle of dry, crackling branches, browned and stripped of life.

Zeph hauled the cart back and forth, while Mari and Kalindi carried the smaller components wrapped in burlap sacks, their arms burning by the end of it. Overhead, Rih flitted back and forth, determined to help by snatching at the smallest pieces—though they inevitably slipped from her grasp, too heavy to carry for long.

That didn't stop her from trying.

She was midair, stubbornly tugging at a large loop of rope and getting absolutely nowhere, when Zeph tossed a sack over her with a muttered curse. Rih gave a muffled squawk, wrestled free, and finally relented, sulking on a nearby beam, her feathers thoroughly ruffled.

By the time they had moved the last load, Mari was ready to collapse on the bottom step of the cellar and not move for at least a candlemark. Zeph hauled the last of the sacks down the confined stairway, grunting with effort as he squeezed past

Mari, who offered an apologetic look but made no move to get out of his way.

"We couldn't have just asked Lana to deliver everything here?" Zeph asked, wiping the back of his hand across his sweaty forehead.

"And risk her being seen? Or worse—risk the elders changing their minds and telling someone where we are?" Mari shot back.

Kalindi leaned against the workbench. "If the Stewards had even the slightest inkling of what we were building, our time in Greenhaven would be over before we could finish."

Zeph winced. "I still don't think Greenhaven has been infiltrated. We would have noticed."

Kalindi appeared unconvinced. "Would you?"

"Yes," Zeph said, but his tone wasn't as certain as before.

Kalindi pushed off the workbench, stepping closer. "Who's your newest citizen?"

Zeph thought for a moment. "Mel and his family. He's a baker. His wife runs a washing service, and their two kids go to the school where my friend Rissa teaches."

Kalindi nodded. "And where did they come from?"

"West Myramin."

"How do you know?" Kalindi's voice was dangerously smooth and she watched him with interest as he considered her question.

Zeph frowned. "He told us so."

"Ah. He told you." A pause, rich with implication. "And he could have told you anything, couldn't he?"

Zeph stiffened. "You think Mel's a Steward?" he asked in disbelief.

Kalindi rolled her eyes. "No, Zeph, I don't think your baker is a Steward. But do you see my point? Anyone could be. A traveler passing through. A merchant making regular supply runs. Anyone who's been outside the village's walls could be compromised."

Poor Zeph had a pained look on his face, the reality sinking in. "I don't like this."

Kalindi's voice softened, just a fraction. "Neither do I."

Mari, standing at the center of the cellar, let them talk. It was the first time she had seen them debate without outright hostility—Zeph, the idealist, resisting the idea of danger lurking within his home, and Kalindi, the realist, shaping his perspective with careful, deliberate words. It was a slow shift, but it was happening.

They didn't have much time for bickering, though. Or flirting. Or whatever was going on here.

"We're on a tight schedule," Mari interrupted. She surveyed the scattered materials, her mind already sorting through the next steps. "Let's get to work."

"I'll head to town and buy the..." Zeph trailed off, a blank look on his face as he searched his memory unsuccessfully. He looked at Kalindi for confirmation.

"Zinc and copper," she reminded him with a slow, encouraging nod.

"Got them here," a voice rang out from behind them.

Rih shrieked wildly, wings flaring as she launched straight into the rafters, sending a cascade of dust and splinters raining down.

The trio spun around, hands half-raised as if expecting an ambush.

At the bottom of the cellar stairs stood Lana, her arms cradling long rods of what Mari assumed was copper and zinc, and a purple pouch hooked around her wrist. She stood frozen, as if she could turn and leave at any second, with a look that could only be described as mildly apologetic confusion.

"We're good, Rih," Mari insisted. "Stand down."

Rih hissed indignantly from above, her feathers puffed to twice her normal size.

"Lana. Thank you for coming." Mari stepped forward, her arms outstretched for a hug.

Lana didn't budge. Instead, she held the goods out at arm's length, making the briefest of eye contact before looking past Mari entirely.

The cellar air, already dense from the humidity required to grow the next generation of date palms, grew thicker. A palpable tension coiled between Lana and Kalindi. Kalindi had straightened from her crouch, moving toward Lana to take the supplies. Lana's grip tightened for just a fraction of a second before Mari swiftly intercepted.

"Appreciate you bringing these," Mari said, flashing Lana a half-smile, hoping to keep the peace before Lana or Kalindi could shoot any more glare-daggers at one another. "You've saved us a lot of time." She made sure to give Lana the most generous nod of thanks she could muster as she accepted the bundle of rods.

Lana barely nodded. "Let's just get this over with."

Mari caught the way Kalindi eyed Lana—part scrutiny, part intrigue—but Lana still refused to meet her eyes as she unhooked the pouch from around her wrist and reluctantly handed it over to Kalindi.

Zeph cracked his knuckles, stepping up beside them with a grin. "Alright, engineer, tell me what to do."

Kalindi raised an eyebrow. "You ever worked a forge before?"

"Not exactly," Zeph admitted. "But I'm good with my hands." He shot her a wink.

Kalindi ignored him and dumped the contents of the pouch onto the worktable beside the rods. "Brass first," she said, sifting through the raw materials. "It's going to take time to get the mixture right."

Lana rolled up her sleeves. "For you, maybe. I know how brass works."

Zeph clapped his hands together. "Great! Love a good teamwork moment. Let's melt some metal."

By dusk, they had set up a makeshift forge using an old iron kiln Zeph had scavenged from an abandoned homestead on the far side of town. They used the last of the water in their waterskins for the cooling bath, careful to leave just enough to make it back to Adavale without needing to dip into their family's rations. Zeph had insisted they move all the saplings to the end of the prop cellar, and by the time the forge was roaring, Mari understood why—the heat it generated was intense. Mari had expected the tension between Lana and Kalindi to boil over into something unbearable, but to her surprise, they worked in focused silence, side by side, falling into a steady, competent rhythm.

Lana gripped the tongs like a seasoned blacksmith as she held a crucible steady over the fire, sweat glistening at her temples. "Higher heat," she said.

Kalindi adjusted the airflow, increasing the forge's intensity. "I know."

A pause. Then, begrudgingly, Lana added, "You have a steady hand."

Kalindi's lips twitched, though she didn't look up. "I know."

The forge glowed, white-hot and furious, as they poured

the molten metal into crude molds, shaping each piece to Kalindi's precise measurements. The sound of cooling brass, hissing as it met the prepared water bath, echoed across the cellar.

Mari stole a glance at Zeph, who had been watching the two women with an amused smile.

"They're either going to end up best friends or kill each other," he murmured.

Mari grinned, wiping sweat from her brow. "Maybe both."

By mid-morning the following day, the propagation cellar was buzzing with productivity. The commotion was, however, entirely too much for Rih, who spent the better part of the morning tapping her beak against the window with increasing urgency, as if personally offended by the clatter.

Eventually, Zeph sighed and let her out, pausing only long enough to remind her, "Stay close."

Mari stood near the cellar's windows, marveling at how quickly their mishmash collection of supplies had become brass gears and copper tubing, and how incredible it was that they in turn had been shaped into Kalindi's vision. It was hard to believe this space, once filled with jars of preserves, fledgling saplings, and an archive of seeds now hosted this temporary workshop.

Her focus drifted over to Zeph and Kalindi. Despite his initial reluctance, Zeph had been drawn into the work, curiosity overtaking skepticism. He crouched beside Kalindi, running a hand along the smooth edge of a brass panel she had just welded into place on the anti-echo device.

"I'll admit," he said, watching the way she worked, "I thought you were full of it."

Kalindi snorted, tightening a bolt without looking up. "You're not exactly alone in that assessment."

"But you actually know what you're doing," Zeph said.

Mari caught the way Kalindi finally glanced up at him, one eyebrow raised, her usual sharpness softening just a little. "Well, I have tried to build one of these before."

Zeph tilted his head. "Yeah? What happened?"

Kalindi paused, just for a second. "It didn't work."

The shift in Zeph was subtle—his usual playful arrogance dimming a little as he studied her. He leaned in, his voice quietly concerned. "But... it will this time?"

A slow, confident grin curled at the corner of Kalindi's lips. "Yeah," she said, meeting his eyes. "I think it will. I've learned a lot about vibrations over the past week, and the adjustments I've made to my original design will do the trick. I feel good about it."

Zeph nodded approvingly and reached for a wrench, passing it to her. "Well then, I feel good about it too." He smiled.

As Kalindi took the wrench, Mari noticed the small, fleeting touch—his fingers brushing against Kalindi's, the moment lingering just long enough for Kalindi to notice, too.

"Careful, Greenhavener," Kalindi murmured. "You almost sound impressed."

Zeph scoffed and flicked his hair. "Yeah, yeah, don't let it go to your head."

Mari stifled a grin. Across the room, Lana's grip tightened around a length of copper tubing she was cutting for the water generator. Her hostility was unmistakable.

Mari stepped closer, lowering her voice. "Lana."

Lana kept her eyes on her work. "I don't trust her."

Mari cast another glance toward Kalindi. "You don't have to."

That made Lana pause. She turned, brows furrowed. "Then why do you?"

"Because she's here. Because she's risking as much as the rest of us. And because, when she says she wants to make things right, I believe her."

Lana studied Mari's face for a long moment, then gave another glance toward Kalindi, who was still deep in conversation with Zeph over some modification to the pressure valves.

Slowly, Lana sighed and turned back to her work. "Life was so great before..."

"Before an evil faction decided to seize control of Patovia's water supply and, ultimately, the Crown?" Mari offered dryly.

Lana chuckled, shaking her head. "Yeah. That."

Mari nudged her with her shoulder, her smile gentle. "We've shared some good times."

Lana nodded.

"But we grow," Mari continued. "Things change. And that's okay."

"You have grown, you know?" Lana smiled.

Mari blinked. "Me?"

Lana looked her in the eye for the first time in what felt like days. "Yeah. I can see it. In your eyes, sure, but also... there's something about the way you move, the way you make decisions... you're so sure of yourself."

Heat crept up Mari's neck.

"I guess kissing the Queen of Patovia will do that to a girl, huh?" Lana teased with a grin. "Zeph told me."

"Of course he did," Mari grumbled.

"I'm happy for you."

Mari snorted, unconvinced.

"No, really," Lana said, and this time, there was no teasing edge to her voice. "Love looks good on you."

Mari lifted a hand. "Woah, woah, Lana, we're not using that word. It's not love, it's..." She paused, searching for the right words. "I can't stop thinking about her. But it's not just infatuation, either."

Lana arched an eyebrow. "It's not Genna all over again?" she teased.

Mari grimaced at the mention of her first real teen-love obsession. "I mean..." She chewed on her lip. "In the sense that I looked at her and the world stopped and suddenly I wanted to burst into a million pieces just so I could envelop her and devour her all at the same time... then, yeah. But it's stronger than that."

"Stronger how?"

Mari glanced toward the clouded cellar windows. "I don't just want to fall to pieces in her arms," she admitted. "I want to come together around her. I want to be stronger, lift her up, and shine for her." Her gaze flicked back to Lana, and her lips quirked into a small, almost shy smile. "I want all of Patovia to see what she makes me want to be."

Lana's smile reached her eyes this time. "Sure sounds like love to me."

Mari blushed and looked down, scuffing her foot across the dirt floor.

"She sounds wonderful," Lana added.

"She is. And she needs my help."

Lana nodded. "Then let's make sure we get this right."

CHAPTER TWENTY-FOUR

By nightfall, the last bolt was tightened ahead of schedule.

The anti-echo device sat on the workbench, its base a rectangular, hollow structure of burnished brass, sturdy yet delicate and meticulously crafted. There were complex levers that could be adjusted to tune the device to the precise frequencies that were required to counteract the Echo Project's vibrations. Nestled atop the brass base was a semicircular cradle that resembled a bird's nest and looked as if it should hold something, though it was empty, the rim sitting flush with the top of the rectangle. From the center of the device, a large gleaming fork protruded. Taller than Mari had expected it to be, its twin prongs curved gently outward, designed to generate powerful vibrations.

Zeph stared at it in quiet awe. "It's beautiful."

Kalindi ran a hand over the device. "It is." She smiled.

"So... what exactly does it do?" Zeph crossed his arms sheepishly. "Counters the Stewards' device just by... shaking the air differently?"

Kalindi chuckled. "More or less."

Mari rolled her eyes. "There goes Kalindi again with her great detailed explanations."

Kalindi tapped the protruding fork on the device, and the anti-echo device let out a deep sound, the entire base humming so deeply that Mari could feel it in her chest.

"Whoa." Zeph stepped back. "I was not expecting that."

Kalindi turned to him with a grin. "She's strong!" She tapped it again, and the noise deepened. The scattered dirt on the propagation tables that were pushed to the sides of the cellar began to jump and scatter, spilling over the edges and onto the floor. "Once it's deployed in the right place, it should nullify the interference caused by their device. The atmosphere will return to normal, and the stars will appear as they always were. The skies will rebalance. And the weather should start to correct itself."

Zeph let out a slow breath and scratched the stubble that was beginning to appear on his jaw. "Sounds like a hell of a risk."

Kalindi gave him a pat on the chest. "I prefer to think of it as a calculated experiment."

Zeph shook his head and chuckled. "You're impossible."

"That's what my father used to tell me," she replied, flashing a crooked grin and a wink, charming enough to distract from what should have been an awkward moment. The energy around them was so lighthearted that they were able to laugh her comment off. Not that Mari thought Kalindi shouldn't unpack the toxic trauma of her youth—just maybe not right at this second.

Kalindi ran a hand along the base of the anti-echo device, admiring their work. "This isn't going to be like last time," she said.

Mari frowned. "What went wrong last time?"

"I was missing something. The frequency wasn't right. I thought if I could just disrupt their device, it would stop everything. When it didn't, I panicked. Smashed everything and ran."

Mari and Zeph exchanged a glance.

"This one won't fail." Kalindi said, determination burning in her eyes.

Mari studied her. "What's different about this one?"

"Remember our little adventure through the Glowing Gardens?"

"The one where you almost had your arm bitten off by a carnivorous plant? Yeah, hard to forget."

Kalindi chuckled. "That's the one. Watching the way the pappus spores generated their own light through their hollow cores gave me an idea."

"Oh, yes, the little fireflies that lit up when the wind hit them?"

Kalindi nodded, excitement creeping in. "Not fireflies, but yes, exactly. The vibrations activated them. And that got me thinking... What if the core of my device was hollow? More airflow, more resonance, more control." She tapped the side of the device. "This base? It's more than a frame—it's the key to everything. The hollow design amplifies the counter-frequencies without interference. Even the Elyrians didn't think of it."

Mari's eyes widened, a grin spreading slowly across her face. "Kalindi... that's genius."

Kalindi beamed. "Yeah. It is. And they're not gonna see it coming."

Zeph cracked his knuckles. "Alright, then. Let's get the water generator set up and see if it works!"

Kalindi gestured toward the water generator. "There's no switch to flip," she said. "We just need to set it up outside and hope it doesn't blow over."

Mari winced. "The storm?"

"Curse it! We should have built it with a stabilization plate so we could drill into the ground." She started pacing, her wild eyes looking at Mari, the panic rising in her voice. "How could I be so stupid? We don't have time to—"

"I can whip up a plate and stabilizing rods." Lana's voice once again cut through the group with a saving grace.

Kalindi stopped mid-stride, blinking at her. "You can?"

"No problem." Lana smiled.

Kalindi extended a hand. Lana took it without flinching and the pair shook hands. "Thank you, Lana."

Lana gave her a single, firm nod. "I'll have it done before midnight."

Kalindi pointed to the bottom of the device. "You'll need to check it in the morning. If it's working as expected, the trough at the bottom will have water in it by dawn."

Lana nodded, still eyeing the device. "And if it doesn't?"

Kalindi shrugged. "Then we know it's useless and we're all doomed."

"Great," Lana said flatly.

Zeph clapped his hands together. "Well, we won't need to worry about it if we can deploy the anti-echo device on time."

"Let's go full General Clar on these fops." Mari grinned excitedly.

"Now, that's something I can get behind," said Kalindi.

❧

THE PROP CELLAR had become their unofficial base over the past few days, and now, with the work done, Mari insisted on setting it back in order before they left. She rolled up her sleeves and began restacking the crates along the walls, grateful for something to do with her hands.

"You don't have to clean all this up, you know. I'll take care of it when you're gone," Lana offered.

Mari shook her head. "If I sit down now, I won't get up again."

Lana watched her for a moment, then let out a small chuckle. "I know when to stop arguing with you."

Mari grinned, but she kept moving. She needed this normalcy, this last act of care before they left, as a way to leave Greenhaven just as she had found it.

Kalindi, meanwhile, was busy arranging jars of seeds on the shelves. "So," she said, throwing a glance at Mari, "once we render their echo device obsolete and enrage an entire army of Stewards, how exactly are we supposed to get out alive?"

Mari didn't pause in her work, but she knew Kalindi was watching her, and she couldn't let the uncertainty she felt all over show on her face. "I'm working on it," she said. "I have some ideas."

Kalindi snorted. "That's reassuring."

Before Mari could retort, the cellar door swung open and Zeph strolled in carrying a wrapped bundle in one hand and an unmistakable grin on his face.

"Dinner," he announced, dropping the bundle onto the nearest crate. "And three horses."

Mari and Kalindi both turned to him in unison. "Three what?"

"Horses! Outside, not in there," Zeph said, gesturing at the brown paper bundle. "They're ours." He grinned and tossed Mari a bridle. "Well, borrowed. The elders agreed it'd be faster this way. No way we'd make it, dragging a cart across the terrain from here to Brindlemyre."

Mari folded her arms. "We?"

"I'm coming with you this time," Zeph said simply. "I had all that time while you were gone to regret my decision, and I'm not going to make the same mistake twice."

Mari could have argued and reminded him that their family needed him and that this wasn't his fight, but she knew better. They needed the extra strength, that much was true, but all she could think about was how the road had changed her and how Zeph might not be ready for it.

She met his gaze, searching for doubt. She found none.

"All right," she said finally.

Zeph grinned, reaching for a long bottle from a shelf behind him. "Then we drink."

DINNER WAS SIMPLE BUT FILLING—ROASTED pheasant, fresh bread (stolen, again), and a generous helping of Zeph's latest experiment: date wine.

Mari eyed the bottle skeptically as Zeph poured her a cup. "This better not taste like last time."

"I refined the process," he assured her. "You'll love it."

Mari took a cautious sip, then another. "Alright, it's actually not bad."

Kalindi raised a brow. "High praise."

Lana leaned back against the cellar wall and raised her cup. "I'll drink to that."

They laughed, and Mari let herself settle into the rare moment of lightness before the road ahead. The wine dulled the edges of Mari's exhaustion, making her limbs heavy but her heart light. For a moment, it was enough. Still, she knew when to stop. She set her cup down and stretched. "Remind me to try this wine again when we get back. After all this is over."

"So you are coming back?" Lana asked.

"We'll finish what we started in Brindlemyre," Mari said carefully. "And after that... I don't know."

Kalindi met her eyes over the rim of her cup but said nothing.

Comfortable silence settled between them, until Lana finally stood. "I should go before I start getting sentimental." She turned to Kalindi, hesitating momentarily. "And... thanks. For looking out for Mari."

Mari, mock-offended, placed a hand over her chest. "I've been looking after Kalindi just as much!"

Lana smirked. "Sure you have."

"Shh, let me have this." Mari whispered.

Lana reached out and squeezed Mari's hand. "Take care of yourself out there."

Mari squeezed back. "You too."

Mari felt her soul relax, and she gave a satisfied hum as she realized things between them were back to normal, grateful for the friendship repair before they parted ways.

As the night progressed, the others eventually settled down to sleep. But Mari could not. She had expected sleep to have come easy after the exhaustion of the past few days, but she lay awake, staring at the blurry moonlight, obscured by the grimy windowpanes above her, her mind restless. She turned the token from Lyra over in her fingers.

Quietly, she climbed out of her makeshift cot on the prop cellar floor and stepped into the cool night air.

HER FAMILY'S aviary stood just as she remembered it, the familiar surroundings wrapped around her like a warm hug. She had told herself she was just going to grab some food for Rih and to say hello to her old feathered friends—a moment to slip in, snuggle some of her favorites, and then she would slip away again. But as she found herself stepping under the wooden beams, she was overtaken by comfort and couldn't bring herself to leave so quickly.

She climbed up into the higher alcove and crouched on the rafters, her knees pulled to her chest, listening to the soft cooing of her family's birds. For a moment, she closed her eyes, letting herself simply exist.

Then she heard it. The door creaked open, and someone entered the aviary. She could tell by the footsteps alone that it was her father. Below, he moved through the space, murmuring to each bird in turn and whistling a melody Mari had known since childhood. It sounded like home; it felt like safety. She exhaled as quietly as she could and reached for the beam below her, seeking the sensation of the ridges in the rafter to keep her rooted in the moment, for fear that she would unravel entirely if she let herself.

She could go to him and fall into his arms.

She could break.

She hadn't let herself think about how much she missed her father. How much she wanted to drop down from the rafters and call his name. And, by the gods, she almost did... Almost. But she knew if she made the decision to reveal herself, he wouldn't be able to keep it a secret from her mother, which meant that, by morning, all of Greenhaven would know everything too. So she held her breath, bit her lip, and remained silent while her father moved through his routine with the same gentle hands he had always used, unaware that his daughter was above him, aching to say something. When he reached for the feed bag, Mari's vision blurred. She willed the tears not to fall down on him and give her away.

She bit her tongue.

The moment hung there, unbearable.

And then it passed.

Her father left, the door closing softly behind him. Mari pressed a hand over her mouth, holding in the emotions that threatened to spill over until she was sure that he was gone, far from earshot. She pressed her knuckles into her mouth and bit down hard, swallowing everything she could not say.

She had made her choice—before first light, she would be gone.

THE ORCHARD SWAYED, the trees groaning under the force of the rising wind. Fruit thudded to the ground like fat raindrops, bruising on impact. The windstorm loomed on the horizon, an ominous wall of creeping darkness, already rustling through the thinning branches beneath the dark night sky. The aurora was so bright overhead that it cast a glow of deep pink across the entire property.

Mari knelt in the dirt, pressing her palm against the soil. Beneath her fingers, she could feel the steady presence of the stabilizing rods Lana had driven deep into the ground, securing the water generator where it was nestled among the vast roots of her grandparents' trees. It was in place. It was ready.

She inhaled deeply and closed her eyes, letting the atmosphere and the smells of the orchard sink in around her. Greenhaven's fate wasn't entirely in her hands anymore.

Mari rose to her feet, and turned toward the prop cellar, ready to finally sleep.

CHAPTER TWENTY-FIVE

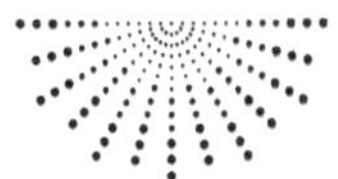

THE DAYS OF TRAVEL BLURRED TOGETHER—NOTHING but aching muscles, endless miles, and the cold bite of sleepless nights. They took the straightest line they could, cutting through dense forests and riding across rivers, pushing their horses as far as they could without causing harm. They stopped for next to nothing. Their rations had dwindled to scraps of dry bread and harder cheese, which they ate in hurried bites before pushing forward again. Sometimes, they didn't even stop to eat.

No taverns. No warm beds. No villages.

Zeph let out a long, suffering sigh as he ducked beneath another low-hanging branch. "I think I've forgotten what 'clean' feels like. We smell like we've been raised by wolves."

"No," Kalindi countered dryly, brushing a leaf from her shoulder. "Wolves at least have the sense to roll in fresh grass."

Mari pulled her hood lower against the chilly wind, scanning the tree line ahead. Above her, Rih soared effortlessly, showing no sign of weariness from the journey.

They were close now. Just outside Joycita's limits.

The thought should have settled her, but it didn't. Unease took root tightly in her stomach in a slow, twisting knot that no amount of deep breathing could loosen.

The queen was here, beyond those city walls. Carrying the weight of the entire kingdom on her shoulders. It felt cruel to be this close and unable to see her or to know if she was safe.

Mari's grip tightened on the reins as the outpost came into view—an unwelcoming mass of dark stone and black iron. It was the kind of joyless place meant to keep people out. Or to keep them in.

She swallowed the lump in her throat and resisted the urge to kick her horse into a canter. They had pushed the animals hard, too hard, and even though every inch of her ached to be off the road, they had no right to ask more of the horses than they already had. They would be at the outpost within a candlemark; she could be patient. Still, the thought of rest tugged at her. A hot meal. A real bed. A night without fear creeping at the edges of her dreams.

THE BARRACKS SAT JUST within the outer walls of the military outpost. Mari barely felt the exhaustion dragging at her limbs until she swung down from the saddle. The moment her boots hit the ground, her legs nearly buckled, her muscles screaming in protest at the sudden shift from endless riding to solid earth beneath her feet. Her groin was apparently very angry with her.

Zeph groaned beside her. "I swear this horse and I have fused into a single being." He arched his back, then immediately regretted it. "Yep. There goes my spine." He swung his leg over and made a clumsy dismount. Then, he started to work the buckles to release the echo-device from where it had been strapped to the back of the horse and hoisted it onto his back.

Kalindi slid off her horse with ease only to immediately stumble sideways, nearly taking Zeph down with her.

Zeph caught her arm. "Steady there, graceful."

Kalindi huffed, wrenching herself upright. "That was on purpose."

"Uh-huh."

She ignored him, sauntering up to the massive iron-bound gates, and rapped her knuckles on the small metal peephole. "By the gods, I think I've forgotten how to use my legs." She yawned and stretched.

The peephole slid open, and a familiar, tediously official voice called out.

"What business do you have here?"

Kalindi cupped her hands to her mouth. "We've come to raid your kitchen and ravish your women."

Mari punched her in the arm. "Calen, open the door. We're falling to pieces out here, and we have seriously precious cargo that needs protecting."

Zeph raised an eyebrow and gave Kalindi a sideways glance. "Women?"

Kalindi nudged Zeph with her shoulder, as if daring him to say more. She nearly toppled over from the impact, barely catching herself before Zeph grabbed her arm to steady her for the second time.

"Women?" Zeph repeated.

Kalindi grinned, still breathless. "You're so easy. I don't discriminate, Zeph. I'll ravish whoever I please."

Mari snorted. "Not smelling like that, you won't."

The trio jumped as the doors opened, revealing a surprised

Calen standing on the other side, his arms crossed, his eyes sweeping over them. They must have been a sight—Mari's sweaty, tangled hair, Rih on her shoulder, Zeph slouching under the large package that was strapped to his back, and Kalindi barely holding herself together but doing a fairly decent job of hiding the fact. Calen fixed on Zeph, the only unfamiliar face. After deciding he posed no threat, his face broke into a wide, welcoming smile. "By the Gods, Mari," he said, shaking his head. "I thought you'd be halfway across the kingdom by now."

Mari pushed back her hood, her hair sticking to her forehead. "So did I." Her voice came out rough, rasping from too many days in the cold air and too little rest. "Plans changed. We need your help." She gestured to Zeph. "This is my cousin, Zeph."

Zeph extended a hand, his usual grin softened by exhaustion. "If you tell me there's food and a halfway decent place to sit inside, I might actually cry."

Calen shook his hand. "If you're that desperate, I won't stop you."

Zeph sighed dramatically. "I haven't eaten anything that didn't taste like rocks in days, and my bones may never recover from that damn saddle."

Mari snickered. "At least you stayed in your saddle. Kalindi nearly fell off twice today."

"The second time was deliberate. I needed to stretch," Kalindi huffed.

Calen chuckled, shaking his head. He eyed the bundled device strapped to Zeph's back. "I take it that this is what needs protecting?"

Kalindi patted the covered device. "Like my own child."

Calen gave a short nod. "Follow me."

CALEN LED THEM INSIDE, down a long corridor and to a private meeting room. The table inside was battered from years of use, but it would do. He gestured for them to sit, but Mari remained standing, too anxious to settle. Beside her, Zeph and Kalindi also stood stiffly, both on edge from days of riding.

Calen poured them cups of water from a metal pitcher at the front of the room, watching as they drained them gratefully. He then signaled to Bartel, a kind looking man who was standing guard outside the room to bring them some more.

"You said you came all the way back here for my help?" Calen asked.

Kalindi rummaged in her pack, pulled out a crumpled map, and slapped it down on the table. The map was basic—just the main roads and landmarks of Brindlemyre and its surrounding areas, but not nearly enough detail.

"We're heading to Brindlemyre," Mari said.

Calen blinked, then let out a surprised laugh. "Brindlemyre? That's home."

"I remember. That's why we're here. We need your insight," Mari said.

His smile faded as her tone registered, and suddenly he was more serious. "You're not just passing through, are you?"

Kalindi forced a fake laugh. "Passing through? We wish."

"How can I help?"

Mari traced a finger along the south easterly road. "This is all we have," she said. "We were hoping you could do better."

"It's... lacking," Kalindi supplied.

Calen snorted and shook his head. "Lacking is an

understatement. That's a traveler's map. It's barely enough to find a tavern, let alone anything useful."

He moved to a nearby chest, flipping it open and rifling through stacks of parchment. After a few moments, he pulled out a large, detailed map, the parchment yellowed with age, and laid it down on the table.

The new map was far more intricate, with roads, forests, and even elevation lines etched into the surface. Mari leaned over it, her eyes scanning the area surrounding Brindlemyre. Zeph let out a low whistle. "Now that's more like it."

Calen pointed to a long line that cut through the mountains. "This is the ridge that separates Brindlemyre from the northern trade routes. The caves run all through here."

Mari frowned. "There's nothing marked."

Calen shook his head. "There wouldn't be. The caves have been around for centuries, but they've never been properly mapped. Too dangerous. When I was a kid, we were forbidden from going near them. Stories about people disappearing in the tunnels were enough to keep most of us away." He hesitated. "Most of us."

"How big are we talking?" Kalindi asked.

Calen shrugged. "Big. Vast, even. They stretch under the entire ridge. Some say they go deeper than the mountains themselves."

Kalindi swore under her breath, her eyes round and wide. "If they're that extensive, and the Stewards have found a way to use them..."

Calen rubbed his chin as he processed the gravity of the situation. "Alright. But... hold on," he said, his brow furrowing. "The Stewards? As in... THE Stewards?!" He shot a panicked look at Mari. "They're still active?" He looked between them, searching their faces for some indication that this was all a bad joke. "What the hell happened while you were gone?"

Mari winced. "A lot."

Calen mopped his brow, his voice tinged with disbelief. "You're telling me that while I've been standing watch at this quiet little outpost, you've been dealing with ancient cultists trying to tear the kingdom apart?"

"Not quite. We've been preparing to...but that's where we're headed next."

"But how... You hadn't even heard of them when you passed through here last." Calen's confusion was written across his face.

Kalindi rubbed the back of her neck, her gaze fixed on the map. "I may have... known a little more about the Stewards than I let on," she confessed.

Calen's wide eyes betrayed his surprise. "You knew?"

Zeph, standing behind Kalindi, crossed his arms and gave her a look. "More than a little."

Kalindi inhaled with frustration. "Can we not do this right now?"

Calen's gaze didn't waver. "How much more?"

"I—" Kalindi faltered.

Mari cut in, making sure she sounded firm enough to keep the conversation moving forward. "The past doesn't matter right now. What matters is finding where they'll set up their next phase of the Echo Project."

Calen stared at her, then at the map. "You're serious."

"Deadly serious," Mari confirmed. "And if we don't stop them, Brindlemyre will be the next casualty."

Calen nodded slowly. "Alright. What do you need from me?"

Mari's expression hardened. "Anything you can tell us

about the caves. Entrances, exits, anything unusual. If you have contacts in Brindlemyre who might know more, that would help too."

Calen stared at the map he had pulled out, deep in thought. After a while, he pointed at a spot on the map with a quick, double tap and a confident nod. "There's an old smuggler's route that might get you close without being spotted. It's risky, but if you're avoiding the main roads, it's your best bet."

Mari nodded, committing the information to memory. "We'll take it."

"Good." Calen's eyes darkened. "If the Stewards are as dangerous as the legends say, you'll need all the help you can get."

Mari was relieved to hear how reassured he sounded. They had come to the right person. She felt herself begin to breathe again. "Thank you."

Calen folded the map carefully and handed it to her. "We need to visit the general."

Zeph rubbed his hands together. "Alright! General Clar; I've been waiting to meet this guy." He set the covered anti-echo device down on the table and arched his aching back into a long stretch.

Calen eyed the large bundle and raised a brow. "What would you like to do with that while we eat?"

Kalindi nodded. "If we can get it secured for the night, I'd be able to relax," she said gratefully.

"Consider it handled," Calen said. "Bartel?"

The soldier who had been diligently standing guard from outside the room peeped his friendly face around the door. "Sir?"

"Would you take these folks to the armory? And let's

double the night guard tonight."

"Aye, sir." Bartel gave a nod and turned toward the armory, down the hallway, motioning for Kalindi and Zeph to follow him. Rih took flight, landing neatly on Kalindi's shoulder, as if declaring herself Kalindi's personal escort for the journey.

Calen turned back to Mari. "Would you perhaps like to wash up before we see the general?"

Mari gave a nod. "You read my mind."

THE DOOR SHUT behind her with a *click*, the sound loud in the stillness of the washroom. The space was small, built for efficiency rather than comfort—just a basin of cool water, a cracked mirror, and a stack of rough linen towels folded on a short stool. A single candle rested in an old bracket on the wall.

She peeled off her travel-worn cloak and let her shirt drop to the floor. Her body ached. Seven days in the saddle had left its mark—her muscles were tight, and her skin was raw where her pack had rubbed, leaving dark bruises along her ribs.

She caught her reflection in the mirror and almost looked away. Her face was thinner, her eyes dark with the kind of exhaustion she knew sleep wouldn't fix. A deep-set exhaustion clung to her features, one that sleep wouldn't fix. Her hair stuck to her temples, the remnants of sweat and dirt making her look like someone she didn't recognize.

Gods, when was the last time I actually looked at myself? Mari turned away before she could answer that.

She dipped her hands into the basin, pushing a whistling breath through pursed lips as the cold water met her skin. She washed slowly, letting the grime of the road melt away but unable to scrub the pressure of everything else weighing down on her.

We could die tomorrow. The thought lodged itself in her chest. She hadn't allowed herself to think about it before—not fully. Not like this.

Her breath shuddered, and she braced her hands against the edge of the basin. Tomorrow, they would ride to Brindlemyre. If the device failed, if the Stewards were stronger than they expected, if their army wasn't enough...

She may never see the queen again.

The thought sent a splintering pain through her, unexpected in its depth. Lyra. Strong, untouchable Lyra. She was still in Joycita, still trapped under Bomi's watchful eye, still out of Mari's reach.

She sucked in a breath. She had spent years reading about Joycita from a distance, never imagining, never daring to imagine, she could stand beside the Queen of Patovia as someone of importance. And now, she had gotten close enough to feel the warmth of her presence, to see past the crown, past the careful walls Lyra had built around herself. And it wasn't enough.

Mari squeezed her eyes shut, gripping the edge of the basin until her knuckles turned white. Her mind drifted to Searsan. For a moment, she was back at the Great Library, sitting across from him at the desk in his office, his quick wit on full display. She could almost hear his voice—gentle, knowing. *You are more than this moment, Mari.*

Mari let out a shaking breath, blinking rapidly against the sting behind her eyes. Then, before she could stop it, a single sob ripped from her throat. It startled her how sudden, how raw it was—a ragged, broken sound, pulled from the depths of everything she was trying to ignore, and it burned as it escaped.

She pressed the heel of her palm to her mouth, trying to silence it, but it was too late. The dam had cracked. The grief, the fear, the exhaustion... It all flooded in. Tears slid down her cheeks, mixing with the water still clinging to her skin. She gasped for breath, trying to keep it quiet, to keep it contained, but there was no one here to see. No one here to judge.

So she let herself break.

For Searsan, who had believed in her.

For Lyra, who might never know how much Mari would have fought for her.

For every person back home in Greenhaven counting on her to get this right.

For herself.

Mari gritted her teeth, forcing a deep breath into her lungs. The entirety of her upper body shook, but the sobs grew quieter. She didn't have time to fall apart.

She wiped a trembling hand over her face. Then, slowly, she pulled herself together. She finished washing and dried herself gently, and then pulled a clean tunic over her head and ran a dry cloth over her arms and her neck.

Finally, she met her reflection again, forcing herself to look this time. Her eyes were red-rimmed but steady. Her heart was still hammering.

She breathed in deeply and then out. She grabbed a towel, dried her face, and gave a short shout of defiance into the mirror.

There was still a war to fight.

CHAPTER TWENTY-SIX

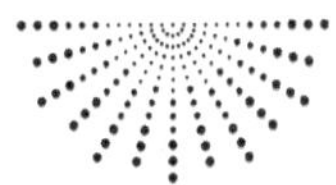

GENERAL CLAR SAT BEHIND HIS DESK, HIS BROAD hands resting one on top of the other, his fingers still, and his breathing slow. Outside, the wind shifted, pushing against the windowpanes, whispering a warning of the approaching storm. Clar's gaze swept over them as if he were studying pieces on a board, and he considered them with curiosity. "You want what?" he asked, clearly not convinced he had understood correctly.

Mari stood firm. "A unit of infantry. Armed soldiers to accompany us to Brindlemyre."

He leaned back in his chair, watching her with the kind of look that suggested she was either incredibly brave or incredibly stupid. "That's a bold request."

She nodded. "It is."

Clar snorted. "The queen's orders were to grant you what you need," he said, though his voice held no certainty. "But this is not weapons or grain. You ask me to send men into battle. People. Lives. You understand that? That is not a decision I can make lightly."

Kalindi shifted, impatient. "General, we're going to finish what you started. Surely, you want to help us."

The general's mouth thinned. He closed his eyes for the space of a breath, then opened them again. "This is a lot to consider. A lot of new information to process."

Kalindi grunted. "We've given you documents stolen from the Stewards' inner circle. Do you not believe us?"

Calen winced. Kalindi's biting tome was clearly out of order, but the general did not rise to it. "My concern is not whether your words are true. It is what this truth requires of me."

Kalindi made no move to protest as he continued to speak.

"If the Stewards have taken root as deeply as you claim, then a small unit will not be enough. If I send soldiers to Brindlemyre, then I must send nearly my entire outpost." The weight of his experience burned behind his bold eyes. "That is not a decision I can make alone."

Clar turned a page in the notebook Kalindi had placed in front of him, though it was clear he was not reading. "And you say Councilor Bomi is involved?"

Mari nodded. "He controls the queen's appointments, her decisions. Even the treasury."

"This is treason."

Kalindi folded her arms. "Then let's end it."

Clar let out a long breath, staring past them blankly. "I cannot mobilize the outpost without approval from Joycita." He sounded regretful with the unfortunate reality as it was. "And if the queen is as compromised as you claim, if we have been infiltrated as the evidence suggests, then I cannot seek approval without tipping them off. We would lose the element of surprise, and we would be stopped before we could even move."

Mari reached for Rih, who was perched tensely on Kalindi's shoulder. The little bird ruffled her feathers, sensing the unease in the room. Then, slowly, the idea barely formed in her mind as the words left her mouth, Mari said, "What if the approval came directly from the queen?"

"Without going through the chain of command?" General Clar tilted his head, not following.

Zeph stirred beside her, understanding immediately. "Are you certain Rih could make it? Aren't skyweavers still getting lost?"

Mari scooped Rih into her hands and held her tightly. "The east is still stable. If the Stewards haven't deployed their device here yet, she will find her way. Plus... Rih isn't a skyweaver. Not really."

Rih puffed herself up indignantly.

"It's a compliment, little one," Mari whispered. She unrolled a small parchment, wrote quickly, and tied the message to Rih's harness. "If the queen herself responds," she said, "will that be enough?"

Clar did not look convinced in the slightest. He considered her with a long, challenging gaze. "And how do you expect to reach the queen without Bomi intercepting the message?"

Mari rose to his challenge as she secured the last knot into place. "Rih will deliver it to Zećira's Tea House in the Lantern District."

She had not expected Kalindi's reaction.

The engineer stilled beside her. Mari turned, frowning at the snarl that had appeared across Kalindi's face.

"You know of the Mycelium?" Kalindi's voice sounded sour, and she looked so pale that, for a moment, Mari worried that she had been hit with a wave of nausea.

"Zećira is part of the Mycelium?" Mari asked, shocked.

Kalindi let out a slow, humorless laugh. Her lips curled, but there was no mirth in her smile. "Zećira is the Mycelium."

Clar's gaze moved between them, his brow furrowing. "I am going to need an explanation."

"They're a resistance group, General. More people are fighting the Stewards than you think. But they aren't some noble, righteous rebellion. They do what needs to be done. No matter the cost." Kalindi's jaw tightened before she added, "I learned that the hard way."

Clar studied her. "How?"

Kalindi didn't look at him, her angry foot tapping against the table leg aggressively. "They used me," she said, her voice venomous. "I thought I was helping the fight." She breathed slowly, as if forcing herself to say the words. "I thought if I told them where my mother was, they would save her. That they'd get her away from the Stewards, that we could finally run." Her face was tight with pain. "But it was never a rescue mission." Her hand curled into a fist. "The next day, she was dead."

No one moved.

Then Clar rubbed his temples and squeezed his eyes shut. "And this is the group you're trusting to get a message to the queen?"

Mari swallowed. "Lyra told me to contact them if I ever needed her. She said we could trust Zećira."

Kalindi inhaled deeply, then let the breath out. After a moment, she waved a hand. "It must be done."

Mari cupped Rih in her hands and lifted her to her face, whispering her instructions and pressing a small, brief kiss against the bird's head. "Does this window open?"

Clar rose, flicked the bolt, and pushed on the frame. The hinges squeaked with reluctance as they opened, and the taste of distant dust blew in with the breeze.

Mari lifted her hand, and Rih took flight. She let out a slow, controlled breath. "Strong threads."

The group watched as Rih became a speck in the distance, her small but powerful wings beating furiously, suddenly the most important bird in all of Patovia.

Clar leaned back and folded his arms, the picture of composure, his decades of military training on display. "If the queen responds," he said, "we move."

Mari nodded.

"But make no mistake." His voice slowed, as if he wanted them to really understand what he was saying. "If we do this, it is not a request for aid. It is war. And war does not end cleanly."

Kalindi's voice matched his. "That is why we must end them for good."

Clar studied her for a long moment. "You three are too young for this."

Mari wanted to show him that she understood what he was saying. She made a point to meet his gaze, keeping her eyes just as steady and unflinching as his. "We don't get to choose when the world needs us, General. When the call comes, you answer it—whether you're ready or not." Then she gave herself a little shake and lifted her chin higher than it was before, as if to make sure he saw what she felt in herself. "And I am ready."

Zeph cleared his throat. "I'd be more ready after something to eat, if I'm being completely honest."

Clar let out a short, hearty laugh. "Calen, get these three to the mess hall before they drop."

Calen stared at Clar with wide eyes, as if he'd never heard the general laugh before. He appeared unsure of whether it was appropriate to join in, and settled on an awkward smile before opening the door.

Clar stood by the window, double-checking the bolt before snapping the blinds shut. He turned back to Mari. "Let's hope your bird flies fast."

Mari swallowed. She had made this promise before—placed her faith in one of her skyweavers and assured someone they would come through. This time, she hoped for a better outcome.

~

THE DINING HALL was alive with murmured conversation, but at their table, the dread of what lay ahead had thinned the conversation to nothing.

Mari barely touched her food, pushing potatoes around her plate, more aware of the clatter of cutlery than the taste of anything in her mouth. She wasn't sure how food could be so good and taste like nothing at the same time, but here they were. Across from her, Zeph stretched out his legs and rolled his neck out with an exaggerated wince. "If I survive tomorrow," he announced, "I'm sleeping for a week. At least."

Kalindi, across from him, didn't acknowledge the comment. She hadn't spoken much since they had left General Clar's office, and not at all since they had sat down. She had barely touched her soup. Instead, she stirred it absently. Then, without warning, she stiffened, dropped her spoon, and shoved back from the table so fast that her chair nearly toppled. The sound of it scraping against the floor was as abrupt as her movements, and she darted toward the edge of the hall. A second later, she doubled over.

The sound of her retching was drowned out by the hum of the dining hall, but Zeph was on his feet in an instant. He crossed the hall and reached for Kalindi, but she threw up a hand before he could get too close. "Don't," she managed between deep breaths. "It's gross. I'm fine."

Zeph did not budge. "You're clearly not fine," he said flatly.

Kalindi shot him a glare, wiping her mouth with the back of her sleeve, her breath still unsteady. "This is deeply unattractive for both of us. Walk away."

Zeph crossed his arms. "Kal."

Kalindi pressed a hand to her stomach. "It's not just nerves," she confessed, although she spoke as if the words were harder to swallow than the dinner she'd just lost. "The mention of the... the Mycelium. It caught me off guard."

Mari tensed.

"I swore I'd never rely on them again. After what they did. After what they took from me."

Zeph nodded with understanding. He moved to Kalindi and placed a tentative hand on her shoulder. She flinched but didn't pull away completely. She closed her eyes, and a tear escaped from the crease and fell onto the floor below her.

"I thought I'd put it behind me. That I could hear their name without feeling like this," she whispered. "Guess not."

Silence settled between them. For once, Zeph didn't try to fill it with some well-meaning quip. He gave Kalindi's shoulder a squeeze and then disappeared without another word.

When he returned, he had a glass of water, and he pressed it into Kalindi's hand. She let her fingers rest on top of Zeph's as she took it.

Mari definitely noticed that.

Zeph looked at Mari and hummed. "Ginger would help."

Mari grabbed the opportunity to be helpful, and also to excuse herself from the intimacy unfolding in front of her. "I'll check the kitchens. I'm sure Brenna will give me some if they have any." She raced off, grateful for the errand, though she knew she shouldn't take too long. Kalindi really did look like she needed that ginger.

When she returned with a small piece of ginger root wrapped in a cloth napkin, Zeph was seated beside Kalindi. His arm was around her, and her head was resting on his shoulder. Without a word, he took the ginger from Mari and started to peel it.

Kalindi gripped her glass, holding it like a lifeline. She watched Zeph work, and Mari could have sworn she saw her blush when he looked at her and gave her a smile, but not his usual cocky grin full of bravado—this one was stripped of showmanship, far more genuine and reassuring.

Mari noticed the way Kalindi stared at him, and hid a smile behind a sip of her own drink.

Night fell and they retreated to their quarters in an attempt to get some rest. The barracks were uncomfortably quiet, and not the kind of quiet that brought calm.

Mari lay on her back, staring at the beams above, counting the knots in the grain in an attempt to quiet her racing mind. Would Rih make it back in time? Would they march into Brindlemyre alone, or with an army at their backs?

She could hear the slow breaths of the others, the blankets tousling as they shifted restlessly. No one spoke.

She knew there was no way to find the answers to any of the questions that were racing through her mind. Nor was there a way to stop herself from asking them. She tensed every muscle in her body, holding the strain until it bordered on cramping and her limbs started trembling, and then slowly let it go. It helped a little. She exhaled slowly and forced herself to accept that there would be no new information in the long stretch of dark before dawn.

At the far side of the room, Zeph let out a frustrated sigh. "I'm trying to sleep, but my brain won't shut up."

Kalindi groaned. "That's because you never use it, and now it's panicking from overwork."

"Thank you, Kalindi. Always a comfort," Zeph said with a snort.

A pause stretched across the quiet room before Mari pushed her blankets off and sat up. "What's it saying?" she asked.

Zeph shifted onto his side. "That this could be the worst idea we've ever had. That we should wait for Rih before we move out. That maybe we're walking straight into a trap."

Silence. Then Kalindi said, "We probably are."

"Great. Love the confidence," Zeph huffed.

Mari swallowed. "We've done everything we can. If we wait for a reply before we leave, we risk missing the alignment with the windstorm. We're going for widespread, maximum impact; we need that momentum. We have to push forward."

"Easy for you to say," Zeph grumbled. "You've lived it already. You've got all the experience of this past moon... I just have this stupid face."

Mari grinned in the dark. "It is a very punchable face."

Zeph gasped in mock offense. "Ah, and here I was worried you wouldn't think of any inspiring words to share. You're always so uplifting."

"Shut up and go to sleep." Kalindi's voice cut across the dark room.

No one did.

The night stretched on, and Mari lay awake still, hounded by the unknown. There was nothing left to do now but wait. If sleep came, it might make the waiting easier, but Mari knew she wouldn't be that lucky.

She stared at the ceiling, a teardrop sliding from the corner of her eye to the corner of her mouth. She sipped it in and hoped to the ancient gods above that Kalindi and Zeph wouldn't hear her cry. None of this was easy. None of it was supposed to be, but this was everything—quite possibly, the most important fight she would ever take on. And when the moment came, she would bring everything she had—her mind, her heart, her fear, her fire...all of it.

She could only hope it would be enough.

DAWN ARRIVED QUIETLY. No fanfare. No messages.

Mari stood in the barracks doorway. The outpost was waking, soldiers moving through their routines, unaware, or maybe uncaring, that she and her friends were about to ride into battle alone.

Her disappointment dulled her spirit. There had been no word from the queen. There would be no army at their backs. It would be just the three of them and Calen, who had boldly insisted to General Clar that he join the party. Clar had agreed it was the least he could do without blatantly breaking the rules.

Zeph approached, fastening the last buckle on his gear. "Still nothing?"

Mari shook her head.

"Figures."

"There's still time," Mari said hopefully, scanning the empty skies.

"No, there's not. It's time to go. We should already be on the road," Kalindi said.

No one argued.

Their horses were waiting, saddled and restless, their breath misting in the brisk morning air.

Zeph mounted first and gave a tight smile. "Well," he said, forcing a grin, "at least if we die, we won't ever have to ride another horse again."

Kalindi swung into her saddle like she had been riding all her life. "Speak for yourself. If we die, I'll go out looking competent. You'll be the one flopping off your horse in disgrace."

Zeph gasped and clutched his chest. "You wound me, Kal. You know I'd at least make a dramatic exit."

Kalindi adjusted her reins. "Let's hope that's the only wound you receive today."

Zeph's grin faltered. Then he leaned in, dropping his voice lower. "Worried about me?"

Kalindi snorted and nudged her horse forward. "You'd like to think so."

Mari cleared her throat loudly in an effort to curtail the not so subtle back and forth between these two, although deep down, she secretly loved it. "I don't plan on dying today."

Zeph gave her a look. "You say that like it's up to you."

Mari met his gaze. She felt powerful and immovable. She was ready to crush the Stewards into oblivion. "It is." She turned her horse toward the road that would take them to Brindlemyre.

With no army behind them, no guarantees ahead, and only each other to rely on, they rode.

CHAPTER TWENTY-SEVEN

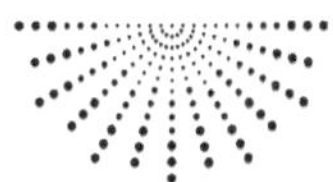

THE ROAD STRETCHED BEFORE THEM, SEEMINGLY endless. The wind carried grains of sand, an early omen of the coming storm, and the group had to work hard to keep their heads down and the grit out of their eyes.

Mari kept her eyes forward, her hands firm on the reins.

They were halfway to Brindlemyre when the ground began to shake. Mari's breath caught. A low, rolling rumble rippled through the earth, deep enough to stir the dust at their feet and make the horses shift uneasily beneath them.

Kalindi twisted in the saddle, pulling her horse to a stop alongside Mari's. "That can't be..."

"The storm?" Zeph finished, his voice tight.

No. surely not... It was far too early. Mari panicked at the thought that her calculations had been so drastically off. She yanked her telescope from her belt and scanned the horizon behind them. A sea of figures, their armor glinting under the sun and their banners raised, appeared as tiny dots in the distance. And at the front of it all... Rih.

The little bird cut through the sky like an arrow, closing

the distance between them in an instant. Mari lifted her arm and Rih landed hard on her shoulder. A scroll dangled from her harness, and Mari fumbled with the knot, her heart pounding as she unrolled it. The parchment was small and hastily written.

It contained two words: "Permission granted."

For a moment, she just stared. Then Zeph leaned over. "Uh, so, is this a good message, or should we start to run?"

Mari lifted her gaze, locking onto the figure at the head of the charge. General Clar, suited for battle, was grinning like a man ready to set fire to his enemies and watch them burn.

Mari couldn't stop the breathless laugh that escaped her. "Oh, it's a very good message."

Clar rode hard toward them, his warhorse kicking up dust, his infantry closing ranks behind him. The sight was enough to knock the wind from Mari's lungs.

Clar reined in his horse beside hers, a broad grin spread across his face, his eyes serious. "I want to make one thing clear," he said, his voice carrying over the rumble of hooves behind him and the restless energy of the gathered soldiers. "This isn't some glorious march into victory." He looked at each of them in turn. "This is war. My men know what they're risking, and I don't take that lightly."

Mari swallowed, nodding.

"But if there was ever a time to end this...It's now." Clar gave a steady, encouraging nod.

The energy shifted, now intense and electric. Zeph let out a loud whoop, pumping a fist in the air and tipping his head back with a grin. Kalindi reached for the hilt of her sword, tapping her fingers against the grip, her only tell that she was feeling anything at all. Mari bit the inside of her cheek and gripped her thighs together, absorbing the raw power of the horse beneath her.

Mari had imagined this moment so many times—riding into battle, the blood rush as she perched on the edge of readiness... Now, however, as she sat astride her horse, feeling the steady rise and fall of its breath and the powerful swell of its ribcage pushing against her calves, she realized something. It didn't feel like she thought it would. A creeping anxiety had slithered in, somewhere between when they had departed the outpost and this moment, dislodging her conviction. There was no grand swell of confidence, no roaring certainty in her chest. Instead, her mind moved too fast, considering every detail, every potential opening and every variable she couldn't control, like the impending windstorm, or the way Zeph was steadying the anti-echo device, or the tension Kalindi was trying so desperately to hide...

And beneath it all, a single, intrusive thought:

What if I get this wrong?

A gust of wind caught the edge of her cloak, yanking her forward just slightly. She inhaled. There was no room for ifs. She settled in the saddle, her voice steady when she finally spoke. "Move out."

Brindlemyre was ahead. Finally. And with the thunder of hooves shaking the ground, they pressed forward.

MARI SCANNED THE FIELDS AHEAD, her hands shaking as she slowed her breathing in an effort to catch her breath. The grass rippled with each strange gust of wind, bending and straightening as though whispering among themselves. The sky had darkened, a combination of the approaching evening and the clouds of dust being carried in by the storm.

There was nothing that stood out—no Stewards, no visible stronghold, and no battle waiting for them.

Behind her, the army stood restless. They had come expecting to fight, but they were met with the unsettling silence of an empty field instead.

"There should be something here," Kalindi whispered

Mari lifted her telescope and focused it on the horizon. There were trees, rock formations, and patches of high grass, but no caves or fortresses, and no sign of the hidden tunnels the stolen notes had led them to believe existed.

Zeph muttered under his breath. "I hate this. It feels like we called an entire army here just to have an awkward picnic."

Mari swallowed, lowering the telescope. "It doesn't make sense."

Clar turned to her, his voice calm. "Take a breath, Mari."

Obeying the general, Mari took a moment to center herself before she started making any more observations. She noticed the way the trees swayed at erratic angles, their branches snapping in directions that didn't align with the wind. She tried to tap into the vibrations in the air. Something felt... off.

"This is the calm before the storm," General Clar said. "And I don't just mean the windstorm." His gaze swept across the open land. "Just because you feel alone doesn't mean you are."

Mari's uncertainty grew stronger. "Calen?" she called, glancing over her shoulder.

Calen nudged his horse forward through the front row of soldiers. "We should be heading for the caves." He gestured toward the mountains in the distance, the Myramin River carving a path across the ridge. "If I had to wager, I'd say that's where they're set up."

Kalindi twisted in her saddle. "No. We need to be sure. We need to find the device. If we don't deploy our countermeasure in exactly the right location, none of this matters."

"If we can pinpoint the general area, the windstorm's timing should do the rest, right?" Mari asked.

Kalindi shook her head. "That's a risk. We don't know exactly where—"

"I do." Mari brought her telescope back to her eye and turned it toward the sky that was deepening into twilight, the first faint streaks of the aurora stretching across the darkness.

The constellations had begun their slow shift westward. She traded her telescope for her astrolabe to trace the movement of the heavens while following the thread of calculation in her mind. She turned slowly, aligning herself with the pull of gravity and the shifting air.

"This way." She nudged her horse forward, leading them toward a rolling hill. Behind her, the army held position as she dismounted and handed the reins to Zeph before making her way up the ridge alone.

Something deep within told her to be cautious. She crouched beside a large tree with low-hanging branches and lifted her scope again. And then... There it was—not caves, but a hillside, carved out unnaturally, shaped by hands rather than nature, exactly like the ones outside Adavale and the Isa Glades.

This was the spot. For a brief moment, excitement and adrenaline surged before it was crushed beneath the weight of realization. She saw fire pits, at least two dozen of them, dotted across the crest. She lowered her scope and cursed.

Clar, standing beside her with his own scope, let out his own choice words at the sight. He was already calculating. "Five men per campfire," he murmured. "We're looking at well over a hundred."

Mari watched the way the group of Stewards laughed easily, completely unprepared for the army that was watching them from just beyond the ridge. "Definitely not tipped off," she said.

Clar nodded grimly. "Good. They don't know we're here."

"So, what now?" Mari asked.

"We made excellent time, General," came the voice of a soldier from within the ranks. "Perhaps we wait until it's darker before we strike?"

"Good instincts, Bartel, but we have no time to waste," Clar responded. He scanned the ranks behind them and then turned his horse in the direction of his officers. "We'll need a moment to communicate the target," he said calmly. "No use charging in if they don't know what they're aiming for, but the troops will be ready to strike on my command."

Mari nodded. "Alright." She turned to Kalindi and Zeph, motioning them closer. "Any moment now. You two ready?"

Zeph adjusted his grip on the straps of his pack that held their device and nodded. "Get this thing in place and hold it steady."

Mari held his gaze. "And?"

Zeph's mouth twitched. "And don't die."

Mari gave him a nod. "Good. Stick to that."

Zeph arched his brow. "I'd love a little recap with a few extra details before we throw ourselves into this Steward death trap," he admitted.

"We get into the cave, locate the device, and place the anti-echo device beside it." Mari glanced at Kalindi. "That sound about right?"

Kalindi hesitated. "Almost."

Mari was concerned. "Kalindi."

"There may be one thing I haven't mentioned yet."

Mari stared at her. "What?!"

Kalindi winced and rubbed the back of her neck. "I wasn't sure how to bring it up... but, I'm... I'm not exactly completely certain that this is going to work."

Zeph threw up his hands. "Kalindi!"

"You said you were confident this would work," Mari said, frustrated.

Kalindi shrugged. "Fake it till you make it?" She gave a weak, sheepish smile.

Mari dragged a hand down her face. "You're telling me we might be risking everything on a gamble?"

Kalindi lifted a hand. "It's not a gamble. Do you remember the stone in my gauntlet?"

"The one that was stolen? Of course." Mari glared at Kalindi. "I knew that was a bigger deal than you made it out to be."

Kalindi nodded hurriedly, clearly trying to move past the point quickly. "It wasn't just a stone. It had vibrational properties. I was going to use it to amplify the frequency of my device. When it was stolen, I lost my best shot at making sure this worked."

Zeph crossed his arms. "Fantastic. So, we're walking into this without the secret ingredient?"

Kalindi shook her head. "Not exactly." She reached into her pocket and pulled out something small, cupping it carefully in her palm.

Mari squinted. The tiny pappus spores sat motionless in the crook of her hand. "You said you were going to use those, right?" she asked.

Kalindi nodded. "When I saw the spores in the Glowing

Gardens, I thought maybe they could work instead. They generate energy like my stone did, just in a different way." She let out a slow breath. "I'll drop them into the cup built into the device. If I'm right, it should work just as well as the stone was supposed to. I just don't know for sure if it will be enough."

Mari rubbed her forehead. "Kalindi, I swear—"

Zeph clapped a hand on Mari's shoulder. "Hey. No turning back now."

"I did say it was a theory, when I first told you about it," Kalindi said, as if that made it better.

Mari sighed. As their only option, they had no choice but to go with it. "Alright. Let's hope this works. Zeph, you get our device as close to theirs as possible, and then Kalindi, you take it from there."

Zeph patted the anti-echo device, offering them a lopsided smile. "Wherever you need it, I'll put it. No matter what."

Kalindi swallowed, eyes flicking between them. Then, quieter, "Thank you," she said. "For believing in me."

Mari reached out and gripped Kalindi's arm. "Thank you for being here."

Kalindi let out a shaky breath. "Guess I got attached."

Zeph poked his head between them. "To whom?"

Mari rolled her eyes.

Then Clar's voice rang out behind them. "Troops, hold position!" Atop his warhorse, Clar's words carried over the soldiers like rolling thunder. "We strike swiftly and decisively," he said. "Our priority is holding the line while the device is deployed. The Stewards don't know we're here. We keep it that way until we are already upon them."

A ripple of murmured acknowledgment.

Clar turned to Mari with sharp eyes, ready to launch. "Tell me when."

Mari met his gaze, then turned back to Zeph and Kalindi. "Strong threads," she said, wiping the sweat from her palms on her pants.

"Bright flames," Kalindi replied with a smile. She tucked the pappus spores back into her pocket and shot Mari a wink.

Clar raised his arm... and the charge began.

THE FIRST ARROW whistled through the air before Mari had even reached the hill. The moment the militia crested the rise, the Stewards realized what was happening. Chaos erupted in the camps. Men scrambled for weapons, for shields, for any semblance of order.

It was too late. The first wave of Clar's soldiers slammed into them, and the sound of steel against steel rang out across the valley. The battle surged forward, bodies colliding, swords clashing, and warhorses rearing.

Rih shrieked as she plunged from the sky, her talons slashing at the exposed, vulnerable places the enemy couldn't protect, quick and merciless.

Mari moved forward. Zeph was at her side, clutching the anti-echo device, keeping pace as they cut a straight path toward the cave opening. Kalindi was ahead, her dagger drawn and her eyes locked in on the three guards stationed at the entrance.

One of the guards saw them coming, but Clar's arrow caught him first. He went down without a sound. The second lunged, but Kalindi met him head on, the steel of her blade flashing.

Mari ducked as the third man swung for her, twisting away just as Zeph crashed into him. Mari turned back and kicked out his knees from the side, his screams piercing above the sounds of battle around them. Zeph delivered a strong punch to the man's head, knocking him out before he even hit the ground.

Zeph and Mari sprinted toward the cave as Kalindi dispatched the second guard with brutal efficiency, sending him crumpling to the dirt. The entrance was clear.

Behind them, the battle raged, and the wind whipped through them as the storm snapped at their heels, arriving almost exactly with the timing that Mari had predicted. She had no time to congratulate herself. She turned to Zeph and Kalindi. "You both ready?"

Zeph gave a nod. "Right behind you."

Kalindi shook out her shoulders and delivered a nod of her own.

Then, together, they plunged into the darkness.

CHAPTER TWENTY-EIGHT

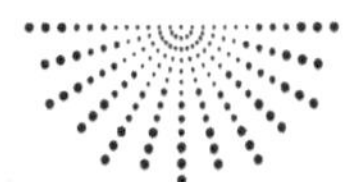

The cave walls were humming.

Mari could feel the pulse of something undeniable in the air, and while she knew this was a mere replication designed for evil, she couldn't help but feel drawn in by the ancient power. The walls around her had been shaped with stolen schematics that were far older than the Stewards themselves. Above, wide openings in the ceiling let shafts of moonlight spill through.

The inside of the cave felt overwhelmingly familiar to Mari. Not because of instinct, but because she had been here before. Not this exact place, but others just like it. The etchings on the walls, the angled passageways, the way the space curved in on itself... It all mirrored the chamber she had explored outside Adavale and again in the Isa Glades. Even in the darkness, she knew where to go.

She let her fingers trail along the stone, mapping the space as she had done before, following the curve of the wall as her eyes adjusted. The path widened, then opened, and she stepped into a vast, hollowed-out space.

As they got closer, the hum deepened. It was a pressure

inside her ribs, a bone-deep vibration that made the hair on the back of her neck stand on end. Her breath stilled. The sound was overpowering.

Zeph staggered behind her, grimacing as he clutched his chest. "Gods, that's—"

"I know," Mari cut in, her voice tight. She felt it too. "I..." She swallowed her words as they rounded a final corner, her eyes widening when she took in what was in front of her.

At the center of the cave, towering and crude, stood the Stewards' echo device. It was nothing like Kalindi's.

Mari didn't need to be an engineer to see that this contraption was wrong. It was a clunky, gutted monstrosity, pieced together with no care or understanding. But somehow, it worked.

Zeph struggled to get the device off his back, fighting the pain caused by the vibrations. Mari and Kalindi rushed to help him, and together they got it unpacked and set up beside the Stewards' contraption.

Kalindi's device was sleek and perfect, built with the care of someone who knew what they were doing, but compared to the chaotic build of the Stewards' device, it looked... small.

Zeph looked to Kalindi. "Is it okay here?"

Kalindi nodded and reached into her pack for the pappus spores, sprinkling them into the chamber. She pulled a bronze tuning rod from her bag and tapped the top of the forked metal protruding from their device. Then, again, lower, near the base.

Their device hummed in response, but the sound wasn't the same as the echo device. It was deeper. Slower.

Kalindi went rigid. Her head snapped up, panic blooming across her face. "No, no, no."

Zeph immediately turned to her. "What?"

Kalindi frantically adjusted the tuning rod and tapped the metal again, once, twice, listening. Her breathing picked up. "The resonance is too weak," she said, her voice high. "It's not generating enough of a vibration to counter the echo device."

Mari tried not to panic. "Fix it."

"I'm trying!" Kalindi snapped. She ran her fingers through her hair, gripping it tight before shoving her hands back into the device. "The frequency is wrong, and the energy transfer isn't stabilizing. It should be working."

Mari ripped open her satchel, digging through its contents with shaking hands. She pulled out a handful of soil samples and sorted through them frantically. Adavale, no. Joycita, no. Elyria's edge, no. "Come on..." She turned over the next soil sample and counted the knots on the tie. Bingo.

She yanked it open, and soil spilled out onto the floor, small pieces of rock and plant buried among the dirt, their faint glow catching the dim light. "You said everything has a hum, right?" She held it out to Kalindi. "Soil from the Glowing Gardens... Will this help?"

Kalindi grabbed it without hesitation and dumped the soil and stones into the chamber on top of the spores.

For a moment, nothing happened. Then, deep in Mari's chest, she felt it. The hum shifted from a sound to a feeling that seemed to pull a resonating force through her bones.

Kalindi grinned, her eyes bright. "She's alive." The satisfaction was short-lived, though, and her face suddenly fell as quickly as it had lit up. Her hands trembled when she tapped the outer box again and listened, her brow furrowing.

Zeph noticed it too. "Kalindi."

She stared at her device, crestfallen. "It's still not strong enough."

Mari felt a jolt of fear. "What?"

Kalindi's voice rose. "Their resonance is still stronger! We're not countering the echo!" She let out a cry of concern. "I—I don't understand. This should be working."

Mari was about to press her when a booming voice made her jump. "You didn't think we would know you were coming?"

The voice curled through the cavern like smoke. Mari whirled, her breath catching as a figure emerged from the shadows, his gait slow, like he had been waiting. He stepped forward into the pale light, his angular face smiling, though there was not a trace of warmth behind it.

"You took such care to travel undetected," he mocked. "Did you really believe we wouldn't know? You think we don't have men inside the outpost?"

Mari's body locked in place, her hand edging toward her weapon as slowly as she could without him noticing. Who was this?

Then, the man looked past her to Kalindi. His smile widened. "You never really did think things through, did you... Kalindi?"

Mari felt, more than saw, Kalindi stiffen beside her. For the first time since she had met her, Kalindi did not have a sharp remark or a quick retort. Instead, she took an unsteady step back, trembling, and that was all the body language Mari needed to understand. This was personal—Kalindi knew this man, and by the way her face had gone ashen...she feared him.

The silence stretched for a fraction too long before Kalindi finally spoke, her voice barely above a whisper. "Kareth."

"Now, now, is that the proper way to greet your father?" Kareth laughed cruelly. "Welcome home, sweetheart."

Kalindi set her jaw. "You're not going to win, you know."

Kareth simply smiled. "Win?" he echoed, as if amused by

the notion. "Kalindi, I've already won. The people deserve control. We're just giving them what they want."

Kalindi's fists clenched. "You have no idea what the people want. And you don't t get to decide what they deserve."

Kareth laughed smugly, the condescension blatant. He appeared entirely unbothered by everything going on around him. "Your little science project is useless, Kalindi," he continued. "We built another device."

The words echoed off the cave walls, wrapping around the deep hum of the devices.

"We built another device."

Mari's heart stuttered.

"It's already running," he continued. "Your brother warned me about that look in your eye, Kalindi. We couldn't take any chances that you might cause us any further setbacks, not when we're so close to the final phase."

Mari frantically calculated her next moves. Beside her, Kalindi remained still.

Kareth took another step closer. "Lucky for us," he said, "you left us a final gift to help us amplify our mission."

The realization came crashing down on Mari and she looked at Kalindi's bare wrist to confirm her fears.

No.

No.

"You stole my gauntlet," Kalindi snarled.

Kareth laughed. "Stole? No, Kalindi. We reclaimed what was always meant to be ours."

Kalindi snapped. "IT BELONGED TO MY MOTHER!" she yelled, and lunged toward him, but Zeph was faster. With a roar of fury, he slammed into Kalindi's father, tackling him to the ground. His fist connected hard with Kareth's jaw.

Mari spun toward Kalindi. She grabbed her wrist, jolting

her back into reality. "We need to get our device outside!" she shouted over the storm, her voice barely carrying over the rising thrum. "The wind will amplify its vibrations!"

Kalindi looked over to Zeph, who was still grappling with Kareth.

Mari shook her harder. "Kalindi..."

Kalindi's eyes locked onto hers. "Do you trust me?" she demanded.

Mari's answer was immediate. "Have we not established that already?"

Kalindi shook her wrist free from Mari's grip. "Then go. Leave me here to deal with my father."

Mari nodded.

"I trust you!" Kalindi called to her as Mari grabbed the anti-echo device, staggering under its weight, and ran.

THE WIND HIT HER INSTANTLY, roaring in her ears as she fought her way against the gusts, looking for somewhere to set up the device. She didn't have many choices as the battle still raged on, but she finally spotted a space big enough to set it up away from the ongoing battle. A Steward caught sight of her and moved in her direction, but Calen was there first. His sword ran the man through before he got anywhere near her.

Calen's gaze met Mari's, and he gave her a quick nod before turning to look for other threats. "You can do this!" he shouted.

Mari dropped to her knees, bracing as she lowered the device onto the earth, setting it down just as a powerful gust tore through the valley. It howled as it funneled through the device's resonance chamber, catching on the tuning forks. She steadied herself just as the first shift occurred—a subtle tremor in the air that made the very ground beneath her seem to vibrate in response.

The soil and spores in the cup flared to life, pulsing with a glow inside the metal casing. Mari cupped her hand over the top of them, worried that they would spill out with the force of the wind, but they remained tightly tucked in thanks to Kalindi's clever design.

The device started working immediately, and Mari felt the frequency deep and steady within her chest. She paused, her breath shallow as she waited for the change to ripple through the valley, expecting some sort of sign that the battle for the skies was finally tipping in their favor.

Something was wrong. Despite the power radiating from the device, the air around her remained thick, pressing down rather than lifting. The atmosphere still felt stagnant, and the auroras above shifted sluggishly as if caught between two opposing forces. Mari felt her body flush with a wave of heat as her anxiety took the reins. Why wasn't it working? The wind was strong enough. The device was in the perfect place. So, why did everything still feel the same?

Then, from the corner of her vision, something emerged, from the opening of the cave, moving swiftly in her direction and closing the distance between them with unnerving speed. It was Kareth, and he looked furious.

Mari's breath caught in her throat, and she looked to Calen, but he was too far away, engaged against two Stewards.

Kareth was bearing down on her, his eyes locked on the device, his intent clear.

She pushed herself upright and caught sight of Kalindi and Zeph, both racing full tilt after him, their weapons drawn and their faces strained with exertion. Zeph's nose was streaming with blood, but he leaped at Kareth and dragged him to the ground.

Kalindi's voice ripped through the wind, her words raw, desperate, barely audible over the roaring storm. "Destroy the other device, Mari!"

As they grappled, Kalindi's eyes searched out Mari's, making sure her words landed. "Even with the wind supercharging ours, as long as there are two, ours will never be strong enough!"

The warning had barely left her lips when her father's fist slammed into her face. Kalindi's head snapped to the side, her body reeling from the impact, dropping toward the ground like a dead weight. Zeph was there immediately. He lunged between them, bloodied and breathless, catching Kalindi with one arm and throwing a punch with the other so hard that it sent Kareth staggering backward. Kalindi shook herself, blinking the daze away, spat blood onto the ground, and launched herself back toward her father, teeth bared.

Mari's body locked up, and suddenly she couldn't move her feet. Every instinct screamed at her to stay and throw herself into the fight alongside Kalindi and Zeph.

Then, through gritted teeth, Zeph roared. "Go, Mari!" Blood sprayed from his mouth as he rounded on Kareth.

Mari tore her eyes away and forced herself to move. She turned, her feet already in motion, and sprinted away from the chaos. She snapped her eyes to the mountains in the distance, where the second device was still running. She could feel it in the way the atmosphere refused to shift, the auroras above were still shining, and the wind struggled against invisible chains.

She pushed harder, her lungs burning as she broke free of the battlefield. The moment she reached open ground, she yanked out her astrolabe and did her best to hold it steady.

The device spun in her hands, aligning with the currents of the air. She scanned the sky, searching... There.

The sky above the distant caves warped, its patterns twisting unnaturally. Now she knew what she was looking for; she could practically see the ripple in the atmosphere. The second echo device was hidden in the very caves Calen had warned them about.

Mari gritted her teeth and took off at full speed, the world narrowing to nothing but her breath, her heartbeat, and the mountains ahead. The Myramin River lay between her and the base of the cliffs, the water black and glassy under the storm-heavy sky, but she didn't slow, or pause, or think.

She plunged into the icy current, the cold gripping her body like a vice, but she pushed forward, kicking against the current, fighting toward the other side. She had to reach the caves.

The wind crackled with static, the vibrations from the anti-echo device resonating through the storm, not quite strong enough to make a difference.

She was nearly across the river when she slipped. The slick stones beneath her gave way, and suddenly, she was falling. Her shoulder crashed into the riverbed, icy water swallowing her whole.

The current was faster than it looked and pulled at her like grasping hands, spinning her under. The world became a chaotic blur of rushing water, limbs flailing, and lungs screaming for air. She kicked against the force dragging her downstream before her fingers snagged something... Reeds.

She gripped them, scrambling against the slick river rocks, and with a final, desperate heave, she dragged herself onto the rocky shore, water dripping from her sleeves. She had no time to waste, so she forced herself upright and ran. The entrance to the mountain caves loomed ahead.

The wind screamed in Mari's ears as she closed the distance, but the moment she neared the opening, she saw them—two guards were stationed at the mouth of the cave, their weapons drawn, very much ready for a fight.

She didn't slow down, though. The guards tensed, realizing too late that she wasn't stopping. She roared with unbridled aggression and threw herself into the fight.

The first man swung high, but Mari ducked low, twisting, her knife already in her hand. Her instincts took over and she sidestepped his strike, pivoting as she slammed the hilt of her blade into his ribs. He staggered, but she was already moving. Her foot hooked behind his knee and she yanked. A loud snap cracked across the cave mouth as he collapsed.

The second guard was faster. He lunged, but Mari pivoted and slipped past his swing, her knife already in motion. She drove it up, straight into his sternum. The man gasped, his eyes wide in shock, but she wasn't done. She ripped the knife free, spun, and with a single stab, drove the knife deep into his eye. His body seized, a garbled cry tearing from his throat, before he collapsed beside his lifeless companion.

Mari staggered back, her breath heaving and fingers slick with blood and water. For a brief second, the world tilted, but she had no time to stop. She forced her limbs to step over the bodies and ran into the dark cave.

The moment she got inside, the sound slammed into her. It was a deep, grating wail, so unnatural that it felt as if the air inside the cave was splintering apart. The walls seemed to tremble with it, pulsing in time with the unbearable frequency, warping the space around her. The pressure was a relentless, suffocating force that drilled into her skull, clawed at the insides of her ears, and vibrated against her ribs. Her teeth ached from the sheer intensity of it.

A wave of nausea hit her so fast and violently that she had to slam a hand against the rough cave wall to stay upright. The churning sensation rose quickly, climbing into her throat, choking her with it. She squeezed her eyes shut and tried to breathe through it, but every inhale felt thin, useless, like her lungs were being compressed by the very air around her.

Still, she forced herself forward. Every step was a battle. Her vision swam, black spots dancing at the edges. The floor beneath her felt unsteady, as if it was suspended by ropes, rising and falling in uneven jolts. She stumbled, barely catching herself before she hit the ground.

She shook her head, forcing herself to focus, telling herself that the ground wasn't moving—it only felt that way. The vibrations here were stronger and deeper than in the first cave, distorting everything around her.

The second echo device sat at the center of the chamber, just as the first had, humming with a deep, terrible power. It was larger than the first. Sleeker and sharper. This wasn't a device haphazardly thrown together. It was their perfected version, fine-tuned to tear the fabric of the world apart, to own the sky, to control the elements. And at its core, glowing faintly in a carved-out chamber and pulsing with power, was Kalindi's stolen stone.

Mari's insides lurched. Even through the haze of reverberations that threatened to split her apart, she recognized it instantly. She choked on a breath. The pressure was unbearable now, pressing down on her from all sides. She barely had time to turn her head before she vomited onto the cave floor. She trembled as she wiped her mouth with the back of her hand, swallowing against the acrid burn in her throat.

Her head throbbed. Squeezing her eyes shut, she willed the pain to stop, forcing herself to focus, to move.

The stone. It was cracked but still functioning, amplifying the vibrations that were currently trying to tear her apart. She had to take it. Before she could give in to the pain, she lunged for it.

Her fingers closed around the gem, her nails digging into the rough edges of the crack. It was warm to the touch, like it was burning from the inside. With a yank, she ripped it free.

The hum stuttered, the frequency dipping as the pressure inside her skull eased just slightly, but not enough.

"OH, COME ON!"

The device was still running. Even without the stone, even with its power weakened, it was still functioning. Mari's heart pounded in her throat. The device thrummed erratically, struggling to adjust, but it wasn't stopping. She needed to change that... now.

She let out a ragged shout, and with the last of her strength, she grabbed the device and heaved it off balance, sending it crashing into the floor. The impact sent a piercing scream through the cave.

Mari staggered, barely able to keep her footing as the cave trembled around her. "Would you just stop already?!" she roared. Her voice was swallowed instantly by the withering wails of the failing device.

She wrenched a metal panel free and then swung it down with all the force she had left. The device buckled under the strength of the blow, crumbling into itself. Then she swung again. And again. And again. Every strike landed with purpose, with rage, with grief.

Her breath came in gasps as she drove her boot into the wreckage, sending shards of metal skittering across the cave floor. She didn't stop until there was nothing left but dust and an empty, hollow silence.

The hum was gone. Mari staggered back, her entire body trembling, wrecked. *Is it over?*

Her ears rang with the aftershock. The pounding in her head was like a drumbeat, throbbing out of sync with her pulse, but something had changed. The weight in the air had lifted. The oppressive, suffocating pressure that had been bearing down on her was simply... gone. She wondered if the sky outside would be different too.

Mari pressed her hand to her forehead, trying to steady herself. Her body ached from the inside out, exhaustion sinking into her soul. She turned unsteadily toward the mouth of the cave and forced herself forward, staggering toward the moonlight until she finally broke free of the tunnel. She stumbled into the waiting night and leaned heavily against the cool stone of the entrance. The sky was changing already. The auroras still twisted above, but Kalindi had been right. The natural balance was slowly settling, and the pressure that had once made the world feel off-kilter was beginning to fade.

·The storm had passed.

CHAPTER TWENTY-NINE

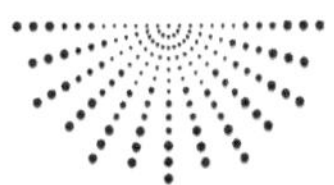

MARI KEPT HER PACE SLOW AS SHE RETURNED TO THE bloodstained battlefield, her muscles stiff, her ears still ringing with a phantom hum. The sounds of the battle were gone, replaced by the murmur of the wounded giving occasional groans of pain.

She scanned the survivors. The Stewards were outnumbered. Some had fled into the darkness, their escape paths barely visible in the fading light. Others knelt in surrender, their hands raised, their weapons discarded, their eyes hollow as they awaited their fate.

She barely noticed the Joycita militia sweeping through the field, chasing down those who still ran. Her focus shifted instead to the anti-echo device.

It was still running, right where she had left it. The frequency that emanated from it was warm and stable—a welcome contrast to the cold, sinister resonance of the Stewards' device.

Mari expected to see Kalindi or Zeph nearby, but they were nowhere in sight. Instead, she spotted Calen, leaning against a fallen log and drinking from a waterskin. His face was streaked with dirt and he had a fresh gash above his eye, but he looked alright otherwise. He pushed himself upright as he noticed her approaching.

He met her with a clasp of the arm and pressed the waterskin into her hand. "Are you okay?"

Mari nodded. She wasn't sure if that was true, but it was easier than explaining. She took a long drink, feeling every cut inside her throat sting as the water trickled down. Lowering the flask, she reached into her satchel and her fingers closed around the stone—Kalindi's stone.

She stepped toward the anti-echo device and crouched beside it. The soil and spores inside the resonance chamber were still glowing brilliantly, their energy unwavering. She let the stone fall into place, settling atop them. The reaction was instant. The frequency deepened, shifting into something much fuller.

Mari turned to Calen, motioning toward the sky. "Look."

The auroras were fading further, receding from the inside out, like breath dissolving into a cloud of smoke.

"This has to be guarded at all times," she said, making sure she conveyed the importance of her instruction. "It needs to run until... I don't actually know how long. We'll have to ask Kalindi."

Calen nodded, and Mari could see that he was pushing through his exhaustion. "Three men, rotating shifts?"

"At least. No one touches it but us."

"I'll run it up the flagpole. We'll make it a priority."

Mari nodded, but her mind was already moving elsewhere. Suddenly, a thought struck her like a cold slap. She remembered Kareth saying that he knew they were coming. A chill shook her spine. Someone had told him.

She turned back to Calen, urgency rising in her voice. "The outpost was infiltrated," she said. "Someone gave away our movements."

Calen's expression darkened.

"Where is General Clar?" And more importantly... Where were Zeph and Kalindi?

Without a word, Calen took off at a run.

Mari's eyes swept the battlefield again, this time faster. Her gaze landed on a passing soldier, his armor battered and his face smeared with dirt and exhaustion. She grabbed his arm, stopping him mid-stride. "You."

The man turned, straightening instinctively at her tone.

"Are you steady?" She waited for his nod before continuing. "Good. I need you to keep watch over this device." She motioned toward the anti-echo device. "It has to stay running. Don't touch it and don't let anyone else touch it. Just stand guard until you're relieved. Understood?"

The soldier nodded again and took up position beside the device.

Mari gave a sharp whistle, and almost immediately, Rih dropped from a high branch, streaking toward her from where she'd been resting, hidden among the leaves. She landed lightly, her feathers streaked with dark blood, but the bright chirp she gave in greeting told Mari she was unharmed. She reached up to brush a hand over Rih's blood-smeared feathers, relief washing over her.

"Good girl," she murmured.

Across the field, Calen's voice rang out. "Mari!"

Her head snapped toward him. Calen was standing beside General Clar, waving her over.

General Clar was kneeling beside an injured soldier, his hands moving swiftly as he tied a tourniquet around the man's bleeding arm. His face was grim, streaked with sweat, but as Mari approached, he looked up at her, his eyes smiling. "It's over," he said.

Mari smiled weakly. "General, I need to tell you something—"

Clar cut her off, shaking his head. "We already know."

Mari blinked. "Know what?"

Clar pushed himself to his feet, brushing the dirt from his uniform. "The outpost was compromised," he said flatly. "We caught him. Bartel. He tried to flee with the Stewards when they scattered."

Mari stopped cold. Bartel—the kind soldier who had helped them secure the anti-echo device in the armory the night before, the man who had shared a meal with them and pretended to be one of them, the man they had trusted. She felt her fury rise. "Where is he? I want to question him."

GENERAL CLAR LED Mari over the hill where Bartel sat against a mossy boulder, his hands tied behind his back. The crest of Joycita had been ripped from his uniform, his eyes were bloodshot, and his lip was split.

A thousand questions swirled in Mari's mind, but she asked the most important one first. "Who gave you your orders?"

Bartel smiled, and something about the way his lips curved gave Mari the feeling that he was holding something back. She felt the urge to punch the smile right off his face.

His head lolled back against the rock, his breath uneven, his body slack with fatigue. He'd been more than just roughed up by the outpost soldiers. He looked like he was on the edge of delirium as he spoke. "You think you've won..."

Mari stepped closer, grabbed the front of his tunic, and pulled him upright. "Were you a plant from the beginning?" Her voice was low, controlled. "Or did someone get to you?"

Clar placed a steadying hand on Mari's shoulder. "Let's take him to Brindlemyre and get him seen to. Once he's had some fluids and rest, we can question him again. We didn't get anything out of him either."

Bartel laughed, but it turned into a cough and he choked on his own fluids that rattled in his throat. Mari stepped back in disgust as he spluttered. "You walk into Brindlemyre and you'll be dead before sunrise." His head rolled lazily toward her, his smile widening, his teeth red with blood. "They're waiting for you."

Mari's frustration overpowered her self-control, and she shoved him back against the rock and turned away, kicking at a patch of grass.

Clar stepped in front of her, his hands firm on her shoulders. "Don't let him get to you, Mari. The battle is won. The Stewards won't recover from this." He gestured around the battlefield, taking in the scattered remnants of their forces—those who had fallen, those who had fled, and those who now knelt in surrender, awaiting their fate. "We obliterated nearly their entire force. Whatever remains is fractured, and their leaders, wherever they're hiding, won't hold power for long. Without an army behind them, they have nothing." His gaze hardened. "Brindlemyre is next. We'll secure the city and weed out any lurking loyalists. If there are still Stewards hiding inside its walls, we'll find them."

He extended a hand. Mari gripped it, shaking firmly. "Then

we move on to Joycita," she said, her voice hoarse. "The capital will need to be cleansed of the Stewards just as thoroughly."

Interrupting the moment, Bartel coughed again, more violently this time, a spatter of blood spraying from his mouth. "Not just Stewards," he rasped.

Clar and Mari exchanged a glance. She crouched beside him, getting as close to him as she could without having to smell his stench. "Who?"

Bartel's eyes fluttered closed. "They're inside." His voice was barely above a whisper. "They're everywhere."

Clar turned to the soldier standing watch. "Keep an eye on his pulse. I want him alive and strong enough to answer questions tomorrow."

The soldier nodded.

Clar turned back to Mari. "We'll secure Joycita. Make sure this evil is banished for good." He held her gaze for a moment before adding, "You did well, Mari."

She should have felt something. Pride? Triumph? At the very least, satisfaction... But all she felt was empty. The battle was won, but Zeph and Kalindi were nowhere to be seen.

As if on cue, a panicked voice cut through the settling quiet.

Mari's heart lurched into her throat. It struck at the gnawing fear that had been sitting deep in her gut that something was still very wrong.

She turned, barely fast enough to see Zeph barreling toward her, his steps uneven, his body buckling under the weight of something heavy and limp in his arms. No... Not something. Someone.

Mari's breath stopped. Zeph's face was white with terror, his body barely holding itself upright as he staggered forward, his arms wrapped tightly around Kalindi's lifeless form.

Mari's vision sharpened. She was moving before she even realized it, sprinting toward them, General Clar right behind her.

Zeph's voice was breaking. "She needs help!" His arms shook under the strain of carrying her, but he didn't loosen his grip, refusing to let up even as his knees nearly buckled beneath him.

Mari barely registered the words before she was there, her hands reaching out instinctively. Kalindi's body pressed into her as she helped ease her down onto the ground. She was so pale. Her skin was clammy and streaked with blood, and her breathing was so shallow that her chest was barely moving.

"Kalindi." Mari's tone was sharp. "Can you hear me?"

Nothing.

Zeph shook his head, his chest rising and falling fast and uneven.

Mari turned to Clar. "Where are the healers?"

Clar hesitated, just for a second, but Mari saw it before he even spoke. His mouth pressed into a thin line, his eyes dark with regret.

And then, everything clicked. There had been no healers tending to Bartel, and no one moving among the wounded, distributing medicine or setting broken bones.

"They were killed in the fight," Clar said. "All of them."

Mari felt the world waver. She leaned back, letting Zeph regain hold of Kalindi as she steadied herself.

No.

No, no, no.

Zeph let out a curse, his voice shaking. "Then, where do we take her?"

"Brindlemyre," Clar said. He turned, already scanning the battlefield, looking for the least-wounded militia members who could assist. "We can get her there fast. Someone there will be able to help."

Mari shook her head. Her hand shot up, stopping him. "No! You heard what Bartel said. We don't know how many Stewards are still inside." Her voice was urgent. "We can't be sure it's safe. Kalindi has a history with them, and I won't risk her running into someone who wants to finish what her father started."

Clar shrugged. "Then your only other option is Joycita, but you're at least a day's ride away."

Mari looked down at Kalindi. She was breathing, just barely. Mari leaned closer, pressing her fingers to her wrist. There was a pulse. It was weak, but it was there. She closed her eyes for the briefest second, just long enough to gather herself. When she spoke again, she forced her voice to be firm. "We have friends in Joycita."

Zeph's grip tightened around Kalindi. "Kalindi would rather die than let the Mycelium touch her."

Mari's throat burned. "She might not have a choice." She refused to lose this argument. Brindlemyre wasn't safe. Not yet. "We're taking her to Joycita."

Zeph looked like he wanted to protest, but instead, he just swallowed hard and nodded.

"We need transportation," Mari commanded.

Clar gave a single nod. "I'll get you two of our fastest horses."

Mari didn't waste another second. She tugged at the chain from around her neck until it snapped and then slipped off the round charm etched with the Healer's Crown constellation—the very same charm Lyra had gifted her at the start of her journey. She fastened it to Rih's harness, her hands steady. She leaned in and whispered, "Find Zećira."

Rih tilted her head in understanding, and with a flash of feathers, she was gone.

Mari looked back down at Zeph. He still sat on the ground, Kalindi cradled in his arms. And then, his voice broke the quiet. "She was amazing, Mari." His words were barely more than a breath. Mari looked at her shattered cousin.

"She threw herself in front of a blow that Kareth meant for me." His voice cracked. "Took the hit. Gashed her up real good. Blood everywhere." He shook his head, his throat bobbing as he tried to steady himself. "But she didn't stop." He pulled Kalindi in closer still. "She kept fighting. Didn't stop swinging. Not until she landed the final blow." His voice turned hoarse. "Not until she killed him."

Clar returned leading two horses, saddled and ready. Mari recognized one immediately—Clar's own warhorse. Zeph passed Kalindi to Clar gently and mounted his horse, moving faster than Mari had ever seen him move before. He shuffled back in the saddle so Clar and Mari could hoist Kalindi over the front of the horse, securing her as best they could.

"We'll be right behind you," General Clar reassured Mari. "We'll return to Joycita for reinforcements before we deal with Brindlemyre."

Mari gave him a taut nod. "Good. You'll need to tell the queen what happened here today. If this isn't enough evidence to act upon..." She trailed off and looked down at Bartel. "Keep him alive." She swung onto the second horse and gripped the reins. She turned to Zeph. "We're not stopping until we get there."

Zeph didn't answer. He just nodded once, holding Kalindi tighter.

CHAPTER THIRTY

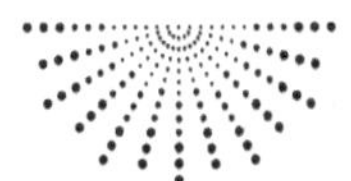

The water enveloped her, muffling the world
until all that remained was the distant patter of her own
heartbeat. Mari let herself sink deeper, her eyes closed, chasing
that thin line between discomfort and silence.

Down here, the battle didn't exist as she bobbed
weightlessly, submerged in the waters of the sweetbath. There
were no bloodied fields or frantic cries, no Bartel, and no limp
Kalindi, cradled in Zeph's arms. There was only stillness and
the occasional tiny air pocket that escaped from her nose. She
exhaled, blowing out the lungful of air that she had been
holding, letting her body rise with the cascade of bubbles that
she released with her breath.

She let herself float on the surface, feeling the waterline lick
at her feet, her ankles, her calves and thighs, her hips, her back
and shoulders, her neck, and her head. Her body scan
produced nothing but the same numb feeling she had
welcomed the moment she climbed off her horse and fell into
Elisa's arms at the entrance of the tea house.

And then... *Drip*. She opened her eyes, blinking against the rippling distortion of the bathhouse ceiling.

Drip. Drip. Drip.

The sound echoed, the steady trickle threading through the silence. It was coming from the far corner of the bath, where a single pipe leaked with slow, rhythmic persistence. Mari lolled her head side to side, letting her hair drag across the water slowly.

The pipe was still dripping. Of course, it was.

A ghost of a smile touched her lips, more realization than amusement, as she remembered how Kalindi had interrupted her very first sweetbath with the intent to fix it. She hadn't realized until now that she was in the same room as before.

Mari closed her eyes, letting herself drift weightless for a moment longer, trying to picture the girl she'd first met—drenched in bathhouse steam, wrench in hand, muttering under her breath as she burst through the door, unaware that the room was occupied. This was the same girl who had spent weeks at her side, holding her own against assassins, against the Stewards... against her own father. The same girl who was now fighting for her life just beyond these walls.

Mari had done everything she could. Now she had to wait. She took another deep breath and let herself float back down under the water, as deep as she could go without exerting any effort, forcing her mind to go blank, but it refused to.

Her mind pulled her back to the moment they arrived.

The room had smelled of smoke and spice, but all Mari had noticed was Rih. She was white and silver again; someone had given her a bath. The bird had been waiting for her, perched on the edge of the long, rectangular table. The moment Mari stepped inside, Rih fluttered to her shoulder and pressed against her neck, her feathers soft and familiar.

Mari had sunk into the comforting smell of seed and feathers, her hand reaching up to Rih's head, stroking her with relief. She had dropped into the chair beside the table, her body aching, weariness threatening to drag her under, but she fought her closing eyelids as she watched Zeph carry Kalindi down the stairs.

Zećira had been waiting, a look of seriousness about her as she gestured them forward, immediately making assessments the moment her eyes set upon Kalindi.

"Kalindi." Zećira had smiled, her head tilted, her eyes tender with sympathy as she recognized who she was.

Zeph had settled Kalindi onto the table gently, ignoring the chair that Elisa had pulled out for him. He leaned over the table, his face directly above Kalindi's, until Zećira pushed him out of the way with gentle force and ushered him into the chair. Elisa had handed him a teacup that steamed, and he sipped it timidly, holding it out from his body as his shaking hands spilled the contents inside.

Rih had nestled against Mari's collarbone, and the last thing she remembered before her eyes finally slipped closed was the steady warmth of Rih's heartbeat against her temples.

Mari pushed up from the bottom of the tiled bath, floating upwards in a straight line for the surface, releasing everything from her lungs. She had thought a bath would stop her mind... but it didn't.

She swam over to the step and climbed out slowly, not bothering to reach for a towel. She wasn't interested in comfort. She let the cold bite into her skin as her wet hair dripped, mirroring the steady sound of the leaking pipe across the room. She stood there, bare and silent, her hand curled under her tucked chin, and she stayed like that for a moment, swaying in place, staring into nothing, listening to the water drops.

Then, with a slow exhale, she turned away and stepped out of the bath chamber and into the changing area beyond. This wasn't working. Nothing would until she knew whether Kalindi was going to be okay.

THE STARK CONTRAST in temperature was the first thing Mari noticed when she entered the warmth of the teahouse. Steeping herbs and something sweet—maybe honey melting in hot water—wrapped around her, grounding her.

She padded down the stairs, the same ones that had once felt unfamiliar now felt like a return to safety. She took a deep breath and pushed aside the curtain to Kalindi's room, bracing herself for what she might find.

Kalindi was awake and propped up in a makeshift bed, her dark curls disheveled and her face tired, but the tension that had lined her face for weeks was gone, replaced by what Mari pegged as relief.

Zeph was curled up at the foot of her bed, asleep. Across the room, Zećira worked meticulously at a small clay pot of steaming liquid.

Mari inhaled deeply, catching the familiar notes of willow bark and peppermint—pain relief. She started to walk further into the room but stopped when she saw Zećira move to Kalindi's bedside, a steaming cup cradled in her hands. Something in Mari's gut told her to wait.

Zećira handed the cup to Kalindi and placed a steadying hand on the pillow that was propped behind Kalindi's back.

Kalindi took the cup tentatively, staring at the liquid inside, deliberately avoiding Zećira's eyes.

A quiet moment passed before Zećira finally spoke. "I know we'll never see eye to eye, Kalindi," she said. "But I won't insult you by pretending I regret what happened with your mother."

Mari watched as Kalindi's hands tightened around the ceramic, her white knuckles visible even at a distance.

Zećira's expression didn't change, but her hands smoothed over the blanket covering Kalindi's legs. "I do regret that it left you vulnerable," she continued. "And for that, I'm sorry."

Mari shifted, suddenly aware she was intruding on something private. She considered stepping back into the hallway, but couldn't bring herself to move, aware that the slightest movement might break the fragile energy that was unfolding between them.

Kalindi finally looked up and into Zećira's eyes. "Thank you," she said with a nod.

Zećira returned the nod, giving the blanket one final press before she turned away, moving toward the bench against the wall. Without another word, she reached for the basin of hot water and began to methodically stir the steaming rags inside.

Mari let the moment settle before stepping forward fully into the room. Kalindi glanced up at her entrance, a familiar grin twitching at the corner of her mouth. "Well, you look like hell."

Mari let out a slow breath, relief coursing through her body. She could burst into tears. "Kalindi..." She rushed to Kalindi's bedside and wrapped her arms around her, holding back just enough to avoid squeezing too hard, although all she wanted to do was clutch her tight and never let go. When she pulled back, her gaze searched Kalindi's amber eyes. "How are you feeling?"

Kalindi sighed, sinking back into the pillows. "Dizzy. But otherwise?" She lifted a weak hand, wiggling her fingers. "Still breathing. No missing fingers. Not dead. So I'd say not bad."

Mari didn't look convinced. She turned to Zećira. "Is that true?"

Zećira set down the steeping herbs and nodded. "Her body shut down from the strain, but it did what it needed to—protected her. She's surprisingly fine, and just as spicy as always." She reached for a small jar, muddling the contents. "A few cuts and bruises. They'll heal, with time and this ointment."

Zeph lifted his head and stretched lazily. "So, basically, she was just being dramatic." He grinned.

Kalindi's arm snapped up. She ripped the poultice from her shoulder and flung it at him. It hit him square in the chest with a wet slap, and Zeph let out an exaggerated noise of disgust, tossing it onto the floor.

Zećira pressed her lips together in clear disapproval and immediately reached for another poultice, placing it back against Kalindi's shoulder with obvious care. "Heroes, the lot of you... yet, you act like children."

Mari watched as Kalindi let her head fall back against the pillow, smiling. It felt strange, seeing her like this—unguarded. Strange, but good.

Zećira left the room, and the moment she was gone, Mari turned to Kalindi. She hesitated before speaking. "I'm sorry we had to bring you here."

Kalindi blinked and then let out a slow breath, tilting her head back against the pillow.

Mari braced herself to receive Kalindi's feelings. She had expected her anger to be overwhelming.

Kalindi only shrugged. "It's okay." She said it so simply, as if it had already been settled in her mind. "I thought I would have more anger, but honestly? After seeing my father, after finding out my brother betrayed me... there's a part of me that was in denial about who my mother was." She looked up to the ceiling. "She was just as brainwashed as the rest of them. If Zećira hadn't..." Her voice trailed off.

Mari didn't press.

Kalindi shook her head. "If things had turned out differently, maybe my mother would have betrayed me too."

Zeph patted Kalindi's knee, as unsure of what to say as Mari was.

"It's okay," Kalindi assured them. "Really. There's a part of me that will always wonder what could have happened if I had gotten to her first, but... there's a bigger part of me that knows the answer. However that story ended, it ended with heartbreak." She took another deep breath. "I won't ruin my life over blind rage and resentment. Not anymore."

Zećira returned with a chair for Mari and set it beside Kalindi's bed. Mari shifted off the mattress and into it, giving Kalindi more space.

Kalindi stretched out against the pillows, rolling her stiff shoulders as Zećira replaced the last poultice. "So, what's been going on while I was getting my beauty rest?"

Zeph, still pulling at a loose thread on his sleeve, shrugged. "General Clar met with the queen last night. She snuck down here for an update."

Kalindi's attention sharpened immediately. "And?"

Mari sighed. "I don't know."

Zećira, making a new bundle of poultice patches, spoke

before Mari could continue. "As far as I've heard, none of the known Stewards inside the castle are aware of what happened in Brindlemyre yet. That gives us the upper hand when we make our next move, but the queen appears... hesitant. My reports say she's too nervous to act."

Kalindi shook her head. "So, the queen is still as weak as ever."

Mari glared at Kalindi before she could stop herself. "Hey. Don't be like that."

Kalindi looked at her, unimpressed. "Am I wrong?"

Mari frowned, searching for a counterargument, but she knew Kalindi wasn't entirely wrong, because even now, with Bartel captured, living proof that the Stewards had infiltrated the queen's own ranks, Lyra still hadn't moved. "She does seem nervous to move against Bomi. Maybe she just needs... encouragement."

Kalindi's eyebrows raised. "Encouragement?"

Mari felt the heat creep up her neck before she could stop it.

Kalindi's smile was instant. "Wait." She grinned, shifting despite Zećira's pointed look. "You haven't seen her yet, have you?"

Mari looked away almost bashfully. "I was asleep when she came by."

Kalindi stared at her, deadpan. "Are you serious?"

Mari shot an unimpressed look at Zeph. "Did no one tell her that we galloped for an entire day without stopping to get her back here?" She dragged her hand down her face. "Yes, I'm serious... I was exhausted."

Zećira, ever composed, simply added, "She asked about you."

A thousand thoughts raced through Mari's mind at once.

Did she ask how I was? Did she seem relieved? Did she seem... disappointed? She swallowed, forcing her voice to stay even. "She did?"

Zećira nodded as she adjusted the last bandage on Kalindi's shoulder. "If you want, Elisa can get you into the castle later tonight."

Kalindi didn't even give Mari a chance to answer. She slapped Mari's arm hard. "Yes. She wants that."

Zećira arched an eyebrow. "Is that true?"

Mari sighed. "Fine."

Kalindi's eyes glittered with amusement. "Don't pretend you're reluctant, Namari of Greenhaven. Go see your woman."

Mari flushed and glanced at Zećira, who graciously pretended to stir her tea, although the corners of her mouth twitched.

"It's not that," Mari mumbled, fidgeting with the hem of her sleeve. "There's a lot on the line right now. She needs support. We finally have solid proof that the Crown has been infiltrated, and she has to act."

"And?" Kalindi prompted, too smug for Mari's liking.

Mari huffed, folding her arms. "And what if it's not enough?" The words left her before she could stop them. "What if I'm not enough? What if I can't be who she needs?"

Zećira smiled knowingly. "You don't need to be what she needs. You need to be yourself. If that's enough for her, she'll lean into you."

Zeph, who had been uncharacteristically quiet, finally spoke. "I never thought I'd leave the date orchard to fight for all of Patovia," he said. Then, looking directly at Mari, he added, "But if there's anyone who can convince the queen to be brave, it's you."

Mari met his gaze and nodded, her stomach flipping in a

way that had nothing to do with nerves and everything to do with anticipation. This wasn't just about politics or about convincing Lyra to act. It was about being near her again. It was about the way Lyra's eyes lingered on her when she thought no one was looking, about the way her voice sounded when she said Mari's name, and how her hands had gripped Mari's waist the last time they had been down here together in Zećira's tea house.

"Please tell Elisa I would like to see Queen Lyra."

THE WINDING underground tunnels beneath the castle were chilly..

Elisa moved quickly through them and Mari hurried to keep up. "These were built decades ago," she murmured. "Back when the Mycelium was just whispers in the kitchen. My great-grandmother used them to pass messages from the castle to the Lantern District."

Mari nodded, absorbing the information, but her focus was already ahead, on the woman waiting for her.

They reached the end of the passage and Elisa pressed against the door in front of them, listening for any sounds on the other side. Satisfied, she eased it open, revealing a darkened corridor lined with barrels and sacks of grain—the castle kitchens. Low voices drifted from somewhere deeper in the room, but with most of the day gone, only a few night staff remained.

Elisa led Mari through the maze of stacked crates and cooling bread loaves, weaving around countertops that were dusted with flour. They reached the far end of the kitchen, where a small door led to a spiral staircase, the kind meant for staff and servants, unseen by noble guests.

Elisa placed a finger to her lips, then gestured upward. Silently, they ascended. At the top of the stairs, Elisa cracked the door open just enough to peer out and then beckoned Mari forward.

They stepped into a long, carpeted hallway with a deep crimson runner. Mari could tell by her surroundings that this was the queen's wing. At the far end, past the grand arched doors, lay the queen's chambers. She tried to ignore the way her heart pounded harder with every step. Suddenly, from out of nowhere, Mari heard thudding footsteps ahead. Someone was approaching from the opposite end of the hall.

In a flash, Elisa moved, shoving her behind a heavy tapestry. Mari pressed herself flat against the castle wall, holding her breath. Through the small gap in the hanging fabric, she watched as a cloaked figure strode past.

It didn't look like it was a guard. The individual was dressed in deep navy robes, the hem embroidered in delicate silver filigree. A member of the queen's council, perhaps?

Mari felt her panic settle as the figure disappeared down another hall. Elisa waited a moment longer and then lifted the tapestry just enough for Mari to slip out. Their eyes met. Elisa's expression was intense. "Move fast."

Mari didn't need to be told twice. Together, they rushed toward the doors of the queen's chambers. Elisa knocked quickly and then stepped back, waiting only long enough for the latch to slide open before pushing the door inward. Mari stepped inside and promptly forgot how to breathe.

CHAPTER THIRTY-ONE

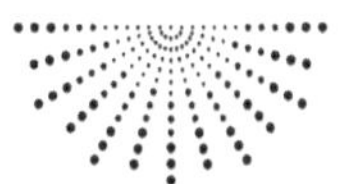

Lyra stood near the balcony, wearing an ivory nightgown, the thin material flowing over her form, leaving little to the imagination. Her hair was pulled back into a braid that curved along the back of her head as if a thick rope of golden hair was draped over her shoulder.

Gods. She was stunning.

She had imagined this moment a hundred different ways. She had fought against imagining it a hundred more. But nothing, not the memory of their stolen moments or the way Lyra had once looked at her across the council table, could have prepared her for this.

The queen turned slowly, and when she saw her, she smiled. "Mari."

Mari nearly melted at the sound of her name on Lyra's lips, at the warmth in her voice and the way her eyes drank her in.

Lyra took a step forward, looking Mari up and down. "I was worried you wouldn't return."

"They didn't make it easy."

Lyra's voice dipped lower as she found Mari's eyes. "You missed a lot, Namari."

Mari held her gaze. "So did you."

The words stopped there, but their eyes kept speaking, roving over one another. Mari fought the pull to close the distance between them.

Lyra stepped closer still. "Is that why you came?" she asked. "To brief me?"

Mari swallowed. "Of course."

Lyra arched an eyebrow, amused. "No other reason?"

Mari met her challenge, her own voice dipping to match Lyra's teasing. "Would you like me to list all my reasons, or would you rather guess?"

Lyra's eyes betrayed her thoughts. "I'd rather you tell me the one that's most important."

"I tried not to think about you," Mari admitted. "Tried to focus on the mission. But in truth?" Her voice dropped. "I thought about you every day."

Lyra's breath faltered. "You did?"

Mari nodded.

Lyra's eyes searched Mari's, overflowing with vulnerability. "I could tell you how often I thought about you, but it would be easier to list the moments I didn't. There were fewer of those." She was now close enough that Mari could touch her if she dared.

Mari's heart ached. She lifted a hand, brushing her knuckles over the queen's cheek. "When we were on the hill in Elyria's Edge, you told me you didn't regret your feelings—just the timing."

Lyra nodded.

Mari's voice was barely above a breath. "How's the timing now?"

Lyra didn't answer. She didn't need to. Her body language shifted, and she took a subtle step forward, her breath drawing a little too sharply. She tilted her chin up toward Mari, who took the action for the silent confession it was. She wanted her. "I can't explain how I feel when I'm near you, Mari. For the longest time, I was searching for strength, for inspiration, and then you showed up, and suddenly I had more of it than I could hold."

Mari's chest tightened.

Lyra continued. "I wanted to be near you—to the point that I risked sneaking out of the castle just to see you again. That's when I realized I was losing control, because even though we had only just met, I couldn't bear to be apart from you. I knew so much hinged on your journey, so I stepped back. I didn't want to complicate things."

Mari smiled. A fire burned in her, spreading through her limbs. "Things are far less complicated now," she said. "The Stewards' strength has been shattered. We hold the power now. It's all yours to wield, Your Majesty."

"When I'm with you, I feel utterly powerless against my own feelings," Lyra confessed.

Mari moved forward again, now inches from the queen. "Let me show you how to harness that power."

Lyra swallowed hard, her eyes never leaving Mari's. "It feels like moons since we were last together."

Mari closed the distance. "I'm here now. And I'm yours."

There was a heartbeat of silence. Mari wondered if Lyra could hear her heart pounding in her chest. Then, there was no more distance—just the slow, inevitable pull of desire, the warmth of bodies drawn together, the soft brush of lips before they fully met.

Mari pressed her body against Lyra's, guiding her back

until they hit the wall. Lyra's head tilted back, her eyes fluttering closed as Mari pinned their interlocked hands above her head.

"Every moment I fought was for you," Mari whispered, pressing her lips to Lyra's throat.

Lyra moaned, breathless. "Mari..."

Mari paused, pulling back just enough to search her face. "Do you want me to stop?"

Lyra shook her head. "No. But are you sure we should?"

Mari grinned slowly, nodding, biting her lower lip, and pressing a leg between Lyra's. "Oh, we absolutely should." She rolled her hips into the queen until there was no space left between them.

Lyra's body melted into Mari's, her head tilting back, exposing the smooth column of her throat—an offering.

Mari took it. She dragged her tongue along the nape of Lyra's neck, feeling the queen shudder under her hands. Her skin was warm and tasted faintly of lavender. She moved higher, tracing a path to the tender spot just beneath Lyra's ear. She felt the way Lyra's breath stuttered, the way her fingers dug into Mari's arms.

Lyra's lips parted slightly, her breath shallow and wanting.

Mari snaked her tongue along the inside of Lyra's upper lip. "You're stronger than you know, Lyra," Mari growled, her voice rough with desire and admiration. She pressed her mouth to Lyra's, swallowing the soft gasp that escaped her.

Lyra moaned, her arms dropping from above their heads, her hands gripping Mari's tunic, pulling her closer.

Mari pushed her tongue past Lyra's lips, tasting her, feeling the way the queen whimpered into her mouth.

Then... Lyra stiffened.

Mari felt her hesitation and pulled back instantly, just enough to search Lyra's face. "What is it?"

Lyra's eyes were wide and conflicted. "I've spent so long being told to hold back. To obey. To be someone else. I don't know if I—"

Mari pressed a palm against Lyra's racing heart. She knew what her queen needed. "Show me now," she whispered.

Lyra swallowed.

"Show me how powerful you are, Your Majesty," Mari challenger her.

Determination flashed across Lyra's face. She took Mari's hands, and pulled them together, holding them in one hand. She then placed her hands on her hips and guided Mari toward the bed, walking backward until the backs of her knees hit the mattress. "Undress."

Mari maintained eye contact, her chest heaving as she obeyed, her fingers already moving to the buttons of her shirt. She had only just pulled it over her shoulders when Lyra stepped forward, placing a firm hand on her chest and pushing her back onto the bed.

Mari landed against the sheets, her arms holding her up at an angle as Lyra climbed onto her lap and straddled her.

The queen looked hungry. "You say you missed me?"

Mari nodded, unable to form words.

"Answer me."

"Yes, I missed you."

"How much?"

Mari's hands found Lyra's hips. "More than you realize."

Lyra hummed, her fingers trailing up Mari's bare torso, sending heat ripping through her. "Explain."

Mari's voice came out uneven and breathless. "What you told me...about how you admired my conviction..."

"I meant it." Lyra pressed her palm back against Mari's chest and pushed her down, pinning her.

Mari gave up trying to speak as Lyra's knee slid between hers, nudging her thighs apart, settling deeper into her. She let her head fall back as Lyra kissed her, deep and possessive.

"You're unlike anyone I've ever known, Namari." Lyra's lips moved lower, trailing across Mari's collarbone, her shoulder...

Mari arched beneath her, gasping. Lyra was unyielding, and Mari had never wanted anyone more.

THE QUEEN'S chambers were quiet now, filled only with the sounds of their breath and the occasional rustle of sheets. Silver moonlight streamed in, bathing them in a dreamlike glow that made Mari feel like she was dreaming.

Mari lay on her side, one hand tracing absent patterns along Lyra's bare shoulder, her touch light. "Tell me what you're thinking," she murmured.

Lyra sighed, burrowing into the soft pillows. "Gods, where to start..."

Mari's fingers stilled against her skin. "Wherever you want to, my darling."

Lyra's lips spread into a slow, tired smile. "Mmm. Darling. I could get used to hearing that."

Mari reached for her, tucking a stray strand of hair behind her ear, her fingers pausing just long enough to coax Lyra's eyes back to hers.

"I was pushed into marrying the king."

Mari's breath caught. She wasn't surprised by the statement, but she hadn't been expecting the subject here, in this moment.

"I've known since I was a girl that I loved women. But my parents... they insisted that the future queen of Patovia would marry a man, that it was my duty, that my kingdom came before my heart." She let out a slow breath. "So, I did what I was told."

Mari's chest ached. She tilted Lyra's chin up, searching her face. "I'm sorry you had to pretend to be someone you weren't."

Lyra stared at her for a long moment and then, quietly, she whispered, "All my life, I've been told how to act and who to be. I'm tired of being a pawn. I'm ready to show the world who I am."

Mari felt her heart swell. She reached for Lyra's hands, interlacing their fingers, squeezing gently. "I love what I see already."

Lyra let out a shaky breath. Then, slowly, she leaned in, kissing Mari deeply.

Mari smiled into it, feeling Lyra press closer, her body warm, her heart steady. She had been in the queen's presence longer now than any time before, and every moment only confirmed what she had desperately hoped—Queen Lyra was everything she had imagined. What an honor it would now be to watch her finally step into her own strength.

"It sounds like you're ready to take control of your crown, Your Majesty."

Lyra turned to her, a devilish gleam sparking in her eyes. "I was always ready," she said, a quiet fire in her voice. "I just needed a reason to stop holding back." Then, with unshakable certainty, she whispered, "No more leashes. No more chains. No more men who think they can rule me from behind a curtain. They built their power on my silence. Let them choke on the sound of my war cry."

Mari's mouth suddenly felt dry.

Gods.

She was so devastatingly, impossibly gone for this woman.

THE FIRST THING Mari noticed was the absence of warmth beside her. The sheets were cold where Lyra had been, the presence of her body long gone. Mari stirred, rolling onto her back, blinking up at the ceiling before turning toward the open balcony.

Lyra stood there, already dressed in a deep sapphire robe cinched at the waist with a golden clasp. Her hair, now unbraided, cascaded down her back, rippling in the morning breeze. Mari admired the commanding way in which she stood —shoulders squared, head lifted, her gaze fixed on the city stretching below her.

Mari wrapped the sheet around her and padded barefoot across the floor. "Admiring your kingdom, Your Majesty?"

Lyra didn't turn. "Preparing to reclaim it."

Mari leaned against the stone railing, watching Lyra's profile. "No more hesitation?"

"No more hesitation," Lyra echoed. She turned to Mari, the light catching in her ice blue eyes. "Did you know there was once a queen who ruled Patovia without a husband?"

Mari arched an eyebrow. "Before you?"

Lyra nodded. "Decades ago. She never took a king. She ruled with strength until the day she died, and the crown passed to her male cousin. Since then, Patovia has never had a woman at the head of its throne."

Mari studied her. "Until you."

Lyra seemed almost surprised by the words, despite the fact

that this was the exact point she had been making. "Until me." Mari watched as Lyra silently built herself up, bit by bit. "I spent so much time trying to make others comfortable, trying to appear the way they wanted me to be. But why? Why should I deny myself to satisfy those who never had my happiness in mind?"

Mari smiled. "Sounds like you're going to make your female ancestors proud."

"Not just them. The girls of this kingdom deserve to grow up knowing a woman can wield power without apology. And I won't let them be told otherwise."

"I know I would have appreciated a role model like you," Mari said, looking at her with admiration. She leaned in to press her lips against Lyra's, but a knock at the door interrupted the moment.

Mari shrank instinctively, pulling the sheet tighter around her, but Lyra stood unmoving. "Enter," she commanded.

A royal official stepped inside, bowing low before offering a sealed scroll. "A message from the council, Your Majesty."

Lyra moved back into her quarters and took the note, breaking the wax seal and scanning the contents.

The official stood, waiting, looking mildly surprised as he took in the sight of Mari. Lyra noticed. She met his eyes directly. "You have something to say, Captain Rellen?"

"I—no, Your Majesty. Only that I did not realize you had company," the official replied.

"And now you do. I trust I can count on your discretion, Captain."

Rellen nodded. "Of course, Your Majesty."

Lyra rolled the parchment, tucking it into the pocket of her robe. "Summon the council. I will address them after lunch."

Rellen gave another short nod, but she wasn't finished.

"Additionally, see to it that Councilor Bomi meets me in the War Room before the meeting."

"You... you want me to deliver instructions to Councilor Bomi?" The official looked a little afraid.

Lyra gave him an unwavering stare. "That's correct. Is there a problem?"

Rellen shook his head and shot her a smile, clearly impressed by her changed presence. "No, Your Majesty. Not at all. Right away, Your Majesty."

As the door shut behind him, silence settled in the room once more. Lyra turned to Mari and stepped closer. She reached out, tracing her fingertips along Mari's wrist. "You're still here," she murmured.

"Where else would I be?" Mari searched Lyra's face. "I don't understand," she admitted. "What was it about me? What made you feel strong enough to finally face them?"

Lyra smiled. "I tried to fight it. The way I was drawn to you. At first, I thought it was admiration. Then, I thought it was need. But the truth is, Mari, I recognized something in you that I've been missing in myself for a long time. You brought it out of me, and in doing so, you also allowed me to see more of you." Her vulnerable words made Mari shiver. "Still, I know I've barely scratched the surface of who you are. You contain multitudes, Namari, and I want to know them all."

Mari was certain that at that moment that she had absolutely stopped breathing.

The queen took Mari's hand in her own and pressed a kiss against her knuckles. The slow, sensual brush of her mouth sent sparks dancing up Mari's arm.

"Who would have thought that the day I bumped into you on the stairs would set all of this into motion?"

Mari forced a teasing smile. "Sounds an awful lot like fate, Your Majesty."

Lyra smiled, stepping even closer. "Sounds an awful lot like trouble."

Another knock at the door.

Lyra sighed but didn't move immediately. Instead, she let her fingers linger against Mari's skin for just a moment longer. Then she collected herself and cleared her throat. "Shall we get to work?"

CHAPTER THIRTY-TWO

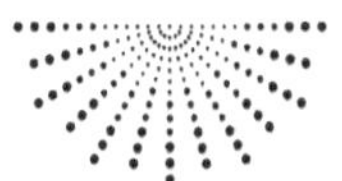

back now.

Mari stood with Lyra and Kalindi just around the corner from the War Room, hidden in the shadows of the stone corridor. The corridor echoed the muffled sounds of distant voices from the great hall, where the council remained at lunch.

Bartel swallowed hard. He was sweating—whether from nerves or the heat of Kalindi's glare, Mari couldn't tell.

"Just do as we say," Mari murmured. "Your cooperation will be considered in your sentencing."

Kalindi didn't offer him the same reassurance. She grabbed his arm roughly, her fingers digging into his sleeve. "Stick to the script, Bartel," she hissed. "One wrong move, or if I don't like what you say, or even the way you say it, and the deal is off and we throw you to the wolves."

Bartel nodded quickly, his throat bobbing as he swallowed.

Mari looked toward the staircase when she heard the sound of footsteps approaching.

Bomi was here.

He appeared at the top of the stairs utterly unaware that he was being watched. With the confidence of a man who had never questioned his own importance, he crossed the hall, pushed open the doors to the War Room, and stepped inside.

Mari looked at Bartel. "Go."

Bartel stalled just long enough for Kalindi to give him a firm shove. He stumbled forward, catching himself before straightening his uniform and stepping toward the War Room doors. They followed at a careful distance, keeping to the shadows, hanging back just far enough to remain unseen as Bartel pushed inside.

Mari pressed herself against the wall, angling her body beside the door, her eyes finding the narrow gap in the hinge. Lyra sidled up beside her, lowering herself to a crouch, her gaze fixing through the same sliver of space just below Mari's. On the other side of the door, Kalindi took position, peering in from a different angle.

They could see everything.

BOMI SAT at the strategy table, his quill scratching against a piece of parchment. He didn't even glance up when Bartel entered.

"Um, ... hello...," Bartel said, the attempted casualness of his voice marred ever so slightly by the tightness that wrapped around his words.

Bomi ignored him and continued writing for another moment before finally setting his quill down. When he looked up and actually saw Bartel standing there, his demeanor shifted to one of surprise at first, and then disdain. "Is that what's left of your uniform, Bartel?" His lip curled. "I'd hardly call that presentable. If you're going to play the role of a soldier, at least try to look the part."

Bartel stood rigid under his scrutiny. He clenched his jaw and moved cautiously toward the table, his hands shaking.

"I heard General Clar arrived in Joycita last night," Bomi said, his voice clipped. "What's going on? I haven't had a single report from anyone about what happened in Brindlemyre. Can you give me an update?"

Bartel looked like he was frozen in place.

Behind the door, Mari held her breath.

Bomi stood slowly. His voice dropped dangerously low. "I asked you a question."

Bartel stammered. "It was a success, sir. The device activated as planned. The disruption worked."

Mari reached for Lyra's hand and squeezed it excitedly. Bartel had delivered the lie perfectly. She tensed, waiting to see whether Bomi would believe it.

Bomi's eyes flashed with satisfaction. "Then why are you standing in front of me like a half-drowned rat? Where's my full report? Status, casualties, territory secured..."

Bartel jumped in quickly, keeping the cover intact. "Kalindi and Mari are dead."

Mari nodded. *Keep going, Bartel...*

A smug smile crossed Bomi's face. "Finally. That took far longer than it should have." He paced confidently. "I suppose we can actually dispose of the old astronomer now," he mused.

Mari's breath caught. *Searsan is alive?!* A sudden wave of heat flushed through her, and her heart began to hammer. She fought the urge to burst into the room and demand Bomi immediately tell her where Searsan was being held.

Beside her, Lyra laid a gentle hand over Mari's, grounding her. She gave a slow, steady squeeze. Mari sucked in a deep breath, forcing oxygen into her lungs. She closed her eyes, willing herself to stay in control. When she opened them, she tried to focus on the room beyond the door, but she heard nothing. The War Room had gone still. Bomi wasn't speaking or pacing.

Mari barely dared to breathe, her body rigid as she strained to listen, terrified that Bomi had heard her and would wrench the door to the War Room open at any second, discovering them.

At last, Bartel shifted. He cleared his throat, the sound loud against the uncomfortable silence. "If I may be so bold, sir, what is the plan now?"

Bomi crossed the room, pausing at the tall window overlooking the castle grounds, his hands clasped loosely behind his back, as if weighing his next words. "We begin phase two—conversion. Growing followers."

Kalindi's lips curled in disgust as he spoke.

"If this is going to work on a widespread scale, we start with those who are easiest to sway," Bomi continued. "The restless, the desperate, the overlooked. Those who already feel like the Crown has failed them." He walked back to the table and leaned over it to glare at Bartel. "Start with the outpost," he ordered. "Give me a list of soldiers weak enough to flip. I'll have Lunn do the same with the Joycita police force."

Lunn. Remember that name.

"Let's focus on the ones with the most influence, the ones in command—officers, captains—those who can shape public trust. The rest will follow." Bomi's eyes gleamed with calculation. "And after that, we move to the civilians."

Mari dug her nails into her thighs to keep herself from moving. Bomi was so certain. So confident.

He flicked a glance at Bartel again and paused. "Why aren't you taking notes?"

Bartel stood stiffly, unmoving. *Too slow, Bartel.*

Bomi frowned. "I assume Kiron and Kareth are still watching over the echo device?"

Bartel hesitated, just for a second, but Bomi caught the pause. His entire demeanor shifted, and suddenly, real suspicion crept into his features.

Just when Mari thought Bomi might realize the trap, he continued. "Have them send me a report," he said. "I want recommendations on where we move next." He turned toward the window, and his voice dropped lower, like he was speaking only to himself now. "Before we know it, it will be time to execute phase three—the downfall of Patovia's beloved queen."

Mari couldn't believe what she was hearing.

"If I am to prove that I am the best person to step up and take over," Bomi said, "then we need to start establishing my authority now." He crossed the room and placed a hand on the map of Patovia, tracing the borders of Joycita. "Have Dayel arrange for the team overseeing the Opal Tower construction to meet me in my chambers this afternoon. I want a deadline for project completion. Oh, and have the astronomer confirm the coordinates he mapped for the location before you...take care of him."

Mari's brow furrowed. The Opal Tower. She remembered Searsan had been consulting on the construction, although at the time she hadn't paid much attention.

She felt a breath of warm air brush against her ear. Lyra, crouching below her, whispered low enough so that only Mari could hear. "It's nothing more than a glorified watchtower posing as a landmark," she murmured, her eyes locked on Bomi as he paced before the map. "He's been pushing for it for years. Claims it will enhance the city's reputation and bring more visitors in, and double as a security measure, but it's just another piece of his illusion of leadership, just a symbol to hold over the council—a way to claim he championed Joycita's safety."

Mari started to understand exactly how the crafty councilor was planning on taking Lyra's power. He was constructing the proof that he deserved it.

"By the time phase three is complete, there will be no doubt that I will have proved to them that I am strong enough to take control of Patovia. Stronger than this queen, anyway," Bomi sneered.

Mari looked at Lyra. They had him. They had everything they needed.

Bomi's eyes suddenly snapped back to Bartel, and he tilted his head, as if he was truly noticing him for the first time. His gaze dragged over the soldier's disheveled uniform, the tension in his stance and the sweat clinging to his brow. "What are you even doing here? Shouldn't you be back at the outpost?"

"I..." Bartel's voice cracked. "I was summoned."

Bomi's eyes flickered with immediate suspicion. "Summoned?" His fingers stopped tapping.

Bartel swallowed. "By the queen."

Lyra squeezed Mari's hand tightly. The trap was closing.

For a moment, Bomi just stared. Then his lip curled. "The queen?" His voice dipped into a mocking sing-song. "She summoned you?" He let out a short, humorless laugh, shaking his head. "Why in the gods' names would she summon you?" His scowl deepened. "For that matter," his irritation was flaring now, "why would she summon me?" He smoothed a hand over his tunic as if brushing off the very notion of being summoned.

"Perhaps," he muttered, "she's forgotten who is really in control here."

The door behind Bomi flew open. "Quite right, Councilor Bomi."

Bomi spun around to look behind him.

Lyra stepped inside, her composure razor-sharp. "For a while there," she started, "I think I had completely forgotten that it is I who wears the crown... not you."

Bomi scoffed. "The wardrobe doesn't make the woman," he said, condescension dripping from his voice. "About time you showed up. You're wasting everyone's time. Do tell, what urgent matter of state compels us all to rearrange our day to indulge you?"

Lyra didn't flinch. She didn't so much as blink.

Bomi took her silence as an invitation to keep talking. "Shall I guess?" he mused. "You want me to smooth things over with the council? Convince them that you're capable?" He clicked his tongue. "I'll give you some guidance for when we meet with them later, shall I? Keep your mouth shut. Let me do the talking." He stepped closer. "You may wear the crown, but we both know who truly holds this kingdom together."

"I'll keep that in mind, Councilor Bomi," Lyra said. "Though I do wonder..." She folded her arms. "...if you're still so certain of your standing when all your pieces are suddenly gone from the board."

Bomi's arrogant posture faltered, just slightly.

From behind the door, Kalindi stepped into the room, claiming her space to the right of Queen Lyra. Her eyes glowed as they locked onto Bomi. "We burned all your damn pieces to the ground," she snarled.

The mockery drained from Bomi's face. "You," he spat.

Then it was Mari's turn to step forward. "And me," she said, flanking the queen's left.

Bomi's eyes darted between them, the realization of the situation hitting him squarely in the chest. Mari hoped it hurt.

The three women stood together, their presence radiating power. Side by side, they were a reckoning.

Lyra's voice was calm and certain when she spoke next. "Thank you, Bomi," she said smoothly. "But your time on my council has come to an end."

Bomi's composure was crashing rapidly. He snapped his eyes toward Bartel, who had started inching away from the group. "I suppose I shouldn't be surprised," he spat. "You were so easily swayed to our side. Makes sense you'd be just as easily swayed back."

Bartel flinched, his eyes darting around the room for an escape as Bomi closed in on him. "They'll never forgive you for this," Bomi threatened.

Mari looked at Kalindi, who seemed equally curious. *Who is he talking about?* She remembered Bartel referencing something similar in Brindlemyre, and the recollection made her stomach curl. Her thoughts were interrupted when Bomi made a sudden lunging move toward Bartel.

His dagger flashed, and before anyone could react, Bomi's blade sank deep into Bartel's chest with a sickening wet crunch. Bartel choked. His hands scrabbled uselessly at the hilt as Bomi wrenched him closer and twisted the knife cruelly, a cold, vicious smirk warped across his face. Then, with one sudden, brutal tug, Bomi spun Bartel around, gripped him by the collar, and threw him out the window, his body plunging to the depths of the quadrangle below.

A scream ripped from Mari's throat. Lyra and Kalindi

screamed too, a chorus of horror as they watched Bartel disappear from view.

Bomi turned back toward them, unshaken. "Now it's your word against mine," he jeered.

Mari's blood burned.

Bomi looked at Lyra, his sneer widening, his arrogance abundant. "The council so easily believes in the strong, confident, intelligent man at the helm," he continued. "I inspire more confidence in them than you ever could." He tsked, shaking his head. "Such a shame, truly—how far you've let things deteriorate... One of your own soldiers, Your Majesty. Overcome with despair. The state of mental health in the outpost must be in dire condition," he drawled. "How desperately you have failed the people of Joycita, Lyra."

The tense stillness that followed Bomi's words was shattered by the slow creak of a door swinging open from the opposite end of the War Room, on the far-right-hand side of the wall. From a room beyond, Councilors Sannah, Varella, and Thammond, the longest-serving members of the queen's council, and the most loyal, stepped forward. They had been waiting quietly behind the door, exactly as Queen Lyra had requested them to do earlier that morning.

Their faces were painted with disgust.

Bomi turned at the sound. His composure wavered for the first time.

"From where we stand, Councilor Bomi, it sounds to us like you are the one who has let down the people of Joycita," said Varella.

"To think that our forces have been poisoned from within... This is the true disgrace." Councilor Thammond seethed with disappointment. "Soldiers have fought and died for Patovia, believing in the cause of their kingdom, and all the while, you were undermining them from behind council walls." He spat in Bomi's direction. "You have tainted not just our forces, but this council. This is unforgivable."

Bomi's face paled as realization sank in. They had heard everything.

Mari could see it happening in real time. The unraveling of a cold and calculated man who had spent his entire life controlling the pieces on the board, only to realize he had just been outplayed.

He whirled back toward Lyra, and he did what men like him always did when faced with the consequences of their own incompetence... He tried to lie his way out of it.

Bomi spread his hands, his voice slipping into something impossibly smooth. "My friends," he began, the condescension creeping back in, "you're mistaken. This is nothing more than a misunderstanding. I have only ever acted in the best interests of Patovia." He searched their faces, looking for a foothold he could use to manipulate them. "The queen is clearly incapable... She needs my guidance." His tone changed—he really was trying every trick in the handbook of manipulation. It would have been impressive if it wasn't so pathetic. "Can any of you truly say she is prepared to rule alone?"

Mari's jaw clenched. Bomi was still grasping for control, still trying to twist their doubt against Lyra, but he had miscalculated. This time, no one would believe him.

Sannah stepped forward last. She didn't raise her voice. She didn't need to. It was already game over. Her clear eyes pinned Bomi in place. "Spoken like a man who still believes himself untouchable." She took another step closer, her tone almost... amused. "Tell me, Councilor Bomi, are you delusional, or merely desperate?"

Bomi's eyes widened with panic as his control over the council slipped from his grasp.

And just like that, the room belonged to Lyra once more. Sannah turned to the queen and bowed her head. "Your Majesty," she said, "what would you have us do?"

Mari felt the shift.

Lyra, standing at the heart of the room, no longer overshadowed, no longer uncertain, spoke confidently. "I want the charges and his sentence expedited. Let's transport him to the council chambers and hold him there until the rest of the council arrives." She motioned toward the window, where Bomi had flung Bartel to his death. "On the grounds of conspiracy against the Crown," her voice did not waver, "and murder."

CHAPTER THIRTY-THREE

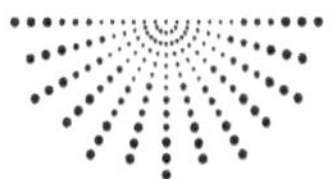

 of the council chamber, their presence muted as they attempted to catch every uneasy glance, every carefully masked expression that would take place as soon as the first person stepped through the chamber doors.

At the head of the council table, bound in chains, sat Bomi. He had stopped denying his involvement. He sat rigid, his face a red ball of fury.

The councilors entered one by one; their reactions varied, each one telling in its own way. Some stopped short, their eyes darting between Bomi's shackled form and the queen standing at the head of the table. Others stared in open shock, their confusion evident. A few, however, were too composed—their expressions were perfectly schooled, a little too careful.

Mari noted them all, wishing she had more names to go with some of the faces.

When the chamber doors swung open again, General Clar entered, his presence solid and commanding, followed closely by two additional guards at his back. Mari didn't recognize them. Behind Clar and his men, Captain Rellen and another man in similar garb entered. Rellen stood with his back to the doors, and Mari assumed that the other man was a scribe, given that he seated himself at a small table off to the side and pulled out a large book and a quill. He opened it to a blank page and turned his attention to the queen.

Lyra took her seat as she considered the entire council before her. "You all know why we are here."

A hush settled over the room. Then... Bomi laughed mirthlessly, mocking the room. "What's the point of this, Lyra?" He spat. "You think you've won. So, just kill me and be done with it."

Some of the councilors grimaced at his open defiance. Others remained stone-faced, as though considering his words carefully.

Lyra didn't even flinch. She stood as steady as an oak. "You are guilty of treason. Of conspiracy. Of murder."

Bomi's look of disdain did not fade. "And you are naive if you think I was the only one."

Mari felt the energy in the chamber shift, but Lyra continued. "If there are others who have betrayed Patovia, let them reveal themselves now." Her voice rang through the chamber, commanding and expectant.

Silence. No one moved.

Mari didn't expect anyone to come forward—not yet—but that didn't mean the moment was wasted. She studied them all, watching the way they swallowed, blinked, brushed hair from their faces, broke eye contact, and shifted in their seats. The scribe sat, his quill hovering a fraction above the page, his eyes darting from council member to council member, waiting for someone to speak.

"We must now decide his fate," Lyra instructed.

Councilor Varella was the first to speak. "Execution is the only fitting punishment," she said plainly, folding her hands atop the table. "We must set an example."

There were a few nods of agreement, but Councilor Oran, a middle-aged man with ink-stained fingers and a reputation for diplomacy, shifted forward. "Death is too final," he mused. " Perhaps imprisonment for life would be the wiser course. He would rot behind bars knowing he had lost. Knowing he would never be free."

"That would leave him available to be questioned further," Councilor Sannah mused.

Then came Councilor Yelveth, a younger man with keen eyes. "Banishment." His voice was clear. "Let him be exiled from Patovia entirely. Let him see what it is to be cast aside from the very nation he sought to control."

The idea was quickly shut down. "Absolutely not," Thammond's voice rumbled. "Do you think a man like him would simply accept exile? Do you think he would not scheme his way into another seat of power elsewhere? We let him live and we give him time—time to crawl back."

Lyra looked across the faces of the council members before she turned to Mari and Kalindi. "A word?" She didn't wait for an answer and stalked out of the room.

Mari and Kalindi followed the queen into the antechamber, and Mari pulled the door closed behind them.

They stood in silence, waiting for Lyra to take the lead. She pressed her fingers to her temple and rubbed hard. "What do you two think?" she asked in a whisper.

Kalindi shrugged. "I thought it would be easier," she admitted. "Thought I'd be able to read it on their faces, but I feel like I'm second-guessing everyone."

Mari nodded, biting her lip. "Same. There were a few who looked rattled, but fear doesn't always mean guilt."

Lyra scrunched up her face in frustration.

Mari added, "We might need to press Bomi for more information. Maybe he'll spill?"

Kalindi cracked her knuckles. "Maybe we can make him spill."

Lyra shot her a pointed look. "Torture is outlawed in Patovia."

Kalindi held up her hands, grinning slyly. "That's a real shame."

Mari tilted her head, her mind already working through possibilities. "We can wait him out."

Both women turned to her. "Lock him away in the darkest cell you have. Give him just enough food to keep him breathing. Let him sit with his failure. Let him feel what it is to be utterly powerless. Eventually, he'll beg to talk."

Lyra seemed to consider the suggestion briefly before giving a slow nod. "I like that."

Kalindi huffed, clearly still favoring a less patient approach, but she said nothing.

Mari smiled, inclining her head toward the door. "After you, Your Majesty."

Lyra returned to the council chamber, her presence commanding, her decision made.

"Councilor Bomi," she said. "You have committed treason against the Crown. You have conspired against Patovia, against its people, against me." She let the words land so that he could feel them. "I will not grant you the martyrdom of execution."

A murmur rippled through the room. The councilors exchanged glances, some in agreement, some still appearing uncertain.

Bomi laughed under his breath, and Mari recognized it immediately as arrogance creeping back in. *Unbelievable. He thinks that he is still in control, and that he can still talk his way out of this.* "Mercy, then," Bomi mused. "I always knew you didn't have the stomach for real leadership."

Lyra did not blink. "This is not mercy."

Bomi's face twitched.

"You will be imprisoned beneath this castle."

His face ripped into a snarl.

"You will remain there until you decide you want to be useful," Lyra said, her voice ringing with authority. "Until you decide you want to give us names. You think you still have power, but you have nothing. No title. No army. No council. No voice."

Mari didn't watch Bomi. She watched the councilors instead. She watched the ones whose eyes dropped to the table, whose bodies tensed, whose breath caught ever so subtly—the ones who might be realizing, at this moment, that their fate could very well mirror his. The problem was that their reactions were so varied, she wasn't sure what to make of any of them.

"You will sit in that cell and wonder," Lyra continued, "when I will come knocking."

Bomi flinched, and at that moment, Mari knew he finally understood what Lyra was doing to him. The sinking realization that his impending punishment would be worse than death washed over his face. He would be erased.

"Take him away," Lyra commanded, turning her back on him as if he were already beneath her notice.

Rellen stepped away from the door, and the armed guards moved at once and grabbed Bomi, still in chains, by the arms. He jerked violently, but they yanked him upright and dragged him toward the exit. Bomi's expression was venomous. Mari had never seen him look so small.

Lyra turned back to the council table, sweeping her eyes across every face as Bomi's shouts faded away down the corridor. When his cries had disappeared to nothing, and all that was left behind was an intense silence, she turned on her councilors, dipped her head, and looked up at them from beneath a threatening brow. "Make no mistake." She did not blink. "I will find out who among you stood with him." She looked each of them in the eyes. "And the consequences will be brutal."

A ripple of unease spread through the room.

Lyra watched as several of them shifted. "You're dismissed." And with that, she walked out.

THE DAMP DUNGEON was flooded with the stench of forgotten traitors. Mari walked through the dark tunnel, her presence echoing through the space as she moved deeper into the prison.

The guards outside Bomi's cell came to attention as she approached. "Open it," she said.

With a bow of his head in acknowledgement, one of them unhooked a key from his belt loop and unlocked the door.

Bomi sat on the wet floor against the far wall, his wrists shackled to iron rings embedded into the rock. His once-pristine council robes had been stripped from him, replaced by a coarse prisoner's vest.

He sneered at her through the darkness.

Mari closed the door behind her and sneered right back at him.

"Come to gloat?" Bomi drawled.

"I don't have time for gloating." She stepped closer. "Tell me where Searsan is."

Bomi scoffed. "And what? You'll have the queen pardon me? Spare me from my incarceration?" He shook his head, laughing bitterly. "You must think me a fool."

Mari shrugged. "You are a fool, but I do have sway with the queen. You tell me what I want to know, and maybe I'll ask her to be lenient."

"We both know that's a lie," Bomi said dismissively.

Mari didn't move for a long moment. Then, so suddenly that Bomi flinched, she gripped the front of his vest, pulling him forward until the chains rattled loudly against the stone. "Then let's play a different game," she cooed. "If you don't tell me where Searsan is, I'll make sure Kalindi pays you a visit."

Bomi went still. His smirk didn't vanish, not entirely, but it faltered, and Mari knew she had him in her grasp.

"You're bluffing," he said, but the certainty wasn't there.

Mari leaned in, her breath warm against his ear. "She watched you manipulate her mother. She heard you celebrate when you thought her dead. You think she won't take pleasure in breaking you piece by piece?"

Bomi tried to mask his uncertainty with pure defiance, as he spat in her face. "Your sad, old astronomer is long gone from Patovia. He's so far from here that he'll rot before you find him," he hissed.

Mari wiped her cheek slowly and glanced down at the floor. When she looked up, she smiled. And punched him square in the face.

The impact sent Bomi's head snapping back against the wall, a grunt escaping him as blood trickled from his split lip.

Mari turned toward the door. "Don't be so sure about

that." Without another glance, she stepped out of the cell, the door clanging shut behind her.

MARI MOVED DEEPER into the tunnels that wound beneath the heart of the castle. She peered inside each cell, her eyes searching the face of every prisoner she passed. Most were strangers—men and women worn thin by time and darkness.

She pushed deeper, trusting the instinct curling in her gut. Bomi had told her that Searsan was far beyond her reach. That was his mistake because the moment he had said it, Mari knew. Searsan was down here. She just had to find him.

The deeper she went, the heavier the air felt, the walls sweating with moisture. Water trickled in thin lines along the stone, pooling into a murky slurry at her feet.

She checked over a hundred cells... Nothing. As desperation tightened in her chest, she threw caution aside.

"Searsan?" she called out.

No response.

"Searsan!" she shouted again, her voice echoing loudly down the curving passageway.

For a moment, there was only silence, but then she heard something, a sound so faint it almost didn't register.

"Namari?" The voice was weak but familiar.

Mari gasped. She ran toward the sound, water splashing up her legs as she raced down the narrowing corridor. "Searsan!" she shouted.

She reached the final row of cells, gripping the iron bars as she peered inside. A figure moved in the darkness and she felt cold, thin fingers wrapping around hers.

"Namari of Greenhaven."

Mari couldn't see his face in the weak light, but she knew without a doubt—it was Searsan.

His voice lifted in something close to a quiet chuckle. "I knew you were coming."

Mari tightened her grip on his fingers. "I'm going to get you out of here."

She spun, bolting back down the corridor, her heart pounding with urgency. She didn't stop running until she had the keys in her hands and Searsan was free.

BACK IN THE LANTERN DISTRICT, at the tea house, Mari found Zeph and Kalindi sitting at a table, peeling licorice root alongside Zećira, the table covered in curled shavings. In the corner, Rih was perched quietly, her eyes closed and her feathers fluffed in rare contentment—a quiet contrast to her usual restless energy. Mari watched her for a moment, smiling to herself. *So this is what it looks like when Rih relaxes.*

Zeph glanced up as she entered and grinned. "Get over here and help me peel. I'm bringing as much as I can back to Patovia with me!" he declared, holding up a long strip of bark. "I can taste it now—licorice dates!"

Mari barely resisted grimacing. There was nothing in the world that sounded worse than licorice dates.

"Sounds delicious," Kalindi said, not a hint of sarcasm to be seen.

Mari slid into the chair beside Zeph, shooting a surprised glance at Kalindi.

Wow.

It appeared she wasn't the only one who had it bad for someone.

Zeph beamed. "So, are we going to enjoy the delicacies of Joycita tonight, or what?"

Mari exchanged a look with Kalindi before answering. "We've been invited to a victory banquet at the castle."

Zeph's smile faltered. "Oh..."

Kalindi rolled her eyes. "You're invited too, you fop."

Zeph sighed with relief, placing a hand dramatically over his chest. "So I finally get to meet this queen of yours?"

Heat rose to Mari's cheeks, creeping up her neck.

Kalindi grinned. "Oh, she's definitely yours. You're not even denying it now."

Mari giggled, tugging her cloak over her face. "Next subject."

They laughed, and Mari felt lighter as the tension unwound from her body.

Zećira stood and gathered the licorice peel shavings into a towel. "I'll leave you three to your scheming." She smiled. "Try not to burn the place down."

Mari pulled back her cloak just enough to flash her a mock-offended look. "If that happens, it won't be my fault."

Kalindi snorted. "Oh, it absolutely would be."

Zećira chuckled as she swept toward the door, tucking the bundle of shavings under her arm before disappearing into the hall.

The laughter faded, giving way to a comfortable quiet.

Mari's eyes unfocused as she sank into the moment, the world blurring at the edges as her thoughts pulled her inward. How much longer would she have to wait before she could fall into the queen's embrace, rest her head against her chest, and listen to the steady rhythm of her heartbeat? She yearned to be back in Lyra's arms. Now that Lyra had demonstrated she was capable of owning her power, Mari found herself wondering just how much further that strength could be explored. How it might manifest in other places and other moments. Or other nights... She shuddered at the thought, goosebumps rippling across her skin.

Zeph noticed. "Alright, cuz. What's that look for?"

Kalindi tossed a forgotten shaving at Mari. "Yeah, you're practically glowing. Thinking about your queen?"

Mari huffed a laugh, shaking her head. "I was thinking about how much she's come into her own. If you had seen her before... "

Kalindi arched an eyebrow. "Yeah. I remember. She's changed a lot already. Thanks to you."

Mari met her gaze. "No. It's all the queen's doing. I might have been the inspiration she drew from, but this came from inside of her. The same as us. No one handed us our strength. We built it ourselves."

Kalindi nodded. "We did it."

Zeph let out a slow breath and grinned. "We really did it."

Mari reached into her satchel and pulled out a small leather charm. "I'm sending Rih back to Greenhaven tonight to deliver the message."

Kalindi's head snapped toward her. "You're sending Rih away?"

Mari smiled. "Not sending her away. Sending her on a mission."

Zeph and Kalindi stopped peeling, and they studied her. Mari could see their minds ticking over, processing her words.

Mari stretched her arms over her head. "There's still more to uncover at the castle—a lot more, but I'm ready for it. I've never felt more alive... I'm excited to stick around and see this through to the end."

Zeph's grin dimmed. He looked at her, something hesitant in his expression. "So... you're not coming home?"

"Not yet." Mari smiled, a quiet certainty settling in her soul. "I'm not done here."

CHAPTER THIRTY-FOUR

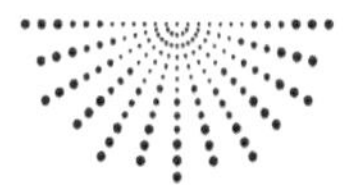

THE CASTLE PULSED WITH LIFE, A STEADY RHYTHM OF movement and energy as preparations unfolded for a grand victory banquet—one Queen Lyra had insisted be held to honor those who had fought to reclaim Patovia's future. Kalindi, Mari, Zeph, General Clar, and Searsan, each had played a pivotal role in dismantling the Stewards' invisible hold on the kingdom, and that night, their names would be celebrated.

Although doubt still remained over whether Bomi had acted alone, investigations were already underway, working through the names he had let slip in his complacency. In time, those still loyal to his cause would be found. The echo device had been destroyed, and the skies above had settled into their natural state. If Mari ever wished to see the auroras again—not that she was rushing to—she would have to journey to Elyria's Edge for the Festival of Still Waters. For now, she was content beneath the quiet sprawl of dark blue stretching over the horizon, unmarred.

She sat on the edge of the bed in the chamber that had been

assigned to her, although the arrangement was mostly for appearances. Lyra had made that much clear when she first led her through its grand doors, her voice dropping low and private as she had whispered, "I don't expect you to sleep here."

Still, Mari appreciated having the space to retreat to and to pretend, even for a moment, that she was still just a girl from Greenhaven charting the stars. Her star charts were spread across the entire mattress, a constellation of ink and parchment, intertwined with the pouches of soil she had collected throughout her journey.

A gentle breeze drifted through the open window, fluttering a stunning emerald-green dress that was draped over the changing screen, waiting for her. She scowled. *Not yet.* The time she had endured during the fitting had been quite enough, thank you. The thought of spending the entire evening trapped in its stiff embrace made her want to bolt back to Greenhaven. Mari may have won against the Stewards, but she was about to lose against a tight bodice and layers of embroidered fabric.

With a sigh, she leaned back, pressing her palms into the plush mattress as she marveled at the room before her. It was a grand space, far larger than anything she had ever called her own. A lush, ornate rug stretched before the fireplace; its elaborate designs couldn't be more different than the simple woven mats of her family home. The fire itself popped quietly every now and then. It needed more wood, but she had asked the attendants not to disturb her while she finished cataloging her charts.

Attendants... She had attendants, a whole wing of them. The sheer absurdity of it made her laugh. She could already hear her mother's voice buzzing with excitement as she retold every detail of Mari's letter home to the neighbors. All of

Greenhaven would know the layout of this chamber within a week.

The thought warmed her. She could almost picture her father standing in the doorway, shaking his head at the sheer extravagance of it all before pulling her into a bone-crushing hug. She ached for that moment.

She made a mental note to ask Lyra to send them an invitation once the formalities of the celebration were over. The idea of her parents breaking open a sealed letter from the Queen of Patovia, reading an official summons to Joycita, was almost too much to bear. She smiled at the thought of running down the castle steps to greet them, her father gawking at the towering spires, her mother fussing over how thin she had gotten.

Mari closed her eyes. A single teardrop fell from her left eye as she fully, truly, let herself relax. Every cut from every vine, every sleepless night beneath the open sky, and every moment of doubt and fear had been worth it.

Stretching, she pulled herself up from her bed slowly and swung her cloak over her shoulders. There was still some time before the banquet began, and she was determined to savor as much bodice-free time as she could before duty called her to the changing room and the formalities of the evening took over.

Attendants hurried through the halls, their arms laden with silver trays and goblets, their shouted orders mingling with the clatter of preparation. The smells that drifted through the halls from the kitchens below made Mari's mouth water as she passed by. After weeks of nothing but dry rations, she was prepared to truly embrace the meaning of the word 'feast' that night. She dipped down the corridor, turning her body against the wall to narrowly avoid a group of people that looked like they were probably members of an orchestra who were filing through, holding large, polished instruments carefully, their eyes darting from the floors to the walls to the high ceilings above, admiring the grandeur of the architecture and interior decorations, and nervously following their leader to wherever they were headed.

She exited through the main castle doors into the streets beyond, the commotion of the banquet preparations falling away behind her, only to be replaced by the sounds of what had fast become one of her favorite places in all of Patovia—Joycita.

Joycitians moved through the streets, preparing for the victory banquet. While the queen's official guest list was limited to the royal court, noble families, and key political figures who wielded influence over Patovia, it was clear that the entire kingdom was celebrating.

Word had spread quickly about how the Stewards had sought to seize control of the land's elements, how they had nearly succeeded, and how, in the end, they had been crushed. The queen had wasted no time to proclaim victory, ensuring that the people of Patovia knew the danger had passed, that their skies remained theirs.

Everywhere Mari looked, there was a palpable buzz of conversation. Whispers turned to excited murmurs, then to impassioned discussions: Who were the Stewards, really? Had they always been lurking beneath the surface? How had they gained power unnoticed for so long? Calen had been right: the truth of the Stewards' presence in Patovia had been buried well. Whoever had orchestrated their silence after Clar's first victory had been meticulous, ensuring that history barely remembered them at all. But history had changed. In the sprawling city beyond the castle walls, houses were being adorned with decorations, communal tables were being set, and kitchens were creating delicious masterpieces. There would be feasts in every home in Joycita that night.

Mari tried to ignore the feelings of self-consciousness that crept upon her as eyes turned her way, whispers rippling through the streets whenever someone recognized her—the astronomer from Greenhaven, the one who had worked with Searsan to uncover the truth before anyone else. She didn't think she deserved the recognition. This victory belonged to Queen Lyra, not her. Tugging her cloak tighter, she lowered her head, hoping to disappear into the crowd. Let them celebrate the queen. Let them celebrate Patovia's future. Tonight wasn't about her.

Hidden under her cloak, she passed through the cobbled streets mostly undetected, slowing on the bridge above the bathhouses she had visited on her first night here, taking a moment to deeply inhale the myrrh she smelled floating up from below. It mingled with the spice of roasted almonds being sold nearby, and she paid for two small cups gladly, her mouth still watering after smelling the dinner being prepared back at the castle. Mari knew this route well now. Once, it had been unfamiliar and daunting, but now it simply was.

She took another deep breath as she looked around at the trees that grew in the center of the streets, a row of rocks encircling them. There were so many details she hadn't even noticed before because she had been so focused on her mission. She couldn't wait to explore every inch of this city.

The bridge to the Great Library loomed ahead. She stopped when she reached it and placed a hand on the smooth railing. Beneath the bridge, the river ran dark and steady below, its waters drifting through the city like liquid onyx, lapping against the bridge's ancient supports.

She had crossed this path before. That night, when she had

first arrived in Joycita, she had been a stranger, an astronomer from a quiet village, stepping into an unknown city with broken stars above. She had walked this bridge timidly, with doubt boiling in her gut, burdened by questions that felt too tangled for someone like her to unravel.

This time, as she crossed the bridge, she felt different. Her journey had sharpened her. She still had questions—gods, she would always have questions—but now, she had the strength to find the answers herself.

She lifted her chin as she reached the Great Library, its towering facade stretching to the heavens, its windows gleaming gold against the dark.

MARI DID NOT KNOCK. She pressed her palm against the oak door of Searsan's office and gave it a push.

Inside, the room was dim. Searsan sat on a worn, comfortable-looking couch before the small fireplace, his frail hands folded neatly in his lap. His eyes were fully clouded now, his vision gone—unable to adjust after weeks in the dungeon's darkness. The healers had done their best, but it was no use. Searsan was blind. His expression was calm, but Mari knew that his mind, as always, was anything but still.

"They're too precise," Zećira murmured, standing near the hearth with a piece of parchment in her hand. One arm was crossed over her waist, the other lifting the page closer to her face. "No merchant keeps records this meticulous unless they have something to hide." She looked up as Mari stepped into the doorway, her words fading.

"Sorry to interrupt," Mari said from the threshold. "I can come back."

Zećira smiled and waved her inside. "No trouble. Come in."

Mari leaned against the doorframe, her arms crossed. "I didn't see your name on the guest list for the victory banquet, Searsan. A grand feast in your honor wasn't enough to tempt you?"

Searsan huffed a quiet laugh. "I prefer my victories quiet." He shifted in his seat, the firelight casting deep lines across his face. "Besides, I need my rest."

Zećira snorted. "He means he doesn't want to waste breath listening to men congratulate themselves for surviving something they barely understood."

Mari smiled. "And here I thought tonight was a celebration."

Searsan's sightless eyes were fixed somewhere past her. "A celebration is only a celebration when one has nothing to fear. Tell me, Namari... Does Joycita feel safe to you?"

The city had been freed. Bomi was in chains. The queen was finally, truly, the queen. So, Mari asked herself... Did Joycita feel safe now? "No," she admitted.

Zećira shot her a knowing look. "Then you understand. We still have work to do." She lifted the parchment again and motioned Mari forward. "We were just discussing pressing next steps. Come in."

Mari pushed off the doorframe and closed the door behind her, her interest instantly piqued. "Tell me."

Searsan gestured for the parchment, and without a word, Zećira placed it into his waiting fingers. He held it with both hands for a moment before offering it to Mari.

She took the document, lowering herself onto the couch beside him, and scanned the contents of the aged parchment. It was a map, intricate and dense, filled with notes scrawled in the margins—shipping routes and a list of ships and their captains who sailed beyond Patovia's borders. She glanced up. "What is this?"

"The Stewards never built that device alone," Searsan said.

Mari frowned. "Right, they used Kalindi, but she helped us destroy everything. What's left to uncover?"

"Not what... who." Searsan gave her a pointed look, disappointed almost, as if she should have thought to ask this question long before he had.

Zećira leaned forward, tapping a finger against the list of captains. "The problem isn't who built it. It's who supplied them. Someone fed the Stewards those blueprints, someone well connected and very well hidden."

Mari rolled the parchment open further, examining the list of routes and the names of merchants. "That's what I don't understand," she admitted. "Historians have been scouring Elyrian ruins for centuries, and all they've ever found are crumbled relics. But somehow, the Stewards managed to dig up enough to rebuild an entire Elyrian device?"

Zećira moved around the back of the couch and leaned in between Mari and Searsan. She smelled of bergamot and woodsy tea, softened by the faintest hint of lavender from her thick black hair, which was pulled into a loose ponytail that draped over her shoulder, half-hiding her ears. She jabbed at the circled trade routes with a finger.

"I was just telling Searsan when you came in—my team pulled the trade ledgers for the last ten seasons. Someone has been covering their tracks for a long time." She tapped the page. "The shipping records are too clean. Too perfect. The average merchant's books are always a mess of scribble, but these?" Her finger dragged along the parchment. "This is someone who wants to slip under the radar so badly, they're practically screaming to be noticed."

Mari pieced the information together, trying to keep up. "So, we're looking for a smuggler?"

Zećira nodded. "Exactly." She stretched her arms behind her back as she moved toward the fireplace. "Apparently, there are murmurs of a smuggler dealing in Elyrian artifacts too. If that's the case, it could explain a lot."

Mari's eyes thinned. "And what's the plan?"

Zećira smirked. "I'll handle it."

Mari arched an eyebrow. "That's not an answer."

Zećira raised her brows right back. "I think you'll find it was," she said with a wink.

Before Mari could argue, Zećira continued. "You think taking out one traitor will silence the threat? It just teaches the rest to whisper more quietly." She glanced toward the door, as if ensuring no one was listening. "There are still whispers in the castle. Maybe they'll fade... maybe they'll grow louder. Either way, we need to keep our ears open."

A shiver crawled down Mari's spine.

Zećira took the parchment back from Mari, tucking it into a hidden pocket. "I need to get ready for the banquet."

"I thought Lyra said you weren't invited? The Mycelium isn't exactly looked upon favorably by the Crown..." Mari paused. "Officially, I mean."

Zećira flashed a wicked grin, adjusting the black cuff of her quarter sleeve. "Who said I needed an invitation?"

Mari folded her arms, intrigued. "You're sneaking in?"

"Let's just say... I have a team keeping an eye on things. Watching the comings and goings. If someone sneaks away, or if certain councilors decide to have a quiet word with one another... we'll know."

"You have spies at the banquet?"

"I have spies everywhere, Mari. You just don't know who

they are yet." Zećira turned toward the door, tossing a casual wave over her shoulder before slipping into the hall, the fabric of her dark dress whispering against itself as she walked away.

Mari turned back to Searsan, who had gone quiet. "What's on your mind?"

Searsan smiled, his clouded eyes locking onto hers with unnerving precision. "I did tell you once, Namari, that the stars whisper their secrets to those who listen. You've proven you speak their language. You did it."

"You don't sound surprised."

"Because I'm not." He patted Mari's hand. "I saw this moment long before it came to pass."

Mari wasn't sure how to respond. "You saw everything that happened? Brindlemyre? Bomi?"

Searsan's lips quirked into a small, knowing smile. "Not quite," he admitted. "I see the shape of things, not the details. It's like watching a ship on the horizon—you know it is coming, but not what it carries."

Mari frowned. "And what do you see for me?"

Searsan turned his sightless eyes toward her again. "Your path is shifting, Mari. The stars above you have settled, but the ground beneath your feet is still restless."

A chill shot through her. "What does that mean?"

"You should be careful." His voice had lost all trace of lightness. He reached for her hand, gripping her steadily. "The queen shines brighter because of you... but you are not her sun."

Mari's throat tightened. The words hit deeper than she expected. "What are you saying?" she pressed.

Searsan only smiled, rising to his feet slowly. "I'm saying that nothing in this world is as fixed as the stars."

Mari scowled. "That was a terrible analogy."

Searsan chuckled, amused. "It was, wasn't it? My apologies."

Before Mari could push him further, he continued. "This old man must take his leave," he said slowly. "I need my rest. Enjoy the feast tonight. You deserve it, Namari."

Mari stood as he did and grasped his hand. "Are you sure you won't come?"

Searsan's mouth curled faintly. "A feast is wasted on an old man with no stomach for pomp." He leaned in, his thin, weathered fingers finding the top of her head, and placed a soft kiss against her hair.

CHAPTER THIRTY-FIVE

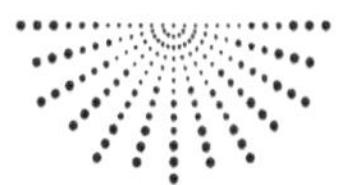

THE GREAT HALL OF JOYCITA'S CASTLE WAS ALIVE with the sounds of celebration. Long banquet tables stretched from one end of the room to the other, laden with roasted spatchcock chickens drizzled in a garlic lemon glaze, bowls of steaming vegetables dusted with the perfect amount of seasonings, and jugs of red wine being constantly refilled by the waitstaff. Deep, rolling notes of music played by the royal orchestra accompanied the laughter that rippled across the stunningly decorated hall. Candles in golden sconces lined the walls, and on either end of the hall, two great fires roared, filling the space with a smoky, warm joy.

At the head of the grand table, Queen Lyra sat with effortless grace in an elegant sapphire gown. She wore her power comfortably now, like a second skin, her laughter light but assured, and her every movement commanding yet at ease.

Mari sat beside her, squirming in the gown the dressers had insisted upon. The fabric was elegant and entirely impractical. She had argued for her usual trousers and a well-fitted tunic, something she could move in and breathe in, but formalities had won out.

They sat shoulder to shoulder, the queen's thigh brushing against Mari's under the table, a touch neither of them moved to break until they absolutely had to.

Dinner was exquisite, a feast so rich and indulgent that Mari would later write home, declaring it the finest meal of her life. As the clatter of silverware quieted and plates were steadily cleared away, Queen Lyra's gaze swept over the long tables, watching as her guests basked in the comfortable bliss of full bellies and flowing wine.

She took a slow breath and then lifted her hands, commanding the room without a word.

A hush fell over the hall.

Mari watched, struck by the sight of her and the effortless way she held power now and how she moved through it like she had always belonged there. For the briefest moment, their eyes met, and Lyra's lips curved in something like acknowledgment before she turned her attention to the hall.

"I want to thank you all for coming tonight," she began, her voice carrying easily, "and for standing beside me. There was a time not long ago when I doubted my own strength, when I allowed others to wield power in my name while I stood in the shadows." She took a look around the room as her admission settled amongst her guests. "But I assure you, I am a changed queen. I am a changed woman."

Lyra paused while the room applauded loudly.

"We come together to celebrate a victory against a threat we never saw coming, a threat that would have continued to spread, unchecked, if not for the efforts of those who risked everything to stop it." Lyra lifted her goblet proudly. "And tonight, we honor them."

Another smatter of applause rippled through the crowd.

Queen Lyra turned toward the end of the high table, where General Clar sat upright and beaming. "General Clar, who has not only defended this kingdom time and time again but stood steadfast in the face of betrayal. A lesser man might have let doubt take root after discovering a traitor in his own ranks, but instead, he..." She paused, meeting Clar's gaze directly. "Tell me, General. How do you feel, standing here tonight?"

Clar set his goblet down with a quiet tap. "Proud," he said. "Proud of the men and women who fought for Patovia. Proud of those who held the line, even in the face of uncertainty." His eyes swept the room, his jaw tightening. "But I'd be lying if I said I didn't have questions. We may have severed the head, but I don't believe we've seen the full body yet."

Lyra let the room consider and respect the power of his words. Then she smiled. "Well said, General." She lifted her goblet but didn't drink. Instead, she turned her attention to the gathered nobles, council members, and honored guests. "I know that, for some of you, this victory brings relief. For others..." she paused. "It brings uncertainty." She took a step forward. "Because you wonder if your name is on a list. You wonder if your loyalty is in question. You wonder if your queen knows."

A hush fell over the banquet hall.

"Let me be clear: I do not intend to rule with paranoia." She paused. "But I do intend to rule with vigilance. The people of Patovia deserve no less." She tilted her goblet toward Clar and then to the rest of the table. "To vigilance," she said, and Mari knew she was baiting anyone who was cocky enough to fall for it. "And to those who know where their true allegiance lies."

Glasses rose and toasts echoed through the hall.

"To Searsan, who has guided Joycita's scholars for decades and continues to serve this kingdom with wisdom beyond measure." Lyra let the applause fill the room and die down before she continued. "To Kalindi, whose mind, brilliant and unwavering, unraveled the secrets of the Stewards' devices and ensured their destruction."

Across the room, Kalindi froze, her goblet hovering just short of her lips. Slowly, she slid lower in her seat, as if willing the room's attention to shift elsewhere. For all her contributions, for all she had risked, Mari knew a part of her still wrestled with the fact that she had built the device in the first place. Mari caught the way her eyes were cast downward, as if she wasn't sure she deserved the honor being given to her.

Sitting beside Kalindi, Zeph nudged her foot under the table, giving her a look that said 'take the damn win.' With a small, begrudging nod, Kalindi finally raised her glass and took a sip.

"And to Namari of Greenhaven..."

Mari tensed at the sound of her name, a hundred pairs of eyes focusing on her at once.

"...who dared to follow the stars when no one else could see where they led. Who fought not only with weapons, but with knowledge, courage, and conviction, and who, in doing so, saved us all."

A cheer rose, led by Zeph, who clapped so loudly it startled the councilors at his table. Clar lifted his goblet in solemn approval, and Kalindi smirked before tilting her glass toward Mari and giving her a wink.

Mari felt her face heat furiously. Suddenly, she understood what Kalindi had been feeling. She wasn't used to this kind of attention. She wasn't sure she wanted it, but when she looked back at Lyra, she saw pride in her eyes, and she was certain she wanted that.

Lyra raised her goblet higher. "To our heroes. To those who stood with me when I needed them most. To those who have proven their loyalty. And to those who will make Patovia stronger in the days to come."

The room erupted in a thunderous toast, goblets clinking together, the celebration echoing off the vaulted ceiling.

As the hall settled into the warm cadence of dessert conversation, Lyra turned, extending her hand to General Clar as he approached, gratitude evident in his weathered expression.

Suddenly and ungraciously, Kalindi dropped into the chair beside Mari with a dramatic sigh. "I have had far too much wine."

Mari chuckled, raising her own goblet before taking a slow sip. "And whose fault is that?"

Kalindi groaned, tugging at the bodice of her dress. "This thing—" she gestured vaguely at the fabric, nearly sloshing what little wine remained in her cup, "—felt so restrictive, I thought a quick drink would take the edge off."

Mari arched an eyebrow. "And how many quick drinks did it take to loosen the seams?"

Kalindi drained the last of her goblet with a pointed look. "I'll let you know when I get there."

With that, she pushed up from the chair, weaving her way toward the nearest jug of wine, leaving Mari shaking her head and smiling into her cup.

∼

As the night wore on, the wine flowed more freely and the room grew more joyful.

Mari was pushing around the remains of a spiced poached pear around her plate, too full to take the final bite that remained. She dipped her finger in the golden syrup and popped it quickly into her mouth before it could drip too far down her hand.

Lyra leaned in toward her, her voice low enough that no one else would hear. "You're enjoying yourself."

Mari licked the last of the syrup from her finger before taking a sip from her goblet. "I am. And you should be too."

Lyra looked past her, still watching the councilors. "I can't stop thinking about what he said."

"Who?" Mari asked, though she already knew.

Lyra scowled. "Ugh, must I say his name?"

"Ah. About us being naive if we think he was the only one?"

Lyra nodded, taking a deep drink from her goblet.

"He didn't specifically say it was someone on the council, though," Mari pointed out.

"I know," Lyra murmured, her eyes scanning the room, "but the way he looked at each of them... It's a gut feeling."

Mari took another sip of her wine. "If there's one thing I've learned, it's that if you have a gut feeling, you should lean into it."

Lyra gave a subtle nod, but it was clear her mind was still elsewhere.

"There's got to be more people involved," Mari continued, watching Lyra closely. "We'll find them. I've already spoken to Zećira. The Mycelium's started looking into the other names Bomi mentioned. We're not going to stop until every traitor is uncovered."

Lyra nodded again, her eyes unfocused. Although she hadn't spent a lot of time with her, Mari recognized that look—she was overthinking.

"Did you see the councilors' faces during my speech?" Lyra asked suddenly.

"Yes, but it's hard to tell whether they betray guilt or if they're just as shocked and impressed as the rest of us that you're settling into your power so nicely."

Lyra arched an eyebrow. "Oh?"

Mari gave a knowing wink. "So commanding. It's very sexy. You're wearing it well."

Lyra pressed her lips together, as if trying to suppress a smile, but Mari could see the way her posture eased.

"I feel like I could read a thousand things into every action," Lyra admitted.

Mari leaned in, just enough that their faces were only a breath apart. "You need to stop thinking, Your Majesty."

Mari didn't give her the chance to reply. "Maybe," she whispered, her breath hot against Lyra's ear, "I need to tell you all the things I plan on doing to you this evening." She made sure to let her lips barely ghost over the delicate strands of hair framing Lyra's skin, the way she knew would send shivers down her spine.

Lyra's mouth quirked into a slow, gleeful smile. "Why, Mari, are you trying to distract me?"

Mari's hand barely grazed Lyra's wrist under the table. "Is it working?"

Lyra turned fully toward her, her eyes glittering fiercely. "I suppose that depends. Are you prepared to face the consequences of distracting your queen?"

"Your Majesty," Mari murmured, "I am counting on it."

Beneath the table, Lyra slipped her fingers beneath the

layers of emerald fabric draping Mari's legs, her touch slow, and expertly found her way to Mari's thigh.

Mari gasped quietly, shooting a panicked side glance to Lyra at the bold move.

"Now, who's distracted?" Lyra whispered with a commanding air. She slid her hand higher up Mari's thigh. "I think you're right, Stargazer. I should be enjoying myself. Talk of traitors can wait."

Mari felt herself melt into an absolute mess.

Lyra's voice dipped lower. "For now, let's just enjoy this evening."

Mari turned her head, meeting Lyra's gaze fully. Her lips curled. "I'd enjoy it more if we were alone. In your chambers."

"We waited for moons," Lyra murmured, her eyes glinting. "You can manage a little longer."

Mari sighed dramatically, swirling the wine in her goblet before taking a slow sip. "Cruel, Your Majesty."

Lyra only laughed and tapped her goblet against Mari's in a quiet toast while her hidden hand settled on the bare inside of Mari's thigh before she turned her attention back to the revelry. The Queen of Patovia was strong, confident, and completely, unapologetically herself.

Mari marveled at the sight of her, transfixed, hardly believing that in mere candlemarks she would have this woman beneath her, unraveling her, making her completely hers. The thought sent a thrill through her, a slow heat burning in the depths of her imagination and lower, insistent and aching.

Lyra's featherlight touch lingered a fraction higher, sending a hum through Mari's veins, and a slow, exquisite burn pooled deep and low in her core with anticipation.

A firm tap on Mari's shoulder interrupted the moment.

Mari and Lyra both jumped, Lyra pulling her hand back so abruptly that it struck the underside of the table. The impact sent the empty dessert plates rattling and the nearly drained jug of wine teetering precariously before settling back into place.

Kalindi stood behind them, her arms crossed and her eyes flicking between them. "I'm not even going to ask what that was about..."

The silence that followed was awkward, and almost certainly entirely deliberate. Mari cursed Kalindi, who let it last just long enough to make Mari squirm before finally breaking it with a grin. "Can I borrow her?" she asked, motioning toward Mari.

Lyra's lips pouted momentarily, but she recovered without missing a beat and composed herself immediately. "Of course." She sounded agreeable enough, but Mari knew she was reluctant to grant the request.

Heat coiled low in Mari's stomach. She leaned into Lyra's neck as she pushed back her chair, her voice a sultry whisper. "When I come to your chambers tonight, I want you waiting for me... in nothing but that crown." Her lips brushed the shell of Lyra's ear, just barely, but the effect was immediate. Lyra shivered, goosebumps rippling across her bare shoulders, her breath catching ever so slightly.

Mari smiled smugly as she stood, pleased. *Let her sit with that.*

Kalindi, apparently oblivious, or simply ignoring it, grabbed Mari's wrist and tugged her toward the balcony doors at the other end of the hall.

~

THE GENTLE NIGHT air enveloped them as they stepped outside. Joycita stretched out before them, streets twisting like threads in a tapestry, the lights on each home scattered unevenly throughout the city. From inside, the din of the banquet continued, but out on the balcony where Mari and Kalindi stood, it was quiet.

Kalindi leaned against the limestone railing, resting her arms over the edge. "I'm going back with Zeph."

Mari's head turned. "Going back?"

"To Greenhaven."

Mari stared at her. She had expected Kalindi to stay. She had assumed, maybe selfishly, that after everything, after the battle, after surviving together, they would stay here, together. "You're sure you want to leave Joycita?" she asked carefully. "Head engineer sounds like a pretty fantastic job title..."

Kalindi smiled. "Come on, Mari. You and I both know I was never meant to stay here."

Mari ran a hand through her hair. "I just... I don't know how to do this without you."

Kalindi nudged her shoulder, her voice softer now. "You're not doing this without me. I'll just be watching from a little farther away."

Mari forced a smile. "Greenhaven better be good to you."

Kalindi appeared wistful as she looked back toward the city. "It's been a long time since I've been somewhere that felt like home..." She paused, as if tasting the words before speaking them aloud. "Greenhaven felt like home."

Mari beamed. "And Zeph?"

Even in the soft torchlight, Mari saw the way Kalindi's ears reddened. "I'll admit it, once," she confessed, rolling her eyes. "Zeph feels like home too."

Mari's smile widened, but it was bittersweet. She reached out, wrapping her arms around Kalindi and pulling her close, holding on a moment longer than necessary. "Take care of him for me."

Kalindi scoffed, her voice muffled against Mari's shoulder. "I'll make sure he doesn't eat anything poisonous and die."

Mari laughed. "That's all I ask."

For a moment, they just looked at each other—two warriors, two survivors, two... yes, Mari realized, friends. Bound by battle, by loss, by a journey neither had planned but both had endured.

Kalindi was leaving. Mari was staying.

LATER THAT NIGHT, as the Great Hall floors were being swept clean of the evening's revelry, Mari found herself scaling one of the lower spires of the castle. She placed a careful foot on the turret's ledge, feeling the shale stone beneath her fingers as she steadied herself. With a quick breath, she leaped the short distance to the castle's roof. Crouching low, she climbed halfway up the sloped surface before finally reclining against it, letting her body sink into the familiar embrace of the night.

The sky stretched endlessly above her, a deep ocean of ink and silver. The auroras were gone, their dancing colors nothing but a memory, and in their place, wisps of pearly clouds drifted lazily, veiling the moon's glow in passing shadows.

A breeze lifted through her dark brown hair, teasing the loose strands across her gently freckled face and tickling her cheeks. She exhaled slowly, and her pulse slowed as she eased into the quiet hush of Joycita after dark.

Mari looked up at the stars and traced their patterns with her eyes, each one an anchor, a promise, a reminder that even after all that had changed, some things remained. The constellations above twinkled, steady and bright.

The stars were exactly as they should be.

THE END

CHARACTERS & GEOGRAPHICAL FEATURES

PRONUNCIATION GUIDE

Adavale: AY-duh-vayl
Amara: uh-MAH-ruh
Bartel: bar-TELL
Bomi: BOH-mee
Brenna: BREH-nuh
Brindlemyre: BRIN-dul-my-ur
Calen: KAY-len
Cel: SELL
Clar: KLAHR
Corrin: KAW-rin
Elisa: eh-LEE-suh
Ellin: ELL-in
Elyria: eh-LEER-ee-uh
Gail: GAYL
Gil: GILL
Greenhaven: GREEN-hay-vuhn
Gura: GOO-ruh
Harcanth: HAR-kanth
Isa Glades: IZ-uh GLAYDZ

Jai: j-EYE
Jannah: JAN-nuh
Jayel: jay-EL
Joycita: joy-SEE-tuh
Kalindi: kuh-LIN-dee
Kareth: KAH-ruth
Kia: KEE-uh
Kiron: KEER-un
Lana: LAH-nuh
Lea: LEE
Lillyford: LIL-ee-ford
Lyra: LIE-ruh
Maiyma: MY-mah
Mari: MAH-reeFull name - **Namari:** nuh-MAH-ree
Midwilds: MID-wyldz
Myramin: MEER-ruh-min
Nesby: NEZ-bee
Outpost: OWT-poest
Patovia: puh-TOH-vee-uh
Rellen: REL-en
Rih: REE
Rowan: ROE-un
Sannah: SAN-nuh
Searsan: SEER-sun
Sharaine: shah-RAYN
Thammond: THAM-uhnd
Varella: vuh-REL-uh
Zećira: ZEH-cheer-uh
Zeph: ZEFFFull name - **Zepharon:** ZEH-fuh-ron

ABOUT PENNY G. CAVANAUGH

Penny is a competitive Capricorn, roller derby enthusiast, and proud mum who wrangles words, people, and the occasional existential crisis. Born in England, raised in Australia, and now braving Midwest winters, she believes in fate—after all, Lucy Lawless accidentally helped her find her wife.

Her greatest pride is her daughter, her greatest joy is inspiring others, and her greatest dream is to never stop dreaming. She's happiest when she's learning, cooking, camping with her family, or watching women's sports. Her adventures, both real and imagined, are fueled by coffee and a love for the stars.

Connect with Penny

Facebook:
https://facebook.com/pennygcavanaugh

Instagram:
https://www.instagram.com/pennycavanaugh/

AUSXIP Publishing:
https://ausxippublishing.com/contact/

AUSXIP Publishing is a small, independent publishing house that was founded on March 15, 2015. We publish books with strong female characters because we believe that women are resilient, powerful and inspiring. Our mission is to publish books that celebrate these incredible women.

Join us on our journey!

Join our AusPub Newsletter:
https://newsletter.ausxippublishing.com/

Discover your next book:
www.ausxippublishing.com

9 781764 085908